Q/c

FOREIGN AGENT

BRAD THOR

FOREIGN AGENT

SIMON &
SCHUSTER

London · New York · Sydney · Toronto · New Delhi

A CBS COMPANY

First published in the US by Atria, an imprint of Simon & Schuster, Inc, 2016
First published in Great Britain by Simon & Schuster UK Ltd, 2016
A CBS COMPANY

1 3 5 7 9 10 8 6 4 2

Simon & Schuster UK Ltd
1st Floor
222 Gray's Inn Road
London WC1X 8HB

www.simonandschuster.co.uk

Simon & Schuster Australia, Sydney
Simon & Schuster India, New Delhi

A CIP catalogue record for this book is available from the British Library.

Hardback ISBN: 978-1-4711-5193-4
eBook ISBN: 978-1-4711-5196-5

Printed and bound by CPI Group (UK) Ltd, Croydon, CR0 4YY

Simon & Schuster UK Ltd are committed to sourcing paper that is made from
wood grown in sustainable forests and support the Forest Stewardship
Council, the leading international forest certification organisation. Our
books displaying the FSC logo are printed on FSC certified paper.

For Scottie Schwimer—
the world's best entertainment attorney and an even better friend.
Thank you for everything you have done for me.

"When bad men combine, the good must associate; else they will fall, one by one, an unpitied sacrifice in a contemptible struggle."

—EDMUND BURKE

CHAPTER 1

At six-foot-four, two hundred seventy-five pounds, Ken Berglund was a massive sight to behold. He had a thick, blond beard and sleeves of tattoos up both arms. "T-bones are almost ready," he called out.

A cheer arose from his teammates in the courtyard and from the women who had gathered around the old stone slab being used as a dining table. Someone fired up a Charlie Daniels song on their iPhone as more beers were pulled from the cooler.

It was a perfect night for a cookout. Above the abandoned desert fortress, the stars shone in the blue-black sky, a cool breeze blew away the lingering heat of the day, and for a moment you could almost forget where you were.

That was until you noticed the modified M4 rifles kept within arm's reach, or the .45-caliber pistols the men carried at their hips. As soon as you saw those, the illusion was shattered. Nobody gunned up that heavy for dinner unless they were in a war zone. Which was exactly where they were.

Ashleigh Foster, though, had downplayed the danger when she spun the trip to her two girlfriends as something out of *Lawrence of Arabia*— a weekend at a romantic desert castle surrounded by nothing but sand and the occasional camel. Of course, as a CIA collection management officer, she knew better. Stationed at the U.S. embassy in Amman, Jordan, she saw the intelligence on a daily basis. In fact, it was her job to sort it, encrypt it, and send it all back to CIA headquarters in Langley, Virginia.

No place in Iraq was safe—and that went double for Anbar. ISIS may not have pushed this far into the province yet, but it was only a matter of time.

Her girlfriends knew better too. As embassy staffers, they were kept up to speed on the security situation not only in Jordan, but also in neighboring Iraq and Syria. What they were doing was dangerous.

But danger had been part of the weekend's appeal. It was an adventure, and adventures were supposed to be exciting. And what could be more exciting than partying at a CIA safe house for two nights?

They had snuck out of work early on Friday, stopping back at their apartments only long enough to pick up their clothes and four enormous Yeti coolers (borrowed from an Embassy storage room) filled with all sorts of food, including steaks, ice cream, beer, and even doughnuts.

With a carefree attitude better suited to a trio of college coeds headed off on spring break, they hopped into Ashleigh's Toyota Land Cruiser, turned up the music, and pointed the SUV toward the Karameh/Turaibil border crossing.

Less than three hours later, they flashed their diplomatic passports and were waved through both the Jordanian and Iraqi checkpoints. Just beyond, Ashleigh's boyfriend and two of his teammates were waiting.

A former U.S. Army Ranger, Ken Berglund worked for the CIA's highly classified paramilitary detachment known as SAD, or Special Activities Division.

He and his six-man team had been sitting in the crumbling desert fortress for over a week, waiting for the CIA to green-light their insertion into Syria to snatch an ISIS HVT, or high-value-target.

Berglund's team was already running low on supplies when Langley informed them that the target had changed locations again and there'd be another delay. The CIA wanted to keep the target under surveillance for a few days to see who he was meeting with. They'd decide what to do after that.

Hurry up and wait. It was par for the course for operators. If Langley wanted to delay this mission, that was their decision.

In the meantime, though, Berglund had made a decision of his own. Why not make their resupply a little more interesting?

He and Ashleigh hadn't seen each other in months. When he asked her, she jumped at the chance. As long as she hit the road by Friday prayers, she'd be all right. There wasn't much to worry about between Amman and the border. She'd have her weapon with her, and if she needed to rock out with her Glock out, she could hold her own.

Her father, who was ex-military, had taught her how to shoot at an early age. On top of her extensive CIA training, she practiced continually and took great pride in outshooting any man dumb enough to underestimate her.

It was one of the many things Berglund loved about her. Not only was she this hot, south Florida stunner, she was also her own woman—unafraid, unapologetic, and unaffected by who or what other people thought she should be.

Her father, though, had his own plans for her. He hadn't wanted her getting anywhere near the Middle East, and had exerted great pressure to keep her back in the United States. But, Ashleigh being Ashleigh, she had found a way to get what she wanted.

She always did, which concerned Berglund. While they'd gotten naughty a lot over FaceTime, he was worried she'd eventually need it in the flesh and find it, either at the Embassy or somewhere else in the diplomatic community.

The thought of her with some Eurotrash diplomat, or God forbid, some *Ooh Rah* embassy Marine, was more than the former Ranger could stand. Any rules he was breaking by bringing her out to the desert were worth it.

But, as is often the case, one bad decision normally leads to another.

The idea of steaks and pretty girls had appealed to the other men on the team, and so two of Ashleigh's friends had been invited as well.

As far as the operators were concerned, what happened downrange stayed downrange. There was no reason anyone at Langley needed to know.

Berglund turned his attention back to the T-bones, giving them a final ninety-degree rotation to sear perfect crosshatch marks into the meat— a technique he had learned one summer in college working at a steakhouse in Dallas.

It was going to be an epic meal. Ashleigh had even laid her hands on the ingredients for a wedge salad. *If only all of their deployments could be like this.*

When the steaks were ready, he stacked them on a plate, slung his M4, and headed toward the table. His helmet, mounted with night-vision goggles, sat in a row with the others.

Berglund was only halfway there when he heard the high-pitched whistle of an inbound mortar. Dropping the steaks, he raced toward the others yelling, "Incoming! Get down! Get down!"

CHAPTER 2

Hot, jagged pieces of rock flew in all directions as the first mortar exploded. It was immediately followed by two more.

Scrambling for their gear, team members yelled out their call signs, and that they were "Up!"—ready to engage in the fight.

As they raced toward the areas they were responsible for covering, Berglund grabbed one of his junior guys, a man named Moss. Pointing at the women he yelled, "Get them to the pit!"

The pit was a subterranean interrogation facility from the days when the Iraqis had used the fort as a detention facility. It was the safest place for Ashleigh and her girlfriends.

"And bring back the belt-fed!" Berglund roared over the din, calling for the team's lightweight medium machine gun.

The mortars continued to rain down, knocking out huge sections of wall and scoring a direct hit on the fort's last remaining tower as Moss rushed the women toward the stairs.

At the bottom was a huge metal door that had been propped open with a large piece of stone. Moss herded the women inside, snatched up the twenty-four-pound machine gun, and grabbed as many cans of .338 Norma Magnum ammo as he could carry.

"Get to the back of the room," he instructed. "And don't come out until one of us comes for you."

Knocking the stone out of the way, he bent his shoulder into the heavy door and gave it a shove. He was halfway up the stairs before it clanged shut.

Outside, on the fort's decrepit battlements, the gun battle was on.

Berglund was firing his suppressed rifle in controlled bursts when Moss charged into the courtyard. "Hurry up with that belt-fed!" he shouted.

Moss ran to him, dropped the ammo cans, and began setting up the weapon.

"Did they get to the pit?"

He was about to respond when another mortar round came screeching in and exploded inside the courtyard. It blew out half the wall near the stairs, only feet from where he had just been.

"Did they get to the pit?" Berglund repeated, yelling above the ringing in his ears.

"They're safe," Moss shouted back.

Berglund pointed with the barrel of his rifle toward the southeast. "There's at least fifty of them. Maybe more. Armed with AKs and RPGs."

"Who the hell are they?"

"*Who the fuck cares?* Start putting rounds on them."

Using the night-vision scope mounted to the top of the machine gun, Moss flipped off the safety and opened fire.

The .338 Norma Magnum round was incredibly accurate and exceedingly powerful. Its effective range was two thousand yards, but it was capable of hitting targets at over six thousand. The General Dynamics lightweight medium machine gun could burn through five hundred rounds a minute, and Moss was letting them have it.

But no sooner had he dropped one group than another popped up. And now they were coming at the fort from different directions. It was a swarm. They were everywhere.

Moss changed position six times as one of the team members rushed to the pit to retrieve the rest of their ammo.

Berglund had already called Langley over his encrypted satellite phone for help. He needed intel badly. *Who are these guys? What are their numbers? And what kind of assets are in the area to come to the team's assistance?* Langley didn't have any good answers for him.

Whoever the attackers were, they had struck as the CIA's drone had come off station. A new UAV wouldn't be overhead for at least twenty more minutes. Retasking a satellite would take at least thirty. Berglund didn't have thirty minutes. He doubted he even had twenty. Pretty soon, they were going to be out of ammo. When that happened, this fight would be over.

Complicating matters was the fact that the SAD team was not even supposed to be in Iraq. This was a completely black operation. The CIA, though, wasn't going to let its people die.

In an abandoned warehouse back across the Jordanian border sat a commercial eighteen-wheel vehicle. Hidden inside its long, white trailer were two heavily modified Hughes/MD 500 helicopters with their rotor blades folded in.

"Let's move! Let's move!" the CIA crew chief yelled as the birds were rolled out and hastily prepped for launch. Their fastest time ever from truck to takeoff was four and a half minutes. If they had any hope of helping Berglund's team, they were going to need to cut that time in half.

The helicopters, CIA versions of the U.S. Army's MH-6 Little Birds, had been pre-positioned on the Jordanian side of the border as a Plan B. Plan A was for Berglund and his men to roll into Syria via three separate vehicles, put a bag over the head of their ISIS target, and roll back out. The helicopters were only there in case something went wrong during the mission.

An attack of this magnitude, at such a remote location, when no one should have known that they were there, had been considered almost impossible. But here were Berglund and his men, with only minutes left to live. The aviation team wasn't even aware of the unauthorized visitors hiding beneath the fort in the pit.

Swinging his index finger urgently above his head, the crew chief barked for the pilots to fire up their birds. "Get 'em hot! Let's go! Now! Now! Now!"

As four support personnel snapped, slapped, and racked the helicopters' weapons systems into place, the noise in the warehouse was pierced by the high-pitched whine of the engines coming to life.

Moments later, loose panes of glass began falling from the warehouse windows as the vibrating rotors chopped hungrily at the air.

When the pilots flashed the thumbs-up, the crew chief gave the signal for the warehouse doors to be opened and he set the birds loose.

Lifting off the concrete floor in unison, the MD 500s hovered over to the exit and took off.

The team had beaten their all-time best record by a minute and eighteen seconds. It was a valiant effort, and might have made the difference, except for what happened next.

Three kilometers out from the fort, as the copilots in each helicopter went hot with their weapons systems, a pair of surface-to-air missiles locked onto the heat from the engines. Neither had a chance.

Berglund didn't need Langley to tell him what had happened. He could see the explosions in the night sky for himself. Emptying the last round of his rifle mag, he set it down and transitioned to his pistol.

In his oversized Texas way, he had thought he was being cute when he had welcomed Ashleigh and her girlfriends to the "Anbar Alamo." Whether that had been prophetic or ironic didn't much matter at this point.

With their vehicles destroyed by mortar fire and the helicopters shot down, they had no choice but to make their stand here. Even if jets could be scrambled out of Jordan, they wouldn't arrive until it was too late. This was going to be it.

Berglund was a warrior. And that's how he would go out—on his feet, taking as many of the enemy with him as possible. He only had two regrets—that he hadn't better hidden Ashleigh, and that he never got a chance to eat his steak.

Sacha Baseyev was impressed. The Americans had fought harder than he had expected. Even after running out of ammunition, they had drawn their knives and tried to fight with their hands.

Only two remained alive. Both were beyond any hope of medical treatment, though. He told the videographers to hurry up and get to work.

Walking across the rubble-strewn courtyard, he approached the coolers. Brushing off a layer of debris, he removed a flashlight and opened one of the lids. Reaching inside he found it to be full of—*ice. An incredible luxury in the middle of the desert.*

He then went to the next cooler, and the next, studying their contents. *Bottles of pink wine? Pastries? Ice cream?* As decadent as the Americans were, these provisions made no sense, even for a CIA paramilitary team.

Strewn across the ground near the last cooler were steaks. Baseyev reached down and touched one. It was still warm. He counted nine of them. *Nine steaks for a six-man team.*

Considering how big some of the Americans were, perhaps a few planned to consume more than one steak. But that still didn't explain the wine he had seen. American men, particularly military men, usually drank beer or hard liquor. If they drank wine at all, it certainly wouldn't be pink.

Something wasn't right. The contents of the coolers looked like catering for a picnic or some sort of American beach party. Then his flashlight caught a reflection a few feet away.

Underneath more debris, he found an iPhone clad in a rhinestone case. Its password-protected screen was cracked, but the image of a woman kissing one of the CIA fighters was clearly visible. This was indeed a blessing.

Holding it up in the air, he called out to his fighters in Arabic. "There is a woman here," he shouted. "An *American* woman. If you find her, you can have her!"

A cheer rose from the jihadists as a handful of them rushed into the stairwell.

In the passageway below, it took two of them to pry open the pit door. The first man to force his way in took two shots to the chest and one to the head. Another gunfight was on.

This one, though, was much shorter. Ashleigh only had two spare magazines.

When her pistol ran dry, the jihadists poured in. Her colleagues were clerical workers. They didn't carry weapons.

It took only seconds for the unspeakable to begin.

CHAPTER 3

Scot Harvath wasn't trying to hide. He expected to be seen. That was the plan. Be brief. Be bloody. Be gone.

There would be handwringing by the Austrians, of course. But the politics of the assignment weren't his concern.

The White House had been crystal clear. Either the Europeans dealt with their problem, or the United States would.

Harvath sat in a corner of the Café Hawelka. A suppressed Beretta rested beneath a newspaper in his lap. Art posters covered the faded walls. The place smelled like chocolate and stale cigarettes.

Taking a final sip of his coffee, he stood and set the newspaper on the table.

His target was sitting with another man, near the window. Both were in their early thirties. Neither looked up.

Approaching the table, Harvath said only, "Paris." Then, placing the suppressor under the man's jaw, pulled the trigger.

Even though the Beretta was suppressed, the shot was still audible, and the man's brains splattered across the café window were extremely visible.

Patrons screamed and knocked over tables and chairs in a rush to escape. Others sat frozen, either in shock, or out of self-preservation—hoping not to attract the shooter's attention.

The CIA Director wanted a Rembrandt—*big, bold, and unmistakable.* Harvath had delivered.

Exiting via the rear of the café, he took off his cap, disassembled the weapon, and slid everything into his pockets.

Six blocks away, he walked into the Hotel Sacher. Tipping the coat check girl, he reclaimed his overcoat and shopping bags. He then used the men's room to clean up and change clothes.

He stood at the sink and washed his hands. There would be multiple descriptions of him given to police. None of them would be accurate. The bystanders had been transfixed by the violence and the speed at which it had happened.

His waiter would remember only that he was a white male, maybe in his thirties, who had quietly placed his order in German.

If they were able to track him all the way to the Hotel Sacher, the coat check girl might describe him as handsome. He doubted that she'd be able to add, "Five-foot-ten, sandy-brown hair, and blue eyes," to her description. Either way, he'd already be gone.

Outside the hotel, he had the doorman hail him a cab for the main train station. There, he laid a false trail by purchasing a ticket for Klagenfurt, a village near the border.

Exiting the station, he walked a few blocks to a nearby U-Bahn platform and hopped on the subway for six stops.

He poked around an obscure Vienna neighborhood for twenty minutes, then found a cab to take him to Ristorante Va Bene near the river. Confident no one was following him, he sat outside and had a beer.

He was cutting it close. The ship would be leaving soon. He needed that beer, though.

More than the beer, it was the five minutes of quiet he needed. Five minutes to get his head out of one game and into the next.

He hadn't run an operation this way before. Trying to serve two masters was never a good idea. It didn't matter how smart you were. You were begging for something to go wrong. And when things started going wrong, mistakes started piling up, along with the bodies.

He looked down at his watch. *So much for five minutes of peace.* Pulling some cash from his pocket, he threw back the rest of the beer, paid his bill, and left.

It was just over a mile to the Port of Vienna. Along the way, he tossed the Beretta and then the suppressor into the Danube.

He retrieved the Ziploc bag he had taped beneath a Dumpster with his passport, key card, and other personal effects. Putting everything back in his pockets, he ran one more mental check as he patted himself down. He didn't want to get caught with anything tying him to what had happened at the café.

Stepping onto the ship's gangway, he presented his embarkment card and smiled at the crew. They put his shopping bags onto the belt of the X-ray machine and had him walk through the magnetometer.

In the four days he had been on the ship, he had noticed a hundred ways a terrorist or other bad actor could wreak havoc. None of them involved sneaking something through the magnetometer or the X-ray machine.

Receiving the "all clear," the crew handed him his items and welcomed him back aboard. One cheerful staffer began to ask if he had enjoyed his time ashore, but he was halfway across the lobby before she could finish.

Arriving at his stateroom, he paused at the door and listened. *Nothing.* Fishing out his key card, he let himself in.

It was dark. He began to reach for the light, but stopped himself. The sliding glass door was open. A figure was standing on his balcony.

CHAPTER 4

H arvath had known this was coming. He didn't want it, but it was inevitable. Dropping the bags on the couch, he walked out onto the balcony.

Lara Cordero was leaning against the rail with a glass of champagne in her hand. Her tight dress clung to her stunning body as a faint breeze moved her long, brown hair. She could have been a model for the cruise line. She looked gorgeous.

"How'd it go?" she asked, gazing across the Danube.

He hadn't told her what he was doing, but she wasn't stupid. He had been bombarded with calls and emails since they had arrived in Europe. He was also carrying a smartphone she had never seen before. She knew enough about him to put two and two together.

He had promised her a vacation last fall, right before a megalomaniac at the United Nations engineered a devastating, global pandemic. While it burned itself out, he and Lara had taken refuge in Alaska. Under the circumstances, it wasn't exactly the getaway either of them had envisioned. A cruise along the Danube was much more like it—at least for Lara. Harvath had a secondary agenda, and that's why he had suggested it.

Islamic terrorism had exploded in Europe. Americans had been killed. The United States had been unequivocal about what it expected its European allies to do. It was time for the gloves to come off. They were at war.

The terrorists hid among the very people they were slaughtering. They used the freedom and openness of the West to strike at soft targets like churches, cafés, restaurants, bars, transit centers, tourist attractions, sporting events, concerts, movie theaters, and schools.

They were not legitimate combatants. They were savages. To expect any mercy from the nations upon whom they preyed was the height of insanity. They respected one thing and one thing only—force.

Abubakar al-Shishani was responsible for a string of terror attacks in Paris that had killed multiple Americans. The fact that he moved about so openly in Vienna showed how little he feared any reprisal. Harvath had taken care of that, though.

It was meant to be a message to the rest of them. If they killed Americans, America would kill them. It didn't matter where they were, or how long it took. Harvath was happy to be the messenger.

Moving in and out of Vienna via boat was too good an opportunity for Harvath to pass up. The cruise provided him with the perfect cover. It also provided him with a chance to have his cake and eat it too.

He and Lara were at a crossroads. They needed the vacation, but they needed it in order to sort out what was going to happen next.

The pandemic, though short-lived, had been brutal. It seemed everyone knew someone who had been impacted. That included Lara. Two of her superiors had succumbed. And because of it, she had been offered an amazing promotion.

The Boston Police Department wanted to elevate her from homicide detective to commander of the entire unit.

It was an incredible opportunity. But it meant she would have to remain in Boston.

In the hope that she might relocate, Harvath had been reaching out to his contacts in and around D.C. They were all feeling a similar pinch. They had lost exceptional people, but wanted to promote from within. The chance Lara was being offered wasn't going to be matched anywhere else.

Although it killed him to admit it, it was the best decision she could make. He respected her sense of loyalty to a department that had always had her back, and to a city that she loved.

There were other factors at play as well. Her aging parents lived in the apartment right beneath hers. They were too old to leave Boston and start over. All of their friends were there. They were a tight family. The idea of

Lara's son growing up in Virginia without his grandparents just down-stairs also didn't sit well. If they couldn't make the move together, she didn't want to make the move at all.

Harvath understood. He loved her enough to want what was best for her—to accept the promotion. He also loved her enough to want their last trip together to be special.

His moving to Boston was pretty much a nonstarter. He couldn't do his job long-distance. The CIA had him under contract now and the President demanded a lot of face time. With the country's aggressive new stance on terrorism, he was only going to get busier.

It wasn't an easy conclusion to come to. Ten years from now, or maybe even just five, his thinking might have been different. But not now, not at this moment. Too much was at stake.

The world was growing more dangerous. Some derided the American Dream. Not Harvath. He knew that the American Dream couldn't survive without people willing to protect it. He had always put the country ahead of himself. He had done it as a SEAL, and had continued to do it in a variety of capacities ever since. That wasn't going to stop, no matter how much it personally pained or cost him.

Right after Paris, he'd had a conversation with the President. In it, he shared his theory that there were wolves and then there were sheep. In order to protect the sheep, the nation needed sheepdogs, and that's how he saw himself.

The President thought about it for several moments before sharing his own view. Yes, the United States needed its sheepdogs, but it also needed wolf hunters. That was how the President saw Harvath best helping to protect the sheep.

"We're not going to wait for the wolves to come to us," he had said. "We're going to go to them, where they live, where they eat, where they sleep. We'll hunt them with a ferocity the likes of which they have never seen. If they so much as look in our direction, we will take them out."

It was one of the most powerful statements Harvath had ever heard. It hadn't been made for the cameras or to score political points. It was the man's core ideological belief. And it only served to deepen Harvath's respect for him.

Take off the chains and let us go do our jobs. It was a statement made over and over again by spies and Special Operations personnel. Now Harvath was getting his chance. He didn't intend to let it slip by.

Pulling the cold bottle of champagne from the bucket, he poured himself a glass.

"Can we at least enjoy Budapest together tomorrow before we have to fly home?" she asked, still facing out toward the river.

He walked over and wrapped his arms around her. Kissing the back of her neck, he was about to respond when his phone vibrated.

CHAPTER 5

Senator Daniel Wells leaned forward and studied the man on the other side of his desk. "Did I stutter?" he asked. His jacket hung on the back of his chair and his sleeves were rolled up.

"No, sir," replied his guest.

"Was I speaking in a foreign language?"

"No, sir," the man repeated, in a frustrated tone, tired of the condescension from the arrogant Iowa senator. He was the worst kind of politician. Even in the aftermath of the pandemic, he was all about furthering his own agenda.

"Thirteen Americans are dead. *Thirteen,*" Wells barked. "And you don't have a fucking clue what happened? Not one piece of information?"

"Sir, if I could just—"

Wells cut him off. "Stop calling me *sir*. I am a United States Senator."

"Yes, Senator. I didn't mean to—"

Wells ignored him and plowed on. "It's your duty, as Director of the CIA, to keep my committee informed."

"We're still trying to unpack what happened."

"Let's start with what the hell you were doing in Anbar."

Their conversation was drifting into dangerous territory. Bob McGee chose his words carefully. "Looking for high-ranking ISIS figures."

"You deployed a six-man SAD team to the Syrian border, along with heavily armed, multimillion-dollar covert aviation assets, just to look around?"

The CIA Director nodded. He was in his late fifties, with wavy salt-and-pepper hair and a thick mustache.

"You're full of shit. That's why we have a drone program. What were you really doing there?"

"Senator, as I said, looking for high-ranking ISIS figures."

Wells glared at him. He was getting nowhere. "And the collection management officer? What about her? What was *she* doing there?"

They were officially in dangerous territory now. Nevertheless, McGee decided to give him a straight answer, "I don't know why Ashleigh Foster was there."

"Bullshit."

"Senator, you have my word that—"

"What about the other two?" Wells interrupted. "The two additional women from the Embassy?"

The CIA Director shook his head. "We're still not sure."

Wells glared at him. "What about the video? Have you even seen it?"

McGee was tempted to glare right back at him. *Had he seen it?* Of course he had. The whole world had seen it by now. ISIS had wasted no time in putting it out. It was beyond barbaric.

The women had been made to do unspeakable things with the body parts of the deceased SAD members. They were then brutally raped and tortured before being murdered. One could even be heard crying for her father to come save her. Even for a group as depraved as ISIS, it was sickening.

"Savages," said McGee, acknowledging that he had indeed seen it.

"Can you imagine what the families are going through?"

"I can't possibly—"

"You're damn right you can't," Wells broke in. "I don't know what kind of game you're playing, but as far as I'm concerned, the CIA is fully responsible for the deaths of those Americans."

McGee could see where this was going now. Wells hated the Agency. He was going to hang everything on Langley, if not on him personally.

The Senator was a petty, vindictive man who had done everything in his power to block McGee's confirmation. He had never thought him a good choice for director. He had wanted someone with more political skin in the game, a careerist he could manipulate.

But that was precisely why the President had selected McGee. He wasn't seen as an "insider." He didn't play the game. He had a long history at the CIA, but on the ops side, not management. That was a plus as far as the President was concerned.

McGee cared deeply about the CIA, and about repairing its broken culture. He was the perfect pick to muck its Augean stables.

As Director of Central Intelligence, McGee had swung the ax without mercy. The Agency needed to get back to its roots. There were too many bureaucrats, too many middle managers more concerned with their next promotion than the men and women in the field.

McGee fired more people at the CIA than had been fired in the last three decades. He went after the waste, fraud, and abuse like the cancer it was. That included people friendly with Senator Wells. People who thought Wells would protect their positions.

The Senator had been quite upset about the layoffs. His pull inside the agency was waning. He was losing good sources of information and influence. People who owed him favors were being cut loose. It didn't take him long to push back by subtly threatening the new director.

"You worry about the CIA and I'll worry about Wells," the President had told McGee. Up until now, it was a strategy that had worked. But Anbar had just changed everything. It would only accelerate the ambitions of Senator Wells.

Though he hadn't yet announced, everyone knew he was going to challenge the President in the next election. Anbar, and that sick video, must have looked like a gift from heaven.

McGee had no intention of helping Wells. "As soon as I have a better picture of what happened," he said, "I'll be happy to brief the committee."

"No, you'll brief me. And I don't care how many asses you have to kick, or kiss, you'd better have something for me soon."

McGee nodded and began to stand. "If that's all, I'll be—"

"Sit down!" Wells bellowed. "I'm not finished."

It took everything McGee had not to throat-punch the man, but he complied.

"What do you know about Vienna?" Wells demanded.

Without thinking it through, he replied, "It's the capital of Austria."

"You want to mess with me, Director McGee? Is that it? How funny do you think it'll be when the CIA gets its funding cut?"

McGee knew better than to be a smart aleck. Wells wasn't just an arrogant jackass—he was an extremely powerful, arrogant jackass. That made him dangerous.

It would be political suicide for Wells to cut off funding. He'd never do it. He could, though, slow it down. If that happened, it would cause all sorts of problems for the CIA.

That was the barrel he had McGee over, and McGee despised him for it. He hated having to kowtow to self-serving clowns like Wells.

But what he hated even more was the thought of his people at the CIA not getting what they needed. Money was oxygen in the intelligence business. If it were to be cut off, everything would cease to function. He couldn't risk that.

"Vienna," McGee said, pushing his ego aside. "You're referring to the hit on al-Shishani?"

"No, I'm referring to their *fucking* schnitzel. Of course I'm referring to the hit on al-Shishani. What do you know about it?"

Everything, thought McGee. *None of which I am going to share with you.*

Looking the Senator right in the eye, the CIA Director replied, "We think the French wanted to send a message."

"*The French?* Because the shooter allegedly mentioned Paris?" said Wells, thinking about it for a moment. "I don't buy it. Not their style. The Israelis, maybe. But they don't have a dog in this part of the fight."

McGee shrugged. "You asked me what I knew."

"And you haven't told me shit," said Wells. "Our government has checks and balances for a reason. If I find out that you, *or* the President, have been operating outside constitutional authority, I'll rain hell down upon you both. Do you understand me?"

"Yes, sir, I do," McGee said, pressing the man's buttons once more as he stood. "Will that be all, sir?"

Wells stared daggers at him. "Get the fuck out of my office."

• • •

Leaving the Senator's office, McGee knew two things. One, he hated Wells more than ever. And two, if Harvath didn't figure out who was behind the Anbar debacle, they were all going to be in a lot of trouble.

CHAPTER 6

In Budapest, the CIA had a gray Mercedes waiting for them at the dock. Lara was going to the Four Seasons. Harvath was going to the airport. They were both exhausted.

Neither had wanted to face the raw emotion of their separation. It had been easier to let two bottles of champagne dull as much of it as possible, and they'd had one final, wild night.

They were a great couple—smart, passionate, and electric together. The fact that they couldn't figure out how to make something so good work in the same city was crazy.

When it came time for the actual goodbye, Lara gave him one of the best kisses he'd ever had. Long, slow, sexy. Then she got out of the car, grabbed her bag from the trunk, and walked into the hotel.

Harvath sat in the backseat and stared at the polished glass doors. *What the hell just happened*, he wondered. It was like all the oxygen was just sucked out his lungs. *Did I really let her walk?*

Several moments passed as he sat there and tried to sort it all out. His driver finally interrupted his thoughts. "Are we ready to head to the airport, sir?"

The short answer was *no*. He wasn't ready to head to the airport. He wanted to chase Lara up to her room, lock the door, and pretend he hadn't said yes to Brussels. But he couldn't do that. He had given his word.

Harvath usually enjoyed traveling by private jet, especially on something as luxurious as a Dassault Falcon 5X. But even its dramatic skylight failed to impress him today.

He mixed salt, sugar, and ground aspirin into a tall glass of tomato juice over ice. It tasted horrible.

After downing another, he stretched out on the white leather couch with a large bottle of water.

The CIA used an encrypted app that only allowed him to watch the Anbar video and view the image files once. It was more than enough.

ISIS was an Islamic death cult trying to usher in an apocalypse. The larger they grew, the more depraved they became.

Their ultimate goal was to meet the infidel in Dabiq, a tiny village in northern Syria. After a decisive ground battle, the Muslim messiah would return. Or so the ancient prophecy went. Harvath was willing to bet that the prophet Mohammed had never envisioned nuclear weapons.

If it were up to Harvath, he'd let the nukes fly. After dropping leaflets warning residents to flee, he'd flatten Dabiq and then Raqqa, the ISIS capital. There'd be no ground battle. There'd only be fields of glass. The ISIS savages were not worth another drop of American blood.

But it wasn't up to Harvath. It was up to the President of the United States, who, for the moment, had a different plan.

He wanted to know how the SAD team in Iraq had come under attack. How had ISIS known they were there?

Harvath had gathered the intelligence for the operation. He was the one who had identified and pinpointed the high value ISIS target. The information had come from his contacts. Now thirteen Americans were dead.

The CIA had launched an immediate investigation. They learned that Ashleigh Foster had been in a relationship with one of the SAD team members. She had convinced two girlfriends from the Embassy to join her for the weekend and party at the safe house. Phone records, texts, and emails all backed it up. It was a case of extremely bad judgment across the board. The ISIS attack, though, was another matter.

The jihadists had come ready for the fight. They had not only overwhelmed the SAD team but had also downed two CIA helicopters. They knew exactly what they were up against. They'd even brought a video crew. Had they known the women were going to be there too?

All of this was what Harvath had been tasked with figuring out. And square one was in Brussels.

• • •

The city was more than twenty-five percent Muslim, and its most con-centrated Islamic neighborhood was Molenbeek. Sitting on the wrong side of the canal, it boasted more than two dozen mosques.

It also boasted one of Harvath's best contacts—a contact who had suddenly gone dark.

Either Salah Abaaoud was in trouble, or Harvath had been double-crossed.

If he'd been double-crossed, there wasn't a hole deep enough for Salah to hide in. Harvath would find him. It was what he did.

Salah was a doctor with a storefront practice. Everyone in Molenbeek knew him. He was the unofficial mayor of the neighborhood. He settled disputes, helped new Muslim immigrants navigate the Belgian welfare system, pulled bad teeth, and even arranged marriages.

He was a generous contributor to local mosques and charities, drove a bright red BMW, and always had tickets to the best sporting matches.

By all outward appearances, Dr. Salah Abaaoud was a successful man. No one in the neighborhood had any clue about his criminal past. Even the Belgian government was in the dark.

Back in the Middle East, Salah had made a fortune as a smuggler. Le-veraging his position as a doctor, he had exploited Red Crescent, UN and a host of other medical relief missions and convoys. He smuggled every-thing, from stolen antiquities, drugs, and weapons, to people. It was the weapons, though, that had gotten him caught.

At one point, he was moving a crate of stolen missiles from Morocco to Lebanon. Harvath had been tracking the cell behind the theft. One piece of information led to another until Harvath ended up on Salah's door-step. The only thing that had saved the doctor's life was his willingness to cooperate.

With all his connections, Salah was in a position to know things. He had an impressive network, and Harvath wanted it.

Salah agreed to a generous monthly stipend and was allowed to con-tinue breathing. Allah had doubly blessed him.

Harvath assigned him the code name Sidewinder, after the missiles

Salah had been caught smuggling. But as time wore on, he realized the actual rattlesnake was an even better fit. Salah's blood was cold, he made a lot of noise when he was upset, and he could strike without warning. The man required delicate handling.

Right now, though, Harvath wasn't in the mood to be delicate. Thirteen Americans were dead. Ten of them had been operating on intelligence he had gathered. The other three had just been in the wrong place at the wrong time. None of them, though, would have been there if it wasn't for him. That was a fact, and it weighed on him. He tried to put it out of his mind as he hunted for Salah.

The first place he checked was the man's house, but there was no sign of him or his red BMW. Next was the clinic.

It was locked up tight. Through the window, Harvath could see a stack of mail piled up on the floor. Had Salah skipped town? Had he fled the country? Harvath's concerns over being double-crossed began to rise. There was only one other place he could think to look for him.

Salah's piety had a limit. It ended right at his erogenous zone. He kept a love nest, along with a well-stocked liquor cart, in the fashionable Saint-Gilles neighborhood. Harvath had followed him there once. The apartment was located just off the Avenue Louise.

If the true measure of a person's character was what they did when no one was watching, Dr. Salah Abaaoud would have scandalized the Muslims of Brussels. In addition to being a semiprofessional alcoholic, he was screwing the very attractive, very much younger, and very married nurse from his clinic, Aisha.

Harvath stood outside the door and listened. What was he expecting to hear? *Sex?* Even a man as gluttonous as Salah wouldn't disappear for days on a bender. He was too careful. He had too much invested in his public image. Not so much, though, that it stopped him from screwing or drinking. He had simply gotten used to a certain level of risk.

Harvath could hear something coming from inside. It sounded like screaming, but it definitely wasn't sex. *A soccer game?*

He twisted the knob of the brass bell in the center of the door and waited. The last time he had walked in on Salah, he had gotten more than an eyeful. Full frontal of any man, much less that fat and that hairy, was something he never needed to see again.

No one came to the door.

After waiting a few more moments, he removed a credit card–sized piece of steel from his pocket. Lockpick tools had been carved into it with a laser. All he had to do was pop out the ones he needed.

Studying the lock, he was in the process of selecting a pick when he decided to try the handle.

The door was unlocked. Salah never left anything unlocked.

Pushing the door open, he could see all the way into the apartment without stepping inside.

Someone had been here. And they had created their own Rembrandt.

CHAPTER 7

There was no sign of a struggle. No torture. Salah sat on the couch in a gold and purple robe with his head tipped back. A corona of blood was splattered on the wall behind him. On the table was a highball, half-filled with what was probably his favorite bourbon. The TV was on. Probably had been for days.

Harvath stepped inside and closed the door. The scent of tea and spices was overpowered by the odor of death. He needed to make this quick.

Standing in the vestibule, he took everything in. The hit looked professional. Salah had been shot once in the head.

As no one had called the police, the killer had probably used a suppressed weapon. That ruled out Aisha's husband and an act of passion.

Making his way into the master bedroom, Harvath noticed an unmade bed, Salah's clothes over the back of a chair, and a woman's clothes draped across a chaise near the window. Faint light glowed from the bathroom. Harvath had a bad feeling about what he was going to find inside.

Moving over to the door, he nudged it open. Aisha lay naked and dead in the tub. Someone had shot her once in the head, just like Salah. The tiles behind her were bright red with her blood, the bathwater a deep rose.

Stepping out of the bathroom, Harvath walked back through the apartment.

It was definitely a professional hit. Nothing appeared to have been stolen. Salah still wore his gold Rolex Daytona, the two Chagalls still hung in the living room, and all the jewelry he had purchased for Aisha, which she could never bring home, sat in a red velvet box on her dressing table.

The killer was not only professional but disciplined. This ruled out most, if not all, of the underworld and jihadist figures Salah conducted business with.

If any of them had had a beef with the smuggler, Harvath would have heard about it. Salah frequently abused their relationship in order to settle his business disputes. He knew there were certain clients that the United States would gladly take out for him.

In fact, the CIA sometimes scrawled *AGFSA* on the missiles its drones used for such assignments—*A Gift From Salah Abaaoud.*

Salah's success rate in identifying and locating terrorist targets was why the CIA had taken his recent ISIS intel so seriously.

But now look at him, Harvath thought as he examined the body. He had definitely been here a couple of days.

So if it wasn't a jealous husband, or a disgruntled business associate, who killed him?

The professionalism of the hit made it look like a state sponsor, carried out by some country's intelligence service.

Harvath immediately ruled out any services allied with the United States. He had flagged Salah across the board. If MI6, the Mossad, or anyone like that had wanted him, it should have been brought to his attention.

Could it have been a Middle Eastern nation like Morocco, Egypt, or Saudi Arabia? Possibly, but they were pretty bad at projecting force much beyond their own borders. And if it *were* one of them, why would they expend that kind of effort over Salah? It didn't make sense.

There were a lot more questions coming to his mind than answers. One thing, though, was certain. Salah was proving just as much a pain in the ass dead as he had been alive.

Harvath continued to carefully move through the apartment as he looked for clues. The last thing he wanted was to leave anything that would tie him to the scene. He wanted Belgian authorities focused on catching the real killer.

And whoever that was, he had chosen to splash Salah here, rather than at his home or his clinic. *Why?*

Based on the evidence, it looked like he had caught Salah by surprise. Having just had sex, he was watching TV and enjoying a drink, while his mistress took a bath. The assassin appeared to have only one goal—to kill him right where he found him.

But if that was the case, why not then turn and leave? Why walk back to the bathroom and kill Aisha? Time.

If he had just turned and left, it wouldn't have taken Aisha long to find Salah's body. Would she, the unfaithful wife, have called police? Maybe. Would she have screamed and drawn the attention of neighbors? It was possible, and a professional would have taken it all into consideration.

This was particularly true of someone who needed to get out of the country. The more time he had before the police even knew he was there, the better his chances, especially if he was leaving by plane or rail.

Pulling out his phone, Harvath took pictures of everything. Geo-Tagging the location, he transmitted the images back to his team in the United States. He included a message with it for his IT expert, Nicholas.

Known to global intelligence services as "The Troll," Nicholas suffered from a condition known as primordial dwarfism. Though he stood less than three feet high, Nicholas was a digital savant who had built a name through the purchase, sale, and theft of highly sensitive black-market information.

He had made powerful enemies in his career. And though he had gone "straight," his two enormous white Caucasian Ovcharka dogs were always at his side, just in case.

Professional job, Harvath's message read. *Possible foreign intel service. Pull surrounding CCTV footage. See if you can track the hitter.*

Returning to the bedroom, Harvath removed the keys from Salah's trousers and exited the apartment.

• • •

By the time he arrived back in Molenbeek, it was already dark and residents were at evening prayers. He decided to check Salah's clinic first.

Unlocking the front door, he stepped over the pieces of mail and slipped inside. Salah's personal office was in the back.

Harvath didn't know what he was looking for. A professional hitter coming after Salah was one thing. A professional hitter coming after Salah, right on the heels of the attack in Anbar, was something entirely different.

Until he had reason to suspect otherwise, Harvath was going to consider the two events connected. You didn't live very long in this line of work by believing in coincidences.

He made a quick pass of Salah's office, but everything seemed to be in place. It didn't look like anyone had been here at all.

Turning on the clinic computers, Harvath inserted a portable flash drive with a program that would allow Nicholas access. Once the program was uploaded, he removed the drive and headed for Salah's house.

It was a bland, three-story brick structure. The ground floor, where Salah held meetings and received people from the neighborhood, was modestly decorated. The second and third stories were much more lavish.

The color scheme for these levels was similar to the robe Salah had been shot in—lots of purple and gold. Overstuffed couches sat on thick Persian carpets, accented by ornate chairs and heavy draperies. Paintings of plump, naked women and bowls of fruit adorned the walls. The musty air was laden with the sickly-sweet, overly perfumed smell of incense.

Harvath used his elbow to open a set of French windows and let in some air. Moving from room to room, he took note of what he saw.

Dirty breakfast dishes sat in the sink. A coffee cup rested on the windowsill in the bathroom. A three-day-old newspaper lay open on the dining room table. It didn't look like anyone but Salah had been here since then.

Either the murder was revenge for something very far in Salah's past, or he had been killed in order to keep him quiet.

Harvath was betting on quiet. *But quiet about what?*

There had to be something in the house that would tell him. Returning to the study, he opened Salah's desk drawers and began going through his personal papers. Most of them were written in Arabic.

It was a language Harvath had some proficiency in speaking, but reading was all but out of the question. He was going to have to bag everything and get it to an Agency translator.

He was coming back from the bedroom with a pillowcase when he got a text on his phone.

Recognize this guy? the message from Nicholas asked. A photograph followed.

It showed a thin, almost feminine-looking young man with pale skin and blond hair that was nearly white. He wore a short sleeve dress shirt and a narrow black tie.

No. Who is he? Harvath typed back.

Within seconds, his phone vibrated. It was a call from Nicholas.

"His name is Sacha Baseyev," the little man said from more than three thousand miles away, back in northern Virginia. "Two years ago, the FBI debriefed a Russian intelligence officer seeking political asylum. He came ready to play. Baseyev was on a list of names he gave up."

"Why are we talking about him?"

"I'm getting there," Nicholas replied. "You remember the Beslan School siege and the Moscow theater massacre?"

Harvath knew them well. They were huge mass-casualty events.

Beslan was a horrific three-day attack in which 1,100 people were taken hostage. Three hundred eighty-five were murdered, 186 of them children.

The attack on the Moscow theater resulted in 900 hostages, 170 of whom were killed.

They were textbook cases studied by America's premier counterterrorism and hostage rescue personnel.

"I remember," said Harvath. "It was carried out by Islamic terrorists. Chechens. Is there some other nexus?"

"A Deputy Director of the GRU, Russia's largest foreign intelligence service, lost his wife and daughter at the theater that night. After a long leave of absence, some believe to hunt terrorists in the Caucasus, he returned to the GRU and received permission to establish a new unit."

"What kind of unit?"

"An assassinations unit."

"Were they part of the response at Beslan?" Harvath asked.

"No, they came after."

"To hunt down the rest of the terrorists?"

There was a pause. "To recruit," Nicholas replied.

"From among the survivors? The children?"

"Who better to send after the devil, than someone who had already been through hell? At least that was their thinking."

Harvath had once recruited a hijacking survivor to help ID a terrorist, but that was different. What the Russians were attempting was insanity. "I'd be stunned if any of those kids were capable of being a functional adult—much less an operative who could follow orders in high-stress environments."

Nicholas agreed. "All of the recruits washed out. They either buckled under the pressure, or were so aggressive that it bordered on psychotic."

"Except for one, I'm guessing."

"Correct. Sacha Baseyev. No matter what they threw at him, he excelled."

"So, now we're back to my previous question," said Harvath. "Why are we talking about him?"

"Because I think he's your assassin."

CHAPTER 8

Plastic surgery had made Sacha Baseyev a man of nondescript features and indeterminate origin. All the better for him to move in and out of places he wasn't supposed to be.

He stood five foot nine inches, but could look taller, or shorter, just by how he carried himself.

He was remarkable in that he was completely unremarkable. Even when he stood next to others, they usually failed to notice him. He was the quintessential "gray man" who faded into the background.

He was one of the best weapons the Russians had ever created against Islamic extremists. He had been trained to infiltrate their ranks and destroy them from within. He was exceptional at it.

But with Anbar, he had taken what he did to an entirely new level. The Russians had laid an elaborate trap for the United States. His job was to bait it. That's why he was now in Turkey.

He was running a cell of ISIS fighters from an old warehouse. It was in a part of the city where few people spoke, and even fewer asked questions—a perfect location for a safe house.

Tonight, Baseyev's oiled hair was black, his eyes brown. His knowledge of the Quran was as deep as the ocean. So deep was it that the brothers chose him to lead them in prayer. It was only natural. In their eyes, he was the most pious, the most devout among them. He was their leader.

Their faith in him was absolute and they had willingly ingested the pills he had given them. Though drugs were frowned upon in Islam, exceptions were made in preparation for battle.

Their bodies relaxed and their minds began to float free. It was a religious experience in itself, a hint of what awaited them in Paradise.

One of the men, his eyes dilated, smiled and said, "*Insha'Allah,* we will be victorious tomorrow, Brother Ibrahim."

Ibrahim al-Masri was Baseyev's nom de guerre. He had adopted it years earlier when he had joined a radical madrassa in the Caucasus. From there, he infiltrated his first Muslim extremist group in Chechnya. They had no idea of the deadly viper they had welcomed into their ranks.

Baseyev collected intelligence on the organization that resulted in several high-ranking members being taken out. He also did some of the killing himself—making it all look accidental.

When he used his jihadist connections to move on to ISIS, his reputation preceded him. Many fearsome acts had already become attached to the name Ibrahim al-Masri.

In Iraq and Syria, he slaughtered many enemies of ISIS. And as he did, his fame and prominence within the organization grew. They came to consider him a fierce lion. But it wasn't always this way. At first, his superiors had been wary of him.

His travel patterns had troubled them. The young fighter came and went, never staying longer than a couple of months. It appeared he wasn't fully committed to the struggle.

But when he started showing up with things they needed, their image of him began to change. He was proficient at finding hard-to-get items like medicines and blank passports, night-vision equipment and infrared laser devices.

He then began helping develop recruiting strategies and planning attacks. Eventually, Brother Ibrahim came to be seen as a valuable asset and a rising star within ISIS.

As the caliphate grew, he was offered a governorship, but he politely turned it down. Rationing fuel, settling petty squabbles, and overseeing councils were not for him. Allah, he explained, had blessed him with the skill and stamina to fight. His sword was meant to sing, not hang in a scabbard on a wall.

The powers that be understood. They were better off with him not sitting behind a desk. They allowed him broad autonomy and continued to be rewarded for it.

Everything had unfolded just the way the GRU had planned. He was on the inside. No one doubted Ibrahim al-Masri's sincerity or devotion to the cause.

Unrolling his rug on the floor of the warehouse, he led the men in evening prayers.

He knew the words so well that he could say them in his sleep. He had been placed with an Arabic-speaking family and fully immersed in Islamic culture since his teens. Now in his late twenties, he could converse like a scholar on everything from the conquests of the Prophet Mohammed to the failures of Pan-Arab nationalism and the rise of the caliphate.

Many core ISIS members possessed advanced degrees, and intelligence, especially at the top levels of the organization, was very highly prized. Intelligent men went far and were handsomely rewarded. ISIS saw to it.

The men he had gathered here in this warehouse, however, would not go far. Any who survived the attack tomorrow he would kill himself. That was his will. Their pagan desert god had nothing to do with it. He would not stretch down a magical hand to protect them and smite their enemies. Allah was a phantom.

He was a myth, a figment from the mind of a disturbed psychopath named Mohammed. The violence and hatred he preached had created over a thousand years of anguish.

Sacha Baseyev looked at the men on their mats. How these bloodthirsty animals envisioned any god that would condone their acts of barbarism was beyond him.

He would always remember that September day in Beslan. It felt more like spring than the end of summer vacation. His father, the school's director, had awakened him and his younger sister before dawn. His mother, an art teacher, was already cooking breakfast.

His father liked to joke that the two best days of the year were the first day of school and the last. Sacha liked to respond that his father was only fifty percent correct.

Who in their right mind wanted summer vacation to end? Even their mother, a schoolteacher, sighed as she moved about the kitchen, pausing as she changed the water in a small vase of flowers they had picked on a recent hike together.

The summer had been full of all sorts of adventures. His six-year-old sister, Dasha, had ridden her first horse. He and Grigori, his best friend, had found a cave with an abandoned jeep inside. They spent weeks pretending to repair it, discussing all the places it would take them.

When Sacha's birthday arrived, his father gave him a beautiful pocket-knife. Catia, the neighbor's freckled niece visiting from Stavropol, let him hold her hand.

Who would trade any of this for school?

The sun was only just beginning to rise when they arrived at their father's office. He poured small coffees for them and allowed them to have extra sugar. It was a reward for getting up so early.

Sacha drank his as he watched the officers changing shift at the district police station next door. Many of them had children in the school. Grigori's father was a police officer. He had taken them into the woods over the summer to shoot his pistol. It was very loud. Not as loud, though, as what was to come.

The traditional start of the Russian school year was known as First Bell, or Knowledge Day. Children dressed in their best clothes and brought their parents and relatives with them. They presented flowers to the teachers and participated in school-sponsored festivities.

Sacha was outside with his parents and sister at eleven minutes past nine that morning. They were welcoming everyone when a police van and a military truck pulled up and his life was shattered forever.

Several dozen heavily armed Islamic terrorists leapt out and began shooting. They were dressed in camouflage military fatigues and black masks. Many wore suicide belts.

Over a thousand people were herded and packed into the school's gymnasium. There, the terrorists separated off the biggest, strongest men and executed them. One of them was Sacha's father.

During the next three days, temperatures in the gymnasium soared. The children stripped down to their underwear. Sacha and his friends drank their own urine from shoes to stay hydrated. His mother was taken away and raped. He never saw her again.

The terrorists had rigged the gymnasium with explosive devices in case they were overrun. On the third day, at three minutes past one in the afternoon, something exploded. Two minutes later, there was another explosion. The roof of the gymnasium was on fire. The terrorists refused to let anyone leave.

Minutes later flaming rafters and large sections of roofing began to fall in. Sacha's sister, Dasha, was trapped. He and Grigori tried to get to her, but they couldn't. She burned to death.

A third explosion followed, knocking out a huge section of wall. Panicked hostages stampeded to get out. Grigori and Sacha fought their way through the smoke and fire to join them. Then, more shooting started.

The terrorists were firing into the crowd, attempting to stop anyone from fleeing alive. Parents, teachers, children . . . bodies fell all around them, but Sacha and Grigori kept running. They had to get out. They had to get free.

There was a *pop*, and then time collapsed. Sacha looked to his left as half of Grigori's face disappeared. One of the terrorist's bullets had tumbled through the back of his head and out the front of his face. He seemed to stare at Sacha as his lifeless body collapsed to the ground.

Someone, he would never know who, grabbed Sacha and propelled him forward.

People told him he was lucky to be alive. That he must live his life not only for himself, but also for his dead mother, father, and sister. Those people were wrong.

There was nothing lucky about his being alive. There was nothing lucky about having lived through what he had. It had broken him—like a watch that had been struck so hard, it had stopped at the moment of a terrible accident. He wasn't alive. He was a walking version of death. He was cold through to his very core. Actual, physical death, if it ever came, would be a relief.

The CIA team and their women in Anbar was just the beginning. An appetizer. The next attack was going to be even more dramatic.

CHAPTER 9

Richard Devon took one last look over the turquoise-blue Mediterranean and breathed in the air. Soon he would be inside a plane for ten hours, and he wanted to sear it all into his memory.

He and his Turkish counterpart usually met at the air base in Incirlik, but Ismet Bachar, Chief of the Turkish General Staff, was on vacation near Antalya. Bachar had no intention of leaving, not even for the U.S. Secretary of Defense. So, Devon had gone to him.

The Turkish Riviera was a part of the country he had never seen before. It turned out to be stunning.

Bachar's villa was positioned to maximize its breathtaking view of the sea. They had lunch on the terrace, surrounded by stone pots planted with lavender. The sun was bright and strong, but the breeze off the water made for the perfect temperature. Devon understood why his colleague didn't want to break away to come meet him.

While the Secretary of Defense looked like a doughy, fifty-five-year-old country club member who should have been spending more time on the treadmill and less time in the grill, Bachar looked like a Hollywood film star. He was tall and thin, with white hair that was perfectly trimmed. His handsome, angular face was tanned and sported a pair of black-framed glasses. Out of courtesy to his American guest, he had put on a suit, but no tie.

It was like being in the presence of a Turkish Cary Grant.

Though Devon had seen only a houseboy, he could imagine a bevy of bikini-clad women hidden upstairs, waiting for him to leave, so that whatever party he had interrupted could continue.

For lunch, Bachar served Mediterranean swordfish with pomegranate and pistachio salad. He paired it with a 2008 Domaine Leflaive Puligny-Montrachet Les Folatières Premier Cru. He was showing off. But considering how far Devon had come, and why, it was the least he could do.

The Turks had the second-largest army in NATO and were an important American ally. Their military also took the threat of fundamentalist Islam seriously.

Four times since Turkey's founding, the Turkish military had stepped in to reduce the power of the Islamists in their country. Bachar was concerned that number five might be around the corner, maybe even before the next election.

Turkey's leader saw himself more as a sultan than a president. He was gathering powers to his office that didn't belong. Other branches of the government, which should have served as a check, had done nothing to stop him.

Of concern to the military was that their president was an Islamist. Of concern to the United States was that he was an Islamist, sympathetic to ISIS.

Turkey had only been putting on a show of fighting ISIS. While its President allowed the United States to launch bombing runs from Incirlik, he ignored the men, money, and materiel flowing to ISIS across the Turkish border.

When Turkish planes flew, they didn't hammer ISIS positions. They hammered the Kurds who were successfully fighting against ISIS. The Turks didn't want the forty million Kurds in Syria, Northern Iraq, and Western Turkey to unite and form their own sovereign nation.

The Turks also hated the Syrian regime, which meant they hated Russia and Iran for propping it up. They no longer thought twice about bloodying the noses of the Russians or the Iranians. If a justifiable situation presented itself, they took it.

Tossing lit matches into puddles of gasoline was a recipe for disaster. If the brinksmanship wasn't deescalated, the world was going to war. All it would take was Turkey getting hit back and then citing Article 5 of the

NATO charter—*An armed attack on one member of the alliance is an attack on all.*

The men spoke for more than three hours. Bachar played his cards close to his vest. For the time being, the Turkish military was following its president's orders. That could change. More than that, Bachar wouldn't say.

He agreed with Devon that ISIS was a growing cancer. It was a cancer, though, eating a neighbor that Turkey despised. Right now, he was content to let it continue.

The prospect of war with the Russians or the Iranians, though, wasn't something he relished. He shared that with Devon and suggested that instead of pressuring Turkey, the United States should focus on those nations. Anything Turkey had done had been in retaliation for something Russia or Iran had done. None of it had been unprovoked. If Russia and Iran wanted to continue their escapades in Syria and if those escapades drifted over the border or threatened Turkish sovereignty in any way, they could expect more of the same. Turkey had a right to defend herself.

Devon understood that it was a matter of national pride. He also understood that by flexing its muscles, the Turkish military was bolstering its image among the Turkish people. That would come in handy if they decided to move against the President and other powerful Islamists.

A complicated chessboard was taking shape in Turkey. If the United States couldn't control the movements, it at least needed to know where the pieces were.

Before leaving, Devon reassured his friend that whatever he chose to do, he would have the support of the United States. That level of support, though, could be dialed up or down, based upon how Turkey handled ISIS and any further Russian or Iranian provocations.

There was no need to read between the lines with Devon. He was always very clear when laying out what he wanted. He didn't want his words interpreted. He wanted them understood. There was a difference.

Bachar smiled. He didn't care for politicians. He liked simple, straight talk. Devon had always been honest with him. He appreciated that. And while there was only so much he could do under the current President, Bachar assured his colleague that he would keep the lines of communication open.

They enjoyed a final cup of strong Turkish coffee accompanied by a plate of ripe figs. Then Bachar walked his guest out to his car.

In the driveway were three black Range Rovers and a police escort. These days, only the President of the United States broadcast his presence abroad in a fleet of American-made vehicles.

The luxury, armored SUVs had tinted, bulletproof glass, run-flat tires, and a host of nasty surprises for anyone foolish enough to attempt an assault on the Secretary's motorcade. In addition, Devon was accompanied by a team of switched-on, highly intense Special Operations personnel.

After thanking Bachar for their meeting, the Secretary of Defense climbed into the middle Range Rover, and the column rolled out of the gated driveway and headed toward the airport in Antalya.

The main road wound its way downhill and then hugged the ocean. With its beaches, glitzy boutiques, and gourmet restaurants, the area reminded Devon of the French Riviera. It was easy to see why it was one of Turkey's biggest tourist draws.

When they arrived downtown, the police escort raced ahead, halting traffic at intersections so the Secretary could move through without stopping.

Antalya was the eighth-largest city in Turkey. It was a combination of Roman ruins and modern architecture, broad boulevards and narrow medieval streets, the perfect mix of the exotic and the traditional: the kind of place his wife would enjoy visiting. Depending on how Turkey handled matters going forward, he could see himself bringing her back.

The motorcade had just passed a quaint outdoor café, its name painted in gold leaf, when two men leapt out of a parked car. They were masked and carrying AK-47s. Immediately, they began firing.

"Contact left! Contact left!" one of the security team members yelled.

Tires squealed and gas flooded into the Range Rovers' huge engines as the SUVs took evasive action.

Secretary Devon was forced to the floor for his safety. Just as his head was pressed beneath the window line, he saw both of their motorcycle escort cops lying dead in the street.

The agent in the forward vehicle was radioing instructions to the rest of the team as another agent alerted headquarters that they were under assault.

They made a sharp right turn, only to discover more gunmen waiting for them. Though the vehicle was practically soundproof, Devon could hear the popping of gunfire from outside and the impact of the rounds hitting his vehicle.

"They're trying to funnel us!" one of the agents warned as more masked gunmen appeared at the next intersection.

"Run it!" another yelled, encouraging the motorcade to barrel through the gunmen.

"Jesus," Devon's driver cursed as he swerved, trading paint with and knocking the mirrors off three cars. "We have to get back to the boulevard! These streets are too narrow."

Speeding into the intersection, the driver of the lead Range Rover pulled hard on the wheel and spun right into the gunfire.

The shooters rained down bullets on it and succeeded in cracking its windshield. Two of them were caught beneath the undercarriage and dragged.

One was dislodged, only to be run over by the vehicle right behind. It happened so fast the driver couldn't avoid it.

Devon felt his heavy Range Rover lift slightly off the ground as it crushed a gunman's body.

At the next intersection, they readied for gunfire, but none came. They appeared to have left the shooters behind. The lead vehicle made a hard left. The others followed.

The street was deserted, just rows of parked cars on both sides. The lead vehicle picked up speed. The others followed suit.

They were halfway down the block when a series of massive car bombs detonated in unison.

· · ·

From a small apartment at the end of the street, Sacha Baseyev captured all of it on camera. The killing of U.S. Secretary of Defense Richard Devon was going to be his most spectacular video yet. And it would be another nail in the coffin of ISIS.

CHAPTER 10

P resident Paul Porter let the moment of silence go on good and long. He wanted them to move beyond shock. He wanted them angry, like he was.

In the wake of the pandemic, a lot of people had changed how they viewed death. Some had suffered such tremendous loss in their personal lives that they had just become numb.

The President had suffered too. He had lost friends and acquaintances, trusted confidants and cabinet members.

He had been forced to rebuild his team quickly. Everyone he had selected had come highly recommended. Some of them he had known before, some were completely new to him.

Many of them were second- and even third-stringers plucked from different agencies—seat fillers until a more formal team could finally be assembled.

Because of his leadership and handling of the crisis, the President was enjoying the highest poll numbers of his career. Even Congress, also stocked with seat fillers who had been appointed by their state governors until the next election, was working with him.

The President knew, though, that there was a limit to all the goodwill. He also knew that bad forces remained marshaled against the United States. The business of being President, of protecting the country, didn't stop, no matter how badly he needed to catch his breath.

Porter looked around the table, and when he felt enough time had passed, he called the meeting of his National Security Council to order. The first person he looked at was his CIA Director. "What do we have?"

Bob McGee hit a button on his laptop and the screens around the Situation Room lit up with crime scene photos. They were stamped with the logo of Turkey's General Directorate of Security.

"The Turks believe that up to ten terrorists may have been involved in the attack on Secretary Devon and his team. According to witnesses," said McGee as he advanced to a new photo, "these three were struck and killed by the lead vehicle in the motorcade. They have been identified as Abdullah Özal, Ahmet Çiçek, and Hüseyin Tüzman. One worked in a pharmacy, one was a schoolteacher, and the third lived at home with his parents."

The Chairman of the Joint Chiefs interrupted him. "Are they wearing GoPros?"

"They are," replied the CIA Director as he zoomed in on one of the dead terrorists and the camera mounted to his chest.

"Where's the footage? Have the Turks shared it with us yet?"

"These cameras didn't have SD cards. Everything was wirelessly up-loaded in real time to the cloud. The NSA is already chasing it."

"But we should expect another video," said the Secretary of State.

McGee nodded.

"Has any group claimed responsibility? Do we know who we're deal-ing with?"

"Shortly after the attacks, multiple photographs were posted to social media showing Tüzman, and maybe Çiçek, fighting in Syria."

"So it looks like ISIS?"

Once more, the CIA Director nodded.

"How the hell did they know the motorcade route?" the National Se-curity Advisor asked. "How does a group like ISIS get their hands on that kind of intelligence?"

"There's obviously a leak."

"Obviously."

"And we have to assume that it could be connected to what happened in Anbar," interjected the Secretary of State.

"We've considered that," McGee replied.

Everyone waited for him to elaborate, but he didn't.

President Porter cleared his throat and said, "In four days, we have had twenty-two Americans brutally assassinated. One of them used to sit in this very room with us. We will not slow, we will not sleep, we will not stop until the people responsible have felt the full force of our wrath. If we have to turn over every damn rock in the Middle East until we find them, we will.

"But while we're turning over rocks, I want to discuss a broader strategy. For every ISIS Muslim fanatic we kill, two more pop up to take his place. How do we defeat them?"

"We deny them territory," the Chairman of the Joint Chiefs responded. "Without territory there's no caliphate."

"And how do we do that?" the President asked.

"Bomb the hell out of them and send in ground troops."

"That's exactly what they want us to do," said the Secretary of State. "We'd need a sustained force of five hundred thousand troops at least."

"To wipe out less than fifty thousand jihadists?" replied the Chairman.

"No, for the decades of occupation afterward."

"How do you figure?"

"ISIS is a creation of Sunni Islam. Part of its appeal is that it's a pushback against the growing Shia influence in the region. That influence is backed by Iran. You're going to end up with twenty-five million Syrian and Iraqi Sunnis looking for protection. If we don't fill that role, they'll run back to ISIS, or something even worse."

"If ISIS is a creation of Sunni Islam," said the President, "how do we get the Sunnis to destroy it?"

"You want Frankenstein to kill his own monster?" the National Security Advisor asked.

Porter nodded.

"You're asking for a complete reformation of Islam."

"Christianity has had one. Judaism too. Why not Islam?"

"Because Islam sees Mohammed as the perfect man and the Quran a perfect copy of a perfect book in Paradise. They have no history of criticism or self-examination. The word *Islam* itself means submission. And the word *Muslim* means one who submits."

The President leaned in, challenging his adviser. "So you're saying Muslims are somehow different than Jews or Christians? That they're intellectually incapable of reform?"

"What I am saying is that the so-called 'radicals' are the ones practicing their faith exactly the way Mohammed wanted it practiced. The moderates are the ones who have contorted it."

"The moderates are the majority, though. How do we push them to reform?"

"I don't know that you could," his adviser replied.

"That's a cop-out. If you could wave your National Security wand and have it done in a day, how would you handle it?"

The man thought about it for a moment and said, "Every time we have been hit by a terrorist attack, we tighten our security. That means Americans wake up the day after an attack and have less freedom. It has been the knee-jerk of every administration since 9/11. Instead of eroding Americans' civil liberties, I'd put the pressure on the Muslim nations themselves."

"How?"

"They profile like crazy. They have no problem with it. In fact, behind closed doors, they laugh at us for being so resistant to it. I say we turn that around on them.

"The American public would be shocked to know how many foreign nationals from Muslim countries have overstayed their visas. We pause all visas for the next twelve to twenty-four months while we hunt them down."

"Do you know what an outrage that would be?" the Secretary of State demanded. "Do you know how badly that would damage relations with our allies in the Middle East?"

"We'd do a carve-out for diplomats," the National Security Advisor replied.

"It doesn't matter. They'd still go ballistic."

"Would the plan hurt well-intentioned, moderate Muslims? Yes. But that's the point. You and I can't reform Islam. Only the moderates can, and they need to be pissed off enough to get off their asses and do something about it."

"But the only people these pissed-off moderates are going to be pissed off at," the Secretary of State countered, "is the United States."

The National Security Advisor shook his head. "Not all of them. Not the smart ones. The ones with business dealings here, and there's a lot of them, will see this for what it is. They know who the radicals in their own families are. They know which mosques are preaching radicalism. They know who is funding it. That's where their ire will be focused. When they start coming down on the radicals in their own midst, that's when reform will be on the horizon."

"Or so you hope."

"That's the beauty of having a magic wand, I don't have to hope. I just wave it."

"That's ridiculous. In fact, the entire idea is ridiculous," the Secretary of State replied. "You'd be giving ISIS exactly what they want."

The President, who had been jotting notes with his Chief of Staff, suddenly looked up and said, "That's it."

"What's it?"

"How we defeat ISIS," Porter answered. "We give them exactly what they want."

CHAPTER 11

The Secretary of State looked at the map on the monitors and shook his head. "I think I'd rather cancel our Visa Waiver Program. The fallout would be minuscule in comparison."

President Porter nodded. "I agree. The fallout from my idea would be massive. So massive, in fact, that something might actually get done."

"And in addition to deep-sixing our diplomatic relations with every Muslim nation in the region, if not around the world, we're going to throw the Brits and the French under the bus too."

"Don't forget Israel," the National Security Advisor stated. "They're going to lose their minds over this."

"Israel is tough," replied Porter. "They can hold their own. Even so, we'll make sure to give them an advance warning."

"Can we back up here a second?" the Attorney General asked. "For those of us rusty on their history, would somebody unpack this?"

The President enlightened him. "Did you ever see the movie *Lawrence of Arabia*?"

"Years ago."

"That's what this is all about. When the Ottoman Empire aligned itself with Germany and Austria-Hungary in World War I, the Brits and the French were worried that the Ottomans would cut off key shipping access and cripple their economies.

"They needed to get the Arabs to fight against the Ottomans, and so the Brits sent in T. E. Lawrence to convince them. They were promised

everything under the sun, including Arab rule over a new, united King-
dom of Greater Syria."

The Attorney General looked at the map on the monitors. It was from
1851 and was labeled *Ottoman Syria*. It encompassed present-day Syria,
Lebanon, Israel, and slices of Iraq and Jordan.

"There was just one problem," Porter continued. "The Brits and the
French never intended to honor any promises they were making to the
Arabs. They'd just be trading one caliphate for another.

"With Russia's blessing, two diplomats—Sir Mark Sykes of Great
Britain and François Georges-Picot of France—secretly formulated a
plan between their governments to carve up the Middle East in the event
the Ottoman Empire was defeated. It became known as the Sykes-Picot
Agreement and resulted in entirely new borders being drawn.

"It threw the region off balance, and by keeping it off balance, the Brits
and the French were able to control it. This control allowed them to carve
out a state for the Jewish people. This is the land ISIS wants. It's why they
have also called themselves ISIL—the Islamic State of Iraq and the Levant.

"What modern countries form the Levant?" the President asked, as he
turned and pointed at the map. "Egypt, Syria, Jordan, Lebanon, and Israel."

Turning back around, he said, "What they want is what the Brits
promised them a hundred years ago. They want their Arab caliphate."

"And you want to give that to them?" the National Security Advisor
asked. "Why?"

"I don't want to give these butchers anything. What I *want*, is to put
the entire damn region on notice. You said it yourself, we can't reform
Islam. Only the Islamic world can. This may be our magic wand."

"If we challenge, or even question, the validity of the Sykes-Picot
Agreement, it could destabilize the entire region. And if we walk away
from it, that's it. Game over. Every single one of those governments will
be overthrown."

The President looked at him. "That sounds to me like a pretty good
reason for them to get their acts together."

"But you'd also be challenging the very validity of Israel. As soon as
this fire starts burning, it'll swallow them up. Their neighbors will overrun them."

"You let me worry about Israel," Porter replied. "This isn't about them. This is about forcing the hand of the Muslim nations in the Middle East to commence reform."

"There's just one thing missing from your plan," the Secretary of State said. "Saudi Arabia. They're not part of Sykes-Picot, but they're the very heart of Sunni Islam. Without them on board, none of this will make it past *go*."

The President looked at his CIA Director and nodded. It was apparent that they had discussed this issue before.

"We can handle the Saudis."

"Excuse me?" the Secretary of State said.

"You heard me."

"Yeah, I heard you. What I want to know is *how* you plan to handle them. I've been around a long time and I don't think I've ever heard the words *handle* and *Saudis* in the same sentence."

"Well," McGee replied, "you just did."

The Secretary of State looked at the President. "Sir, what the hell are we about to do?"

"You're going to have to trust us," Porter responded.

"With all due respect, what I'm going to *have* to do is answer for all of this. I can't do that if I don't know what's going on."

"One step at a time. First we go after the people behind the Anbar and Antalya attacks. Then we go after everything else."

Looking then at the Chairman of the Joint Chiefs, the President added, "I want an immediate response plan drawn up. I want to see a strike package on my desk within the next two hours. Who, what, where we'll hit in ISIS territory. The American people expect us to respond."

"So does ISIS," replied the Chairman.

"Then let's give everyone something they'll never forget."

•   •   •

As the meeting broke up and people began filing out, the President's Chief of Staff motioned him back to the head of the conference table.

"What's going on?" Porter asked.

"This came in during the meeting. I didn't want to bother you with it."

The President looked down at the man's laptop. Senator Daniel Wells of Iowa had not only put out a video statement about the murder of Secretary of Defense Richard Devon, but his campaign was subtly using it as a fund-raising mechanism.

"That's a new low, even for him," Porter said.

"Normally, I'd suggest we ignore it, but this is pretty egregious."

"Where'd you find it?"

"I use a bogus email address to subscribe to his newsletter."

"So, in other words," said the President, "this is only being sent to the choir."

"At the moment," his Chief of Staff replied. "But I guarantee you all the Sunday shows subscribe to his newsletter as well."

"Right now, Sunday is a lifetime away."

"It may feel like that, but it isn't. Trust me."

"And you need to trust me, a lot can happen between now and Sunday."

CHAPTER 12

Tracking Sacha Baseyev wasn't easy. Nicholas had done an amazing job. He had begun by searching all of the CCTV footage around the neighborhood where Salah Abaaoud kept his love nest. Nothing appeared out of the ordinary, until he added an additional layer to his search.

He next pulled the footage from around Salah's home and the clinic. His assumption was that the killer would have conducted cursory surveillance before making his move. His assumption was correct. But Nicholas had almost missed him.

He was running a series of algorithms in the background of his search. One was an emerging piece of biometric technology called gait recognition, which measured how subjects walk.

Baseyev was indeed a pro. He had altered everything about his appearance. The man watching the clinic was unrecognizable from the assassin who entered the apartment building. Even the walks were different. But it was the walk that had turned out to be Baseyev's undoing.

Faking how you walked was one thing. Faking it consistently was something entirely different. Gait recognition technology was able to spot even the smallest changes. It was also able to look for patterns. If you were captured on camera with an inconsistent walk, it flagged you. That was how Nicholas realized the two figures he had spotted were one and the same.

He had tracked a disguised Sacha Baseyev to a mid-sized hotel in downtown Brussels. When Baseyev emerged on camera hours later, he was dressed in a Lufthansa uniform and accompanied by five other flight attendants.

They placed their luggage in a minibus and were driven to the airport. Baseyev moved through security with the other flight crew, was in and out of a couple of shops, and boarded a plane for Frankfurt.

When the plane landed, Nicholas was able to reacquire the passengers and the other flight attendants, but not Baseyev. He had disappeared.

People didn't just disappear, especially not at a major international airport like Frankfurt. At least not without help. And so, Nicholas had dug in.

Posing as a flight attendant was excellent cover. It was better than posing as a businessman. Flight attendants often received expedited screening, could hide in plain sight, and were viewed by airport staff everywhere as "one of us."

When the United States had learned of Baseyev's existence, there'd been no mention of his cover. It was possible that the Russian intelligence defector hadn't known. Or that the cover had been established later.

As far as Nicholas was concerned, it didn't matter. He was onto him. He wouldn't stop until the noose was pulled so tight that Sacha Baseyev couldn't breathe.

To begin, he needed a name. He watched the Brussels airport footage again. Baseyev had bought something in one of the shops before boarding his plane. He had paid with a credit card. It took Nicholas less than ten minutes to get inside their system.

The assassin appeared to have a sweet tooth. He had purchased six bars of Belgian chocolate with a Visa card. The unassuming name on the card was Peter Roth.

With that name, he was able to set his sights on Belgium's customs and immigration database. Two hours later, he had a full scan of Peter Roth's German passport. Then he went to work on Lufthansa's systems.

Lufthansa owned one of the largest passenger airline fleets in the world. They served nearly 200 destinations across 78 countries worldwide. Each year, they transported more than 100 million passengers.

Over 100,000 people worked for Lufthansa. Four of them were named Peter Roth. All were based out of Frankfurt, Lufthansa's main hub of operations.

Once Nicholas had access to the employee files and their photos, he was able to narrow the four Peter Roths to the exact one they wanted— Sacha Baseyev. *The noose had just tightened.*

He appeared to be very part-time and flew only a handful of routes, mostly international.

What income Baseyev did earn from Lufthansa was direct-deposited into an account in Frankfurt. The address he gave as his residence was a match with five other Lufthansa employees. Nicholas passed it on to Harvath.

It was a crash pad, or "stew zoo," as it used to be called. Having dated a string of Scandinavian Airlines flight attendants as a SEAL, Harvath had been in and out of several of them.

It was a house or an apartment rented by a group of flight attendants who either didn't live in the city their flights were based out of, or who traveled so much they wanted to save money by spreading the rent across multiple roommates.

For Baseyev, though, it would have helped layer his cover and function as a quasi safe house.

According to Lufthansa's scheduling system, he didn't have another flight on the books until next month. *Was he hiding out in the apartment until then?* There was only one way to find out.

Parking his car at the end of the block, Harvath turned off the ignition and popped the trunk.

CHAPTER 13

According to Nicholas, the other Lufthansa flight attendants who shared the apartment were all on active trips outside the country. None of them were expected back tonight.

Harvath had been given a street address and an apartment number. That was it. He had no idea what the interior layout looked like.

He did a discreet reconnaissance, noting the entrance, exits, and which apartments had lights on. When he was ready, he picked the lock of the rear door at the parking lot and snuck inside.

Pausing in the lobby, he checked the mailbox for the apartment. It was empty. Someone had recently picked up the mail.

He found the stairs and walked up to the second floor. Looking at the number plates, he figured out which one he wanted. The only units he had seen from outside with lights on were at the other end of the hall. But just because he hadn't seen any lights didn't mean nobody was home.

Jet lag was an occupational hazard for pilots and flight attendants. The airlines were also very strict about how many hours of sleep they were required to have before flights. Many employees invested in blackout curtains.

Approaching the door, Harvath used his right hand to adjust the .40-caliber Glock 22 tucked in the Sticky holster at the small of his back. The CIA had arranged for it to be left for him at a small hotel near the airport. In his left hand was a bouquet of flowers.

Looking at the flight schedules of the roommates, he noted one who had been assigned at the last minute. After a quick review of her Facebook and Instagram accounts, it was obvious the attractive young woman liked to party and had a lot of male friends. It wouldn't have been a stretch to believe that she had forgotten to cancel a date before leaving on a trip.

Standing outside the door, he listened for a moment. There were no sounds from inside. He knocked and waited. No one answered. He tried once more. *Nothing.*

He tried the knob, but the door was locked. Removing his picks, he let himself in.

The apartment was lit by the faint glow of the streetlamps outside. He gave his eyes a moment to adjust.

Setting the flowers down, he removed his Glock and began moving from room to room.

The decor was sleek and minimalist. The artwork tasteful, but inexpensive. It looked like an IKEA ad. The only place where any real money had been spent was in the kitchen.

From the Le Creuset cookware to the expensive Japanese chef's knives displayed like museum pieces, it was obvious that someone took their cooking seriously.

There was a row of cookbooks with titles in German, French, and English. In one drawer he found a stack of food magazines. The fridge and cabinets were filled with a wide array of gourmet food items, including caviar, truffles, and foie gras.

There was clothing in the closets and a smattering of personal items scattered about, but other than that, the apartment was much more hotel than home.

On his second sweep, Harvath looked for places Baseyev could have hidden an emergency cache. Any operative worth his salt would have kept one nearby. They usually included cash, a burner phone or clean SIM cards, and a weapon. Medical supplies, disguises, and even fake identification might be a part of it as well. It was all based upon what the operative or his organization thought was needed.

Harvath was incredibly thorough in his search, but turned up nothing. If Baseyev did have an "oh shit" kit, it wasn't in the apartment.

The entire trip to Frankfurt was a bust. It pissed Harvath off. He hated dead ends and wasted time. The best the CIA could do at this point was to wire up the apartment and sit on it. If Baseyev came back, they'd need a team ready to put a bag over his head and transport him to a black site for a nice long chat.

In the meantime, the CIA would also want to approach the room-mates to see what they knew. Even the best operative could make a mistake. Baseyev might have screwed up at some point and let something slip that might be helpful.

Putting everything back exactly as he had found it, Harvath retrieved the flowers and left the apartment. He needed to report in. The chain of command, though, was a bit murky.

Technically, he worked for a private organization called The Carlton Group. Reed Carlton was an iconic spymaster who had established the Central Intelligence Agency's counterterrorism center. He put the *old* in "old school."

After decades of faithful service, he had gotten out. He couldn't stand the careerists and the bureaucracy anymore. He saw a real future for an organization able to operate without red tape and beyond the reach of Congress. The Defense Department and the CIA turned out to be two of his best customers. They, in turn, always wanted his best operative.

Carlton had taught Harvath everything he knew about the espionage business. Coupling that with his SEAL background, Harvath had vaulted to the top of the food chain. He was an apex predator, a hunter without equal.

Tucked away, compartmentalized, was the man himself. He liked his work. He probably liked it too much.

It cast a shadow over everything else in his life. And the problem with shadows was that it was very hard for anything to grow in the shade.

He wanted the American Dream, but he had been called to protect it. There were wolves and the wolves needed to be hunted. He had a lot of hunting left in him.

What he didn't have a lot left of was time to start a family. It was slipping away. He had spent his entire adult life being loyal to everyone. Everyone but himself. At some point, the torch had to be passed. At some point, he had to let someone else take his place on the wall.

Not today, though. There was way too much at stake.

Back in his rental car, Harvath used his encrypted phone to text the CIA's Deputy Director, Lydia Ryan. Ryan was Bob McGee's right hand at Langley and, like McGee, had been an outstanding field operative, hand-picked by the President to help rebuild the Central Intelligence Agency from within.

By using The Carlton Group, the CIA was able to push the boundaries of what they were legally allowed to do. It also presented them, and, more important, the President, with plausible deniability if any of those actions came to light.

Dry hole, he typed. *No sign of Pitchfork.*

Pitchfork was the code name they had assigned to Baseyev.

Stand by, Ryan replied.

Several seconds later, his phone rang.

"Was it empty?" she asked when Harvath activated the call.

"No. It's furnished and in use."

"How long since he was last there?"

"No clue. We could do a search for CCTV cameras and pull the footage if you want."

"Right," said Ryan, distracted.

"You should also put a full surveillance package on the building."

"Right."

Harvath could tell she wasn't paying attention. "Do you want to call me back?"

"What? No. I'm sorry."

Something was up. "What's going on?"

"More intel just came in regarding what happened in Turkey," she said.

"*Turkey?* What happened?"

There was a pause. "Nobody told you?"

"Told me what? I've been in the field."

He could hear her let out a long exhalation. It sounded like air being let out of a tire.

"Defense Secretary Devon is dead," said Ryan. "His motorcade came under attack."

"Where? When?"

"Antalya. About four hours ago."

Harvath had known Richard Devon and had liked him, *a lot*. He had also known several of the men on his protective detail. "Did anyone survive?"

"No," Ryan replied. "They're all dead."

He couldn't believe it. "How the hell did this happen?"

"We don't know. There's a lot of moving pieces. We're trying to get our arms around it."

"Who's behind it?"

"It looks like ISIS."

"Come on, Lydia," he replied. "First Anbar, and now this? ISIS isn't that good. And *nobody* is this lucky. Who the hell is helping them?"

"That's the question we're all asking."

There were a ton of things he wanted to say. None of them were helpful, or appropriate. Holding his anger in check, he asked the only question he could: "What can I do?"

The Deputy Director of the CIA didn't hesitate. "Find Pitchfork," she said. "Fast."

CHAPTER 14

I f Baseyev was using Lufthansa as cover to move from country to country, the Russians had to have had someone inside. Harvath had charged Nicholas with figuring out who that someone was.

The biggest obstacle Nicholas faced was wrapping his head around how Lufthansa booked its passengers and scheduled its crews. Once that began to crystalize for him, his search picked up speed.

As someone who dealt with data, Nicholas was obsessed with patterns. Even when there was no pattern, that was a pattern, he would say. And the more he studied Baseyev's travel, the more he began to figure the man out. He definitely had someone on the inside. It was someone very good at covering his tracks. *Very good*, but not perfect.

Now that they had his employee identification number, they could track all of Baseyev's Lufthansa travel as Peter Roth. That included not only his work trips but also trips where he was traveling for free as an airline employee or "dead-heading" to another destination in order to work a specific flight. There were even instances where he showed up in a foreign city somewhere and hopped onto a Lufthansa flight without any indication as to how he got there.

Throughout it all, Nicholas kept looking for a constant, something that repeated itself—something that would point them to whomever the Russians had inside. Finally, he found it.

Jörg Strobl was a senior IT specialist who worked in Lufthansa's crew management division. He oversaw one of the many teams that handled crew scheduling. Though he had done an intricate job hiding his involvement, he was the one behind all of Baseyev's flights.

But that wasn't all. Strobl's wife, Anna, was Bundespolizei—a uniformed federal police officer stationed at Frankfurt airport. It looked like the Russians might have gotten two for one with the Strobls.

The town they lived in was known as being a hub for tourism and IT companies. Per his file, Jörg Strobl had worked out of the Lufthansa Aviation Center at the airport until four years ago, when he began telecommuting from home.

Anna's Bundespolizei file wasn't particularly impressive. She had graduated in the middle of her class and had spent several years protecting federal buildings, before being transferred to airport duty.

What *was* impressive about her, though, was her service photo. She was an extremely attractive woman, with straight brown hair, high cheekbones, and an enviable body that even her boxy government uniform couldn't keep hidden.

She and the handsome, blond Jörg Strobl seemed made for each other. From everything Nicholas could gather, they appeared to have met at the airport. And as far as he could tell, they didn't have any children.

The Strobls lived on the outskirts of Oberursel, not far from the A 661 motorway. Their home was easy enough to find.

The neighborhood of single-family homes was quiet. Privacy hedges separated the yards. Some houses had garages. Others had carports.

Under the Strobls' carport was a new Mercedes van. The spot next to it was empty.

The van seemed an odd choice until Harvath saw a ramp next to the stairs. He wondered if they were caring for an aging parent.

That might explain why Jörg had begun working from home. What it wouldn't explain, though, was why he was working for the Russians.

Crouching below the window line, he crept around the side of the house toward the back.

There wasn't much going on. All he could see was the faint glow through one of the ground floor windows of what looked to be a television set.

At the rear of the house was a small brick patio with three stone steps leading up to a door. Climbing the stairs, he peeked through a window into the kitchen. Suddenly, movement caught his eye and he pulled back into the darkness.

He was still able to see into the kitchen and watched as a figure in a motorized wheelchair came into view. He was ready to have his assumption about an aging parent proven correct when he realized that it was Strobl himself.

There had been nothing in the file to suggest he was disabled. *Why is he in a wheelchair? And where is his wife?*

Harvath waited until the man had left the kitchen and then went to work on the back door.

Once he had the lock picked, he opened it slowly. The house wasn't that big and Strobl was probably in the other room, where he had seen the TV glowing.

He stepped inside and gently closed the door behind him. There was half a bottle of wine on the counter. Beside it were the remnants of packaging for a microwavable meal. From the next room, he could hear music. It was a very old recording. It took him a minute to recognize the singer. *Sarah Vaughan.*

He took out his Glock and moved slowly, quietly toward it.

At the edge of the kitchen he could see the glow from the other room. Three steps more and he realized that it wasn't coming from a TV. It was coming from three, long, flat-screen computer monitors arrayed in a semi-arc on a long table in the den.

Sitting in front of them was a man who looked nothing like the file photo Harvath had seen. Jörg Strobl was thin and frail, a shadow of his former self. In his left hand was a glass of red wine. His eyes were closed as he listened to Vaughan singing "Don't Blame Me."

"Interesting choice," Harvath said, scaring the hell out of the man.

Strobl dropped his glass of wine and it shattered on the floor.

He spun his wheelchair to face him. "Who are you?" he demanded.

Harvath raised his index finger to his lips. "Where's Anna?"

"What do you want with Anna?"

"Where is she?" he repeated.

"I don't know."

Harvath didn't believe him. "Last chance," he said, leveling the pistol at his chest.

"She's at work."

"When will she be home?"

The man shrugged. "She should have been home an hour ago. Sometimes she goes out with her colleagues."

"She doesn't call you?"

Strobl used the joystick to move his wheelchair toward his intruder.

"That's close enough," Harvath warned him.

"Who are you and what do you want with Anna?" the man asked again.

"I didn't come for Anna. I came for you, Herr Strobl."

"For me? Why for me?"

"You have been handling travel arrangements for a very dangerous man."

"*A very dangerous man,*" Strobl replied with a laugh. "You obviously have made a mistake."

"I don't make mistakes," Harvath said. "You're the man I'm looking for and you know exactly why I'm here."

"I wish I could help you, but I cannot."

"You can help me and you *will.*"

"I am calling the police," Strobl stated, turning his chair and moving back toward his desk.

Harvath grabbed a handful of the wheelchair's electrical cable and tore it out. The machine came to an immediate halt.

"You're making me angry, Jörg."

"And you have the wrong man!" he insisted, raising his voice. "I want you to go. Now!"

"Not until you tell me everything I want to know."

"I know nothing," the man said, averting his gaze.

"Jörg, the more you lie to me, the worse this is going to get. Believe me. Your condition will not win you any special treatment. You have been aiding and abetting a killer. I want the details. All of them."

Strobl was preparing to speak, but was interrupted.

"I want the details too," said another voice.

Looking up, Harvath saw Anna Strobl standing in the doorway. She had a pistol and it was pointed right at him.

CHAPTER 15

Anna Strobl wasn't a great cop, but she wasn't a bad one either. Like anything else in life, police work had everything to do with timing, and instinct.

On her way home, she had decided to get fuel. Up ahead, she had noticed a car slow down in front of her house. It didn't stop, but whoever was driving had taken a good, long look at her property before driving off. It was enough to raise her antennae.

After passing her home, the car had returned to a normal speed and turned the corner. She watched and let it drive away.

Even if she had been driving an official Bundespolizei vehicle with lights and sirens, rather than her personal vehicle, she still would have needed more in order to justify a stop.

Returning from the filling station, she was still bothered by the car's actions. She decided to take a roundabout way home and look for it. She found it parked in front of a church, two blocks from her house. The driver was nowhere to be seen. *Something was going on*.

One of the neighbors was traveling and had asked Anna to keep an eye on their house. She parked in their driveway and made her way through the backyards until she got to her own. There was no sign of anything wrong, but her gut told her otherwise.

When she found her back door unlocked, she drew her weapon, slipped off her boots, and crept inside.

She had heard the entire conversation. What bothered her even more than the intruder's knowing her name was that Jörg wasn't even a good liar.

"Drop your weapon," she told the man holding her husband at gunpoint.

"You first," Harvath replied.

Anna leaned her shoulder forward so he could see the patch. "Bundespolizei," she said. "More officers are on the way. Drop your weapon. *Now*."

"No thanks. I'll wait until they get here."

"I am not asking you. I am ordering you. Do it now."

Harvath looked at the man in the wheelchair. "My superiors know everything, Jörg. They know why I'm here and what you've done. If the Bundespolizei become involved, it's over for you."

"What is it you know, exactly?" Anna asked.

"Ask your husband."

She looked at Jörg, and for several moments he refused to meet her eyes. Finally, he said, "Everything I did was for you."

"What did you do?"

"I wanted to make sure you were taken care of."

"What did you do?" she repeated.

"It's nothing. Only a small thing."

"Tell me, Jörg. Now."

He was beaten, ashamed. He cast his eyes down toward the floor. "I manipulated some of the crew rosters."

"Why?"

"For money. So that *you* could have the things that you need when I am gone."

Anna didn't understand. "You took money from crew members?" she replied. "For what? To arrange the trips they wanted? More vacation time?"

"If that's all this was," said Harvath, "I wouldn't be here."

"Tell me why this man is here, Jörg."

"I told you. I accepted money to manipulate the rosters."

Anna looked from her husband to Harvath. She still didn't understand. Harvath laid it out for her. "He took money to help an assassin travel undetected by international law enforcement."

"I had no idea that—" he sputtered.

"How much?" she interrupted.

"Anna, you have to believe me that I—"

"How much?"

"Two hundred thousand euros."

"My God," she responded. "Two hundred thousand Euros and you had no idea, what? That it was wrong? That criminals would be involved?"

"I am dying!" he yelled. "I did this for *you*."

"Do *not* blame me. You did this for yourself, because you feel guilty. I don't need money."

Jörg Strobl laughed. "And your new car? The expensive van that accommodates my wheelchair? Where do you think those came from?"

"You told me you were doing IT work on the side."

"And now you know the truth."

Anna fished the car key fob from her pocket and threw it at her husband. He couldn't get his hands up fast enough to catch it. The fob hit him in the chest and landed in his lap.

There was an uncomfortable silence as the Strobls stared at each other.

Harvath didn't have time to stand around while they worked out their issues. "How were you approached?" he asked. "Who pays you? How do you get contacted?"

Strobl looked at his wife, who holstered her weapon. "I think you should answer him," she stated. Then, turning to Harvath she said, "There are no Bundespolizei officers coming."

Harvath hadn't thought so. He had been taught how to pick out microexpressions, the little tics people subconsciously give off when they weren't telling the truth. She was a very good liar. Her tic was almost imperceptible.

"If I talk," Jörg said to Harvath, "they'll kill me. If I don't talk, *you'll* kill me. I don't see any upside in any of this."

"If you talk, I'll protect you. You *and* Anna."

That was a wrinkle Jörg hadn't expected. He thought about that for a moment. "How do I know I can trust you?"

"You don't."

Jörg shook his head. "I don't even know who you are."

"Which is how I am able to protect you," Harvath replied. "Now, either you start talking, or I am leaving and taking any hope you and your wife ever have of safety with me. Your choice."

Looking up at Anna, Strobl asked, "Will you please pour us some wine?"

CHAPTER 16

The neighborhood known as Bahnhofsviertel included the main railway station, as well as Frankfurt's red light district. It also included the apartment of the man who had recruited Jörg Strobl.

Harvath didn't need or want Anna Strobl there, but she had insisted. She had also made a strong case for being able to authenticate the information that he hoped to extract.

Sigmar Eichel worked in airport operations. And as such, he had access to terminals, runways, hangars, and every other facet of Frankfurt airport. He could move in and out of secure areas without arousing suspicion. He knew all of the security protocols, which cameras were working, and which were down. Anna also commented that he likely could access and even alter the CCTV feeds.

An added benefit of having Anna along was that she was a federal police officer. As soon as Sigmar saw her, he was going to know that it was all over for him. The trick would be in convincing him to turn against the people he was working for.

Harvath hadn't expected the Russians to deal directly with Jörg Strobl. They didn't need to. They would use a go-between, or a cutout, as it was known. That was Eichel's job. He passed along the instructions and Strobl carried them out.

Eichel was higher up the food chain. As such, he would have had more training, and likely more to lose. That meant that he might end up being a harder nut to crack.

Strobl had explained that he had gotten to know Eichel back when he had been working out of the Lufthansa Aviation Center. As Strobl opened up to Harvath about his medical condition, Harvath knew almost exactly how the story of his recruitment would unfold.

Shortly after being diagnosed with amyotrophic lateral sclerosis, Eichel had begun bumping into Jörg in different places, both at work and outside the airport. It didn't happen often, but it happened often enough.

Soon, the pair had struck up a friendship and were getting together for beers after work and occasionally doing things on the weekend. It usually happened, though, when Anna was on duty. She had only met Eichel once or twice.

Figuring that as a cop, she must have had a halfway decent bullshit detector, Harvath had asked her what she thought of him. Her assessment didn't disappoint.

Physically, Anna remembered Eichel as being overweight and having poor eyesight and dry skin. He dressed like a man who didn't have a woman in his life and didn't want one. Personality-wise, he had an over-inflated opinion of both his talent and his worth to the airport. His jokes were chauvinistic and not very clever.

To top it all off, Anna detailed that Eichel wore a corrective shoe on his left foot and that his left leg was probably shorter than his right. She commented that because of this, Eichel may have been teased as a child and have subsequently developed poor self-esteem, which resulted in his disagreeable personality and lack of interest in maintaining his physical appearance.

As a final postscript, Anna noted that Eichel might just have been born an asshole, and therefore everything else was simply peripheral.

Harvath had tried not to smile, but couldn't help it. She had rendered an amazingly insightful assessment and was keenly observant.

Though Harvath was tempted to ask why she had missed so many things about her own husband, he didn't go there. While love could often be blind, the debilitating illness of a loved one was a no-holds-barred cage match. The blows came so fast and so furious that you were lucky to survive, much less grasp everything that was going on around you.

To expect someone in the middle of an emotional tsunami to sense subtle shifts in their spouse and not chalk it up to the illness was beyond insane. Every day was a new battle. Every day you expected the unexpected. Harvath didn't blame Anna. Having been on her side of the equation before, he felt for her.

"You're not married?" she asked.

He was standing at the window of Eichel's dingy apartment near the Kaiserstrasse, waiting for him to come home.

"No," Harvath replied. "I'm not married."

"Why not?"

He smiled. "I don't know."

"You don't like women?"

He laughed. "No, I like women. That's not the problem."

"Then what is it?"

"I'm married to my job, I suppose."

Anna shook her head. "That's ridiculous."

"My work is important to me."

Before leaving the house in Oberursel, Anna had changed out of her uniform into jeans, a T-shirt, and a leather jacket. Peeling off the leather jacket, she set it on the arm of the sofa and approached him.

"Do you have a woman now?" she asked.

Harvath heard alarm bells going off somewhere in the back of his mind. He'd had more than a few women. Many had walked out without even closing the door. "I'm not sure," he replied.

"What does that mean?"

"We are going to be living in separate cities."

"But you live in the same city now?"

"No."

Anna looked at him.

"It's complicated," Harvath conceded.

She held his gaze and was about to reply when Harvath signaled for her to be quiet.

He had heard something. "Someone's coming," he whispered.

CHAPTER 17

Eichel kicked the door shut behind him, threw his keys in a bowl on the dining room table, and dropped a large bag of takeout food onto the coffee table.

He hung his coat on a peg near the door and then walked into the kitchen. There was the sound of a fridge and a cabinet door being opened then closed. He returned to the living room with a tall glass and a large bottle of beer.

As soon as he had made himself comfortable on the couch, Harvath stepped from the bedroom.

Eichel almost had a coronary. *"Scheisse!"* he gasped.

Harvath pointed his Glock at him and told him to shut up.

"Who are you?" he asked. "What do you want?"

"I'm here to talk with you about Peter Roth."

"I don't know any Peter Roth," said Eichel.

Harvath smiled. "That's not what Jörg Strobl told me."

"I don't know any Jörg Strobl."

"So that's how this is going to go. Fine by me."

Eichel watched as Harvath produced a roll of duct tape and approached the couch. The man was already perspiring, his heart beating rapidly. "You can't do this!" he exclaimed.

"I *am* doing this."

"Just tell me what you want."

"I did," Harvath said, "but you decided you wanted to play games. That's fine by me. I like games."

"I am a German citizen. You cannot do this to me."

The fat man seemed hardly in a position to be telling anyone what he could or could not be doing.

When Harvath tried to secure his wrists, Eichel resisted, so he punched him in the mouth.

Tears immediately formed in the man's eyes. "Why?" he moaned.

"You know why. And you should also know that this is only going to get more painful the more you resist me. Do you understand?"

Eichel didn't reply, so Harvath struck him again.

"Okay. Enough. Enough. I understand."

After securing the man's hands, Harvath asked, "Who is Peter Roth?"

"I told you, I don't—" Eichel began, but stopped when he saw Harvath balling his hand into a fist and cocking it back. "Okay, okay."

"Okay, what? Who is Peter Roth?"

"He works for Lufthansa."

"Who does he really work for?"

"I don't know!" the man exclaimed.

Harvath punched him again, much harder.

Eichel spat a broken tooth onto the coffee table. "You have to believe me. I don't know what any of this is all about."

Harvath drew his fist back, and Eichel shut his eyes. But instead of punching him, Harvath grabbed him by his bound wrists and dragged him into the kitchen. The last thing he needed to do was break his hand repeatedly punching this idiot in the face.

He threw Eichel down on the floor and rummaged through the cabinets until he found what he was looking for.

Before the fat man could cry out, Harvath had the plastic bag over his head and had pulled it tight. Oxygen deprivation often did wonders for people's level of cooperation, not to mention recollection.

Lying on top of his hands, Eichel was unable to reach up and claw at the plastic bag. As he writhed wildly on the floor, Harvath sat down on top of him, increasing the intensity of his suffocation.

When he felt the man had had enough, he gave it an extra three seconds and then pulled the bag off his head.

Eichel gasped, but couldn't get any air into his lungs until Harvath got off his back. As soon as he did, the airport operations manager sucked in air like a thirsty man at a desert oasis.

No sooner had he started catching his breath than Harvath said, "That's enough," and began to put the bag over his head again.

Eichel shook his head vigorously from side to side. "No," he managed to rasp.

"You had your chance when I asked you about Roth. But you wanted to be a smartass. This time the bag stays on twice as long."

Eichel thrashed even harder than before. "Please!" he begged. "Please. Stop."

Harvath knew this game. Begging him to stop was not the same as answering his question. Eichel knew it too. So, the bag went fully back over his head.

As soon as it did, he began screaming a name. "Malevsky!" he yelled. "Mikhail Malevsky!"

Harvath removed the bag and waited for the overweight German to begin to catch his breath. Then, rolling him into a seated position, he leaned him against the wall and said, "Who is Mikhail Malevsky?"

"He's Russian."

"No kidding," Harvath replied. "Who is he?"

"He's a businessman."

"What kind of *business*?"

"I don't know."

Harvath grabbed a fistful of Eichel's flabby jowls and twisted. "Tell me who he is, or I put the bag back on and it doesn't come off."

"*Mafia!*" he cried out. "Russian mafia."

Harvath let go of his face. *Russian mafia could mean anything.* The Russian mob was full of Russian intelligence agents. Some were retired. Some were not. All of them maintained good relations with Moscow. It was the Kremlin, after all, that put the *organized* in Russian organized crime.

"Where do I find him?" Harvath demanded.

"You don't. He's very cautious. His security is the best."

"We'll see about that. How does he contact you?"

"He texts me a code," Eichel replied. "I unscramble it and then do what it says."

"What else do you do for him, besides manipulating Lufthansa's crew roster?"

"Nothing. I swear."

He was lying. Harvath reached for the plastic bag.

Eichel quickly added, "Sometimes, I helped move Herr Roth through certain parts of the airport."

"To avoid security or passport control?"

"Yes."

"What else?" asked Harvath.

"Sometimes it was to help him get to the private aviation area."

This got Harvath's attention. "How often did Roth fly private?"

"A handful of times a year."

"Why not use Lufthansa?"

Eichel shrugged. "I don't know."

"When was the last time?"

"A few days ago."

Harvath looked at him. "Where did he fly to?"

"Turkey," said Eichel.

"Where in Turkey? Specifically."

"Antalya."

CHAPTER 18

The attack on the American Secretary of Defense had been spectacular. Everything had gone perfectly.

Baseyev had been prepared to lose all of his men. Instead, he had only lost three. That meant he was left with some cleaning up.

When the men gathered back at the warehouse, they were still jacked up on the new drugs he had given them that morning—pills to make them aggressive and hyperalert.

Drugs to mellow out the night before an attack and drugs to get amped up the day of executing an attack had become prevalent in terror circles. Now, Baseyev explained, it was time for them to come back down and relax. If they were nervous or overexcited, they would never make their escape.

He passed out bottles of water and tiny paper cups with a single pill in each. The men were smiling over their victory and chanting "Allahu'akbar," *God is great!*

They asked Baseyev questions about what life was going to be like in Syria, in the caliphate. He painted a rosy picture in return.

The men would be lauded as heroes, as lions. Already, word had traveled back to the Caliph himself about their success. Lavish apartments and wives had been chosen for each of them. Men would be placed under their command. They were nothing short of Islamic rock stars.

Even more important, Baseyev explained, Allah himself was not only pleased, but had blessed their performance today. He had protected them. He had made them victorious in battle. It was to him that all of the glory was due.

The men halted their self-congratulatory fervor and asked Baseyev to lead them in prayers. He agreed, then made sure everyone had swallowed their pills.

Once they performed their ritual cleansing and had rolled out their prayer rugs, Baseyev began.

Muslims were not allowed to fidget or look around. They were to recite their prayers as if they were in the presence of God. It demanded a state of total concentration.

Where he was allowed to contribute additional verses from the Quran, Baseyev recited the longest ones he could remember.

Throughout their prayers, the men performed all of the required postures from bowing their foreheads to the ground in Sujud to rocking back and sitting on their haunches in Tashahhud.

Eventually, their movements began to slow and become more languid. Eyelids grew heavier and eyes began to glaze over. Baseyev slowed his speech and lowered his volume.

When the prayers were finished, he asked the brothers to remain sitting. Without explaining to them why, he began a lecture about one of the fathers of one of the wives of Mohammed. It was one of the most boring subjects he could think of. Soon the men's heads were bobbing as they fought off sleep.

Standing, he continued his lecture and walked around behind the men. None of them noticed. Their blood was saturated with the heavy narcotic he had given them. The only thing easier than stealing candy from children was handing it to them.

He removed a .22-caliber SIG Sauer pistol from beneath his shirt and attached its suppressor. The Mosquito, as it was known, was ninety percent of the size of its famous big brother, the P226, but Baseyev didn't need that much firepower. He didn't need the noise, either.

With the suppressor attached, the only sound anyone would hear would be the movement of the Mosquito's slide as it ejected spent shell casings and seated each new round.

It was time.

Praising the wisdom and glory of the prophet Mohammed, he walked the line, shooting each of the men in the back of their heads. After the last one, he turned and looked at his work.

All of the men were dead, slumped forward on their prayer rugs, facing Mecca. Baseyev glanced at his watch. He was right on schedule.

After prepping the explosives, he then conducted one final check of the warehouse before leaving.

When his private jet had been cleared for takeoff, he placed a call from his cell phone and initiated the countdown.

On the climb out from the airport, he got to see the warehouse explode. It was an amazing sight.

A gigantic fireball rolled up into the night sky over Turkey. The authorities could comb the site for months, but all they would find was what he wanted them to find.

Settling back in his seat, he reflected on what lay ahead. The best, most dramatic attack was yet to come. But the stakes were going to be much higher, the margin for error narrower. With each step forward, the risks and the danger would compound.

Baseyev was unafraid. In fact, he welcomed the opportunity. Operating on American soil was going to be his greatest achievement ever. And hopefully, it would bring the mightiest military in the world crashing down upon ISIS.

CHAPTER 19

S enator Daniel Wells rolled over and picked up his iPhone from the nightstand. "What time is it?" he asked as he answered the call.

"A little after three a.m.," his Chief of Staff said.

Her name was Rebecca Ritter and she could play the Washington game better than anyone he'd ever met. She was smart and aggressive, and never took no for an answer.

She was also a damn good-looking woman. She could play up or tone down her looks based on what any situation called for.

Rebecca could go from a sweet, demure Iowa farm girl any man would want to take home to meet his parents, to a show-stopping blonde in a little black dress who would have even the most devoted of husbands questioning whether she might be worth the risk.

Wells, though, had never touched her. It would have been like mixing alcohol and firearms. Guaranteed to be a lot of fun, right up until it wasn't.

The Senator had greater ambitions than bedding the twenty-six-year-old graduate from the John F. Kennedy School of Government who sat on the other side of his office door. Besides, the more powerful he became, the more she wanted him. Once he was in the White House and certain of a second term, then maybe he'd entertain a little fun. Until then, though, there was too much to be done.

"Three a.m.?" he replied. "You must have something good."

Rebecca had been warming the bed of a young man by the name of

Brendan Cavanagh. Mr. Cavanagh just happened to be the executive assistant to CIA Director Bob McGee.

"Do you want a blow-by-blow, or should I skip to the bottom line?"

Propping a pillow behind his head, Wells made himself comfortable. His wife, Nancy, was back in Cedar Rapids. He had the king-sized bed and the apartment all to himself.

Reaching for his cigarettes, he said, "Give me the blow-by-blow. Regale me."

Rebecca did, in sordid detail.

She started with what she had been wearing, knowing that her boss's taste ran to that kind of thing—especially stockings and heels. Suffice it to say that despite her husband's appetites, Mrs. Wells was much more subdued.

Rebecca described dinner, drinks, and then everything else that had happened back at Cavanagh's. She took her time and was particularly descriptive.

When she finished talking about the sex, she got to the real reason for waking Wells at 3 a.m.

The Senator took another drag off his cigarette and sat up straighter in bed. "Are you positive?"

"I was right there. I heard the entire conversation."

"Then what happened?"

"We had sex once more in the shower and he rushed off to Langley."

Wells shook his head. She was incorrigible. "You're not still at his place, are you?"

"I wouldn't have called you if I was."

Smart girl, he thought. Picking up his watch, he looked at what time it was now. "Get some sleep."

"What are you going to do?"

"I think I may go for a run."

"Right now?"

"I need to think," said Wells.

"Okay," Rebecca replied. "I'll see you in the office in a few hours."

"Sounds good. And by the way? Excellent job."

She didn't reply. She simply hung up. Her boss was happy and she needed some sleep. Come 6 a.m., Red Bull and a pretty face would only get her so far.

Wells, though, knew there was no going back to sleep. Not with what he had just learned. McGee should have been much stricter with the information floating around at the CIA.

Even then, Rebecca probably still could have gotten it. She was the smartest hire Wells had ever made. He didn't care how much his wife hated her. Women like Nancy were always going to hate women like Rebecca. They were seen as threats. But in the right hands, they were gold mines.

Rebecca was his hard-bodied, big-titted golden calf. How he was going to get her information to market was another issue entirely.

What he had was too good not to use against President Porter. Rebecca, though, needed to be insulated. If they reverse-engineered it back to her then the jig was up. They would know Cavanagh was the source and the CIA would can him. Wells would then be left on the outside looking in. He had to figure out something else.

Changing into his running gear, he left his apartment and rode the elevator down to the lobby.

Stepping out onto the sidewalk, he looked around. It was still dark. The sun would be up soon, but he knew this was the most dangerous time of day. Criminals were like vampires. They shrank from daylight, but the hour before sunrise was when they were most desperate.

He decided to run parallel to the Mall. There was plenty of street traffic. He'd be all right.

After loosening up, he began his run. It was always the best part of his day. No phone calls, no email, no pathetic alms-seeking constituents. Just him and the pavement.

He was always amazed at how poorly the grounds of the Mall were maintained. The sidewalks were cracked, the curbs crumbling. There were weeds in the grass and entirely too much garbage.

A shining city on a hill it was not. For the capital of the greatest nation in the history of the world, it was disgusting.

Cleaning up D.C. was going to be one of the first things he did as President. Better yet, he'd have Nancy make it one of her initiatives as

First Lady. She needed a pet cause anyway. This was a good one. It was good and nonpartisan. Perfect for her.

Within minutes, he had run two blocks. His heart rate was elevated and his endorphins were flowing. It was such a delicious rush. As far as he was concerned, a runner's high was almost as good as sex. *Almost.*

Usually he let his mind wander on his runs. Today, though, he needed to focus. He had discovered a potential chink in the President's armor. It was just begging to have a knife shoved through it.

But before he did that, he had to make sure the information was solid. What if Rebecca was wrong? What if she had misunderstood what she had heard?

There was some truth to the phrase *If something sounds too good to be true, it probably is*—especially in Washington.

As Wells continued to run, he saw a lone figure sitting on a bench. *Homeless,* he thought to himself. That was another thing his wife could get involved in. Good way to score points with the press and the public.

Passing the figure on the bench, he realized that he wasn't homeless. He was an older man, buttoned up in a trench coat. He looked like something out of a spy movie. A newspaper sat folded in his lap.

That was when it hit him. Wells didn't need to confirm Rebecca's information. He needed someone else to do it. And he had the perfect person in mind.

That person, though, didn't do anything for free. They would want something in return.

Looking at his watch, Wells decided to turn around and head back. There was a lot he would need to pull together.

CHAPTER 20

From Frankfurt it was a five-hour drive, nine if there was traffic. Harvath did it in four. And he did it with a body in the trunk.

Lydia Ryan had kept him waiting for an answer so long that he'd finally said *fuck this*, had gotten in his car, and had taken off. When seconds counted, too often the decisions at the CIA were hours away.

The name Mikhail Malevsky, though, was setting off alarm bells across Washington. Bad ones. Politics were now in play. Malevsky was related to the Russian Prime Minister.

They were second or third cousins, but close enough that Malevsky had managed to secure a position as a commercial attaché. By all accounts it was a charade, but it came with a diplomatic passport. And that put him in a gray zone.

He was suspected of being involved in a money-laundering operation in Munich. Everything was being run through a Russian-owned real estate investment company. While their transactions appeared legitimate, the source of the funds did not.

German authorities knew the money flowing into their country was tied to Russian organized crime. Proving it was another matter entirely. For the moment, Malevsky was beyond their grasp. But he wasn't beyond Harvath's.

The United States also knew Malevsky was dirty. They had seen enough evidence. His connection to Sacha Baseyev was one of the most damning details of all. Handling his diplomatic status and his family ties to the Russian PM, though, were the hard parts.

The Russians played a brutal form of hardball. If Harvath was caught, not only was he a dead man, but it would be open season on American diplomats everywhere. The Russians weren't ones to let bygones be bygones.

In any other situation, the CIA would have found a way to work around Malevsky. Unfortunately, this wasn't any other situation. There wasn't a workaround. The path to Baseyev went straight through Mikhail Malevsky. He was the bad actor. They had no other choice than to take the chain off Harvath and trust him to do what he did best.

And what he did best was get results. No matter how much security or protection Malevsky had, Harvath would get to him. Where things went from there was entirely up to him. But considering the Russian's background, Harvath didn't expect him to be cooperative.

Based on the phone number from Eichel, Nicholas had been able to track Malevsky to a picturesque village in the Bavarian Alps called Berchtesgaden. The house wasn't hard to find. It was a massive stone hunting lodge, painted lemon yellow, with its own private drive and wrought iron gates.

There was a FOR SALE sign in front. A check of German property records indicated that a real estate investment company two hours away in Munich owned it.

In addition to a twelve-million-dollar price tag, the home had a twelve-million-dollar view. It looked south over the valley toward the third-highest mountain in Germany, the Watzmann. Its jagged peaks still covered in snow, the rolling Alpine meadows below it were filled with spring flowers.

Towering above the village was a mountain known as the Hoher Göll. Along its rocky sweep, Adolf Hitler had built his expensive vacation residence, the Berghof.

The village itself was a beautiful symphony of pastel-colored buildings, sloped cobblestone streets, and pitched rooftops. Here and there, hand-painted murals depicted traditional Bavarian life. Centuries-old church steeples soared skyward.

The Aga Khan, the Duke and Duchess of Windsor, and Neville Chamberlain had all passed through Berchtesgaden to visit Hitler. Mussolini, Goering, and Goebbels had come too. Now Mikhail Malevsky was calling the village home.

It was hard to imagine that a place of such beauty could play host to such evil. Harvath, though, knew better.

He knew that evil could exist anywhere. And that evil was attracted to beauty. It was like a magnet and he had always wondered why.

He guessed it was because evil was incapable of creating anything. It only destroyed. And beauty, being the ultimate creation, was prized and desired by evil above everything but power.

Beauty was a prize, a pet—an illusion, meant to fool the rest of the world into believing evil was something else. It was why truly evil men craved it. It was an addiction that radiated from the very center of their dark souls. Don't look at me, look at this. *Now* look back at me. See the beauty I am capable of?

Art collections, wives, mistresses, cars, homes, golden guns—even diamond-encrusted motorcycles—evil always wanted more, bigger, brighter, better. It was a self-perpetuating cycle, a need that could never be truly fulfilled. Harvath had seen it over and over again. There was only one, terrifying exception—*jihadism*.

Islamic fundamentalists rejected beauty. Women were to be kept covered. Depictions of the human form were forbidden. Ornamentation and ostentation also forbidden. Theirs was a monastic fanaticism.

And while their acts of savagery were *unquestionably* evil, within their own faith, these were seen as pious tributes to God. Their warriors were practicing the truest, most basic form of Islam. It was the Islam that their prophet, considered the perfect man, had taught them. It was the Islam laid out clearly in the Quran. They were not perverting their religion—they were purifying it.

The jihadists believed themselves to be true keepers of the Islamic faith. Their time on this earth was fleeting. Everything they did was in service of their god. How they dressed, how they ate, how they bathed, how they prayed—every action, no matter how small, was a step on the stairway to Paradise. That was where their reward lay.

The greater their acts in honor of Islam were here on earth, the greater their chances of reaching Paradise.

They were the worst enemy civilization had ever faced. And in its history, civilization had never been weaker.

The Western world had withdrawn, gone soft and cold. There were very few left to protect it. Fewer still who were willing to risk political careers over hard, consequence-ridden choices.

America's President, though, was willing to take the risk. He didn't have a choice. The survival of the United States depended on it.

Green-lighting the operation on Malevsky was the right decision. A bloody trail of American bodies, including the U.S. Secretary of Defense, might have started with ISIS, but it didn't end there. It kept going, right to the Russians' doorstep. He had no idea why, but he intended to find out. He also intended to end it. Right here, right now.

Harvath checked his GPS and continued on. He only wanted a quick look at the house. The sooner he got to his destination and emptied the trunk, the better he was going to feel.

CHAPTER 21

The old farm was fifteen kilometers outside the village. Harvath pulled around behind the faded barn and parked. It felt good to get out and stretch his legs.

The location couldn't have been better. Tucked back into the mountain, it was surrounded on three sides by sheer rock walls. The meadow sloped down, away from the house, and provided a clear view of the road. There were no neighbors.

Looking inside the barn, he saw a black 7 Series BMW. A pile of home improvement supplies was stacked next to it. He didn't see the owner and so struck off for the house.

It was a two-story chalet with flower boxes. Its massive roof overhung a long balcony on the second floor. The back door was unlocked. Harvath let himself in.

A large pair of boots sat on the tile floor. A leather jacket hung from a wooden peg. The walls were covered in rough-hewn planks. Low beams lined the ceiling. From deeper inside came the smell and crackle of a fire in a fireplace.

Harvath removed his smartphone. He wanted to handle the confirmation first.

Moving forward, he peered into each room as he passed. Good habits were good habits, regardless of the situation.

It was in the living area that he found the BMW's owner—an enormous, six-foot-four grizzly bear of a man. He was seated at a table near the fire. In front of him were a laptop, two Beretta pistols, and a large bottle of beer.

Harvath typed *CONFIRMED* and hit Send on his phone.

Moments later the man's computer chimed. "I like that," he said over his shoulder. "Do it again."

"Half now. Half when the job's over," Harvath replied. "Is there anything to eat?"

"Kitchen," the man grunted.

The fridge was stocked with meat, lots of it. There were also several dozen eggs, bottled water, and more beer. On the counter were bags of nuts and what looked like packages of German beef jerky.

Harvath prepared a plate, opened a bottle of beer, and returned to the living room.

The giant at the table stood to greet him. He had a gray beard now. His hair was salt-and-pepper, but still cut short. "You've gotten smaller," he said.

Harvath pointed at the man's stomach and joked, "You too."

"No carbs. No sugar. No fun," he replied. Then, looking at his beer added, "Okay, maybe a little fun."

Harvath smiled and joined him at the table. No sooner had he set his plate down than the man wrapped his huge arms around him. "You look good," he said. "Older, but still good."

The bear's name was Herman Toffle. He had been a member of Germany's renowned counterterrorism unit, GSG 9. They had met in a cross-training exercise back when Harvath was with the SEALs. Herman had an irreverent sense of humor, and they had become friends almost instantly.

"How's Diana?" Harvath asked once Herman had released him from the vise.

"She's good. She sends her love."

"Tell her I said thank you for setting all of this up."

Herman waved it off. "No problem. It belongs to some girlfriend of hers from Munich. She and her husband and kids come down a couple of times in the winter to ski. Maybe once or twice in the summer to swim in the Königssee. That's it. The rest of the time, they rent it out to vacationers."

"Hopefully, the fee will cover it."

The man laughed. "It will more than cover it."

Now that he had gone into the contracting world, Harvath had access to a substantial discretionary account. Herman was a professional. He should be paid. Not only did he warrant a premium for making himself available at the last minute, but he also deserved a little extra for all of the times in the past he had helped out and had received zero compensation in return.

He was a good friend. And now that Harvath was in a position to pay him back, it was the very least he could do.

After being shot and left with a permanent limp, Herman had been forced out of GSG 9. He went to work for a German arms manufacturer and did very well, parlaying his money into several successful ventures—including a private security company.

With the success of his businesses, he and his wife, Diana, were able to bounce back and forth between a luxury apartment in Munich and an impressive home in Berlin.

It had been years since Harvath had seen him, and in a true testament to their friendship, they picked right up where they had left off.

Herman asked about Harvath's good friend and former boss, Gary Lawlor. Harvath asked about Max and Sebastian—two commandos Herman had enlisted to assist them on a previous assignment.

Soon, though, the conversation turned to Harvath's current assignment. "I saw the gear in the barn. Was that everything on the list?" he asked.

"I had to improvise a little," said Herman. "I think we'll be okay."

Harvath trusted him. "Where do you want to put our guest?"

"If we leave him in the barn, he's going to freeze to death."

"I might be okay with that."

Herman shrugged and took a long pull from his beer. This was Harvath's operation, not his. He'd do what he was told.

"We're going to need surveillance," Harvath continued. "Langley is having a satellite retasked, but I want to get some actual eyes on."

"What are you thinking?"

"The ideal situation would be to pose as a potential buyer and actually get a tour of the property."

Herman took another sip of beer before responding. "A home that expensive, though, is only going to be opened to pre-approved buyers. You'd not only need financial statements, but a relationship with an established realtor."

He was right, and Harvath had already thought of that. "There might be a way around that."

"Such as?"

"The CIA has assets everywhere, but especially inside the United States."

Herman looked at him. "I thought that was illegal."

"Technically, they can't run operations in the U.S. But they can, and they do, recruit Americans to help with operations outside the country."

"So how does that help us?"

"There's a real estate firm in Beverly Hills. They cater to an exclusive clientele and specialize in high-end estates. The CIA has used them before."

"And they'll vouch for you as the buyer?"

Harvath shook his head. "Not as the buyer. As someone who *works* for the buyer. Someone passing through who thinks the home may be perfect for his employer. They'll pitch it that I'd like to get in to see it before I fly home."

"When are you *flying* home?"

"Let's say, tomorrow. If they're serious about selling, I'll get a showing."

"And if they aren't?" Herman asked.

"We go to Plan B."

"What's Plan B?"

Harvath smiled. "I haven't figured that out yet."

"Terrific."

"We'll be fine."

"*Sure we will,*" Herman replied as he stood to get some food for himself. "I think my fee just went up."

"In that case," said Harvath as he tossed him his car keys, "you get to empty the trunk."

"Where'd you park?"

"Behind the barn."

"I promised Diana we wouldn't do anything illegal."

That made Harvath laugh. "You shouldn't lie to your wife," he said as he dug into his plate. "It's bad for your marriage."

Herman went for his boots and jacket. "Don't let the fire die. And don't go anywhere. When I get back I want you, the bachelor, to tell me all about how marriage works."

Harvath flipped his friend the finger.

A few seconds later, he heard Herman open the door to go out to the barn and shouted, "He's pretty heavy. So remember to lift with your legs!"

CHAPTER 22

T he trunk of Harvath's car smelled terrible. He didn't know if Malevsky employed dogs, but just in case, he thought it better to drive Herman's BMW. He didn't need dogs going bonkers over his car. The more at ease everyone was, the better it would all go.

The owner of the real estate company in Beverly Hills had done an excellent job. She had worked with enough high-net-worth individuals to know exactly what to say, and what not to say.

An appointment had been set and Harvath had been told to drive up to the gate and ring the call box. Someone would be available to take him on a tour. Whether or not that someone would be Malevsky was yet to be seen.

He left his Glock with Herman, tossed his suitcase on the backseat, and drove back into Berchtesgaden. If they patted him down, or went through his bag—both of which he expected—he needed to fully look the part. If they were even the least bit suspicious of him, things were going to get real ugly, real fast.

The one thing that Harvath had going for him, the only thing, in fact, was that Malevsky was a businessman. The Russian mob had a very expensive property it needed to unload. Once it was sold, millions of clean dollars would be flowing back to their organization. Harvath only needed to be believed for the length of the showing. What happened after that wasn't his problem.

Rolling to a stop next to the call box, he depressed its silver button.

"Da?" a voice replied, but then corrected itself with the proper German. *"Ja?"*

"Hi," Harvath replied. "It's Tommy Molteni. I'm here for a property showing?"

The voice didn't welcome him or give him directions on where to park. There was a short tone, like the sound of a telephone key being pressed, and the gates began to swing inward.

Harvath waited for them to open fully and then followed the driveway up to the house.

The grounds were meticulously maintained. He noticed the placement of landscape lighting, as well as how many trees there were. From a security standpoint, there were a ton of things Harvath would have done differently. But from an investment standpoint, he could understand why Malevsky and the money-laundering operation might not have wanted to make the changes. Mess with the natural look and feel of the property too much by tearing down trees and other such things, and it might be harder to sell.

At the top of the drive, it opened onto a large motor court. Harvath spotted two Porsche Cayennes, a classic Rolls-Royce Silver Spirit, and an Audi R8 convertible. There was no telling what else lay behind the closed garage doors. He wondered if the cars were part of the money laundering as well.

He had expected to see muscle, and in that department, Malevsky didn't disappoint. But instead of slabs of beef in bad suits straight out of Moscow's version of central casting, the men were fit and well tailored. *Were they Spetsnaz—former Russian Special Forces?* They certainly had the look. They also had the vibe.

Predators could smell other predators from a mile away. Harvath made sure not to hold eye contact. Pasting a smile on his face, he waved and gestured for them to direct him where to park.

The men seemed more annoyed by his presence than anything else. They waved him over to the side and had him turn around so his vehicle was facing the correct direction to leave. Before he even had it in Park, one of the men was at his window, motioning him to lower it.

"Identification, please," the man said, once the window was down.

Harvath patted his pockets. "Like business cards? Sorry. I don't have any. The realtor from Beverly Hills should have told you that I—"

"Passport," the man requested, cutting him off.

He was polite, but firm. A professional. Harvath was getting the full-on Spetsnaz feeling from him. "Sure," Harvath replied turning to reach for his bag in the backseat. "I've got my passport right back here."

"Stop," the man said.

Harvath did as he asked.

The man gave an order to his colleague and then asked Harvath to shut off the engine and step out of the car.

The other guard removed Harvath's bag from the car and brought it around to him.

"Passport, please," the first man repeated.

Harvath zipped open the front compartment of his suitcase, pulled out the passport the CIA had issued him, and handed it over.

The Russian studied it, looking back and forth from Harvath to the picture and information contained inside. Finally, he handed it back.

Harvath smiled.

The other guard said something into a handheld radio and motioned for Harvath to follow him. Once more, he did as he was told.

They walked up a stone pathway to the front door, where, just as he had expected, he was checked for weapons. Another switched-on, bespoke security guard waved him with a metal-detecting wand.

Once he was content that Harvath didn't have any weapons, he opened the door, an alarm panel chimed, and he showed him in.

It was like walking into Versailles, on crack. Everything was covered in gold leaf—the railings, the balustrades, the furniture, the mirror frames, the light fixtures, the capitals on the pink marble columns, the crown molding, the door hardware, even the four-foot-high griffins at the bottom of the staircase.

To call it "overdone" would have been a massive understatement. Harvath had only one word for it all: "Wow."

"Mr. Molteni, welcome," said a small, obsequious man with a Russian accent. He had dark, curly hair parted on the side and wore an ill-fitting blazer with a polo shirt. "My name is Jakob. I am the estate manager."

Harvath shook his hand and thanked him for seeing him.

Jakob gazed appreciatively around the entry. "Isn't it something?"

"It's something, all right," Harvath replied.

"Where would you like to start?"

"Any place you wish. I don't want to take up too much of your time."

"Let's start in the great hall."

Harvath followed and listened as the man recounted the history of the house. It had been built in 1908 by a Russian—General Nikolas of Malzoff—who hailed from St. Petersburg.

At the mention of St. Petersburg, Jakob caught a flicker of recognition in Harvath's expression. "Have you been to Russia?" he asked.

Harvath had been to Russia multiple times, but only for assignments. Smiling, he nodded his head and replied, "St. Petersburg, actually."

Jakob enjoyed hearing this and they chatted for several minutes about the city before he got the tour back on track.

Picking up where he left off, he described all the craftsmen that had been imported for the Villa Malzoff's construction. He made particular mention of the artists from Italy who had painted the ceiling frescoes in each of the rooms.

Harvath had never heard of General Nikolas of Malzoff, but whoever he was, he had spent a lot of money.

When they arrived in the great hall, it became obvious why Jakob had wanted to start there. It was a showstopper.

The great hall had been converted into a long living room with six different seating areas. But its most dramatic feature was the view.

Floor-to-ceiling windows could be retracted, lanai-style as they were now, opening the room to the outside. The view of the snow-capped Watzmann was breathtaking.

It was one of the best views Harvath had ever seen. Jakob was quite pleased to hear it.

As they continued, it was apparent that Jakob loved the home. There wasn't a single detail that he hadn't familiarized himself with. Harvath asked if his services as estate manager were included in the sales price. Jakob was flattered, but explained that he moved from property to property as his employer required.

Harvath attempted to quiz him about his employer, but Jakob wouldn't bite. He just kept the tour moving.

Room after room, Harvath took stock of the Villa Malzoff's security measures. So far, he hadn't seen anything he couldn't handle.

Once they were done with the house, Jakob took him on a tour of the grounds.

The property was just under seven acres. It included a swimming pool, a pool house, a guesthouse, and a residential building for staff with seven apartments.

During the entire time, he saw no hint of Mr. or Mrs. Malevsky—other than the clothes hanging in their master bedroom closet.

Harvath had been hoping that the wife and children were back in Munich. They were a contingency he didn't want to deal with.

The final stop on the tour was a small gamekeeper's cottage. It looked like something out of a fairy tale. Like "Hansel and Gretel" or "Snow White."

The cottage was made from fieldstone. It had a thatched roof, a large chimney, and little stained glass windows with wooden shutters.

Harvath was thinking what an attractive playhouse it probably was for Malevsky's children, when the door opened and he got the shock of his life.

CHAPTER 23

"You're sure?" Herman asked. The sleeves of his sweat-stained shirt were rolled up to his elbows. One of the Beretta pistols was tucked in his waistband. His work had been cut out for him over the last hour.

Leaving Eichel back in Frankfurt had been out of the question. There was too much trouble he could have caused.

So, with Anna Strobl on point, Harvath had put his pistol in Eichel's side and walked him downstairs and out to the street. At the car, he forced him into the trunk where he bound and gagged him with duct tape. He and Anna then drove back to her house in Oberursel.

They had chatted for several minutes in the driveway. As gorgeous as she was, she radiated loneliness from every pore. She was not dealing with her husband's illness well.

His prognosis wasn't good. The disease had moved much faster than anyone had anticipated. She confessed that she had never lost anyone before, not even among the cops she worked with. Harvath had lost a lot of people and he shared some of that with her. Most important, he shared the regret he carried and how it weighed on him. He encouraged Anna to make the best of the time she had left with her husband.

She was frightened, but there was also strength inside her. Whether she believed it or not, she was tough. She was a warrior. She would make it through this, and Harvath told her as much. She thanked him.

As he reversed out of the driveway, she stood on the ramp and held his gaze. He hoped for her sake and for Jörg's that they'd be able to find a little bit of happiness together.

What Strobl had done was wrong, very wrong, but Harvath understood it. Wanting to take care of his wife after he was gone was a noble impulse. There weren't many options open to a man in his condition, with the clock winding down. That didn't excuse what he had done, though. Not by a long shot.

But in the time Jörg had left, maybe there was a way he could atone for his sins. Maybe he could be of assistance to Harvath. Anna certainly had the makings of a valuable asset. Harvath would have to think about it.

In the meantime, Herman had done him a huge favor. At some point during the drive down from Frankfurt, Eichel had needed a bathroom break, but was bound and gagged in the trunk and not able to communicate.

Harvath's car was not only cleaned up, but so was Eichel. He had been changed into what Harvath assumed were a pair of Herman's pajamas. A hood was over his head and he was sitting, bound to a sturdy chair, in the barn.

Sheets of plastic had been suspended from rafters and rolled out along the floor. An average person might have suspected that the pair was going to paint something. Mikhail Malevsky wasn't average. He would know exactly what was going on and what all of the plastic was for.

"You're absolutely positive?" Herman asked again as Harvath double-checked Eichel's restraints.

"Are you sure he can't hear us?" Harvath replied, nodding toward their prisoner.

Herman pulled the hood back to show that not only was Eichel blindfolded, he was also wearing professional earmuffs that had been duct-taped to his head. Sensory deprivation. It would keep him off balance, scared. Along with his battered face, he would make an excellent prop. Once Malevsky saw the state he was in, he might be more open to cooperating.

A bit more at ease, Harvath said, "Am I *absolutely positive*? Of course I am. She saved my life. That's not someone you forget."

Harvath replayed the scene in his mind. It was more than ten years ago. They were three miles from the White House. A tactical nuclear weapon had been hidden in Congressional Cemetery. If it wasn't for her, the bomb would have gone off and he would have been dead. He had doubted her loyalty and she had proven him wrong.

"Okay," Herman continued, "let's say you're right. After all of these years, it's *her*. But did she recognize you?"

"After everything we went through?"

"What I *mean*, is, did she acknowledge you?"

He shook his head. "She was cold as ice. A pro."

"So what's she doing here? Why would she be a nanny for some Russian mobster?"

"Malevsky isn't just *some* Russian mobster."

"I know," said Herman. "He's related to the Prime Minister. But even if he was related to the Pope, why would a Russian SVR agent be babysitting for him in Bavaria?"

It was a good question. The SVR was Russia's version of the CIA. Pitchfork, aka Sacha Baseyev, was a product of the GRU, Russia's version of the Defense Intelligence Agency. *Why would the two agencies be crossing paths like this?*

None of it made any sense. "I have to find out why she's here," Harvath replied.

"Wait. What?"

"You heard me.

"*After* we grab Malevsky," said Herman.

"What if she knows something?"

"In and out. That's what you said."

"I know that's what I said. But that was before she saw me. We can't grab Malevsky now—not until we know what's going on. If we go in there and snatch him, the Russians will know the United States is onto them."

"I hate to break it to you, my friend, but they already know. You don't think she's going to report seeing you?"

"I don't know what she'll do," Harvath responded. "That's why I need to talk to her. Alone. Tonight."

Herman thought about it for several moments. Finally, he looked at his watch. "It will be dark soon," he said. "How do you want to do this?"

• • •

Harvath hadn't seen any sign of dogs during his tour of Villa Malzoff. That didn't mean Malevsky didn't have any. If he did, they were personal protection dogs that traveled with him, not guard dogs who worked a perimeter. That was good.

The other thing Harvath had going for him was that the property was not enclosed. There was no wall, no fence, nothing—only the gate at the bottom of the driveway.

There were landscape lights, but no floodlights. There was an in-house, wireless security system, but it wasn't very sophisticated—mostly motion detectors. He hadn't seen any cameras.

Malevsky appeared to have a lot of confidence in his guards. And if that was the case, Harvath needed to as well.

Reviewing the satellite footage Langley had provided, he identified all of the likely avenues of approach and scratched them off his list. They were too obvious. Malevsky's guards would have planned for them already.

The most difficult, and therefore the least likely way in, was to come up and over the rocky terrain behind the estate. Harvath liked it for multiple reasons.

Any view of the house was blocked by a narrow stretch of forest. That meant it was a lousy perch for a sniper. There was also no way to get a vehicle anywhere close back there. Thieves or kidnappers wouldn't want to be that far away from a vehicle.

The only person coming in from the back would be someone planning to kill Malevsky, probably up close, somewhere on the property.

That meant a professional, like Harvath, and it would be very difficult to know he was there.

If the guards were Spetsnaz, that meant they had a military background and likely approached problems by looking for military solutions. If it were Harvath, he would plant ground sensors and tune them to ignore anything at or below the weight of the most common local animals. This way, if a deer came bounding through, things wouldn't get sent into DEFCON 1.

With the kind of money Malevsky had, though, his people could afford an even more sophisticated system. They could conceivably go full military grade with a product that not only automatically distinguished between animals and humans but also had a motion-sensitive camera that tracked the intruder and transmitted a real-time feed.

Those cameras transmitted via hardwire, satellite, or radio frequency. Based on what Harvath had seen, he doubted they'd go through the trouble of trenching and burying wires—not on a property Malevsky was enjoying only until it could be sold.

Harvath's money was on a satellite signal or RF and he lobbed that ball into the CIA's court while he finalized his plan.

When it was complete, he shared it with Herman. "Where am I positioned?" he asked.

Harvath pointed to the map and drew a circle around the farm. "You're staying here with Eichel."

The massive German furrowed his brow. "Bad plan."

"It's a good plan. It'll work."

"Until it doesn't," said Herman, taking his pen and turning the map around. "You expect to leave the property the same way you came in."

"So?"

"What if your access is blocked?"

Harvath looked at the map and replied, "I'll go around this way."

"Which doubles the distance back to your car. What if you're injured?"

"I'll improvise."

"And if the local police find your car parked up on the road?" Herman asked.

"It won't be on the road. It'll be off. I'll make sure they don't find it."

"But if they do?"

"I'll improvise."

"I can see it now," Herman said, splaying his hands. "Here lies the body of Scot Harvath. *He improvised*."

Herman was beginning to get on Harvath's nerves. Harvath didn't need his help. He knew what he was doing. "I want you with Eichel."

"That's fine," Herman replied. "We can duct-tape Eichel in blankets and put him in my trunk. I'll drop you off behind the property and then pick you up wherever you want."

"And if the police find you? With Eichel?"

Herman smiled. "I'll improvise."

CHAPTER 24

I t took the CIA longer to get back to Harvath than he had hoped. But they had come through. Actually, it was a combination of agencies that had come through.

Detecting whether or not there were devices on the perimeter of the property, and if so what kind of signal they were emitting, wasn't an easy task. Satellites didn't hover. They moved around the earth in an orbit and had limited windows within which to gather information.

After consultation with the National Reconnaissance Office and the National Geospatial-Intelligence Agency, a request was made to the German military for a pair of U.S. F-16 Falcons out of Spangdahlem Air Base to be allowed to modify the flight path of their evening training maneuver. They claimed to be testing a new terrain mapping system and wanted to do so over the mountains of Bavaria.

The Germans granted permission and within fifteen minutes both jets were airborne.

The sophisticated system they carried with them did a lot more than just map terrain. The jets were like Google's "street view" cars, but on crack. They vacuumed up every single scrap of electrical information they came in contact with—Wi-Fi signals, cell phone information, radio traffic and satellite communications, even the RF codes for garage door remotes. It was an incredible piece of high-tech.

The jets had needed only one low-level pass. They turned on their vacuums, swept in over Berchtesgaden, and by the time anyone had heard them and knew they were there, they were already gone.

After landing back at Spangdahlem, the drives were pulled, the data was encrypted, and then it was all transmitted back to the United States.

Harvath had been correct. There were multiple objects around the perimeter of the property communicating with a satellite network.

Now that they knew where and what they were, the NSA got to work on how to interrupt them.

The operation was highly compartmentalized, contained to only a handful of personnel. That was good for secrecy, but not so good for a rapid turnaround. When they finally had it ready to go, Harvath heard a voice over his earpiece.

"Norseman, this is Round Top. We are ready to proceed on your command. Over."

Harvath had gotten as close to the property as he dared. Until he knew the signals from the ground sensors had been interrupted, he didn't want to go any further. "Roger that, Round Top," he replied. It was cold. He could see his breath. "Stand by. Over."

"Roger that, Norseman. Round Top is standing by. Over."

In addition to all the supplies sitting back in the barn, Herman had delivered for Harvath in another department—tactical equipment.

He did one last check of his gear before saying, "Round Top, this is Norseman. On my mark. Over."

"Roger that, Norseman. On your mark. Over."

Adjusting his night-vision goggles, he counted backward aloud from five.

When he got to one, the voice over his earpiece said, "Norseman, this is Round Top. The satellite signal is interrupted. I repeat, the satellite signal is interrupted. You are good to go. Good luck, Norseman. Over."

Harvath didn't respond, he was already up and moving.

The ground was steep, the rocks sharp. He was wearing hiking boots, dark jeans, and a black North Face jacket. The sensors were only going to be down for a short time. He needed to move fast.

Twice, he lost his footing. Twice, he caught himself. If he hadn't been wearing Herman's gloves, his hands would have been hamburger.

At the bottom of the rocks, he sprinted for the woods. Once he was in the trees, he relayed a situation report, or SITREP for short. "Round

Top, this is Norseman. I'm on the beach. Going to zero comms. Over."

Round Top acknowledged that Harvath had reached the trees and wanted radio silence by responding with two squelch clicks over his earpiece. It was now *game on*. There would only be communication if he initiated it.

He removed the 9mm Heckler & Koch USP SD Herman had given him and spun a GEMTECH suppressor onto its threaded barrel. It was loaded with subsonic ammunition and he carried two extra magazines. If bullets started flying, though, that meant something had gone very wrong.

His goal was to channel the Sierra Club—get in, get out, and leave no trace.

It was a serious gamble. If Malevsky discovered that his security had been breached, he was going to be a lot harder to get to. He was either going to add additional layers, or go to ground. Neither option made Harvath's ultimate assignment any easier.

This foray, though, was an acceptable, and even necessary, risk. It had to be done. No one back at Langley disagreed.

With Herman's gloves tucked in his pocket and his hands wrapped around the butt of the weapon, he picked his way through the remaining trees and got ready to make a sprint to the first structure.

"Round Top, this is Norseman," he whispered. "Home plate to first base. All good?"

He waited and one squelch click was returned. *All good*. Via their current satellite, they weren't seeing any trouble between him and his first target.

Harvath swept his night-vision goggles back and forth over the stretch of meadow he would have to cross. It looked clear. Taking a deep breath, he counted to three and took off running.

The ground was uneven, but mostly grass and much less rocky. As long as he didn't hit any holes, he'd be fine. He could already see the residential building not too far ahead. There were no lights inside. It looked like everyone was—

Suddenly, two digital squelch clicks chirped over his earpiece. Harvath dropped, flipped off his goggles, and buried his face in the ground. Some-body stateside had seen something.

He didn't move a muscle. He didn't even breathe. All he could do was listen. But there was nothing. *What the hell had they seen?*

He laid there on the cold ground wondering, until the wind gave him an answer. Above the smell of cold, damp earth, he began to detect some-thing else—cigarette smoke.

Somebody was taking a smoke break and must have wandered in his direction.

He took slow, controlled breaths, trying to gauge the smoker's dis-tance, but the scent faded. *Did the smoker walk away?*

Almost in answer to his question, he received the "all clear" from Round Top—three squelch clicks.

Replacing his goggles, he allowed his eyes to readjust and then slowly looked up and assessed his situation.

There was no one in sight. The smell of cigarette smoke had also all but evaporated.

Pushing himself up, he moved toward the structure. Quickly. Quietly. As he moved, he swung his head from left to right, scanning for threats, his suppressed pistol up and ready to fire.

The main door for the residential building was unlocked and he let himself in. He had rebuilt everything from memory—what he had seen in each room, what staff members belonged to each apartment. She wasn't in this building. Malevsky and his wife would want her close to them, close to the children. She would be inside the main house, but there was someone else of value that slept here. *The chef.*

Harvath had seen him while touring the kitchen with Jakob. He had noticed the broken capillaries of the man's nose, the tremor in his hand, the coffee cup nearby, filled with something other than coffee.

As Jakob had taken him through the residential building, Harvath had identified the man's apartment by the personal photos on his dresser, the Russian cookbooks on his bookshelf. The poorly hidden vodka bottle in the bathroom had confirmed his suspicions.

Standing outside his door now, Harvath could hear the man's snoring. It sounded like the bellows of a gigantic blast furnace. In and out, in and out. It was like someone was trying to parallel-park a mile-long freight train.

Harvath tried the chef's doorknob. It was unlocked. He slowly pushed the door open so as not to make any noise and then stepped inside.

The man hadn't even made it to his bed. He lay passed out on his couch. There was a half-eaten plate of food on the coffee table, accompanied by the "coffee" cup Harvath had seen him with earlier. He was still wearing his uniform.

Harvath shook his head and scanned the living room until he found what he was looking for. The chef had dropped his keys on the floor.

Carefully, so as not to make a sound, he picked them up.

Now all Harvath had to do was to get into the house—something that was going to be much easier said than done.

CHAPTER 25

Harvath had secured enough buildings, events, and estates in his time to know that the key was to limit entry and exit points. With estates, that normally meant the owners came and went via the garage or front door. Servants came, went, and normally received deliveries via some unseen service entrance.

In the case of the Villa Malzoff, it was the grand, restaurant-sized kitchen in back. It was connected to the staff apartments by a small service lane that split off from the driveway.

Harvath used the trees for concealment as he made his approach to the main house. During his tour, he had seen staff coming and going through the main kitchen door.

Unlike the other doors in the hunting lodge, the alarm system didn't chime every time it opened or closed. It probably saw so much traffic that the chime had been disabled.

But was it reactivated at night? That was Harvath's biggest question mark at this point.

It didn't matter that he had a set of keys and that one of them likely opened the door in question. If opening the door meant setting off the alarm, things would instantly go from game on to game over.

He checked out the fifty-meter dash he was going to have to make to a row of garbage cans near some stairs outside the kitchen. Stopping behind the last tree, he requested a SITREP. Three squelch clicks came back in response. *All clear.*

A couple of lights were on in the kitchen, but he couldn't see any activity. The rest of the house was asleep, its windows dark. Harvath decided to make his move.

Unlike his last sprint across open ground, this one went down without incident. Flattening his back against the outer wall of the house, he crouched down between two of the cans and waited.

There were two things Russians could always be counted on to do—drink and smoke. The chef had been passed out drunk, just as Harvath had anticipated. Based on what he had seen during his tour, there were no ashtrays in the house and it didn't smell of cigarettes. Wanting the place to show well, Malevsky had likely issued a ban on smoking indoors.

All Harvath needed now was someone to step out for a cigarette break. Once they used the kitchen door, he'd be able to ascertain a lot about its security.

Twenty minutes went by. The temperature continued to drop. The air was frigid. It was like a saw made out of ice, slicing at him, carving into every fold of clothing it could find.

He had long since given up crouching. It was too rough on his knees. Nobody could hold that position for that long.

Sitting, with his knees pulled against his chest, he continued to wait. In the back of his mind he began to formulate a Plan B. If no one came out, what would he do? *Would he risk the door? Abort the operation?*

He was running through his options, when he heard someone unlock the kitchen door. Quickly, he got into a crouch.

A man stepped outside with an unlit cigarette dangling from his mouth. Removing a Zippo from his pocket, he flipped open the top and struck the flint wheel against the side of his leg. Raising the lighter, he lit his cigarette. Harvath was so close he could almost smell the lighter fluid.

Once the cigarette was lit, the man flicked his wrist, the lid snapped shut, and the flame was extinguished. The man took a deep, long drag. He filled his lungs and put his head back, savoring the hit from the nicotine as it raced into his system.

The man stepped the rest of the way out, and closed the door behind him. Harvath noted that there had been no sound of a chime from the alarm pad just inside. The door appeared safe.

The man was larger than the security guards he had seen earlier. He was bald with a thick neck. He looked like a circus strongman minus the handlebar mustache. When Harvath pictured low-rent, Russian mob muscle in his mind, this was exactly the kind of person he envisioned—gold jewelry and all.

He looked to be in his late fifties, maybe older. It was hard to tell. Russians lived hard and aged badly, particularly in the criminal arena.

In his crouch, Harvath tried to slow his respiration. He didn't want the sight of his breath rising into the cold night air to give him away.

The man took a couple more puffs off his cigarette and then stubbed it out. But instead of flicking the remainder somewhere into the service lane or the grass, he began walking toward the line of garbage cans.

Fuck was the first word that came to Harvath's mind. *What's this idiot doing?* Was he going to throw his recently lit cigarette in the trash?

But when he heard the first lid open, it only took him a matter of seconds to realize what was up.

There was the sound of glass against glass as the Russian fished a bottle of who knows what out of the trash and unscrewed the cap.

Whatever he had found, there wasn't much of it because the bottle went quickly back into the trash and he moved to the next can.

He was close now. Way too close. *Fuck,* Harvath said to himself again. Even with subsonic ammo in his suppressed H&K, the 9mm pistol still made a lot of noise. It would sound even louder this close to the house. Somebody was going to hear it. And whoever did was going to come to investigate. *Fuck.*

He tried to think. *Improvise,* he told himself as he looked around. He could hear the large man fishing another bottle out of the can two down from where he was hiding.

Harvath was going to have to shoot him. There was no getting around it. The man seemed determined to rut through every garbage can before he turned and went back inside. *Booze and cigarettes,* he thought. *Fucking Russians.*

Leaning against the wall, he shifted his weapon into his left hand. This was going to screw everything. He'd have to find a place to hide the body and hope it bought him enough time to do what he needed to do inside.

Somehow, he'd have to figure out how to grab Malevsky and get him out of the house. He hated the idea, but he was going to have to use one of the mobster's kids. *Damn it.*

The Russian was one garbage can away now. It was only a matter of seconds before he came to the gap between the cans and saw him.

Harvath would have to move fast. In order to muffle the sound of his weapon, he'd need to get it up against the man. He planned to shoot him in the back of the head or the heart—multiple shots in quick succession. Then he would drag his body around the side of the house and place it out of sight.

This was not how any of this was supposed to go down. There had to be a better way. *Think,* he told himself. But it was too late. He had to act. The man was now on top of him.

Launching full force up out of his crouch, he came at him like a battering ram. He delivered a searing punch into the best target he had, right up between the man's legs.

The air whooshed from the man's lungs and he doubled over. As he did, Harvath slipped past, turned, and then drove his elbow as hard as he could into the base of his skull, knocking him the rest of the way to the ground.

He drew back his foot to kick him in the head, but stopped. The man was lying on the ground, on his stomach, not moving.

Harvath figured he was out cold. Leaning forward, he placed his pistol to the back of his head and began applying pressure to his trigger. Then he noticed his eyes. They were open, but he wasn't breathing.

He reached down and checked his pulse. He didn't have one. He was dead.

Harvath could smell the alcohol wafting off him, and that gave him an idea. *The stairs.*

Grabbing the huge man under the arms, he dragged him over to the flight of six stone stairs that led downhill and took him to the bottom. He posed the body as best he could and then ran back up to the garbage cans to fish out a bottle of liquor.

Returning to the body, he tucked the bottle halfway underneath. He then placed his knee on the corpse and applied his weight until the bottle broke.

The accident scene was complete. Whether or not Malevsky would buy it was another matter entirely.

All Harvath knew was that he had caught a break. He didn't expect to catch another one. Moving quickly up the stone steps, he headed for the kitchen door.

Slipping into the house, he closed the door behind him and quietly climbed the back stairs. He had a good feeling he knew which room was hers.

The door was unlocked. He opened it slowly.

Despite the hour, she wasn't asleep. She wasn't even in bed. A small, semiautomatic pistol was in her hand. She looked at him as he entered the room and said, "You shouldn't have come back."

CHAPTER 26

President Porter nodded and the lights were dimmed. The glowing presidential seal on the monitors was replaced by the black flag of ISIS. There was the sound of wind. Slowly, the flag began to ripple.

Haunting music in Arabic poured from the overhead speakers. A picture of the Secretary of Defense faded up from the black.

Public photos from the last thirty years of Richard Devon's life began to appear. Each one materialized quicker than the last.

As the pacing of the photos built to a crescendo, so too did the music. Then everything went black.

Everyone in the Situation Room braced for the worst.

But, like a terrifying horror movie, it was a feint—a move meant to keep its viewers off balance.

Secretary Devon's voice now filled the room. The screens pulsed with digital snow, as if trying to capture some faraway signal. Then the video came into focus.

It was the Secretary's swearing-in ceremony at the Pentagon. The words were his oath of office, administered by the Vice President.

But the swearing-in video was soon replaced by images of war and carnage. American tanks, troops, and planes were shown intercut with dead and dismembered Middle Eastern men, women, and children. All the while, Secretary Devon could be heard proudly and confidently reciting his oath.

There was applause as the Vice President congratulated Devon and the screens in the Situation Room went black once again. *Now the worst would come.*

A fraction of a second later, the video roared back to life. The motorcade was under attack. The attackers shouted *"Allahu'akbar"* as they stepped into the street firing their fully automatic rifles.

The attack was covered from multiple angles. Not only were the terrorists wearing GoPro cameras but there was also footage of the carnage taken from up above. Cameras must have been placed in windows or on rooftops.

It was slick and well produced. It looked like something out of a Hollywood action movie.

It was gut-wrenching to watch.

No one in the Situation Room spoke. They were saddened and sickened by what they were watching play out on the screen.

Everyone knew how it ended, but no one could turn away. They were all mesmerized, prisoners of the violence and barbarity unfolding in front of them.

When the final moment came, and the first car bombs exploded, the video transitioned into slow motion. If there was an Academy Award for evil, ISIS would have taken home an Oscar. It was as if the Devil himself had gotten into the film business.

The video ended with a masked figure standing in the desert, taunting the President. He spoke English like an American. He was different from the Brit and Aussie spokesmen the world had seen before.

"Unite your coalition. Mobilize your armies. Exact your revenge," he said. "You know where to find us. We're waiting for you."

And with that, the video shrank into a single point of light and disappeared—like an old television set being switched off.

The lights in the Situation Room came back up. The members of the President's National Security Council sat stunned. No one spoke. They were all without words.

Then, as if a starting gun had gone off, they all began speaking at once. Tempers were hot.

President Porter called for quiet and directed CIA Director McGee to bring everyone up to speed on the latest.

"The video you just saw was published by the media arm of ISIS less than two hours ago," the Director said. "We're in the process of analyzing it now. In the meantime, I want to update you on the explosion last night in Antalya, Turkey."

Activating his presentation, he put a slide up on the monitors that showed two pictures. One was the smoking, burned-out hulks of at least fifteen vehicles. The other looked like a huge bomb crater.

"The photo on the left," the Director narrated, "is a crime scene photo from the car bomb attack on Secretary Devon's motorcade. The photo on the right is from an explosion, about six-and-a-half kilometers away, that happened several hours later."

"We're assuming they're connected?" the Vice President asked.

McGee nodded. "The FBI had already sent forensics teams to Antalya to gather evidence from Secretary Devon's attack. When the second explosion happened, a small contingent of FBI technicians agreed to aid Turkish police in their investigation.

"The explosion leveled almost half a city block. It was an industrialized area, mostly warehouses. No word yet on casualties."

"What's the connection?"

"The FBI's preliminary finding is that the explosive signatures match," McGee replied. "We think ISIS was using one of the warehouses as a bomb factory."

"And judging by the size of that crater," the Chairman of the Joint Chiefs stated, "they still had a lot of ingredients left."

"Which Turkish intelligence assumes was meant for further attacks inside Turkey. They see this as a major escalation. Ismet Bachar, the Chief of the Turkish General Staff, has even canceled his vacation and returned to the capital."

"Good," the National Security Advisor chimed in. "If they'd actually been serious about ISIS from the get-go, maybe Secretary Devon would still be alive."

Maybe, but McGee didn't want to get into hypotheticals. "At this point, they're bending over backward to give us everything we need."

"What about the man in the video?" the Secretary of State interjected. "He sounds American. Do we have any idea who he is?"

"Not yet."

"How about where they got their intelligence?" the Attorney General asked. "Have we identified a specific leak yet?"

"No. Not yet."

"What about the three Turks that Secretary Devon's team plowed down during the attack? Have we learned anything more about them? Anything that might be helpful?"

McGee shook his head and repeated, "No. Nothing yet."

"Has the NSA had any luck isolating what part of the cloud the attackers uploaded their GoPro footage to?"

The CIA Director shook his head. It was demoralizing for everyone present. A silence fell back over the room.

The Secretary of State decided to take advantage of the lull. "Mr. President, if I may ask. Are you still planning to renounce recognition of the Sykes-Picot boundaries?"

Porter had been expecting the question. "I am," he replied.

"Have you decided when?"

"No. Why?"

"This is going to unleash unprecedented chaos," the Secretary of State said. "It'll make the Arab Spring look like a fifth-grade field trip. Israel is our ally. They deserve more than just a heads-up. They need time to get ready, to dig in. And if we—"

Porter motioned for him to stop. "I told you that I would worry about Israel, and I will. I know they're our ally. I also know this is going to be difficult for them. But we're going to make sure they have the biggest stick in the sandbox."

"I don't understand."

"You will," he said. "In the meantime, I believe the Chairman of the Joint Chiefs has something for us. Are you ready?"

"We are, Mr. President," he responded.

Porter nodded.

"Anticipating that ISIS was responsible for the attack on Secretary of Defense Devon, and in retaliation for the attack on the CIA's SAD team in Anbar, the President asked the Pentagon to draw up a response plan."

Nodding to an aide, the Chairman had a target map uploaded to the monitors as he continued. "Code-named Iron Fury, the attack focuses on the following—known ISIS command and control centers, training facilities, and most importantly, oil infrastructure."

The Secretary of State studied the map and then asked, "And it will launch when?"

The Chairman looked at the President, who again nodded.

"Right now," the Chairman replied.

The three-hour attack, code-named Operation Iron Fury, began with two waves of B-2 Spirit stealth bombers, each carrying a payload of eighty 500-pound Mark 82 bombs.

As they destroyed a series of critical oil refineries, volleys of Tomahawk missiles were fired from a U.S. guided missile destroyer in the North Arabian Gulf and a Los Angeles Class attack submarine in the Red Sea.

As those found their targets across Syria and Western Iraq, Reaper drones armed with Hellfire missiles and accompanied by F-22 Raptor fighter aircraft took out hundreds of tanker trucks at multiple points along the Syrian border as they prepared to smuggle oil into Turkey and Iraq.

Not since the last Gulf War had anyone in the Situation Room seen such a massive air assault.

When it was over, and all the pilots were out of Syrian airspace, they sat in silence for several minutes.

Then President Porter told his Chief of Staff to have the Press Secretary ready a statement, and then he declared the meeting over.

As the attendees gathered up their papers and filed out, Porter pointed at the CIA Director and asked him to hang back a moment.

Once they had the room to themselves, he gestured for McGee to take the chair next to him and they sat back down.

"Now," said the President, "I want to hear for real. Where are you on the leak?"

"Same list of names," McGee replied. "It hasn't changed."

"Yet."

The CIA Director nodded. "I know it feels like nothing is happening, but we've got a lot of wheels in motion. Believe me."

"I know. I just have a very bad feeling."

"About the leak?"

"About all of it," said the President. "I don't think we've seen the worst of it yet. Not by a long shot."

CHAPTER 27

The room wasn't much, but it didn't need to be. Sacha Baseyev was only passing through.

There was bottled water in the fridge, along with a few beers. Not enough, though, to get drunk and do something stupid. Probably a smart move on the owner's part. His wasn't the kind of business you wanted to draw attention to.

Dinner had been dropped off by a heavyset Mexican in a white cowboy hat. He didn't speak.

The food came from the restaurant down the street. It tasted like baby goat. Baseyev ate a few bites, then set it aside. He didn't have much of an appetite.

A doctor came by and gave him a physical. The old man reeked of tequila. He listened to his heart and lungs, took his blood pressure, and had him blow into a spirometer.

He had him walk from one end of the room to the other, do a set of deep knee bends, some push-ups. He then asked a series of questions in very bad English. Baseyev lied in response.

The doctor wrote everything down in a small blue notebook.

When he was done, the doc patted Baseyev on the shoulder and made the sign of the cross over him. He had passed.

A couple of hours later the Mexican in the cowboy hat came back and motioned for Baseyev to follow him. He had a truck outside. They climbed in.

The man drove him to an old machinist's shop. They entered from the back and only turned on a couple of lights. It was after-hours and they were the only ones there.

In the main work area, a collection of scuba equipment had been laid out on a stained table. Nearby was an old television set and an even older VCR.

The man in the cowboy hat pointed to a folding chair. Baseyev took a seat. The man turned on the TV, inserted a VHS tape into the dusty machine, and pushed Play.

The screen sputtered to life with a scuba demonstration video that looked like it had been filmed in the 1980s. Baseyev attempted to explain that he didn't need to watch the video, but the man in the hat was quite insistent. Apparently, his organization had standards.

The video ran for forty-five useless minutes. When it was complete, the man in the hat had Baseyev assemble the scuba equipment and put it all on.

He pantomimed for Baseyev to demonstrate his familiarity with the gear, that he understood how to purge his mask and clear his ears. Baseyev did as instructed.

He then removed a tailor's tape and measured him, entering the numbers into a text message on his cell phone and sending them off. And with that, they were done.

The man in the cowboy hat took Baseyev back to his room and dropped him off, all without uttering a single word.

That was fine with Baseyev. He wasn't paying for conversation. In fact, the less anyone spoke to him, the better.

The man in the hat had pointed at his watch, indicating what time he would be back, and then motioned for Baseyev to get some sleep.

Sleep sounded like a good idea. He was going to need his strength for what lay ahead.

Removing his clothes, he stretched out on the bed. He had cracked the window to get some air in the room. Now, from off in the distance, he could hear the low rumble of thunder.

There had been a chance of storms in the forecast, but he had hoped they would slow before they arrived over this part of Mexico. There had already been too much rain. If the next storm was big enough, it might shut things down altogether.

His mind raced as he lay there on the bed—something he didn't usually let it do. He could feel the walls closing in on him, the air being squeezed from his body. *Claustrophobia.*

The more he tried to get his thoughts under control, the more they raced.

Getting up, he retrieved one of the pills he had brought and snapped it in half. Just enough to help him sleep.

Opening up a bottle of water, he swallowed it and lay back down. Still the same problem.

He had never spoken of his claustrophobia. It wasn't anyone's business. Professionally, it had never been a problem.

Personally, it was another thick, white ribbon of scar tissue that he carried from that horrific day in Beslan. He knew it was all in his mind—that it was a toxic by-product of being crammed into the gymnasium, in the heat, with all of those people. Then the fire. Then the stampede. Losing his sister, Dasha. His best friend, Grigori.

It was his psyche, what little he understood of it, looking for a way out. A way to protect itself, to protect him, from the trauma.

He had learned to deal with it, like everything else. Things were what they were. He could either adapt and overcome, or wither and die. He was too angry to die. There was far too much that still needed doing. His veins needed to flow with ice water.

He had survived, while his family, friends, and teachers had died. He had a responsibility—an *obligation* to persevere.

• • •

The sedative eventually took hold and quieted his mind enough for him to fall asleep, but only fitfully.

When the knock came upon his door, he felt worse than if he hadn't gotten any sleep at all. The man in the cowboy hat brought him tamales, with a large cup of coffee, and indicated that he'd be back at the bottom of the hour.

Baseyev knew it was important to eat. Setting the coffee aside, he focused on the food.

After finishing half of the meal, he wiped down the room and the tiny attached bathroom. Whether anyone would ever know he had been here or not, he didn't like to leave a trail.

He finished his food just as the man returned. Grabbing his coffee, a bottle of water, and the few possessions he had on his person, he followed him downstairs and out to his truck.

It was dark, but Baseyev could see that the ground was soaked. In the few hours he'd been asleep, it had rained—a lot. Despite the chilly air, he began to perspire.

The drive took more than three hours. They headed north toward Laredo and the Mexican border with Texas. Their destination was a region called Llanos Esteparios Noreste.

The area was home to Lake Venustiano Carranza and the Salado and Sabinas Hidalgo Rivers, as well as the Camarón and Galameses creeks. It was also home to the only known entrance of an extensive natural cave system that burrowed beneath the Rio Grande and stretched just across the border into the United States. It was accessed via a man-made tunnel on a privately held ranch.

Driving up to a service gate, the man in the hat hopped out, removed the chain, and drove his truck through. After he locked the gate behind him, they continued on.

It took twenty minutes on a dirt road that seemed to stretch forever, before they saw what they were looking for.

The clustered ranch outbuildings were made from cinder blocks and corrugated metal. The man in the hat parked in front of the widest one, but only long enough to activate the large overhead door and drive inside.

An old Jeep CJ7 was already parked there. Baseyev's guide was in the process of unloading all of the equipment.

The greatest risk Baseyev faced, besides decompression sickness or drowning, was getting lost in the cave system. Hence the guide.

Most of the system was flooded. Because of the narrow passages they would have to navigate, they would be carrying their diving cylinders "sidemount"-style, along their hips, as opposed to on their backs. And the cylinders would be smaller than what open-water scuba divers normally used. They would have to be judicious with how much breathing gas they consumed.

That had been one of Baseyev's biggest concerns. If there had been too much rain and the "dry" portions of the cave system had filled up with water, they wouldn't have enough breathing gas to make the trip.

Once all of the gear was stacked on a flatbed cart, the man in the hat removed a set of keys and opened a door on the other side of the garage-like space.

The man-made tunnel hairpinned back and forth and was lined with bare bulbs covered with wire baskets. It was a no frills venture, the money having been spent on excavating the tunnel and navigating the cave system.

The ranch, and thereby the cave system, belonged to Los Zetas—commandos who had deserted the Mexican army to become enforcers for the Gulf Cartel. Eventually, they established their own criminal syndicate. The U.S. government considered them to be the most technologically advanced, sophisticated, and dangerous cartel operating in Mexico.

When the previous owner of the ranch had stumbled upon the caves, he figured Los Zetas would jump at the chance to use them to run drugs. But being underwater with so many tight passages made it ineffective for moving drugs. That didn't mean, though, that Los Zetas didn't have other ideas.

They were smart enough to realize that certain people would pay big money for a sure-thing entry into the United States—especially people who considered being smuggled overland by a coyote too fraught with risk. Baseyev was one of those people.

He could have used his Lufthansa alias, but he didn't want any record of his having entered the United States. Not with what he had planned. It was too risky. In order to not leave a trail, he had to do it this way. He had no choice.

At the bottom of the tunnel was a ramp that dropped into a pool of crystal-clear water and disappeared beneath the far wall of the cave. Baseyev could feel his heart rate beginning to increase.

The guide, who couldn't have been more than eighteen or nineteen years old, tossed him a dry suit and told him to get dressed. Baseyev popped one of his pills and washed it down with the rest of his water.

As he got ready, his guide unrolled a waterproof map and walked him through the route they were going to take. They confirmed hand signals and went through a host of final checklist items, including the triple-checking of their gear.

With everything ready, the guide spoke a few words to the man in the hat, turned on his primary light, and stepped forward into the water.

Baseyev followed as the man in the hat took the flatbed cart and returned back up the tunnel.

Taking several deep breaths to saturate his lungs, he put the regulator in his mouth and dropped below the surface.

The moment he did, the claustrophobia began to wrap its ice-cold arms around his chest and squeeze. He told himself to focus on what lay ahead—on the United States and what he would achieve.

As he scissored his legs through the water, his heart began to pump, his body began to warm, and the sedative moved through his bloodstream. Slowly, his panic started to recede.

As it did, his mind cleared, and he began to contemplate how to handle his guide once they were safely on the other side.

CHAPTER 28

G et out," Alexandra Ivanova said as Harvath stepped into her room. *"Now."*

He ignored the request, as well as the gun she had pointed at him. "You and I need to talk first."

"We don't have anything to talk about."

Harvath closed the door behind him. "We have lots to talk about. Starting with what you're doing here."

"What *I'm* doing here? What are *you* doing here?"

"House hunting."

"Get out," Alexandra repeated, cocking the hammer of her Czech-made CZ pistol. "Before you ruin my assignment."

"Care to tell me what it is?"

"Let me think," she said. Then, after an extremely brief pause, she replied, "No."

He had forgotten how good English could sound when spoken by a Russian woman, especially one so attractive.

Alexandra had always been a striking woman, but she was even better-looking than he remembered. She was tall, with long blond hair, and a very fit body.

"Maybe we can help each other," he said.

"I doubt that."

"C'mon, Alex."

"Do you have any idea how long it has taken me to get this close to

Malevsky?" she asked. "What I've had to put up with? The risks I have taken?"

"*Risks?* What are you talking about? Malevsky is one of yours."

Alexandra glared at him. "Are you sure you have the right Malevsky?"

"Are you?"

"Mikhail Malevsky. *Mafia* from Moscow."

"Correct," said Harvath.

"And how do you know that *you* have the right person?"

"Because I've debriefed two assets on his payroll."

"Russians?"

Harvath shook his head. "Germans. One works at Lufthansa, the other in operations at the Frankfurt airport."

"*I knew it,*" she said. "I knew he had to have people on the inside."

"Well, he does. Now will you put the gun down, please?"

Alexandra lowered her pistol. "So he's using Frankfurt airport and not Munich."

Harvath nodded. "You guys are worse than we are. Don't your agencies talk to each other?"

"What are you talking about?"

"The SVR and the GRU. Don't you communicate with each other?"

Alexandra looked worried. "What does the GRU have to do with Malevsky?"

Jesus, Harvath said to himself. *They really don't talk to each other.* "Malevsky works for them."

"Doing what?"

"I don't have the full picture. That's why I'm here."

"So paint a partial one for me," Alexandra replied.

Harvath was reluctant to give up too much, too soon. He and Alex might have had a history together, but they played for completely different teams. "The GRU has an operative we've taken interest in."

"That's it?" she asked when he didn't elaborate. Pretending to search for her weapon, she said, "Where'd I put my gun?"

Harvath knew her better than that. She knew exactly where her weapon was. "You heard about the U.S. Secretary of Defense?"

She nodded. "I did. I'm sorry."

"We think the GRU operative we're looking for had something to do with it."

Alexandra was taken aback. "You think the GRU was behind the assassination of your Secretary of Defense? That's insane."

Maybe. But Russia had plotted worse, much worse in the past—and Harvath and Alexandra had untangled it together. He shot her a look that said all that and more.

"For argument's sake," she replied, "let's say you're correct. What's your interest in Malevsky?"

"He is the middleman," said Harvath. "He's the link between the operative and the GRU."

"Which you put together via your sources at Lufthansa and the Frankfurt airport."

"In part," he replied. "Now you tell me something I don't know. What the hell are you doing here?"

Alexandra drew a deep breath and let it out, slowly. "ISIS."

Harvath waited a beat, but when she didn't continue, he said, "Keep going."

She lowered her head. *Shame? Embarrassment?* He wasn't sure, but right now he didn't care. He wanted answers.

"The largest contingent of non-Arab ISIS fighters is made up of Russian speakers. Chechnya, Dagestan . . . I could keep going, but you get the point."

Harvath certainly did get the point. Foreign jihadists, Chechens in particular, had flooded into Iraq during the war like a pustulent, festering sore that had been popped with a red-hot needle.

The Chechens had brain-dumped into the Iraqi resistance all the devious and deadly techniques they had developed fighting the Russians. It had been a huge game-changer and the American death toll had soared. People Harvath knew and cared about had been killed. He hated the fucking Chechens.

They had cycled their fighters through Iraq, they had gotten real battlefield experience, and then they had returned to Russia to kill.

"It's Iraq all over again," said Harvath. "You're worried they'll come back and cause trouble at home."

Alexandra nodded. "It would be very bad for Russia."

"Bad for Russia? Or the Russian government?"

"When innocent Russians get killed, it's bad for Russia. That's what I care about. The Russian government can kiss its own ass."

After all this time, she hadn't changed. She was still the same woman. The government had screwed her father—also an intelligence operative—and she still hadn't forgiven them. She cared about her people and her country. Her government could go to hell—or, as she had said, kiss its own ass.

Hopefully, Harvath could still trust her. "I'm waiting for you to tell me something I don't know. Why are you here? What drew you to Malevsky?"

She took a moment to compose her thoughts and then said, "He's part of their finance mechanism."

"Malevsky?"

Alexandra nodded. "He helps them get things they need. Medicine, night-vision goggles, parts for their aircraft."

"What's in it for him?"

"A bottomless well of priceless antiquities."

Harvath felt a knot form in the center of his chest. "What do you mean?"

She shook her head. "Seriously? The Moscow syndicate has been moving billions in priceless artifacts for ISIS. They move it out of Syria and Iraq up into Europe and Russia."

It was like someone had punched a hole right through the center of him. "Smugglers."

"Some of the best."

"What else do they move?" he asked.

Alexandra smiled. "Weapons—lots and lots of weapons. And not just low-end items like rifles and RPGs. They also move serious high-tech product. Ground-to-air missiles, air-to-air missiles—they are a high-speed operation."

The knot in Harvath's chest was spreading. "How did they move it?"

She reflected for a moment and said, "Most of the artifacts come through Turkey, hidden in ISIS oil tankers."

"No. The weapons. How'd they move the weapons?"

Alexandra laughed. "They were actually very clever. They allegedly had a Muslim doctor on their payroll. He was able to exploit countless medical relief missions and convoys. The Red Crescent. The United Nations. You name it."

Harvath, who had never had a weak stomach in his life, suddenly felt like he wanted throw up.

CHAPTER 29

I t was all happening way too fast. What she was asking was way too dangerous. And it was off-the-charts stupid. They needed to take a breath. Step back and take a breath. Take a minute and assess. But they didn't have a minute.

"I'm only giving you one shot," Alexandra said. "So make it count."

Harvath drew back his hand and struck her, hard. She bounced off the nightstand and the bedframe as she fell down. Her nose bled profusely.

He reached down and pulled her panties away with a *snap*. Tucking them in his pocket, he then ripped off her bra and dropped it next to her. She'd had her own idea of how she wanted her lipstick to smear, and he'd already given in. It was the least he could do.

Rubbing it off his mouth and onto his sleeve, he exited her room and headed down the back stairs. Outside, he found the bald man's corpse right where he had left it. He transferred Alexandra's panties to one of the man's pockets. After getting a SITREP that showed everything was clear, he then ran like hell.

Out of breath and near the edge of the property, he reached back to the United States. "Round Top, this is Norseman."

"Go ahead, Norseman."

"Coming out."

"Roger that, Norseman. On your command."

"Do it now."

"Roger that, Norseman," the command center replied as they scrambled the satellite signal from the ground sensors. "You are good to go."

As he scrambled up the boulders, the sharp pieces of rock slashed at him, but he kept his footing and kept moving forward.

Bursting from the trees at the top of the ridge, he took Herman by surprise. "Let's go," he ordered. "Let's *fucking* go."

"Are you okay?" Herman said. "What happened?"

Harvath collapsed in the passenger seat and managed to shut the door. "Drive," he said.

"But—"

"Just drive!" Harvath snapped.

Herman did as he was told.

•   •   •

Minding the speed limits, stopping where indicated, and not giving local law enforcement any reason to pull them over, Herman returned them to the farm.

He pulled in next to Harvath's car behind the barn and said, "You want to tell me what happened?"

"No."

That was all he said. Climbing out of the car, he shut the door with a reasonable amount of force and headed toward the farmhouse.

Herman sat there for several minutes wondering what he should do. Finally, he turned off the engine and followed him inside.

He found Harvath sitting near the fireplace, a glass in his hand with two fingers of bourbon over ice.

"Ready to talk?"

Harvath didn't respond.

The giant shook his head, walked back to the kitchen, and got himself a drink.

Returning to the living room, he took an adjacent chair and sat down. He didn't care if Harvath didn't want to talk. They could play the silent game for hours. His friend shouldn't be alone.

Harvath came to the end of his bourbon and started to rise. Herman waved for him to remain seated.

The German returned moments later with the bottle and a bucket of ice. Harvath refilled his glass. Apparently, they would not be putting a bag over Mikhail Malevsky's head tonight. And so, Herman had poured himself another drink too.

They continued until the bottle was empty. Herman tossed it into the fire. It shattered and the flames leapt.

"Music?" Herman asked, buzzed.

Harvath didn't reply. He sat and stared at the fire.

Herman found his iPhone and pulled up a random playlist. Seconds later, Don McLean's "American Pie" began.

Harvath's eyes closed and Herman was worried he had done something wrong.

"Why'd you pick this?" Harvath asked.

"I don't know," his friend said. "I like it. It's a good song."

Harvath's eyes remained closed, "Do you know what it's about?"

Herman shrugged. "The day the music died. The death of Buddy Holly."

"It was actually a warning."

"*A warning?* About what?"

"About the future and what was coming if America didn't wake up."

Herman looked at his friend. "What the hell happened tonight?"

Harvath didn't respond. He seemed content to listen to the music. Herman decided to leave him alone.

Throwing another log on the fire, Herman sat back and sipped his drink. When Harvath wanted to talk, he'd talk.

Half an hour had passed when Harvath began counting something on his fingers. "What are you doing?" Herman asked.

"Counting."

"I can see that," the German replied. "What are you counting?"

"How many people I got killed."

"Over your career, or just recently?"

"Just recently," Harvath answered. It was deadpan, without any emotion.

"What's the number?"

"Thirteen," he said. "And still going up."

"*And still going up,*" Herman repeated. "Does that mean you're still in the fight?"

Harvath nodded.

His friend leaned forward. "What the hell happened tonight?"

For a moment, Harvath looked like he had no idea how to answer the question. His mind was somewhere else, drifting. "I got played," he finally explained.

"*Played?* What are you talking about?"

"I blew the number one rule in the intelligence game—don't get played."

Herman looked at him. "I still don't know what you're talking about."

"I had what I thought was an incredible asset," Harvath replied shaking his head. "A doctor from North Africa. He was moonlighting as a smuggler. His name was Salah Abaaoud. He produced some incredible intel for us. Turns out, he worked for Malevsky."

"And thereby," said Herman, "the GRU."

Harvath nodded. "The CIA team we staged in Anbar to nail a high-value ISIS target? That was based on intel developed through Salah."

"Why would the Russians want a CIA team wiped out?"

"It's not just the CIA team. Salah is dead. His mistress is dead. The Secretary of Defense and his entire protective detail are dead."

Herman still couldn't figure it out. "But why?"

Harvath shook his head. "I don't know. All I know is that it's my fault."

"Why is it your fault?"

"Because I didn't see it. I'm trained to see it and I didn't."

Herman offered to refill his glass and Harvath brushed him away.

"The Russians can be clever," Herman offered. "Very clever. Don't let them get in your head."

"Get in my head? The Russians are on a fucking killing streak and it's my fault. How do you not let that get in your head?" said Harvath.

Herman threw up his hands and leaned back in his chair. "Take your time. Be angry. When you're ready to get even, let me know."

Harvath stared into the fireplace and watched the hot, blue flames lick at the thick, dry logs. Orange embers smoldered in the gray ash beneath.

He drank his bourbon and thought of the men and women who had died. And as he thought about them, his anger grew.

He hated the Chechens, but he hated the Russians even more. No matter how many times they had pounded them into the ground, they kept popping back up. They were as serious a threat as the jihadists.

But now, they appeared to be using the jihadists—using them as a proxy to do their extremely dirty work for them.

Drinking his last swallow of bourbon, Harvath felt it burn as it rolled down his throat. He then turned to Herman and said, "I can see only one way to handle this."

"I'm listening," the German said.

"There's just a problem, though."

"What's that?"

"Your wife won't like it," Harvath replied. "We're going to do something illegal again. Very illegal."

CHAPTER 30

L illiana Grace was an attractive woman in her late thirties. Chestnut hair, perfect teeth, and just the right amount of makeup. She had made it her business by being twice as smart and twice as hungry as any of the other reporters at the *Washington Post*.

She didn't like sneaking around, but from time to time, it was a necessary part of the job. Senator Wells had chosen the location. A seedy bar in southeast D.C.

"You're positive?" Wells asked. "One hundred percent?" As he talked, he jabbed the tiny squares of ice in his cocktail with a bright green plastic straw.

They were seated in a small, stained booth with duct tape over the rips in the seats. The table between them was covered with cigarette burns. The lights were low and the place smelled like spilled beer and urinal disinfectant.

"You take a lot of meetings here, Senator?" Grace asked, waving her own straw around the dimly lit bar.

"Only the important ones. Now, keep your voice down and answer my question."

"I told you. I came up with nobody."

"Not one single person?"

"That's usually the definition of *nobody*," she replied as she took a sip of her gin and tonic.

"Fuck."

"It doesn't mean the information you were given isn't true. It just means none of my contacts know anything."

Wells had not survived in D.C. as long as he had without being very careful. He wanted to believe Rebecca was right—that what she had picked up at her CIA boyfriend's apartment was right—but it was so damn risky.

If the President and the CIA had known about the threat to Secretary of Defense Devon in Turkey and had done nothing about it, it was a huge story. He couldn't break it, though, hell—he couldn't even hint at it, unless he was sure it was true.

Grace was the chief intelligence correspondent for the *Washington Post.* Before that she had been assigned to the Pentagon. She had the best damn sources in town. If she couldn't substantiate Rebecca's claim, it wasn't worth taking public.

"I believe you have something for me?" she asked as Wells fell silent and played with his ice.

"Excuse me?"

"We had a deal. I look into your rumor and in exchange you give me the background on what happened in Anbar."

"Right," said Wells, refocusing on their conversation. "Anbar."

Grace removed a pen and notepad. She knew there was no way the Senator was going to let her record this.

"It was a CIA operation. They were hunting high-level ISIS members," Wells began. "A lot of mistakes were made."

• • •

The conversation didn't last terribly long. Senator Wells still didn't have much information.

The only new piece of information he had was on Ashleigh Foster, the CIA officer from the U.S. Embassy in Jordan. McGee had sent over a memo explaining that Foster had been dating one of the men on the CIA SAD team. She had convinced the other two women from the Embassy to travel with her to Anbar. From start to finish, it had been an exercise in extremely poor judgment.

"That's it?" Grace exclaimed, once Wells fell silent and went back to stirring his ice.

The Senator nodded.

"How about the names of the specific ISIS members the CIA was looking for? It sounds like they dispatched a pretty high-level team. They also sent two very covert helicopters. They must have had some idea of who they were going after."

"No clue," said Wells, who raised his empty glass and signaled the bartender to bring him another. "The CIA Director wouldn't tell me."

"You mean he wouldn't tell the committee."

"No, I mean *me*. Personally. My committee was never briefed, nor was the House committee."

Grace leaned forward. "Excuse me?"

"Director McGee only came to me after the attack in Anbar."

"That doesn't make any sense. Even if the President decides covert action is necessary, he has to issue a signed, *presidential finding* authorizing it. And that finding has to be presented to both committees ASAP, before any activity begins."

"It didn't happen."

Grace thought for a moment. "If memory serves, the President can delay reporting, but only in extraordinary circumstances. He can also limit who the report goes to. At a bare minimum it would have to go to the House and Senate leaders of each party, as well as the chair and ranking member of each intel committee. Were they briefed?"

Wells nodded. "But only vaguely, and not until after, with no explanation for the delay."

"Interesting," the reporter replied as the bartender set down the Senator's drink. "No, I'm good. Thank you," she said when he gestured at her glass.

She was hard for Wells to read. There was blood in the water. She should have been able to smell it. She was a media shark.

"So?" the Senator asked.

"Like I said, it's interesting."

"Interesting enough to do an article?"

Grace set her pen down. "You're running for president."

"I have made no such determination."

She smiled at him. "A story like this could be damaging to your opponent."

"It could also generate some excellent revenue for your organization and be good for your career," Wells countered.

"Maybe."

Maybe? What the hell was she talking about? He was offering her a scoop. He hated how inscrutable she was. He didn't like when he couldn't read people. "Perhaps I made a mistake coming to you," he said.

"You made a mistake, but it wasn't in coming to me," she replied. "Your mistake was in thinking I'd take what you told me and run with it."

He leaned forward and smiled. "Have I ever steered you wrong in the past?"

No, he hadn't. But this was different. He was gearing up for a possible run at the presidency. Anything he offered that was damaging to the current administration had to be viewed through that lens.

She shook her head. "You've always provided me with solid information."

"And I am doing so again."

"What is it, specifically, that you think the White House is up to? Why are they playing coy with Congress?"

"Off the record?" the Senator asked.

"Off the record," she agreed.

Wells leaned in even further. "I think President Porter, in conjunction with the CIA Director, is running his own extremely black ops program and intentionally keeping it from Congress."

Picking up her pen, the reporter signaled the bartender that she was going to need another drink after all. It was going to be a long night.

CHAPTER 31

T he bald man Harvath had killed at the estate was a guest of Malevsky's named Valery Kumarin.

He was a drunk and a womanizer. He was also a very influential figure in organized crime. He and Malevsky were in the same syndicate but different branches, which were often at odds, particularly when it came to territories.

Kumarin had flown in from Moscow to discuss taking some of the ISIS business. The fact that he had died while visiting Malevsky was going to cause problems. Big ones.

Worried about a hit, Malevsky might very well go to ground. If he did, he wouldn't be taking his wife and children with him. He'd find someplace else for them.

That someplace else would include Alexandra. If there was any way to prevent it, she had to try.

When Harvath had explained what had happened outside, she was ready to kill him. In a matter of hours, he had ruined more than two years of work by the SVR. She had to come up with a plan, quickly.

With Kumarin dead, there was only so much she could do. The key was in helping reinforce the narrative that it was an accident.

All of Malevsky's men had seen Kumarin eyeballing Alexandra. Even Malevsky's wife had noticed. The Russian mobster wasn't exactly subtle. Alexandra decided to use that to her advantage.

He was drunk. He forced his way into her room. He struck her in the face and tried to have his way with her. She fought back, kneeing him in the groin to get him off of her. Groaning, he had retreated from her room.

That was the story she told after Malevsky's men had beaten down her door and found her curled up sobbing on the floor of her bathroom.

While everyone agreed the situation wasn't good, it was beyond obvious what had happened. Kumarin was a pig. Trying to force himself on Alexandra was beyond the pale. He had taken the easy way out by falling down the stairs outside and breaking his neck. If he hadn't, Malevsky would have killed him with his bare hands.

That left them with one final item to deal with—the body. If they called the police, they would be inviting all sorts of problems. If they didn't, they'd be inviting an entirely different set of problems. Malevsky was damned regardless. The only way out was to shift the responsibility to someone above him.

Back in Moscow, the powers that be were not happy. He had taken all the appropriate precautions with making contact, but this was a dead body, on his property, in another country. They might have been criminals, but they hadn't gotten to where they were by being stupid. Malevsky was putting them in a very difficult position.

His superiors turned it right back around on him. *What if*, they suggested, *it wasn't an accident and someone is trying to frame you?* That didn't do much to ease Malevsky's anxiety. If he hid the body, he could be in trouble. If he didn't hide the body and he went to the authorities, he might still end up being in trouble, especially if someone was trying to frame him.

They told him to stay by the phone. They would call him back. Malevsky looked for some vodka but couldn't find any. They were out. *Fucking Kumarin.*

Finally, the phone rang. A decision had been made. Get rid of the body. And as soon as that was done, they wanted Malevsky to return to Moscow so they could question him in person. That could mean several different things—many of them not good. Not good at all. *Fucking Kumarin.*

Malevsky saw to the disposal of the body, then he packed a bag. Ever since he had hung up the phone, he had been thinking about running. He had enough money hidden in different banks in different countries. He could live quite well.

But if he ran, it would be an admission of guilt. He wasn't guilty. He hadn't done anything. If he were going to kill Kumarin, he certainly wouldn't have been stupid enough to do it on his own property. He also wouldn't have been stupid enough not to have an airtight alibi.

He would go to Moscow, state his case, and return home. He wasn't going to run.

He had half a mind to take the nanny with him, to let her explain what had happened, but he decided against it. It would make him appear weak. His word should be enough.

If they required any more corroboration than that, two of his security team would be with him. He'd bring one of the men who had found the nanny on the bathroom floor and one of the men who had found Kumarin at the bottom of the stairs. It had been an unfortunate accident, but it was an accident nonetheless.

If anything, fucking Kumarin had brought it upon himself by getting so blind drunk. There wasn't a one of them back in Moscow that didn't know how bad his drinking was. Malevsky doubted this was the first time the old fool had fallen. In fact, he'd probably tripped and fallen too many times to count.

If they were honest with themselves, many of them back in Moscow would have to admit that it was a wonder Kumarin had survived this long. The problem with Moscow was that they were rarely honest with themselves.

• • •

Exiting the house, travel bag in hand, Mikhail Malevsky found his men in the motor court milling around the Rolls-Royce. "Let's go!" he barked in Russian.

The five-foot-seven barrel-chested mafioso had been a wrestler in his youth. Now, in his mid-forties, his thinning blond hair was going gray, he was plagued with psoriasis, and he had to pop tons of Viagra just to get an erection.

Those factors, combined with his already distasteful personality, made him perpetually angry, abusive, and predisposed to acts of extreme violence. Even the four-letter-word descriptions used by his enemies didn't come close to doing him justice.

Adding to his foul mood was the fact that it had taken forever to arrange a jet to fly him back to Russia. He hated flying commercial, but he hadn't been able to justify the cost of owning his own plane. So, he had split the difference and bought into a private jet program.

As was typical of criminal syndicates, he knew a guy who knew a guy—and that was whose advice he took.

The company Malevsky had bought into was fine for trips planned weeks in advance. But if you needed to fly right away, they were a disaster. He nearly had an aneurysm yelling into the phone at the client "service" representative trying to find him a plane.

Eventually, the company found him a Gulfstream G650. And they not only agreed to waive the upgrade fee for such an exclusive aircraft but also to have it pick him up in Salzburg, rather than his having to drive the further distance to Munich.

Respect, Malevsky had thought as he had hung up the phone. *Some people expect it, others demand it.*

He was going to look like a rock star traveling in that aircraft. Not only to the men who were traveling with him but also to anyone meeting him at the airport in Moscow. And he was going to make sure there were people waiting to meet him in Moscow. Only a fool would blow an opportunity to make that kind of an entrance.

Rolling out of the wrought iron gates of the estate, they made a right turn and headed down into the village.

Privately, Malevsky had been pleased that the old hunting lodge hadn't sold yet. His wife and two children enjoyed it here. It was a simpler pace. Cleaner and less hectic than Munich.

There were also no Muslims. He didn't mind doing business with them in their part of the world, but he certainly didn't want to raise his family around them. They were animals—unclean, uncivilized. At least in Russia, they knew how to deal with them. Russia recognized all too well the threat that they posed.

Malevsky sank back into the quilted leather seat and tried not to think about Muslims, Kumarin, or having to deal with his superiors back in

Moscow. He was in one of the most beautiful places in the world, being driven in a Rolls-Royce, on his way to board a sixty-five-million-dollar aircraft. He had come a long way in life and he still had much further to go.

If he had time, there was a girl he wanted to see in Moscow—a dancer. She was the complete opposite of his wife. She didn't complain. She liked to have fun. And she had a tight ass. *Oh, that ass.* He would have to make the time to see her.

Malevsky closed his eyes for a moment in order to picture her. As he did, he felt the car slow.

"*Chyort voz'mi,*" the driver said. *Damn it.*

"What is it?"

"*Politsiya.*" *Police.*

They were being pulled over.

The words *Chyort voz'mi* passed through Malevsky's mind. But what came out of his mouth was something completely different.

"Fucking Kumarin," he said, as he reached for his diplomatic passport.

CHAPTER 32

There were two parts of Harvath's plan that he regretted. If he had been able to find a better way, he would have taken it. But time was against him.

Alexandra's texts had been sporadic. Everyone at the estate appeared to believe her story. Kumarin had been drinking and had tried to rape her. They had found his body outside, at the bottom of the stone steps.

Whether he had hit his head or had broken his neck, it didn't matter. He was dead. They had decided not to call the police, and had gotten rid of the body themselves. Malevsky's bosses had called him back to Russia for a full accounting of what had happened.

There was concern over an internecine conflict in the organization. Malevsky was not well liked. Kumarin's people were likely going to want revenge. The crime family was trying to stop things before they could get started.

Had it been anyone other than Alexandra on the inside, Harvath wouldn't be getting this kind of intel. Even though her assignment was potentially in turmoil, she kept gathering information and feeding it out to him.

What he had told her about Malevsky, the GRU, and the operative named Sacha Baseyev was very serious. Too often, Russia's military ambitions extended far beyond what was best for the rest of the country.

Alexandra was willing to help Harvath, but only to a point. It needed to be a two-way street. As long as he continued to cooperate, so would she.

With Alexandra having committed to the story of Kumarin attacking her, Harvath couldn't return to the estate and snatch Malevsky. They would immediately suspect she had played a hand in both situations. It was too dangerous.

Herman hadn't seen another option. Harvath, though, had.

He didn't have a problem with lightning hitting the same bad guy twice, just not in the same place. They would have to get to Malevsky outside his estate.

Alexandra had confirmed that Malevsky's security detail were former Russian Special Forces. Harvath had been right not to underestimate them. These were not guys he wanted to go head-to-head with unless he absolutely had to. It would be better to outmaneuver than to outgun them. Which brought Harvath to the two most regrettable parts of his plan.

The first involved Anna Strobl. If she had said no, he would have understood. He knew, though, that there was a part of her that wanted to right the wrongs her husband had committed—even if that meant putting herself in further jeopardy. Within twenty minutes of receiving Harvath's call, she was on the road.

The next element was the wild card. It was the riskiest step in his plan and the one he disliked most. Unlike Anna, the participants in this phase weren't being given a choice.

They found a Bavarian State Police vehicle twenty minutes outside Berchtesgaden. Two young officers were clearing a dead deer from the road.

Harvath took their duty belts and radios at gunpoint. Then he marched them into the forest and had them handcuff themselves around a large tree.

He left them with a couple bottles of water and returned to the road. Herman had already departed with their vehicle.

Removing his balaclava, Harvath hopped in his car, dropped a pin in the GPS app on his phone, and followed. He wanted to make sure they sent the authorities to the right location.

• • •

Back at the barn, Anna inspected the vehicle. "I probably shouldn't ask where this came from."

"Probably a good idea," Harvath replied.

"I'd also keep your gloves on," said Herman.

"You're aware that the Landespolizei use a tracking system for all of their patrol cars, correct?"

Harvath held up a pair of wire cutters. "Not this patrol car."

"Where's Eichel?"

"In my trunk," Herman replied. "We don't go anywhere without him."

"Is he still alive?" Anna said. "Or is that also something I shouldn't ask?"

"He's still alive," Harvath stated.

"What are you going to do with him?"

"That depends on what happens with Malevsky."

"So, in other words, you don't have a plan at this point."

Harvath smiled, then nodded at Anna and Herman. "Everything is going to depend on you two."

Taking over, Herman led them through the next steps.

Harvath felt his phone vibrate and removed it from his pocket. It was a text from Alexandra.

He read it and then said, "Malevsky is getting ready to move. Let's get going."

Anna got behind the wheel of the State Police car. She was wearing her Bundespolizei uniform, but the name tape had been removed. Herman climbed into the passenger seat next to her. Harvath exited the barn and slid inside Herman's BMW.

There was really only one route to the Salzburg airport. And while Malevsky's team might conduct a surveillance detection route to make sure they weren't being followed, Harvath wasn't afraid of losing them. He was more concerned with where they were going to spring their trap.

They had to do it before the border with Austria, and Harvath wanted it in an area with no witnesses. And on top of those two parameters, the State Police would soon be out looking for their two missing officers and their patrol vehicle. The sooner they could get this over with, the better.

They picked up Malevsky's Rolls-Royce halfway through Berchtesgaden and followed it out of the village. There was a stretch of farmland that the road passed through before it came to the next village. That was where they were going to take them.

Harvath had hung back so as not to arouse suspicion. He was also acting as a screen, blocking any potential view of the police vehicle.

A few kilometers out from the takedown location, Harvath slowed and Anna passed him. She was now in the lead.

She trailed the Rolls-Royce for a bit before beginning to close the distance. Then, once she was ready, she activated the light bar on the roof of her vehicle and pulled them over.

Harvath had hung way back and now pulled over to the side of the road as well. He could see the flashing lights ahead, but that was it.

They had decided that it wasn't worth running the risk that one of the men with Malevsky might have been on duty when Harvath toured the estate. If he was recognized, that would ruin everything. They wanted this to go as smoothly as possible.

Herman had promised to keep his microphone open. Harvath would have to be content to listen in as everything went down.

Harvath knew enough cops to know that in police work, there was never such a thing as a "routine" traffic stop. And what they were doing right now was highly dangerous.

The unknown was whether or not Malevsky's men were armed. His diplomatic passport all but guaranteed that the transition across the border would be a non-event.

They had to assume there were guns in the car. Not only that, they had to assume the guns would be close at hand and Malevsky's men would be ready to use them if they had to.

But Malevsky's men were professionals. They were smart enough to know that the officer would call in their license plate before getting out of the patrol vehicle. They were also headed toward Salzburg and the border. If they got in a shootout and killed a police officer, they were going to have a hell of a time getting across.

They would play it cool—at least, until it was time not to play it cool. Harvath was sure about that. They would figure out why the cop had pulled them over and then make their decision on what to do.

"We're making our approach," said Herman over the radio.

The plan was for Anna to move up along the driver's side and for Herman to move up on the passenger's side.

Harvath could hear wind and the rustling of clothing over his earpiece as Herman moved forward. Moments later, Anna identified herself as Bundespolizei. Herman, who was in plainclothes was identified as a member of "Kripo," short for Kriminalpolizei, the detective branch of the Landespolizei.

There were plenty of joint task force operations in Germany. It would also explain, if necessary, why a uniformed federal police officer was in a State Police vehicle.

The Rolls-Royce's driver asked why they had been pulled over. Anna replied by requesting everyone's documents. Malevsky immediately produced his diplomatic passport and started trying to take control of the situation.

There was something else Harvath knew from having friends who were cops. The first test in any encounter with law enforcement was the attitude test. If you failed that test, things only got worse for you.

As Anna collected their documents, she continued to question the driver. Where were they coming from? Where were they going? How long had they been in Germany? What was their business? Who owned the vehicle? What were they transporting?

Malevsky grew impatient and began to tell Anna off. She was solid as a rock, though. With her game face on, she locked eyes with him and told him to get out of the car.

When he refused to, she pulled open his door, put her right hand on her pistol, and asked him again.

One of Malevsky's men made a move Herman didn't like. Sweeping his coat back, he drew his own weapon halfway out of its holster. "Everyone," he said, "get your hands where I can see them. Do it now."

"Out of the car," Anna repeated to Malevsky.

"Do you know who I am?" he demanded. "Who my family is?"

Anna drew her weapon. *"Now,"* she commanded. Her authoritative tone left no doubt as to who was in charge.

"I will own you after this. Do you understand me, girl?" he said as he complied and exited the vehicle.

"Place your hands on the rear of the vehicle and spread your legs."

"This is an outrage. I am a diplomat. You have no right to do this."

"According to the laws of Germany, I have every right to do this. Now place your hands on the rear of the vehicle and spread your legs."

Malevsky began speaking rapid-fire Russian into the car. One of the men inside lowered his hands.

Herman pulled his weapon fully from the holster and pointed it into the Rolls-Royce. "I shoot the next person who moves. Are we clear?"

Everyone in the vehicle froze.

Harvath's voice crackled over Herman's earpiece. "There's a car coming. You need to wrap this up."

Herman looked at Anna and said, "I think we should continue this discussion at headquarters."

"Headquarters?" Malevsky protested. "I have a flight to catch."

"You can catch the next one," Anna replied as she snapped a set of handcuffs on him. "Your men are free to follow us in their vehicle. We'll settle all of this there."

Malevsky was pissed off, yelling to his men in Russian as Anna led him back to the police car.

Herman waited until she had gotten him in the backseat, then he backed toward her, his eyes glued on the men inside the Rolls.

Getting into the seat next to her, he shut his door and looked behind them. Harvath was already gone. "Make a U-turn and start heading back."

"Are you sure?" she asked.

Herman nodded. "They'll never make it."

CHAPTER 33

Three kilometers later, the Rolls-Royce pulled off to the side of the road. Its two rear tires were flat.

During the traffic stop, Herman and Anna had each shoved a specially milled screw into the tire on their side. The screws had a hollow shaft and a hole in the head to let the air out.

Once the Rolls-Royce had fallen behind, they pulled off on a side road, put a hood over Malevsky's head, better secured him with duct tape, and placed him in the trunk.

When they got back to the barn, Harvath was ready for them. Eichel sat naked, bound to the chair he had been bound to previously, surrounded by the plastic sheeting. The only windows in the barn had been covered over with black garbage bags.

Eichel was illuminated by four pairs of 1,000-watt, tripod-mounted work lights. Despite their blinding-white light, they did little to warm the drafty old structure. Equal measures of fear, exhaustion, and cold were causing Eichel to tremble. That was what Harvath wanted.

Anna had driven the police vehicle back inside the barn so that it couldn't be seen from outside or overhead. She wanted to stay, but it was going to get ugly.

Malevsky would be harder to break than Eichel. It wasn't the kind of thing Anna needed to see.

Her assistance in the traffic stop had been invaluable. She had done a perfect job. Right now, though, the best thing she could do was to return to Frankfurt. Harvath would take things from here.

They said their goodbyes inside the barn. Walking her out to her car would only have been asking for trouble.

He liked her—and that bothered him. It bothered him because she was married. And not only was she married, but her husband was critically ill. It wasn't right.

It also bothered him because he felt disloyal to Lara. Their situation was in flux, but it wasn't necessarily over.

He shook his head at that thought—*not necessarily over*. What else could it be? She had chosen her career and he had chosen his. It meant two different cities—Boston and D.C.

Could it work? Anything was possible. *Would it work?* That was the real question.

If your career was the central force in your life, the thing that defined you, how much time were you going to allocate to a long-distance relationship, regardless of how much you loved that other person?

Supposedly, love conquered all, but would it counter countless security checkpoints, delayed flights, and all that time spent in travel?

Being in a relationship that was geographically undesirable didn't seem to make much sense. It would be one thing if it were temporary—a holding pattern while the parties figured out how to end up in the same city.

But Harvath and Lara had already been through that. In fact, they had been transitioning out of it. Now they had been dragged back into it.

There was a lot to be said for having the person you loved close. Being able to walk into the kitchen and just see their face. Spending a Sunday morning doing nothing but reading the paper together. A Saturday night watching an old movie in front of the fire.

People needed what they needed. And they usually needed it when they needed it. Getting together every other weekend—if they were lucky—plus vacations, wasn't a relationship. At least, it wasn't the kind he was looking for.

Harvath loved Lara. He didn't, though, love the idea of loving her from a distance. As a couple, they were moving backward.

"She has good instincts," said Herman.

Harvath had been standing at the barn door, watching Anna leave. His friend's voice brought his attention back.

"With the right training, she'd probably make a halfway decent operative," Herman continued. "She's being wasted at the Bundespolizei."

There was a lot of promise in Anna Strobl, *on multiple levels*, but Harvath didn't want to think about that. Not right now. He needed to focus on Malevsky.

Drawing Herman out of earshot of their captives, he explained how he intended things to go.

Once everything was set, they pulled Malevsky from the trunk of the police car.

Harvath nodded and Herman pulled the hood from the Russian mobster's head. Malevsky blinked several times trying to get his eyes adjusted.

He looked from side to side. He saw the other prisoner, naked and restrained to a chair. He was shivering and had a hood over his head. Malevsky was nonplussed and stared daggers at his captors.

Harvath walked over and tore the duct tape off his mouth in one quick rip. As soon as he did, Malevsky started cursing him in Russian. Harvath waited for him to finish.

But Malevsky didn't finish. He was only just getting started. Harvath spoke some Russian but not as much as he would have liked. He could pick up a few foul words here and there. The rest he just guessed at via the mobster's tone.

When he couldn't get a rise out of Harvath in Russian, he switched to German. Here, Harvath was a little stronger linguistically but not by much. Herman, though, found the man's threats amusing and chuckled at some of the more creative ones.

Harvath drew back his fist and punched Malevsky in the mouth as hard as he could.

There was a spray of blood and the force from the blow knocked the Russian over backward in his chair. His head cracked against the floor.

Harvath let him lie there while he found a towel and wiped off his hand. He was setting the tone. He wanted Malevsky to know that he could keep this up as long as he wanted. He was in no hurry.

The man grunted something that he couldn't make out. "English, please," said Harvath.

"Fuck your mother."

Harvath smiled. It would be a real battle of wills with this guy. He was a street thug. All he understood was brute force. He would talk, it just came down to how much suffering he was willing to endure before he did.

"You are a dead man," Malevsky added. *"Dead."*

He drew the word out as if that would make it more frightening. He had no idea who he was talking to. That was about to change.

Harvath perused a line of tools he had sitting on a long table. He stopped at the ball peen hammer Herman had purchased and picked it up. It had a bright yellow handle and a black rubber grip. He tested its weight. "Left or right knee?" he asked.

"Fuck your mother!" Malevsky spat.

Harvath turned the hammer sideways and ran it along the outside of the Russian's left leg. When he found his knee, he bounced the hammer against it a couple of times.

Malevsky wound up to issue another *Fuck your mother,* but Harvath was faster.

With lightning speed, he swung the hammer and shattered the man's knee.

The Russian screamed at the top of his lungs. Tears flooded from his eyes and down his face.

Harvath returned the hammer to the table and said, "Tell me about Sacha Baseyev."

Malevsky let loose with another string of curses in Russian.

Harvath indicated for Herman to tip the mobster back upright in his chair. When he was sitting up, Harvath repeated the question.

"You are a dead man," Malevsky replied. "Dead man."

"Have you ever been to Iraq, Mr. Malevsky?" said Harvath, looking over his tools.

"Fuck you!"

Harvath paused. Then he smiled and went back to selecting his next tool. "Many years ago, a Russian diplomat was kidnapped. The Iraqi government tried for a week, but couldn't locate him. The Russian embassy brought in a team of 'specialists.' Men, I would imagine, like you.

"They quickly figured out who one of the kidnappers was and went to his house. Of course, the kidnapper wasn't there, but his family was.

They grabbed one of the men. It was his brother, I believe. And then they drove off.

"An hour later, the Iraqi family heard a knock on the door. When they opened it, there was a small box sitting there. Inside, they found the brother's ear.

"One piece of the brother—his nose, a finger, his lips, the other ear, was delivered every hour until the Russian diplomat was released.

"The Russians had been able to do in one day what the Iraqis couldn't do in an entire week."

Harvath stopped at a straight razor and picked it up from the table. "How many of your body parts would it take for your family to cooperate?"

A flash of panic rippled across Malevsky's face. It had only been there for a fraction of a second before he got it under control and masked it. But the micro-expression—*the tell*—had manifested itself nevertheless.

That gave Harvath an idea.

CHAPTER 34

Harvath had been against using Malevsky's kids if at all possible. It wasn't their fault they had a shitbag for a father. They were innocents, and as much as Harvath bent and often broke the rules, there were still some lines he was against crossing.

If there was any way to leave the Malevsky children out of this, he wanted to. But there wasn't. In fact, it was Malevsky himself who had opened the door to their inclusion.

The man was like a block of Russian granite. Harvath could chip off piece after piece, but it was going to take a long time for him to break.

There was also the risk that Malevsky might go into shock, or even die. Things happened. Kumarin was a perfect example. Murphy, of Murphy's law, had a funny way of popping up when you least expected him.

Malevsky was in a trap he had built for himself. The pain and agony it would cause him was only just beginning.

Harvath didn't have any reservations about chipping away at him all day long, if that's what it took. The man had information he needed. Malevsky had been facilitating an assassin who had taken American lives.

Harvath wanted that assassin, and Malevsky was going to tell him everything he knew. By using his children, Harvath hoped to get to the endpoint a lot faster.

"You have two lovely daughters, Mr. Malevsky. They looked to me to be about five and seven years old," said Harvath. "Am I close?"

The tell once again flashed across the Russian's face. "If you touch my family," he hissed, "I will kill you. Do you understand me? I will kill you, motherfucker."

Harvath ignored his threat. "Who is Sacha Baseyev?"

"I'm going to watch you die. Then I'm going to find the people you care about and I am going to watch them die."

Harvath backhanded him, hard, and repeated, "Sacha Baseyev. Who is he?"

Malevsky spat a gob of blood on the ground. "I have no idea who you are talking about."

Harvath gestured to Herman, who walked over and removed the hood from Eichel.

"So what?" said the Russian, unfazed.

Harvath cracked him again, even harder. "Eichel told us everything. Now it's your turn."

Malevsky looked up at Harvath, blood running from his nose and mouth, staining the front of his shirt, and smiled through gritted teeth.

Harvath drew back his hand to strike him again, but stopped. Instead, he stepped away, cleaned his hands with the towel, and removed his phone.

"Do your children have any pets, Mr. Malevsky?" he asked.

The Russian refused to answer. Harvath sent a quick text message and then leaned back against the table as he waited for a response.

When his phone chimed, he looked down and read the message out loud. "Your older daughter is allergic to cats. But they have two goldfish."

The smug smile on Malevsky's face barely wavered. "With enough money, you can find out anything. Cats, fish. I could even tell you what color underwear your wife is wearing."

Harvath smiled back at him and sent another text.

Minutes passed. Finally, his phone chimed once more. Harvath read the text and opened the attachment.

Turning the phone around, he showed it to Malevsky. It was a photo of his two daughters. They were holding up pictures they had drawn. One was of a yellow hammer. The other was of a barn. The smile immediately disappeared from the Russian's face.

"Satisfied?" asked Harvath. "Or would you like to know what color underwear your wife is wearing right now?"

"*You*. You're the American who toured my house. What have you done with my family?"

"All that matters is what I am *going* to do. Anything that happens to them will be *because* of you. If you cooperate, we'll let them go."

"Who is *we*? America?"

Harvath cupped his hand and struck Malevsky in the left ear. It made a loud *pop* and the mobster cried out in pain.

"I ask the questions, not you. You give answers. Anything else and I will instruct my colleagues to go to work on your family. Is that clear?"

Malevsky nodded.

"I can't hear you."

"Yes," the Russian relented. "Clear."

"Good," said Harvath. "Now, who is Sacha Baseyev?"

CHAPTER 35

N ext to the attack during his childhood, swimming through the cave system had been one of the most terrifying things Sacha Baseyev had ever experienced. He never wanted to do anything like it again.

Flooding from the rainwater had been a serious problem. Multiple areas that should have contained pockets of breathable air had been completely submerged.

In one area, where they had been able to surface, his guide had discussed turning back. The young man was afraid that they wouldn't make it.

Quietly, Baseyev made plans to kill him and take his diving cylinders. There were guidelines and line markers to point the way. He could have made it without him. *Unless something went wrong.*

The doubt gnawed at him and so he pushed the young man to see the journey through. The young Mexican was extremely reluctant, but he must have seen something about Baseyev. He must have seen that his own life hung by a very tenuous thread at that moment. Wisely, he chose to press on.

When they emerged on the U.S. side of the border, a smuggler was waiting for them. He had protein bars, bottles of water, and a fresh change of clothes for Baseyev.

Even though he had been wearing a dry suit, he was drenched, having sweated through what he had on beneath.

He washed himself in the cold cave water, put on the new clothes, and followed the smuggler out to his battered Ford F-150 pickup.

Everything he owned at that moment was in a small, sealable bag he had carried inside the suit. He had cash, credit cards, false identification, and a smartphone with spare SIM cards.

The smuggler drove Baseyev into the nearest town, Laredo, Texas, and dropped him at the bus station on Salinas Avenue. From there, Baseyev was on his own.

With plenty of stores within walking distance, he was able to purchase everything he needed. Once his shopping was complete, he hailed a cab and headed out to the airport. A Cessna Citation M2 business jet was waiting for him when he arrived.

After shaking hands with the captain, he climbed aboard and stowed his bag.

The interior was tight, but the caramel-colored leather seats were wide enough and could be folded flat. All he cared about was sleep. As soon as the jet lifted off, he closed his eyes. Within minutes, he was asleep.

When he awoke, the jet was on final approach to Manassas Regional Airport in Virginia. He had slept the entire trip.

He cleaned himself up in the restroom of the FBO and then had a cup of coffee while he waited for his Uber vehicle to arrive.

The explosion of apps like Uber and Airbnb had been a godsend in his line of work. No matter what hat he wore—assassin, terrorist, spy—he didn't need a complicated support network of safe houses, cars, and dead drops. And many of the things he did need, especially in America, were only a click away.

The credit cards and bank accounts he used wound through false holding companies and addresses around the globe that were empty, or simply didn't exist. Trying to track him based on his financial activity was useless. The GRU had created a maze of blind alleys and dead ends.

And considering what Baseyev was about to undertake, they fully expected the Americans to pick every single transaction apart. But by then, it would be too late. The damage would already be done.

• • •

The distance from the Manassas airport to downtown Washington, D.C., was only thirty miles, but it took almost two hours in traffic.

Baseyev had the Uber driver drop him at the Marriott Marquis on Massachusetts Avenue. It was adjacent to the convention center where he said he was attending a conference for human resource managers.

In the lobby, he found a bellman and checked his bag in their temporary luggage storage. He then exited the hotel through another entrance.

Somehow, he had thought Washington, D.C.—the seat of American power—would feel different. He had expected to be awed. He wasn't.

Turning right, he walked down New York Avenue. One thing he was struck by was how many cameras there were. Cameras were excellent for solving crimes, not necessarily for preventing them.

With that said, software had gotten to the point where computers could tell if a bag had been left unattended, or could be directed to find things like a "man on a yellow bicycle." Computers were not going to stop what he had planned.

At 15th Street, New York Avenue ended and Baseyev stepped onto Pennsylvania Avenue. Instantly, he could feel an electricity course through his body.

The defenses, the countermeasures, the things most normal people would never notice, were all around him now. The lengths to which the Americans had gone was ridiculous. *All this to protect one man. One building.*

But that man and that building were both symbolic—facts not lost upon Baseyev.

When he had drawn even with it he had to stop and look. The awe was there now. The White House and all it represented was staring right back at him through its wrought iron fence. It was dramatic.

A tourist standing nearby asked him to take her family's photo. He declined, politely, and began walking again.

Four blocks later, he removed his phone and checked his GPS. Looking up, he saw the building he was headed for.

Not too close and not too far. It was just right.

By the time the United States figured out what it had been used for, he would be long gone.

CHAPTER 36

M ikhail Malevsky had identified his handler as Viktor Sergun. Whether or not that was Russian for *big fucking headache*, Harvath wasn't sure, but that's exactly what the man was.

Colonel Viktor Sergun was Russia's military attaché to Germany, based out of the Russian Embassy in Berlin.

Malevsky had also confirmed that Sergun was also Sacha Baseyev's handler. The GRU routinely placed operatives as military attachés in order to garner them protected, diplomatic status. If they were caught engaged in espionage, the worst a host country could do was to kick them out.

Sergun, though, had been involved in much more than espionage. He had been involved in terrorism—including the murder of the U.S. Secretary of Defense and his protective detail.

In Harvath's book, that voided him—just as it had Malevsky—of any protections whatsoever. The call, though, wasn't his to make. It had to come from D.C.

Going after Sergun meant raising the stakes again, dramatically. The Russians could consider it an act of war.

While they could have attempted the same argument over Malevsky, it would never stick. Not when the Germans had an investigation going into his organized crime practices and the United States had enough to paint him as a mobster as well. Sergun, though, was another matter.

Harvath had worked his way up the chain to get to Sergun. All he had to implicate the Colonel, though, was the coerced confession of Malevsky, the aforementioned mobster.

Russia could deny everything and paint Malevsky as a criminal who had gotten caught and would say anything to make a deal.

It would be a mistake for any of it to be made public, and the United States didn't intend to. Harvath had been tasked to work outside the system—*any* system—and that's what he would continue to do.

Once the word came back from D.C., Harvath set his own wheels in motion. They would have to move fast. If Sergun didn't know Malevsky had gone missing, he soon would.

After cleaning up the barn, they ditched the State Police vehicle and anonymously tipped Bavarian law enforcement on where they could find their officers. Then Harvath and Herman drove their own cars to Berlin.

Harvath spent the entire six-plus hour drive on his phone, engaged in encrypted conversations with the United States. He'd been away from any source of news and had no idea that ISIS had released a video of the Secretary of Defense being attacked. Pulling off into a rest area, he and Herman watched it together.

Feelings of guilt washed over him anew. It was all connected. Somehow he was a factor in the equation. He was certain of it.

Beyond pissed off, he got back in his car and got back on the Autobahn. For a while, he couldn't talk to anyone. Hearing that the Secretary and his detail had been assassinated was tough enough. Seeing it was gut-wrenching.

He let himself marinate in his anger for a while longer and then forced his mind to get refocused on what he needed to do. It wasn't easy. The anger ate away at him like acid.

Getting back on the phone, he tried to let the demands of figuring out a strategy divert his attention. Slowly, a plan began to come together.

But even as it did, there were elements too sensitive to be discussed—even via encrypted communications. Those would have to wait until he arrived in Berlin and could speak with the CIA station chief directly.

One of the other issues Harvath had to figure out was what to do with Eichel and Malevsky—both of whom were making the trip in the trunk of Herman's BMW. They couldn't be released. Yet hanging on to them was not only a security risk but also a major pain in the ass.

As he neared Berlin and saw signs for the airport, a possibility took root in his mind. A lot would have to happen between where he was now and what he was thinking about.

Looking in his rearview mirror he saw Herman flash his high beams. Harvath moved over to let him pass.

Herman had been on his phone for a good chunk of the drive too. He didn't want to keep the prisoners at his home in Berlin. That was a no-go. He promised Harvath he'd find them another location. And he had.

Harvath followed him off the motorway and into an old, east-side neighborhood called Friedrichshain. When the wall went up in 1961, the boundary between the U.S. and Soviet sectors had run right along its edge. In World War II, Friedrichshain had been one of the most heavily bombed areas of the city, as the Allies targeted its factories.

Now it was a funky neighborhood filled with young people and artists. There were cafés, pubs, and clubs, mobile phone stores, bank branches, and apartment buildings. For all its gentrification, it still had pockets of derelict and abandoned buildings. It was one of those buildings that Herman had been able to secure.

With bars over the windows and its walls covered with graffiti, the building appeared to have once housed a produce distributor. As soon as Herman pulled into its loading area, there was the sound of a winch being engaged and the rolling steel service door beginning to rise.

Inside were four rough-looking men dressed in black combat boots, jeans, and the black nylon flight jackets popular with the skinhead crowd.

These men weren't skinheads, though. They had tight, military-style haircuts and wore black tactical watches. If Harvath had to lay odds, his guess would be that they were former commandos, just like Herman.

He followed the big BMW inside and parked next to it. Getting out, he joined his friend.

Herman shook hands with the men and then introduced Harvath.

Their names were Adler, Kluge, Bosch, and Farber. They had been members of Herman's old counterterrorism unit, and now worked for his private security company. With the assignment growing more dangerous, and complex, Herman thought it would be a good idea to have a few more hands on deck.

Three of the men—Alder, Kluge, and Bosch, would have fit in anywhere in Europe or the United States. Farber, though, stuck out.

He had dark skin, dark hair, and very dark eyes. He looked like he would have been right at home on the streets of Riyadh or Tehran. "How's your Arabic?" Harvath asked.

"*Bismillah al rahman al Rahim*," he replied. *In the name of God, most Gracious, most Compassionate*.

Harvath knew the phrase. Every chapter in the Quran, except for the ninth, began with it.

"*Ash-hadu an laa ilaaha illallah*," he continued. "*Wa ash-hadu anna Muhammadan rasulullah*." *I bear witness that there is no god except Allah. And I bear witness that Muhammad is the messenger of Allah*.

Herman looked at Harvath and smiled. "Not bad, eh? German-Jewish father and Lebanese mother. They met in Hamburg."

Not bad at all. In fact, his Arabic was excellent. Perfect for what Harvath had planned. As long as witnesses bought it, that was all that mattered. Whether or not the Russians would buy it was something else entirely.

Harvath glanced at his watch. He was meeting the CIA's Berlin station chief at a bar. It was only a few kilometers from the embassy and he wanted to get there first. There were a couple of things he and Herman needed to go over, though, before he could leave.

The man named Bosch gave them a quick tour of the building. There wasn't much to see.

Two defunct walk-in coolers would be used to house the prisoners. They were virtually soundproof and could be locked from the outside.

A system of tiny, wireless cameras had been placed around the inside of the structure, as well as outside on the perimeter. They would be monitored around-the-clock.

Two offices had been set up with cots and sleeping bags. The toilets worked and there was even a shower, though no hot water. They'd have to rough it.

Once the tour was complete, they established a procedure for communications. Then Harvath left the building.

•   •   •

Walking the streets of Berlin, he felt an uncomfortable sense of déjà vu. A lot of blood had been spilled here—by him and because of him. One of Herman's people had even been killed.

Harvath didn't like that the Russians had drawn him back. No matter how badly they were punished, they kept returning for more. Their expansionist desire to reconstitute the glory of the Soviet Union was as bad as the Islamists wanting to re-create their caliphate.

It reminded Harvath how necessary it was to confront both. Without a counterbalance, he had no doubt the world would descend into darkness and chaos.

But what was Russia's play now? What did Salah, ISIS, Sacha Baseyev, Sergun, and the others have to do with it? What was the endgame?

Arriving at number 4 Mansteinstrasse, Harvath hoped to get some answers.

As he pushed open the door of the Leydicke pub and stepped inside, it was like walking back in time—right into the heart of the Cold War itself.

CHAPTER 37

The E. & M. Leydicke had been owned and operated by the Leydicke family for more than one hundred years. It was a traditional German pub—dark with heavy oak tables and lots of carved wood. Its most significant feature, though, was barely visible.

Behind the bar was a beer stein. Its base was wrapped with a piece of barbed wire. The wire had been cut in the middle of the night from the Berlin Wall itself.

The words *Für die Sicherheit* was inscribed upon it. *For the security*. It was the motto of an elite, highly classified American black ops unit that had been stationed in Berlin during the Cold War.

The members posed as everyday Berliners. Across the city, they had hidden weapons, gold coins, explosives, and radio equipment. If the Russians had ever overrun the wall, it had been their job to launch guerilla warfare.

The Leydicke had been the team's unofficial headquarters. As part of his initiation, each operative was required to sneak up onto the wall using night-vision goggles, snip a piece of barbed wire, and return without being caught by the Soviets.

Each man then received his own, numbered stein with his piece of barbed wire wrapped around the base. Hellfried Leydicke, the bar's owner, received his own special mug as a thank-you for supporting the unit.

As far as Harvath knew, there were still items buried in the basement and sealed up behind the plaster walls. The entire establishment was a living time capsule.

When Harvath had last come to Berlin, it was to rescue one of the team members. Though years had passed and the unit had been shut down, it had been reactivated. In the process, a good friend of Harvath's—a man who had been like a second father to him—had been taken hostage.

A complicated trail of clues had led him to number 4 Mansteinstrasse and Hellfried Leydicke—a short, balding man with wire-rimmed glasses, a gut that hung over his apron, and a wildly unkempt mustache.

He had a reputation as a man not to be trifled with and was extremely rough with patrons he believed were not drinking enough.

On the first day Harvath had arrived, Leydicke had given him a tough time. He pretended to have no idea what Harvath was talking about or whom he was looking for. Everything changed, though, as soon as Harvath pointed out the stein, and recounted its significance.

Looking around now, he was disappointed. Leydicke was nowhere in sight. The pub was half full. Mostly locals, taking up all the spots at the bar.

Harvath found a small table tucked in the back. It had a halfway decent view of the front door, but more important, would allow for a private conversation.

Though it was what he wanted, he knew better than to order a cup of coffee. He asked for a beer and if Herr Leydicke was in.

"Nein," his server replied, before heading off to get his drink. It was good to see that their customer service standards hadn't changed.

Once the server returned with his beer, Harvath settled in to wait for the station chief to show up.

• • •

Helen Cartland appeared twenty minutes before their appointed rendezvous. She walked in, removed the hat she had been wearing, and began to scan the pub.

She was an attractive woman in her late forties with short brown hair and a hip sense of style. In boots and a moss-green hunting jacket, she came off as more British than American.

Stopping at the crowded bar, Cartland ordered a glass of white wine and took her time. She had seen Harvath, but she wasn't in any hurry to approach. She was a professional. She wanted to get a good feel for the room and who was in it before she joined him.

Five minutes later, she picked up her glass and walked over.

"I'm sorry, but did we meet last year in Munich, at Oktoberfest?" she asked.

Harvath studied her for a moment. "I think we did. It was in the Käfer tent, wasn't it?"

Cartland nodded. "May I join you?"

"Please," he replied, standing, as she took the seat across from him. Once she was seated, he thanked her for coming.

"Washington didn't give me much choice. Would you like to tell me what's going on?"

"I'll tell you what I can," said Harvath.

"Why don't we start with who you are?"

"You can call me Phil."

Cartland paused, then replied, *"Phil."*

She obviously didn't believe him. That didn't matter. She didn't need to know his real name. The less she knew, the better.

"Okay, Phil," she continued, "I assume you're a green badger of some sort?"

Green badger was a term used to describe outsiders hired by the CIA. Harvath nodded.

"Corporate or independent contractor?" she asked.

"Does it make a difference?"

"It might help me understand the scope of this."

Harvath drained the last sip of his beer and held up the empty glass when the server went by. "You want another?" he asked, pointing at her wine.

She shook her head.

Harvath indicated to the server that only he needed a new drink and then turned his attention back to the station chief.

The CIA's Directorate of Intelligence and its National Clandestine Service were full of contractors. Many of them were even Agency alums who had retired, only to return on special contracts that paid tons more.

"You looking to jump ship?"

"Me?" she replied, her voice kicking up an octave. "Just curious. That's all."

She *was* interested. That was dangerous. There was nothing wrong with someone thinking ahead career-wise. A station chief doing it openly with a stranger, though, was unsettling.

Harvath shifted the conversation to the reason they were there. "What can you tell me about Sergun?"

Cartland rattled off his dossier from memory. "Divorced. Well educated. Fifty-eight years old. No children."

"Girlfriend?"

She shook her head.

"Boyfriend?"

"No romantic involvement in Berlin that we know of."

"How about an address?"

Cartland removed a package of cigarettes from her purse and placed them on the table. "There's an SD card in there. It has the whole work-up we did on him when he got posted here."

"Photographs?" Harvath asked.

She nodded.

"How does he get to work? Does he have a driver?"

"No," Cartland answered. "The Russians are notoriously cheap. Only the ambassador gets a full-time driver. Anyone else who needs a vehicle has to request a Volkswagen from the small pool they keep at the embassy."

"So does he walk? Ride a bike? Taxis?"

"He walks. His apartment isn't far from the embassy."

That was a piece of good news. Taking Sergun from a vehicle, with or without a driver, was something he didn't want to hassle with.

"Anything else?" Harvath inquired. "Hobbies? Does he like sports? Is he a drinker?"

Cartland laughed. "What Russian *isn't* a drinker?"

She had a point. "What I meant was," Harvath clarified, "is there anything we can use to our advantage? Does he have a place he frequents?"

"Pasternak."

"As in Boris Pasternak? The author?"

The station chief nodded. "Restaurant Pasternak. It's named after him. They specialize in Russian food. A lot of the older Russian embassy employees go there for drinks and dinner on Friday. Normally, Sergun's with them."

"And after?"

"He zigzags back to his apartment."

"Meaning he's drunk?"

"He may have downed a couple, but he's still switched on. He runs a good SDR to make sure he isn't being followed. He's always on his guard, so be careful. Don't underestimate him."

"I won't," Harvath replied, his plan crystalizing in his mind. "What can you tell me about the area around the restaurant?"

"On a Friday night? It's busy. Real busy. Not a place to be if you're looking to stay under the radar. Going unnoticed around there is almost impossible."

Good, Harvath thought, as the server returned with his beer. Going unnoticed was the very last thing he had in mind. As in Vienna, he wanted their act to be seen.

The one thing that concerned him, though, was, could they afford to wait until tomorrow night?

They needed to get to Sergun sooner rather than later. He was the key to tracking down Baseyev. The longer they waited, the greater the chance that something might happen.

Harvath glanced at his watch and did the math. They could make their attempt in the morning, but Sergun was a soldier. If he was the "up and at his desk before anyone else" type, they might not have the public audience they needed.

The only thing that made sense was to grab him on the way home— either from the Embassy, or better yet, from the restaurant.

Harvath understood that he didn't have a wide latitude of choices. He just prayed that he wouldn't regret his decision.

CHAPTER 38

Baseyev had chosen Zainab because she was a woman. In addition to being young and attractive, she was also fast. *Very* fast.

They had met in Syria. She had come to join the jihad and fight for ISIS and the caliphate. The recruiter she had made her way to was highly intelligent. He realized that sending a woman like Zainab to the front lines would be an unforgivable mistake.

When Allah blessed you with such a gift, it was because he intended for it to be used, appropriately. Zainab was placed in a house and protected, kept away from the other recruits until a decision could be made.

The leadership, as it had been doing more and more, had consulted with Baseyev. And as he had proven to them time and again, he did not disappoint when it came to strategy.

Zainab possessed dual American/Kuwaiti citizenship. She was a student at Georgetown University who had returned to Kuwait on her American passport and then traveled on to Syria with her Kuwaiti passport.

For all intents and purposes, her trail was clean. The Americans had no way of knowing that she had gone anywhere other than Kuwait to visit relatives. It was too good an opportunity to pass up.

Baseyev and several ISIS leaders spent considerable time interviewing her. They needed to be absolutely certain she was devoted to the cause. She had made it to Syria, determined to fight, but what would happen when she returned home to America? Would she lose her resolve? Would she change her mind?

After much deliberation, it was decided that she was incredibly resolute and that she could be counted on to fulfill her mission.

When her mission was decided upon and her training complete, she was sent back to the United States and told to wait. Now, here they were.

Zainab only needed to make it thirty yards. From the fence to just beyond the fountain. Anything more than that was welcome, but under no circumstances, not even if the door was wide open, was she to cross the threshold and enter the White House. If she did, it would ruin everything. She needed to remain outside, in full view of the cameras.

Baseyev knew the Secret Service wouldn't shoot. They wouldn't turn their canine teams loose on her either. The White House was too politically sensitive. Images of a young, female protestor of Middle Eastern descent being shot or attacked by dogs on the White House lawn wouldn't play well on television.

Thirty yards. That's all he needed. She promised that she wouldn't fail him.

Despite the bright sunshine, the crisp April day had never gotten out of the low fifties. Everyone was wearing a jacket, including Zainab. As she walked, she could make out the sweet, rose-like scent of the cherry blossoms beginning to peak around the Tidal Basin. It was a good omen. Allah had blessed this day.

The banner she carried was a work of art. It was made of silk and would stream beautifully behind her as she ran across the grounds. All the eyes of the world would be upon her. It was the most incredible opportunity she had ever been given. She was excited and intensely nervous all at the same time. *Only thirty yards,* she reminded herself.

Baseyev had studied the Secret Service. He had watched all the videos and had read all the articles regarding breaches of White House security. And after he had analyzed them, he had shown them to Zainab. For her to be successful, she needed to know what she was up against and how to deal with it.

They took tea together one last time. It was at the apartment he had arranged within walking distance of the White House. They talked for hours, stopping only to pray for Allah's protection and continued guidance.

After giving her a pill to help her sleep, he made himself comfortable on the couch and waited out the rest of the night in case she changed her mind. She did not.

The next morning, he rose early, shaving his dark stubble and changing into a fresh shirt he had purchased in Texas.

When Zainab finally entered the kitchen, he smiled warmly and offered her a cup of coffee. The drug he had given her the night before had been strong. It took her a few minutes to clear away the cobwebs.

He produced a small pillbox and offered her a different item this time. "Something the brothers and sisters in Iraq and Syria have found helpful," he said as he pushed the thick pill toward her. "It packs the courage of a lion and the strength of ten men."

Zainab didn't argue. Accepting the drug, she placed it on her tongue and washed it down with a mouthful of coffee.

"Is there anything I need to do about the apartment?" she asked after swallowing. She was moving her hand in a wiping motion.

"You mean clean it for fingerprints?" Baseyev responded. "I'll take care of it. You focus on the greatness you are about to achieve."

They prayed together once more before he told her it was time to get ready.

Because it was such a special day, there were certain additional rituals that needed to be performed, including how she was required to bathe.

Once she was fully dressed, she stepped back into the living room so that Sacha could look at her one last time.

Everything was perfect. *She* was perfect. She would not fail him. Of that, he was certain.

They had grown close during their time together in Syria and he was not afraid to make a show of his affection. Like a brother or a cousin, he placed one soft kiss upon her forehead as he pressed two more pills into her left hand. "Take these just as you are about to leave."

They exchanged a few more words and then he was gone.

Sitting alone in the kitchen, she watched the clock on the microwave. It was almost surreal. To have the knowledge of what was about to happen, when no one else did, exhilarated her. The drugs only enhanced her excitement, causing her to feel almost euphoric.

When the appointed time arrived, she couldn't wait to get moving.

Pouring a glass of water from the tap, she swallowed the pills Ibrahim had given her, zipped up her jacket, and left the apartment.

She had been told not to alter her route unless she believed she was being followed. With nothing to give her that impression, she continued on.

"You will not see me," Baseyev had told her, "but I will be close. I will be watching over you."

She stole occasional glances as she walked, to the side and behind, hoping to catch one last glimpse of him. But true to his word, he was nowhere to be seen.

The pills he had given her, though, had heightened her awareness. Even though she couldn't see him, she believed she could feel his presence. He was all around her.

Zainab followed her route to Lafayette Square Park, just across the street from the White House. There she saw the permanent array of protestors, each hoping to catch the attention of the President and the media. She was about to teach them how to do both.

She didn't need to remind herself to smile. There was a radiance pouring out of her that she simply couldn't contain. She felt more alive, more certain of herself and her purpose in life than ever before.

CHAPTER 39

Viktor Sergun left his apartment building at 7 a.m. sharp, walked to the end of his block, and turned left.

He was wearing a gray suit and a navy-blue trench coat. His black shoes were polished and his hair neatly combed. A small piece of toilet paper marked where he had nicked himself shaving that morning.

Harvath's instructions had been crystal clear. He didn't want Sergun followed. He only wanted confirmation.

Once Sergun disappeared around the corner, Adler radioed Kluge. As soon as Kluge saw Sergun enter the embassy, he radioed Herman. It was on.

They numbered six men total. Two needed to stay back with the prisoners, which meant they were left with four operatives at any given time in the field.

Surveilling an embassy was no easy task. Surveilling the Russian Embassy specifically was an open invitation to get caught.

For all their faults, the Russians weren't stupid. They weren't careless either. In addition to being heavily invested in electronic countermeasures, they spent a lot of time focused on good, old-fashioned human tradecraft.

The Embassy lay just east of the Brandenburg Gate on a grand boulevard named Unter den Linden. It was one of the busiest, most popular areas in all of Berlin.

In addition to being packed with shops, cafés, offices, and assorted tourist sights, there was a tree-lined allée, replete with park benches, that ran right down the middle of the boulevard, which offered multiple places where someone could position themselves to conduct surveillance.

To combat this issue, the Embassy sent out roving teams of observers. They were dispatched sporadically, which made them hard to spot. *Hard*, but not impossible.

There was a look to them—something that said eastern European. The causal observer might miss it, but not someone who knew what to look for. Herman's men *knew* what to look for.

As such, they had been able to rotate in and out of the area. One at a time, they kept an eye on the Embassy while avoiding detection by its CCTC cameras and observation teams.

Around noon, Harvath and Herman headed to the Restaurant Pasternak. They took their time looking for a parking space, driving around the neighborhood in order to get a feel for it.

There were multiple bottlenecks and chokepoints, but there were also multiple side streets and opportunities to disappear. It was a mixed bag, but Harvath and Herman both agreed that net-net, it was too good a location to pass up.

The restaurant sat on an odd-shaped corner where several streets met. A long outdoor terrace like that of a Parisian café wrapped around the front. Across the street, an old water tower that had been converted into apartments rose from a thick, green park.

They took a table under one of the red awnings outside and ordered lunch. Herman had a beer. Harvath drank Red Bull.

Watching the traffic pass, they quietly discussed what the neighborhood would look like tonight and what kind of problems they might encounter.

When their meals came, they ate and then each man used the restroom in order to scope out the restaurant from the inside.

After walking all the way around the long block, they retrieved Herman's BMW and drove back to the old produce warehouse in Friedrichshain.

Farber and Bosch were finishing up their shift keeping an eye on the prisoners.

Harvath pulled up an overview of Berlin on Herman's laptop and walked them through what he had seen.

They discussed primary and alternate routes, as well as what should happen if police became involved or if they were unable to get back to the warehouse. All of them knew that anything was possible.

They key to success was being ready for anything. That included having a backup plan in case Sergun didn't go to the restaurant. If that happened, they were going to have to take him at his apartment.

All things considered, grabbing him at his apartment was a safer option, but it would not have the benefit of being a public spectacle.

Harvath wanted witnesses because he wanted them to talk. If it looked like Sergun had been grabbed by a team of Arabic speakers, the Russians wouldn't know what to think, much less what to do. They might think it was a ruse, but they wouldn't be certain. It would keep them off balance, doubting.

The second layer of the onion was Malevsky's driver and bodyguards down in Berchtesgaden. According to Malevsky, no one in his organization knew that he was doing work for Sergun and the GRU.

Harvath found that highly unlikely. In fact, he knew it would only be a matter of time before word filtered back to Moscow that Malevsky had been apprehended. When that eventually happened, the Russians would be chasing their tails wondering what Germany's involvement was and whether it stretched beyond Malevsky's money-laundering activities.

It only had to keep them tied up long enough for Harvath to get to Sergun. Once he had his hands on him, he didn't really care what the Russians knew. At that point, it would be game over for them.

When he was finished, Farber floated several questions, along with a couple of suggestions. There were two security cameras Harvath had pointed out that he was concerned about.

Since they would be wearing masks and taking other precautions, he wasn't worried about being ID'd. What he was concerned with was appearing *too* professional.

They needed to come off as lucky. Good, but not great. It couldn't look too polished or too choreographed. Not only would the German security services not believe it, neither would the Russians, once the CCTV footage was shared with them.

There had to be a little sand in the gears—a mistake or two, rookie moves that no pros would engage in. From front to back, it had to feel like a jihadist production. Harvath agreed and was already three steps ahead of him.

He laid out his ideas, and then went back and forth with both Farber and Bosch. Finally, they came to a meeting of the minds.

Some of the things that Harvath had suggested meant the operation would take longer than it should, but they would add legitimacy.

The hardest part would be going against years of training. There were certain things that had been drilled into all of them—certain things that they didn't even consciously think about. They just instinctively knew to do them.

Tonight, though, they were going to have to turn several of those things upside down.

The big thing they had in their favor was that they had all spent countless hours dissecting tactical videos. Both the good guys, and the bad. They knew what the professionals would be looking for. That, they hoped, would give them the upper hand. As long as they all played their rolls as scripted, it should come off exactly as they wanted it to.

The last thing Harvath raised was footwear. It was a small detail, but an extremely important one. He didn't want any of them wearing tactical boots.

Their big, black watches had to stay behind as well. Anything that could even remotely tag them as pros was off-limits. He didn't care what some terrorists had been caught wearing in the past. None of that stuff could be part of this operation.

Farber and Bosch agreed. It wasn't worth it. The entire team had already ditched their distinct boots and jackets for more low-key street clothes anyway. They were well trained and knew that their surveillance of the Russian Embassy required them to blend in.

With everything settled for the time being, Harvath got ready to take up his post when his phone rang. It was Lydia Ryan calling him from Langley.

"Hey," he said, answering the call, "what's up?"

"Turn on your TV," the Deputy CIA Director replied.

"I don't have one."

"Do you have a laptop?"

"I do," Harvath answered, as he opened Herman's back up and pressed the space bar to wake it from sleep mode. "What's going on?"

"The White House has just been attacked."

CHAPTER 40

Harvath didn't want to believe her, but he knew Ryan wasn't kidding. "Tell me what happened," he said as he opened the computer's browser and surfed to one of the cable news sites.

"Suicide bomber," the CIA Deputy Director replied. "She leapt the fence on Pennsylvania Avenue and—"

"Wait," he interrupted. "*She?* It was a female bomber?"

"Yes. She got all the way across the north lawn and detonated on the driveway just outside the north portico."

"How the hell did she get that far?"

"Somebody screwed up," Ryan admitted.

"You're damn right somebody screwed up. Anyone hurt?"

"So far there are three fatalities. All uniformed Secret Service. They were moving in to take her down when she clacked off. We can't even estimate the number of injured yet."

"Goddamn it," Harvath replied. He had been recruited to the Secret Service from the SEALs. He had worked presidential protection. "Was the President there? Is he all right?"

"He was in the West Wing when it happened. They evacuated him to the bunker. He wasn't harmed. They're deciding whether to remain in place or move him to the COG facility."

COG stood for Continuity of Government. The facility Ryan was referring to was a secure fallback location for the President during times of attack or national emergency.

"How long ago did this happen?" he asked.

"Five minutes."

Harvath could now see a live feed streaming from Washington. Herman, Farber, and Bosch gathered around him.

"Mein Gott," Herman exclaimed. *My God.*

They stared, stunned, as the camera panned across the charred iconic façade of the White House.

"That's not all," Ryan added. "Seconds before she got to the driveway and detonated, she unfurled a long black banner."

"Let me guess. With white Arabic writing on it?"

"Yup. Never slowed down for a second, just kept running."

Harvath took a breath. "Have you confirmed this as an ISIS attack?"

"Publically? No. Internally? Absolutely."

"Do you think this is connected to our guy?" he asked.

"Pitchfork?" the Deputy Director replied. "We don't know, but you can add this to your list of questions to ask his handler."

"So it's still a go?"

"One hundred percent. It's even more important now. Do whatever you need to do. Understood?"

"Understood," Harvath replied, as Lydia Ryan disconnected the call.

• • •

Harvath knew it was a serious, maybe even deadly mistake to let his anger get the best of him. Nevertheless, he fumed.

ISIS had struck inside Washington and now even more Americans were dead.

They had hit one of the greatest symbols of the United States. It was a target they had been threatening, and lusting after, for years. Now they had actually done it.

Harvath's anger was tinged with shock. They were getting exponentially better. Each attack was more dramatic than the last. He didn't have the proof yet, but he knew the Russians were involved with this one too.

First Turkey and now D.C. Harvath didn't want to think about what might be next. It was all the more reason to grab Sergun and get him talking ASAP.

The attack in D.C., though, made Harvath doubt his plan. Every TV in Berlin—actually, every TV in the world—was filled with the images of what had happened at the White House. Everyone was aware of it now.

That didn't mean that terrorists around the world would take the night off, but a public kidnapping of a Russian military attaché in Germany would not come off as a coincidence.

It would get hyped even more than if it happened just by itself. The media thrived on fear. He could hear it now, "First Antalya, then D.C., now Berlin. What political target will the terrorists strike next?"

Harvath was beginning to think that perhaps the entire plan should be scrapped. Instead, just slip into Sergun's apartment, grab him in the dark, and carry him out. Screw the witnesses. Let the Russians think whatever they wanted. It wouldn't make any difference. Sergun would be gone.

Harvath discussed it with Herman. "What do you think?"

The man shrugged. "It's your operation."

"That's not an answer."

"You're right."

Harvath waited, but his friend didn't say anything further. "If we snatch him from his apartment, the Russians are going to suspect Germany was behind it."

Herman shrugged again. "Not my problem."

Harvath had seen this attitude growing across Europe. So many people struck him as unhappy with the way things were going. And while some were pushing for massive changes to straighten things out, others had completely given up, resigning themselves to the idea that their nation's best days were in the past.

Harvath refused to ever allow himself to think like that. As long as you could fight, you were in the fight, and that meant the fight wasn't over. Nothing was impossible.

To a certain degree, it was easier for him to feel that way. America wasn't Germany. It wasn't Europe either. Despite the tragic blows the United States had suffered, things were different. How long they would remain that way was the question.

With each attack, there was a call for more security. What had happened at the White House was going to shake Americans to the core.

Harvath knew President Porter, though. His instinct wouldn't be to batten down the hatches, at least not at the expense of people's individual freedom. He would want to reassure the American people, to bolster their self-confidence, and instill in them a sense of control over their own lives. Government wasn't the answer and he wouldn't pretend it was.

Even so, there would be a call for the President to do something. That was how people reacted to situations that frightened them. *Something must be done.* Doing something was a panacea.

It didn't matter if the most popular thing being proposed wouldn't have stopped the attack in the first place, many would still demand that it be done. *Do something, anything.* It was all about people *feeling* safer.

Harvath was reminded of a quote attributed to Ben Franklin—*Those who would trade a little liberty for a little added security, deserve neither and will lose both.*

Maybe the President would be able to reassure America. Maybe not. What Harvath did know was that if they didn't get to the bottom of these attacks and stop another one from happening, the clamor to do something would only get louder, and what they would call for being done would be even more dramatic.

Too many people had died, too much had already been lost. Enough was enough.

Harvath looked at Herman. He had made up his mind.

CHAPTER 41

When Viktor Sergun entered his apartment, the first thing he noticed was that his electricity wasn't working.

Old East German Building, he thought to himself. *Old wiring.* He was Russian. He was used to things not working.

He made his way to the kitchen. The electrical box was in the pantry. So was his flashlight. There was another in the bedroom, but he didn't feel like walking through the dark to retrieve it.

He knew the apartment well enough to navigate into the kitchen without one. It was like all the other cheap apartments his government had placed him in around the world.

He couldn't really complain, though. He had lived in places much worse. At least he was in Europe.

Laying his coat over the back of the lone chair at the breakfast table, he crossed over to the pantry. Hopefully, it was just a fuse. He had a small box of spares sitting on one of the shelves.

He opened the door of the pantry and *POP!*

Sergun heard the sound at the same time he saw the red light of a laser pointed right at his chest. That was the last thing he remembered before the searing-hot pain shot through his entire body.

• • •

The Taser still in his hand, Harvath sprang from the pantry as Sergun's body hit the kitchen floor. He didn't bother to remove the barbed metal probes from the man's chest. There wasn't time.

Rolling him onto his stomach, he placed plastic EZ Cuff restraints over the Russian's wrists and yanked them tight. He then did the same with his ankles.

He finished by tearing off a piece of duct tape from the roll in his coat pocket and placing it over the military attaché's mouth. Looking up, he nodded.

Herman began radioing commands to his team as he laid out a black plastic body bag in the hallway. It had been punctured with airholes so that Sergun would still be able to breathe.

As they bent down to pick him up, he began to struggle. Harvath waved Herman back and depressed the trigger of the Taser again.

The painful burst of electricity raced through the Russian's body like shards of broken glass and he went completely rigid.

When the pulse ended, they rolled him over and picked him up. Harvath had his shoulders and Herman his feet.

They carried him into the hall and laid him on top of the unzipped body bag. Harvath patted him down, going through his pockets, around his waistband, the seams of his trousers, everywhere. Russian intelligence officers were notorious for the escape and evasion materials they hid on their persons.

In addition to his passport, credit cards, and a roll of cash, Harvath found a handcuff shim, a small razor blade, and a length of diamond-encrusted string that could be used to saw through restraints.

Once those items were removed, he and Herman half-mummified the man with duct tape. The less he was able to move, the better.

When he was sufficiently immobilized, Herman let his men know that they were ready to roll. Zipping up the body bag, they waited for a knock on the apartment door.

Seconds later, there was a soft rap. Herman let Bosch and Farber in, everyone grabbed a handle, and they exited the apartment, closing the door behind them.

They moved quickly to the stairs and headed down the three floors to the street.

As soon as they stepped outside, Adler rolled up in Herman's BMW and popped the trunk.

Harvath looked up and down the sidewalk. There was no one in sight. Nodding, he gave the order to move.

They threaded the space between two parked cars, and threw Sergun in the trunk.

Herman then shut the lid and climbed in back with Harvath and Farber. Bosch jumped into the front passenger seat and Adler drove off. The entire operation had taken less than ten minutes.

CHAPTER 42

T he drive from Berlin to Frankfurt was just over an hour and they were careful to obey the speed limit. By the time they arrived at the airport, it was shortly before sunrise.

Moving people and black-market antiquities through any airport, much less one the size of Frankfurt International, required a network of people on the take. Eichel had given all of them up.

Hoping to purchase his freedom, he had surrendered the names and phone numbers of everyone at the airport who was working for him. He would have to do a lot more than rat his associates out, though, and Harvath had explained what it was. Eichel had nodded in agreement and had begun making phone calls.

There was a small checkpoint entrance on the far northeast side of the airport. When they pulled up, it was unmanned.

Within seconds, the yellow concrete bollards in front of them lowered, the gate drew back, and the red- and white-striped security arm blocking their way was raised.

"Open sesame," Herman remarked as he drove onto the airport grounds and headed for the civil aviation area.

Outside a windowless gray hangar, a German Customs and Immigration official sat in a white Mercedes waiting for them.

When they pulled alongside, the man rolled his window down and Harvath handed over an envelope.

After counting the money, the official wished them a good flight, rolled his window up, and drove away.

"It pays to know people," said Herman as he watched the Mercedes drive off. "I never get through the airport this fast."

It hadn't been cheap. While Eichel's man was crooked, he wasn't stupid. He had made sure he was well compensated for his risk.

Helen Cartland, the CIA's Berlin station chief, had flat-out refused the amount of money Harvath had requested. Lydia Ryan had to call from Langley and order her to release it.

When Cartland showed up at the produce warehouse to deliver the cash, she presented Harvath with a receipt and demanded that he sign it. She didn't want her ass on the line for such a large sum.

Harvath shook his head and signed her slip of paper.

"Are you kidding me?" she asked when she read his signature. *"Justin Credible?"*

He winked at her and had Bosch walk her back out to her car as they finished getting the prisoners ready.

Then, once they were all prepped, they were loaded into the trunk of the BMW. Bosch and Farber followed in Harvath's vehicle, which they would be returning for him.

Inside the hangar, a sleek Bombardier Global 6000 business jet owned by the CIA was waiting. Herman and his men helped him board and secure the prisoners. All three were wearing blindfolds, hoods, and earmuffs.

Herman offered to come along to help with security, but Harvath turned him down. It was a short flight. He'd be fine.

They said their goodbyes at the bottom of the airstairs. Harvath thanked Herman and his men for their help.

Fifteen minutes later, he had a mug of hot coffee in his hand, the powerful aircraft was thundering down the runway, and the sun had begun to rise.

Harvath sat back in his chair and watched out the window as the pilots banked and turned the jet south toward the Mediterranean.

Normally, this would have been a prime opportunity for him to get some sleep. But with prisoners on board, that was out of the question.

Instead, he used the time to let his mind wander. There were still so many questions he didn't have the answers to.

No sooner had he begun to list them than they began to crash up against each other like a pile-up on a busy interstate. He had questions about Salah, Malevsky, and Sacha Baseyev. What the Russians knew. What they didn't know. What was next and who was responsible.

It was all Harvath could do not to start interrogating Sergun right there on the plane. Lydia Ryan, though, had been absolutely specific on how it was to be handled. The instructions had come from her boss, Director McGee. And Harvath knew that McGee had issued the orders based on the wishes of the President. He would have to wait until he got to Malta.

As he watched the blue-black sky turn orange, he thought about Lara. It had been days since he had spoken with her. She'd be back in Boston by now.

Knowing her, she'd probably spent a little time with her family and then headed right into the office, jet lag be damned.

Staring at the three hooded figures in the back of the plane, he took a sip of his coffee. It was hard to say that this was better than being in Boston with Lara.

For a moment, he thought about what moving to Boston might be like. D.C. was where his career was. At least that was what he had always told himself.

Working at The Carlton Group had a lot of upside. His boss was a legend in the spy game, the money was fantastic, and even though the Old Man had not directly said it, he was grooming Harvath to take over one day.

But what did that mean? It was a question he knew the answer to but had never really thought about.

It meant running the business. Schmoozing politicians. Glad-handing agency heads. Winning contracts.

He'd be trading in fieldwork for paperwork. Covert operations for conference rooms.

He knew plenty of guys who had gone corporate. Men who had traded being Tier One for the Fortune 500. Or who had completely set up their own businesses.

In return, they had received a semblance of stability. Freed from the relentless tempo of being elite operators, they could now have their chance to enjoy the American Dream.

They bought boats and summerhouses. Took long vacations and went on epic hunting and fishing trips. They were living the dream.

But get a couple of drinks into them and they'd tell you that they missed the action. That nothing matched it. That as much as they loved their new careers and being with their wives and families, the old life never stopped calling. It was an itch that just couldn't be scratched.

There was also the sense of purpose. None of the men Harvath had known had been in it for the money. They were there because they believed in the mission and the men who were fighting alongside them. It was a calling and, as such, extremely difficult to walk away from.

Harvath took another sip of coffee and looked back out the window.

He had never considered that Reed Carlton might pull him from the field before he was ready to leave it behind. It was crazy that it hadn't crossed his mind before.

When the Old Man was ready to hang it up, he was going to hang it up. It wouldn't matter where Harvath thought he was more valuable or where he wanted to be. Carlton would have already made up his mind.

He would have thought everything out. He would have anticipated every rebuttal Harvath might raise. He'd have an offer for him and it would be fantastic. And knowing Harvath as well as he did, he'd have an ironclad justification ready as well.

The Old Man would appeal to Harvath's sense of duty and patriotism. He'd explain why the country needed him to give up fieldwork and helm The Carlton Group. Finally, he would appeal to his sense of loyalty.

None of it would be pretty. And frankly, Harvath had no idea how he might respond. What he did know, was that once the offer had been made, their relationship would have crossed a Rubicon.

There would be no going back to the way things were before. That wasn't how Carlton operated. He was incredibly stubborn and single-minded when it came to the business and what he thought best served the needs of the country.

You either followed his advice, or he advised you to hit the road. Things were black, or they were white. There was no gray.

But while there was no gray with the Old Man, there was with the Agency. In fact, there was *green*—and in more ways than one.

Harvath was reminded of his conversation with Helen Cartland in the pub back in Berlin. She had asked him what kind of green badger he was. Was he a private contractor or corporate?

In his time working with the CIA, he had learned about a hybrid type of contractor. Something called SpecTal, a combination of someone who was sometimes a private contractor and sometimes a corporate contractor.

But for that to happen, Carlton would have to want to keep him around. If Harvath said no to moving into a leadership role at the company, he doubted that was going to be an option. The Old Man would cut ties. That was just the way he was.

If he wanted to stay in the field, going the private route might be the answer. He would be giving up a lot by leaving The Carlton Group, but he stood to gain so much in return.

The CIA wouldn't care if he lived in Boston or Bangladesh. All they would care about is that when they called, he picked up the phone.

Becoming a private contractor for the Agency would allow him to do what he loved to do, and do it from Boston.

He'd have to give up his house. And there was also the chance that the President wouldn't be happy with his decision, but how much would that matter?

He wasn't hanging up his cleats. He'd just be using a different locker room. If the President wanted him for something, he could still find him. He just wouldn't be right down the road.

The more he thought about it, the more the pieces started falling into place. For a moment, he had to stop himself and ask if this was really what he wanted to do. Was he actually going to leave The Carlton Group?

He was tired. His head wasn't on straight. It was a crazy idea. Certainly not something he should be thinking about in the middle of an operation. Pondering the future wasn't something he could afford to do right now. He needed to focus on the present.

He turned his mind back to all the questions that had been piling up like a chain-reaction car crash in his brain. He pulled at a thread here, a thread there, trying to unravel what it all meant.

He was on his third cup of coffee and no closer to any answers when the plane began to descend and Harvath looked back out the window.

They were over the water, just south of Sicily. Double-checking the prisoners, he returned to his seat and buckled up.

It felt odd to be returning. His last visit had marked a low and very dark time for him. He had stayed drunk for days and had even taken a shot at the man he was about to see.

Hopefully, he'd already put that behind him. If Harvath had wanted to kill him, he would have. It had been only a warning shot.

Some people, though, had a way of carrying a grudge. Especially those who had been shot at.

CHAPTER 43

The interrogation facility was located about a half hour outside the town of Valetta. It had been built to resemble a rural Maltese farmhouse. The guts of the operation were belowground in a series of tunnels and windowless cells that had been nicknamed the Solarium.

A man named Vella ran the program. He had PhDs in psychiatry and neurochemistry, and was considered one of the best interrogators in the business.

He was the one Harvath had shot at. Vella and his team were waiting as the jet landed and taxied inside the private hangar.

As soon as the pilots shut down the engines and lowered the stairs, Vella and his team came aboard.

"Flight okay?" Vella asked, as his men got the prisoners ready to deplane. "Any trouble?"

Harvath shook his head.

"Good. My car's outside," he replied, waving Harvath toward the cabin door.

He was a couple of inches shorter than Harvath, lean, with dark hair and glasses. He didn't look like some mad scientist. He looked like an accountant.

Harvath grabbed his bag and followed him out to the car.

"Hungry?" he asked as they climbed into his silver Jaguar.

He was. "Can we pick something up on the way? I want to get started with the interrogation as soon as possible."

"Don't worry. We've got time."

When Harvath had been given permission to transport Sergun and the other two to the Solarium, the Old Man had explained that Vella would be running the show. Harvath was expected to follow his lead.

"Breakfast or lunch?" he asked as they left the airport and pulled out onto the main road.

"Lunch," Harvath replied.

Vella nodded, pressed the button to open the sunroof, and pushed down on the accelerator.

Harvath lowered his window. The sun was bright and it was warm outside. He could smell the ocean. It felt good being close to the water.

Twenty minutes later they pulled off onto a dirt road and kept going. There were no houses, no shops, nothing. They were in the middle of nowhere. Harvath's antennae were beginning to stand up. Then he saw it.

It was half beach cottage, half shack, surrounded by a faded picket fence. A brightly colored rowboat was pulled up onto the beach in front. Two old men worked repairing a large fishing net.

Vella parked his car and motioned to follow him inside.

The front of the restaurant was open to the ocean. They were shown to a small table and offered menus.

"Is there anything you *don't* eat?" Vella asked.

"Brains and intestines," Harvath replied.

Vella laughed and ordered in Maltese for both of them.

When the waitress left to place their order, Harvath said, "Listen, I owe you an apology."

Vella held up his hand. "No, you don't."

"I shot at you."

"If you had intended to hit me, would you have?"

Harvath nodded.

"Then you didn't shoot *at* me. You shot near me. There's a difference. In your case it was a *subtle* difference, but a difference nonetheless."

"I apologize."

"It's in the past," Vella replied. "Let's talk about the present."

"What do you want to know?"

"How you broke Eichel and Malevsky. And then what, specifically, it is you want me to get from Sergun."

"Did they send you my reports?" Harvath asked.

Vella nodded. "I read everything. I just wanted to see what else you could provide. Even small things, things that may seem inconsequential, can sometimes help me."

Harvath began speaking, but paused as the waitress returned with their drinks. Once she had gone again, he continued. Vella didn't write anything down. He simply listened, only breaking in when he wanted clarification.

By the time their food arrived, he had told him everything he could remember about all three prisoners.

The lunch was fantastic. Fresh prawn carpaccio, "aljotta," which was a traditional fish soup, and for their main course a rib eye of veal with wild mushrooms.

By the time Harvath was done eating, he felt even more tired than he had on the flight in. Vella ordered espressos—a double for Harvath—and paid the bill.

When they were done with their coffees, they returned to the car and continued on to the Solarium.

Even with his knowledge of Arabic, the road signs were difficult to read. Maltese was an interesting language, to say the least.

Arriving at the farm, Vella checked Harvath in, issued him a security card, and showed him to his room.

"I'm going to start with Malevsky first," the interrogator said. "I want to gather as much intel as I can before I sit down with Sergun. Okay?"

"Your house. Your rules," Harvath replied.

Vella smiled. "Give me two hours and then come down."

"Will do."

As the man left and closed the door behind him, Harvath tossed his bag on the end of the bed and began unpacking. He then texted a quick update to Lydia Ryan and took a long, hot shower.

After shaving and changing his clothes, he set the alarm on his phone and lay down on the bed. Within seconds, he was asleep.

An hour later, his alarm went off. Though he could have used a lot more sleep, he at least felt a little refreshed.

Pulling a bottle of water from the small fridge in the room, he drank half of it and headed downstairs. He knew his way from the last time he had been here.

It was at the end of his last assignment. He had been given a list of kills to carry out. They were elites, untouchables scattered across Europe. They had been responsible for the terrible pandemic that had swept the globe.

The last person on his list had been a South African. A prisoner at the Solarium. Harvath had brought him to Malta himself.

The South African had worked for the elites. He had helped make their plan possible. He had killed scores and scores of innocents. He was the last link in the chain and Harvath had killed him with his bare hands.

Then he had chased everyone out of the Solarium and had gotten drunk. He had stayed drunk for days. It was the only way he could deal with what he had seen and what he had done.

When Vella came to check on him, that's when he had fired a shot at him. Thirty-six hours later, a friend walked into the cell Harvath was camped in and sat down. They drank and they talked. They sat there until Harvath was ready to leave.

It was indeed one of the lowest points of his life. He had done what he had needed to do, what he had been assigned to do. Once he felt ready, he had flown back home.

He and Lara, along with her parents and little boy, had retreated to Alaska. Harvath had friends there who had a fishing lodge. It was a good place to ride out the next four weeks, a safe, remote place to hide from the infection.

Then, as quickly as the disease had appeared, it disappeared—all but burning itself out.

Every nation had suffered, some worse than others. The amazing thing was how quickly "normal" life had returned. No matter what nature threw at mankind, mankind always seemed to find a way to rebound.

Nevertheless, Harvath still carried the demons with him. He saw the faces of the dead and the dying. He felt responsible, as if somehow he could have changed the outcome. Somehow stopped it.

But based on what he had known, and how far he'd had to go to get answers, he couldn't have stopped it. The wheels had already been in motion. The virus had been set loose before anyone knew what was happening. The men behind the attack didn't send out polite announcements drawing attention to what was coming. It wasn't his fault.

What about Anbar, though? The SAD team was there because of the intelligence Harvath had received from Salah. They were so convinced it was solid, they had bet everything on it. Then the team and the helicopter contingent had gotten wiped out.

Next came the assassination of the Secretary of Defense, his security team, and the suicide bombing at the White House. All of that led from Salah to Sacha Baseyev, and now to the man in a cell downstairs, Colonel Viktor Sergun. He was the man with the answers Harvath wanted.

In light of that, it probably made sense that Vella was in charge of this interrogation. Harvath wouldn't have been subtle. He would have been brutal.

The death of Valery Kumarin had been an accident. Harvath hadn't intended to kill him when he showed up at Malevsky's estate, but that had been the result. Perhaps D.C. was trying to safeguard against any more accidents.

Whatever the reasoning, the call had been made. He was an observer now. Vella had full authority. He was the one calling all the shots. Harvath would act accordingly.

As he walked down the stairs, he looked forward to watching the interrogation of Viktor Sergun.

CHAPTER 44

Almost twenty-four hours had passed since the suicide bombing. The North Portico, which functioned as the front door to the White House, was badly damaged. Scaffolding had been erected to block it from view. Emblazoned across it was a billowing American flag.

In a trend just as disturbing as the Secret Service's reluctance to apply maximum force to trespassers, the President had refused to be evacuated.

He had been in the West Wing when the bomber detonated. His security detail had immediately rushed him to the underground bunker formerly known as the Presidential Emergency Operations Center. They watched the unfolding pandemonium on the cable and television networks whose cameras were permanently encamped on the North Lawn.

Once it became obvious that it was a suicide bomber and that several minutes had passed with no follow-on attack, President Porter had wanted to leave the bunker to assist the wounded. The Secret Service didn't need to restrain him. His entire senior staff jumped up to stand in his way.

"Absolutely not," his Chief of Staff said. "No way."

When Porter tried to push past, his National Security Director stated, "You know how these people operate. The first bomb draws everyone in. The second takes everyone out."

"Look at the feeds," Porter insisted, pointing to all the television monitors in the room. "The first responders are already up there. There isn't a second bomb."

"We don't know that," the Vice President replied. "Please, Paul. Let's just wait."

"Those are our people up there," he fired back. "I am not going to have it said, 'The President of the United States cowered in a bunker while they needed help.'"

Now it was the Press Secretary's turn to step in. "Nobody will say that, Mr. President. Right now, though, you need to be kept safe. The nation is going to want to hear from you."

His lead Secret Service agent, a man named Chudwin, drew the Chief of Staff aside and made his case to evacuate the President to the Continuity of Government facility in West Virginia.

Porter saw them speaking and interrupted. "Agent Chudwin," he said. "We're not leaving. That is final. Am I understood?"

Chudwin looked at the Chief of Staff and then to the President. "Yes, sir."

What he liked even less than cowering in the bunker was abandoning ship. With the issue settled, he looked at his Press Secretary. "I want to give a national address."

"When?" she responded.

"As soon as possible. Just a few brief remarks to show everyone we're still here and to reassure the American people that we will respond to this attack."

The Press Secretary looked at her watch. "Give me twenty minutes to write something up."

"And I want to do it from the Oval."

The Press Secretary looked at the President's lead Secret Service agent.

Chudwin shook his head. "I don't think that's a good idea, sir."

"Duly noted," replied Porter, who looked back at his Press Secretary and stated, "We're doing it from the Oval."

An hour and a half later, stations around the world broke into their programming to carry the President's brief address.

Porter was a gifted speaker and had struck the right tone. He praised the Secret Service for its bravery, extended his heartfelt prayers for the dead and wounded, as well as their friends and families, and then announced his resolute determination to avenge the attack.

It was a very specific choice of words. Some of his predecessors had preferred the phrase *bring the perpetrators to justice*. Bringing perpetrators to justice was what you did with purse snatchers or bank robbers.

This attack hadn't been a criminal act. It had been an act of war. Porter didn't want to put the perpetrators in prison, he wanted to put them in the ground. If, once America found them, there were enough pieces left to justify using a casket.

When the address was complete, the President joined his National Security Council in the Situation Room. They had been practically living there ever since.

With Washington's network of security cameras, the FBI had been able to gather a significant amount of intelligence.

They already had CCTV footage of the bomber as she walked several blocks to the White House, though her point of origin was unclear.

The bomber's walk had started somewhere within an area where there were no cameras. They were assuming that she had exited from either a building or a vehicle.

The two-block area in question had been completely sealed off. FBI agents were combing it methodically, which meant the search was very slow-going.

The Bureau's biggest concern was that when or if they found a car, a van, or an apartment belonging to the bomber, it might be rigged with explosives. They were using robots, dog teams, and everything else at their disposal, to get to the bottom of it.

In the meantime, the banner the bomber carried had been identified as the flag of ISIS. They had all suspected as much.

The big question now was whether the bomber had been inspired by ISIS or actually directed by them.

For his part, President Porter had grown unforgiving of the distinction. As long as ISIS called for attacks against the West, America in particular, the responsibility was on them.

But what about the Russians? Harvath had been able to draw a line from his murdered informant in Belgium to the GRU. He had even learned that a GRU operative had flown from Frankfurt to Antalya right around the time of the attack on Secretary Devon.

That didn't mean, though, that the Russians had been involved. In order to allege, much less act on, something that serious, he was going to need proof. *Ironclad proof.*

Right now, though, they had to assemble a response to ISIS. America's previous attack had dominated global headlines for the last seventy-two hours. The phone at the White House was still ringing off the hook from world leaders.

But in the blink of an eye, the United States had lost the propaganda initiative. ISIS had been able to strike the White House itself. It was an amazing coup.

The Joint Chiefs of Staff had been assembled at the Pentagon. A secure videoconference link connected them with the bunker.

Porter addressed the Chairman. "Your thoughts regarding a response, General?"

The man tapped his pencil onto the pad of paper in front of him. "My guess is the attack on the White House was in the works before we hit them with Operation Iron Fury."

"Agreed."

"And all the intel we're getting here says that we kneecapped them pretty good. We can put together any kind of response you ask for, Mr. President. But what we'd need to know is what you're looking for."

"Meaning?"

"Meaning," the General replied, "do you want something that's proportional? Or disproportional?"

It was a fair question, and one that Porter had already been thinking about. "Let's say we wanted to deliver an equally symbolic message. What would it take to blow the front doors of ISIS headquarters right off their hinges?"

"Well, for starters, we'd actually have to find their headquarters," said the General.

"And if we can do that?" asked the President.

"If you can do that, we'll give you the most unbelievably symbolic response you've ever seen."

CHAPTER 45

Y ou really messed him up," Vella said as Harvath joined him in his office. "His knee is shattered. He's probably going to walk with a limp for the rest of his life."

Harvath picked up the scan and looked at it. "Do you offer dental exams too?"

"We work up each one that comes through. We don't want any unforeseen medical conditions tanking an interrogation."

Despite some of its stomach-churning practices, the Solarium was highly scientific. Harvath understood the need to give prisoners workups. It not only helped identify potential problems but also provided baselines, which allowed them to identify when techniques were working.

"Did Malevsky give you anything useful?" Harvath asked.

"A couple of things," Vella replied. "Mostly background, but I think it could be helpful. In the meantime, I need updated proof of life. Can you get your contact to take photos?" Consulting his notes, he added, "He wants a picture of each girl in the kitchen near her favorite appliance."

"What does that mean?"

"He says the girls will know."

Harvath removed his phone to text Alexandra. "What's the password for your Wi-Fi?"

Vella gave it to him, Harvath entered it into his phone, and sent the message. "I'll let you know as soon as I get something back from her. Now, what about Sergun?"

Vella picked up a remote and clicked on one of the TVs hanging on the wall. A hooded figure sat with his feet chained to the floor and his wrists cuffed to a track that ran down the center of a stainless steel table.

"What are you waiting for?" Harvath asked.

The interrogator opened a drawer in his desk, removed what looked like a small pill bottle, and handed it to Harvath. "Open it."

The moment Harvath did, he regretted it. He only caught a small whiff of what was inside, but it was enough to cause his chest to tighten and his pulse to race.

Replacing the cap, he handed it back to Vella. "That's awful."

"Now you know what fear smells like."

Harvath shook his head to get the lingering odor out of his nostrils. "What are you talking about? What is that stuff?"

"It's a synthetic."

"Synthetic *what*?"

Vella thought for a moment and replied, "Certain species are capable of excreting chemical factors which can trigger social responses."

"Pheromones," Harvath stated.

"Precisely. And when these chemical factors are released, they impact the behavior of the receiving individual. There are many different kinds of pheromones in the animal world that affect behavior and physiology. There are alarm pheromones, sex pheromones, and even fear pheromones.

"This last pheromone is particularly interesting, especially as it relates to human beings, both in groups, as well as in individuals. Essentially, what we have learned is that fear can be chemically induced. And it can be done so via smell."

These guys were way too into their work. They were always developing new interrogation techniques, ways to break people and get them to comply.

"Let me guess," said Harvath. "You're pumping the interrogation room full of it right now."

"Are you kidding me?" Vella replied. "I wouldn't be able to work in there if I did."

"So how are you introducing it?"

Vella walked over to the monitor and pointed to the hood Sergun was wearing. "See this part here? Right around his nose and mouth?"

Harvath looked. The fabric appeared darker. "What about it?"

"That's actually a pocket. We placed pieces of fabric inside, soaked with the synthetic pheromone."

"So he's breathing it."

Vella nodded.

"Does that actually work?" Harvath asked.

"We'll see."

• • •

Fifteen minutes later, Vella turned up the volume on the monitor and excused himself. Harvath remained behind in the office to watch.

Moments later, he heard the heavy bolt on the interrogation room door being pulled back and then the squeal of hinges as it was opened.

One of the guards closed and locked the door behind him after Vella had entered.

It was interesting for Harvath to watch how someone else conducted an interrogation. Normally, he was the one doing it. He didn't usually get to observe other people work.

Vella took his time. He moved quietly to the far corner of the room, leaned back against the wall, and watched his prisoner.

By now, the earmuffs and the blindfold would have been removed from Sergun. The only deprivation he was suffering was due to his restraints and the hood over his head.

During his medical workup, adhesive sensors had been placed at different points on his skin. Now, somewhere in the Solarium, a tech had hit a button and the man's vital signs could be seen across the bottom of the TV monitor.

Sergun's heart rate had gone up since the door had opened and Vella had entered the room. He was keenly aware of the man's presence. Vella, though, did nothing. He remained in the corner, leaning against the wall, watching.

Harvath could only imagine what was going through Sergun's mind at the moment. Most likely, he was trying to remember all of his training. Deny, deny, deny and launch counteraccusations. That's what all good spies were taught.

After five more minutes, Vella approached. He stood very close, almost on top of him. Harvath leaned forward to figure out what he was doing. Then Vella carefully removed the hood and stepped away.

The fifty-eight-year-old Sergun was a good forty pounds overweight. His pasty white face was round and puffy. His jowls shook as his eyes adjusted to the light and he twisted his head left, and then right. His gray hair was cut in a buzz cut, military-style.

"I understand that you speak English," said Vella.

As his eyes focused, they came to rest on his interrogator and he nodded.

"Good," Vella continued. "Do you know where you are?"

Sergun shook his head.

"It has many names. Some have compared it to Dante's seventh circle, where the violent are bathed in a boiling river of blood and fire. Others, though, have compared it to Paradise. A place where their prayers are finally answered. Where they find release."

The Russian remained still. His face was stony and impassive. His eyes, though, told a different story. Harvath could see it even on the CCTV footage. And if he could see it, that meant Vella did too.

"What would you like to accomplish here?" Vella asked.

It was a bizarre question, almost better suited for a job interview or a self-help seminar.

Vella moved back to his corner of the room, leaned back against the wall, and waited. He was in no hurry.

Harvath glanced back at the graphic with Sergun's vitals. His heart rate had increased.

Sergun eventually summoned the will to speak. "What do you want?" he asked.

Vella smiled. "I want you to answer for your sins."

"I have no sins."

The interrogator's smile never wavered. "We all have sins, Viktor. We all must atone. I'm here to help you."

"You are *not* here to help me," the Russian insisted. He was growing more agitated. His voice cracked as his vitals climbed. "Let me go. I want to leave."

"Everyone wants to leave."

"Let me go!"

Harvath watched the monitor as the man became more distraught. He could see the whites of his eyes, wide with fear. The pheromone was working.

Vella moved off the wall and reached for a spare chair. Drawing it gently over, he sat down next to the prisoner. "I understand that in Russia, you read Dante. Do you recall *The Inferno*?"

Sergun began to tremble.

"Who was in the ninth circle, Viktor?"

"The devil," he whispered. *"Lucifer."*

"That's right. You're with the devil now. And no one knows you're here. No one is coming to save you," said Vella. "You can scream. You can cry out. But only I will hear you."

Removing a pair of pliers, he then ordered, "Spread your fingers."

The stainless steel table Sergun was shackled to was like a medieval rack. The track down the center was mechanical.

When the Russian refused to comply, Vella depressed a button that pulled his wrists forward while his ankles remained chained to the floor.

He began screaming almost immediately.

•   •   •

Twenty minutes later, the Russian had been broken. Vella looked up at the interrogation room's camera in a subtle acknowledgment of Harvath.

Then, returning his gaze to Sergun, he said, "Tell me about the GRU, Viktor. Let me help you leave. Let me help you go home."

CHAPTER 46

Harvath used the Solarium's SCIF, a small secured room for transmitting top-secret information, to provide a full report to Washington. He had been in there for hours.

No one wanted to believe it. Harvath didn't want to believe it. But once the shock of Sergun's revelations began to wear off, they started discussing what their response should be.

There were many serious decisions to be made. Not the least of which was whether the United States should declare war on Russia.

The President wanted to confer privately with his advisers. It was decided that everyone would reconvene in an hour.

Stepping out of the SCIF, Harvath saw Vella and flagged him over.

"How'd it go?" the interrogator asked.

Harvath needed a case of water and a fistful of aspirin. Pinching the bridge of his nose to relieve his headache, he replied, "Not well."

Vella had extracted a stunning confession from Sergun. Russia not only had a mole deep inside American intelligence, but had also orchestrated the attack on the SAD team in Anbar, the assassination of the Secretary of Defense, and the suicide bombing at the White House.

All of the attacks had been designed to draw America into an all-out ground war with ISIS. Russia had been playing a media relations game— pretending not to be fully engaged in Syria, when the truth was they absolutely were. They needed ISIS defeated, but they couldn't do it on their own.

There were two major factors at stake for Russia. One foreign. One domestic.

Russia's only deep, warm-water port was located in the Syrian coastal city of Tartus. From this Mediterranean facility, Russia could project its naval power anywhere in the world.

All of its other main ports were either ice-locked for large portions of the year, or landlocked, which required Russian naval vessels to pass through straits controlled by other countries.

If ISIS took over Syria, there was no telling what would happen to the treaty allowing the Russian naval facility at Tartus and their air base north of there. It was in Russia's best interest that the status quo be maintained.

But to do that, Russia had to focus most of its energy on defeating the CIA-backed rebels trying to topple the current government. It couldn't afford to open up a second front against ISIS. The United States, though, could.

All America needed was a strong enough push. If it were repeatedly and dramatically humiliated, it would have no other choice but to act.

Even America's war-weary citizens would eventually call for something to be done. Russia was certain of it.

The attack on the White House was the icing on the cake. It would make for a dramatic ISIS propaganda video, but its real mission was to be an affront to America's patriotic sense of honor—a provocation that could absolutely not be ignored.

Russia's other reason for wanting ISIS destroyed was domestic. The greatest population of non-Arabs traveling to Iraq and Syria to fight for ISIS were Russian speakers.

They came in the thousands from Russian satellites like Chechnya and Ingushetia, Dagestan, and Abkhazia.

Fighting with ISIS, they gained extensive, hard-core combat experience. They learned how to build IEDs, as well as nuclear, biological, and chemical bombs.

Eventually, many would return home to their unstable regions. They would train others, foment unrest, and launch revolutions. And as soon as one revolution started, others would follow. Russia would be overwhelmed, unable to respond. It was a nightmare scenario. One for which they could see only a single exit—getting the United States involved.

It was stupid, outrageous, dangerous, deadly, and unquestionably a direct act of war. Nobody during Harvath's secure teleconference inside the SCIF had debated that. What they had debated was the appropriate response.

As far as Harvath was concerned, the only appropriate response was to hit the Russians so hard that they never attempted anything like it ever again. But that's what America thought it had done a decade ago, when small, man-portable nukes had been discovered secreted across the United States. The message, though, didn't appear to have gotten through. America was going to have to come up with something bigger.

The problem at the moment was figuring out how far up the chain the plot went. Was it limited to just the GRU? Or had it been sanctioned at the very top, from inside the Kremlin?

There was only one way Harvath could see for them to figure that out. And he wanted to be the one to do it. But before he did, he wanted to know how Vella had been able to break Sergun so quickly and so thoroughly.

"Your sense of smell is able to go straight to the part of the brain that stores memories," Vella explained. "It can also impact your mood and performance and does so without asking your conscious mind for permission.

"Essentially what we've created is a chemical Trojan horse. It gets us into the brain, specifically to the amygdala, where fear memories are stored and potential threats are determined.

"It short-circuits the 'fight' portion of the fight-or-flight mechanism. All the patient cares about is surviving. They become highly cooperative, malleable."

"Why were you talking about Dante?" Harvath asked.

"When I interrogated Malevsky, he mentioned that Sergun liked to brag about how smart he was—the kinds of books he read. He spoke a lot about Dante, so I used that."

"Used it how?"

Vella knew Harvath was highly intelligent. He also knew that science could be boring and so used the simplest analogy he could think of. "Fear is like an icepick," he said. "The deeper I can get it, the more acute the sensation. If I can work with images that are *already* in the subject's mind, it helps speed things up. That's why I try to gather as much background as possible."

"Would it work on a stranger?"

"I suppose," Vella said. "But it's probably going to take longer."

Harvath thanked him and headed for the stairwell. He wanted to get some fresh air before he had to return to the SCIF.

A plan was beginning to take shape in his mind and he hoped taking a short walk around the property might help the rest of the pieces fall into place.

CHAPTER 47

President Porter waited until everyone else had left the Situation Room and then had Reed Carlton escorted down from upstairs. CIA Director McGee and Deputy Director Ryan were the only people who had been asked to remain behind.

When they were all seated at the conference table, the President asked, "So what does everyone think?"

Carlton spoke first. "I think it's doable. Harvath has operated multiple times in Syria."

"While augmented by Peshmerga fighters," Porter clarified.

"Yes, sir. That's correct."

"So he wasn't one hundred percent on his own."

"No, sir."

"The Agency has a pretty reliable network of locals," McGee offered. "We can plug him in."

The President looked at him. "What does *pretty reliable* mean?"

"For Syria it means the best you're going to get."

"Meaning the best that money can buy."

The CIA Director nodded.

"What about inserting a team with him?"

"One white guy," Ryan replied, "one set of problems. Many white guys? Many problems."

"But it could be done."

"Anything is possible. Yes, sir."

Porter looked back at Carlton. "Obviously, I have concerns and would feel better knowing someone had his back. Ultimately, though, this is your call. He's your man."

Carlton appreciated the President's candor. "Thank you, Mr. President. It's undoubtedly a trade-off, but I think the smaller the footprint, the better. I know he'd tell you that too."

Porter gave one last push. "This won't be like Berlin. We're talking about one of the GRU's top people. Harvath won't have any reliable backup in Damascus."

"Correct. This won't be like Berlin. But we're going to have something we didn't have there."

"What's that?"

"Bait."

The President leaned back in his chair as he weighed his options. It was not an easy task. There was no instruction manual that came with this job. No index that directed you to page *y* when faced with crisis *x*.

When trouble came, it seemed to come pounding down all at once, like a hailstorm, or, more aptly—like a tidal wave.

He had kept his circle to just the people with him in the room right now. He couldn't trust anyone else. Not with something this sensitive, and not while the leak was still unidentified.

Which made the President ask McGee, "How are you going to plug Harvath into the Agency's network in Syria without any of this getting leaked?"

It was a fair question and one that the CIA Director had already anticipated. "Eyewash," he replied.

"Eyewash?"

"We'll put out a memo into a few of our internal channels that says we have reason to believe that multiple CIA intelligence sources in Syria have been compromised. Until further notice, reporting from any Syrian sources is to be considered suspect.

"If the Russians do get ahold of the information, it'll leave them with the impression that we're in disarray when it comes to Syria. It'll also create some smoke for Harvath. If it gets reported that he's in Syria, the report will automatically be suspect.

"And just to keep them guessing, we'll distribute a second memo to an even tighter circle higher up the food chain. That memo will put everyone on notice that we're sending in specialists to assess all of Syrian sources and that it's to be kept absolutely quiet."

"Won't your people resent being lied to like that?" Porter asked.

"Not as much as I'll resent having to do it. But in the intelligence game, sometimes it has to be done."

Carlton and Ryan both nodded in agreement.

"And what about the leak itself?"

"We're still working it from our end. But at this point, Harvath may end up being our best chance to uncover it."

"Meaning he gets a name," the President replied.

"A name, an email address, a cell phone number. I'd be content just to know what kind of shampoo the guy uses. At least that would be a start. Because right now, we really don't have anything."

Porter didn't like hearing it, but that was the situation. The people he was looking at were not paid to lie to him. "And what about the second half of Harvath's proposed operation?"

"Obviously, that will depend on how successful he is in Damascus," Carlton replied.

Ryan then added, "Suffice to say that if Damascus goes sideways, we're not going to be left with any choice."

The President let that sink in for a moment. A silence fell over the room. Finally, he said, "Then we'd better do everything we can and hope like hell that he's successful."

CHAPTER 48

Getting Harvath into Syria was the first challenge McGee and Ryan had to tackle. There was a secret airstrip the Pentagon had been using in the north of the country, but it was hundreds of kilometers away from Damascus.

They contemplated flying him into Iraq and moving him across the desert, but that was fraught with problems, including potential contact with ISIS.

The best bet was to land him in Amman, Jordan. From there, it was only two hundred kilometers north to Damascus. All they had to do was get him across the Syrian border.

A white Embraer Legacy 600 business jet with crimson stripes delivered Harvath from Malta to Amman in less than three hours. Upon his arrival, a covert CIA operative named Williams met him at the airport.

Williams was a NOC, operating in Jordan without any diplomatic cover. McGee had known him for decades and told Harvath he could trust him.

Williams drove Harvath to a small apartment that the CIA kept off the books. After setting up a white backdrop, he took Harvath's picture in front of it, and then another in profile looking out the window. He told him to help himself to whatever he found in the kitchen. He'd be back in the morning with a new passport and to drive Harvath to the border.

The tiny apartment was stuffy and probably hadn't been used in a while. Harvath opened a couple of windows and walked into the compact kitchen.

Searching through the cabinets, he found a bottle of Bulleit bourbon. How Williams had laid his hands on it in a place like Amman was beyond him. But that's what made a NOC a NOC. They were highly resourceful.

Pouring himself a drink, he grabbed a few pieces of pita bread and a container of hummus and walked back into the living room.

The sounds of motorbikes, car horns, and radios ebbed and flowed through the open windows like a tide. The music was distinctly Arab.

Turning out the lights, he pulled up a chair and took it all in as he ate.

He referred to these moments as "precompression." It was another term for getting his head in the game—of focusing in on where he was and what he needed to do. It was the opposite of "decompression," which happened after an assignment was complete and he tried to put everything out of his mind and behind him.

Getting up only to fix another drink, he sat at the window for over an hour taking it all in, especially the conversations in Arabic as locals came and went along the sidewalk below.

He was in a totally different world now. Different people, different motivations, different rules. No matter how many times he had been sent to the Middle East, it always felt alien to him. There was no other way to describe it. And there was no other place in the world like it.

After taking a shower, he lay down on the bed. An old ceiling fan turned slowly overhead, barely moving the air.

He had hoped the bourbon would help him sleep, but his mind drifted to Lara.

"Married?" she had asked him when they first met. "Any kids?"

"No," he had replied.

"Divorced?"

"No."

"I knew it," she had said. "The haircut and the suit were a dead giveaway."

"Of what?" His hair was short and he was wearing an expensive Brooks Brothers suit.

"Don't be so defensive. Boston's a progressive city. We've got gay cops on the force."

He had laughed. "I'm not gay."

"So what's your problem, then?" she had asked. "Never grew up? Peter Pan syndrome?"

"Just never met the right girl."

"You shouldn't be looking for a girl. You should be looking for a *woman*."

She was, of course, completely right. Then she had added, "If you've come this far in life without finding the right person, the problem isn't them, it's you."

Three sentences. That's all they were. But they had completely changed his life.

She reminded him that a "perfect ten" doesn't exist, which at the time seemed almost funny coming from such an attractive woman. But he grew to understand what she meant. "If you're hitting on five out of six cylinders with someone who truly cares about you," she said, "you should run all the way to the bank with it."

She was right. She was also an amazing woman. He knew he'd never meet someone like her again.

And with that, he finally knew what he was going to do once this assignment was over.

• • •

Williams showed up at dawn with two cups of Starbucks coffee and a large shopping bag.

"Sorry," he said, handing one of the cups to him. "The knock-off Dunkin' Donuts shop wasn't open yet."

Harvath smiled and took the lid off his cup. He hadn't been to Amman in a while. "Which one has better coffee?"

"I don't like that they're ripping off an American brand, but they have damn good coffee. Cheaper too. Doughnuts aren't bad," said Williams.

"Is that what's in your shopping bag?"

The NOC grinned. "Fancy guy like you gets a muffin," he replied, reaching into the bag and tossing one to him.

"Thanks," Harvath said. "Anything else?"

Williams peered into his shopping bag like an office party Santa Claus.

"I don't know. Lemme look. Did you order a new set of Louis Vuitton luggage?"

"Not really my style."

"I didn't think so," the CIA man replied as he removed a hard-sided Pelican briefcase and set it on the table. "There you go. Special delivery."

Opening the lid, Harvath recognized the logo inside immediately. Palafox Solutions Group was a company out of Gulf Breeze, Florida.

It was run by a SEAL who had retired as a master chief, gone into the private sector, and now had all sorts of interesting contracts. One of them was to build "capability kits" for the Central Intelligence Agency.

Capability kits were loaded with all the things an intelligence or counterterrorism operative might need, but couldn't enter a foreign country with.

Sometimes all Harvath needed was a weapon; sometimes he needed more. There was no one-size-fits-all solution.

The first thing Harvath removed was a sand-colored, modified Palafox 9mm SIG Sauer P226 pistol. It had bright green TRUGLO Tritium/Fiber-Optic Day/Night sights that allowed for fast target acquisition regardless of light conditions. Portions of the slide had been milled away to lessen the weapon's weight. It also helped to reduce muzzle flip and better assist recoil management.

Accompanying the pistol was a Sticky-brand inside-the-waistband holster, spare magazines, and several boxes of TNQ frangible 9mm ammunition.

There was also a jet-black, ultra-compact, single-shot Taser X26P, a flashlight, a compass, and a small trauma kit. It was a first-class set-up.

The last item Harvath removed was a stunning, fixed-blade knife by Daniel Winkler called the Spike. The team at Palafox obviously knew what it was doing because the knife came in a leather sheath. Leather not only stropped the blade each time it was drawn, it was whisper quiet. Kydex looked cool, but it made a lot of noise.

Next, Williams handed over Harvath's passport and an envelope full of pocket litter—receipts, a canceled boarding pass, a handful of business cards that looked like they had been in someone's wallet for a while—that would back up his new identity.

He looked at the passport and memorized the information. He was a Canadian, from Ottawa. Williams handed him a series of articles, authored under his assumed name, dealing with conflict zones and humanitarian crises.

They had been backdated to a faux blog the CIA sat on a commercial server in Canada. The photo Williams had taken the night before of him at the window served as his profile photo.

He then handed Harvath a laminated international press credential on an Associated Press lanyard. It was the best the Agency could do in such a short amount of time.

Harvath looked it over, knowing it didn't have to be perfect. All it had to do was get him across the border.

Once he was ready, he followed Williams downstairs to his car.

CHAPTER 49

T
he Nasib Border Crossing marked the international border between Jordan and Syria. It sat right on the Amman–Damascus highway and had long been known as one of the busiest crossings for either country. But while the Jordanians had been able to keep their side under control, the Syrians hadn't been as successful.

The Syrian side of the checkpoint had changed hands so many times throughout the civil war, there was no telling which interest might be in charge once you rolled up on it, or if it would "technically" even be open.

But in Jordan, as in Syria, and everywhere else, the right amount of money opened all doors.

Williams had arranged for Harvath to ride up to Damascus with a Syrian truck driver. The agency had used him multiple times in the past.

He's "reliable." That was the best that Williams could say about him. "Don't expect him to stick his neck out."

Harvath didn't expect anything more than a ride.

Williams pulled into a small roadside gas station and café a few kilometers from the border. He had one more thing to give Harvath.

Reaching behind his seat, he retrieved a gray nylon camera bag and handed it to him. "The camera is to further backstop your cover, but whatever pictures you can get, the Agency would be glad to have."

"Got it," Harvath replied.

"There are two envelopes in the outer compartment. All the border guards know the going rate for safe passage. One envelope is for the Jordanian side, the other is for the Syrian."

"And the rest of the money?"

"Inside the shoulder strap," said Williams.

Harvath felt along the padding. They had done a good job layering the bills between the thin pieces of foam.

"You'll keep that in the cab of the truck," he continued. "Along with your backpack. The gun and everything else, though, is going in a hidden compartment in back."

Harvath had figured as much. That said, he had already removed the knife and was going to keep it with him. If they caught him with it, then they caught him with it. Culturally, a knife for the Jordanians or the Syrians was not that big a deal. A gun or a Taser, on the other hand, *was* a big deal.

"If you want to hit the head," Williams said as he put his car in park and turned off the ignition, "now would be a good time."

He nodded and followed him inside. As Williams went to locate his contact, Harvath used the restroom.

Removing the camera from the bag, he checked to make sure the batteries were charged and a memory card was installed.

Satisfied that everything was in order, he left the men's room, bought a bottle of water at the counter, and walked back outside to the parking lot.

Williams was chatting with a heavyset Syrian in a green, sweat-stained T-shirt, gray polyester trousers, and tan sandals. When he saw Harvath, he waved him over. "Yusuf, this is Russ. Russ, this is Yusuf."

The men shook hands and Williams spent several more moments speaking with Yusuf in Arabic.

When he was done, Williams looked at Harvath and said, "Best of luck on your article. Don't forget to take lots of pictures."

"I won't. What about the rest of my gear?"

"Already taken care of," Williams replied. Then, pulling Harvath in for a hug, he quietly said, "False compartment above last set of wheels. Passenger side."

"Got it," said Harvath as Williams backed away and waved him toward the cab.

"Ready?" Yusuf asked.

He had a mouthful of yellow teeth and wide eyes that showed the whites all the way around. He swept them back and forth, constantly assessing his surroundings.

"Ready," Harvath responded.

They climbed into the cab of the truck. It was thick with the odor of cigarettes. The ashtray was crammed with butts. Several strings of beads hung from the rearview mirror.

Harvath's backpack had already been placed behind his seat. He laid the gray camera bag at his feet.

Yusuf started his vehicle and pulled out of the parking lot. Lighting a cigarette, he pointed out the window at the sky. "Good day for making a drive."

Harvath nodded. "Yes. Good day. Where did you learn English?"

"University," the man replied. "Aleppo."

"What did you study?"

With the cigarette hanging from between his lips, Yusuf changed lanes and said, "Transportation engineering. Now I drive truck."

"Do you have a family?"

He nodded. "It is *why* I drive this truck."

"Someday, the fighting will stop."

"*Insha'Allah.*"

"*Insha'Allah,*" Harvath repeated.

"*Hal tatakallamu alloghah alarabiah?*" *Do you speak Arabic?*

"*Qualeelan.*" *Only a little.*

Yusuf smiled and took a drag on his cigarette. "Why you want to go Syria?"

Harvath fished out his press credential from beneath his shirt and held it up. "Journalist."

They both knew that wasn't true. "*Why* Syria?" he repeated.

"I'm looking for some people."

"Bad people?"

Harvath nodded.

"Syria has many of those," Yusuf replied, removing the cigarette from his mouth and picking a piece of stray tobacco from his tongue.

"What about you, Yusuf? Are you a bad man or a good man?

He thought about it for a moment and then, flashing his yellow smile, said, "It depends on the day."

Harvath liked him and smiled back. "How big is your family?"

Yusuf's smile faded as he saw the Jordanian checkpoint up ahead. "We talk after we cross," he said.

Harvath nodded.

"You have the money?"

Harvath nodded again.

"Give to me."

Unzipping the side compartment of his camera bag, he removed the first envelope and handed it to him.

"No talk," Yusuf cautioned. "No Arabic. No *Insha'Allah*."

Harvath understood. Better for him to play dumb. Let Yusuf do all the talking. This is what he was paid to do.

Arriving at the checkpoint, they were surrounded by a team of four very serious-looking Jordanian soldiers. Yusuf cranked his yellow smile up to full wattage.

They spoke for only a few moments. Then Yusuf discreetly passed the envelope out the window.

After looking inside the envelope, the lead soldier tucked it inside his tunic, smiled, and waved them through.

Yusuf put the truck in gear and accelerated forward.

As they rolled past the last of the troops and military barricades, Harvath looked in his side mirror. "That was easy," he remarked.

Yusuf crushed his cigarette out in the ashtray and quickly lit another one. "Jordan is always easy," he said. "Now comes the hard part. Now comes Syria."

CHAPTER 50

Wide, green fields interspersed with razor wire and long walls of concrete block created a no-man's-land separating Jordan from Syria. Through the windshield, Harvath could see their next checkpoint up ahead.

"Money, please," Yusuf said, extending his hand.

Harvath removed the final envelope and handed it to him.

"Thank you. No talking. Okay?"

Harvath nodded as they neared the checkpoint and Yusuf began to slow down.

Things looked a lot different here than they had on the Jordanian side. Every single structure bore battle scars. All the buildings were pockmarked with bullet holes. Many had been charred by fire or explosions. They were unquestionably entering a war zone.

Eight armed men swarmed the truck as they rolled to a stop under a large concrete awning. Yusuf cranked the smile back up.

The men were unshaven, their fatigues dirty and wrinkled. They clutched their Kalashnikovs in their hands, fingers on the triggers. They were sloppy, undisciplined. It was a powder keg just waiting for a spark. A very bad feeling began to grow in Harvath's gut.

His Arabic was good, but not good enough to keep up with the rapid-fire dialogue being shot back and forth. Things were definitely not going as well as they had on the other side.

Finally, Yusuf nodded and put his truck in gear. Harvath had not seen any money change hands. "What's going on?" he asked.

"They want me to pull ahead so they can search the truck."

Damn it, thought Harvath. He had known this was a possibility, but he had hoped it wouldn't happen.

As they pulled over to the side, men surrounded the truck. Yusuf was told to shut the engine down and get out. Harvath's door was yanked open and he was ordered out too.

A man with horrible breath stood inches away from Harvath demanding his passport. Harvath held up the laminated press credential hanging around his neck.

The man slapped it away and repeated in heavily accented English, "Pazport. Pazport."

Slowly, Harvath removed his Canadian passport.

The man snatched it from him and took a step back. He looked back and forth from Harvath to the picture several times. One of his buddies walked over and joined him.

The man seemed to be preoccupied with something. He directed his colleague's attention to the photo and then over at Harvath. He then tugged on his own hair.

Fuck, Harvath thought. *Not good.* The guy didn't like how recent his photo was.

"Journalist" Harvath stated, trying to take control of the situation. "Photo?" he asked, pantomiming the use of a camera. Turning, he reached back toward the truck for his camera bag.

The men did not like his sudden move. "Oh! Oh! Oh! Oh! Oh!" they began yelling in unison, bringing their weapons to bear on him.

Harvath raised his hands, palms out. "No photo? That's cool. No problem. Journalist," he repeated, pointing at himself and then the laminated card around his neck. "Journalist."

Whoever these men were, they were very badly trained. Reaching for his camera bag had been a smart move. It had drawn them in closer.

Two of them were so close that he could have disarmed either and shot the rest before any of them had any idea what was happening.

Looking to his left, he saw that Yusuf had isolated a commander. They were off to the side discussing something. *Probably money.*

Everyone in the Middle East assumed Westerners were rich. And, by their standards, most were, which made them a prime target for extortion and kidnapping.

If for some reason the cash in the second envelope turned out not to be enough, Harvath had extra in the camera bag shoulder strap. But that was supposed to see him through the rest of his operation. If he showed up in Damascus without any cash, he was going to run into serious trouble.

Harvath watched their body language. Yusuf's conversation with the commander didn't appear to be going well.

As the commander turned and began to walk away, Yusuf reached out and put his hand on the man's arm. No sooner had he done so than the commander spun and struck him.

The blow hit so hard that it knocked him out. Yusuf fell to the ground and his head slammed against the pavement.

Harvath moved to help him, but two of the men grabbed him by his arms and held him in place.

The situation had just gone from bad to worse. Then the commander came over to deal with him.

Harvath could tell that he was the alpha of this pack of wolves. He had cold, dark eyes. His brown, leathery face was crisscrossed with so many scars it looked like a road map. He sported a thick mustache so black that it had to have been dyed.

The armed man holding Harvath's Canadian passport handed it over to the commander. He commented in Arabic about Harvath's appearance in the photo.

The commander studied both him and his passport. He then scrutinized his press credential.

While he was doing so, Harvath's mind was working overtime. He had kept the Winkler knife with him. It was tucked in his waistband, at the small of his back.

The men holding him had no clue what they were doing. He could easily break their hold. At that point, he could grab the commander, put the knife up against his throat, and it would be an entirely new ball game. But the chances of an overzealous, undisciplined recruit deciding he might try to take a shot anyway was pretty high.

What Harvath wouldn't have given at that moment for a sniper covering him, over on the Jordanian side.

The commander looked up from the passport and locked eyes with Harvath. It was obvious that there was something about him he didn't like. The feeling was definitely mutual.

Lowering his eyes, Harvath glanced over at Yusuf. He was still flat on the ground, out cold. He wanted to knock this commander's block off.

When Harvath returned his gaze, the man held it for several seconds and then, without breaking eye contact, ordered his men in Arabic to open the trailer.

They all dispersed, except for the two holding on to Harvath.

Throwing the trailer doors open wide, several of the men climbed inside. When one of the men popped his head out to report what they had found, the commander yelled for them to empty it out.

Instead of traveling back with an empty truck, Yusuf had bought goods with his own funds. He had hoped to sell them in Damascus for a profit. There were cases of water, bags of flour and rice, batteries, toilet paper, soap, and shampoo—luxuries that citizens in the war-torn country would have paid handsomely for. Now he was getting cleaned out.

Yusuf had expected to lose some of the goods on the way back. It was the cost of doing business. Everyone took a cut. He hadn't, though, expected to lose everything.

As the men unloaded the trailer, Harvath's blood pressure continued to rise. Poking out of the commander's tunic was the corner of the white envelope Yusuf had handed him. The man had accepted it, but he still wanted more. *The greedy son of a bitch.*

Harvath was pissed. He wanted to reach out and snap the commander's neck. He hated men like this. Men who preyed upon the weak.

There was nothing, though, that Harvath could do about it. He had to suck it up and take it—*all* of it.

With the trailer emptied out, the commander told his men to search the cab. The vultures weren't done yet.

But just as the men were climbing into the vehicle, two new trucks approached from the other direction.

The men paused and looked at their commander. He glanced at the incoming trucks. They were rolling heavy, which meant they had a buyer on the Jordanian side. They'd be carrying cash in order to be allowed to pass. It was shaping up to be a good day.

He handed Harvath his passport back, but held on to it for a fraction of a second longer than he should have as he fixed him with his icy stare.

Finally, he released the document and nodded for his men to turn Harvath loose. They turned and headed to the other side of the checkpoint to fleece their next victims.

Replacing the passport in his pocket, Harvath moved quickly to Yusuf, who had slowly regained consciousness.

"Are you okay?" he asked, helping him to his feet.

The Syrian nodded, but he was unsteady and needed to lean against him.

Harvath helped him back to the cab and loaded him into the passenger seat.

"What are you doing?" he asked.

"Don't worry. You need to rest."

"Can you drive?"

"*Insha'Allah,*" Harvath replied, closing his door.

CHAPTER 51

I t was a rugged, desolate landscape. The brown, rocky soil was punctuated by thin, sickly trees. The only other life was an occasional goat
tied up outside a crumbling, mud brick dwelling. The pitted, four-
lane highway they were on had seen better days.

When Harvath felt he had put enough distance between them and the
checkpoint, he pulled the truck over to the side of the road.

"What are you doing?" Yusuf asked.

"I want to check you over. Make sure you're okay."

"I am okay."

"All the same—"

"No," the Syrian insisted, opening his door and climbing down.

Harvath opened his door and followed.

Yusuf walked to the back of the trailer and opened the doors. He knew
they had taken it all, but he needed to see for himself.

He stood there for a long time, staring at the emptiness. A heavy black
bruise had begun to grow beneath his right eye. Harvath stood next to
him, but didn't speak.

"I have nothing now," he uttered.

"You'll make the money back."

The man shook his head. "This was my last chance."

"What do you mean your *last chance*?"

"I have no more money. I used everything we had to buy products in
Jordan. Now those are gone."

"You'll figure something out."

"I don't think so," Yusuf replied. "I owe too many people too much money."

Removing a package of cigarettes, he lit another and looked out across the fields. "Syria," he said, shaking his head.

Harvath felt terrible for the guy, but there wasn't anything he could do. He let him have a couple more moments of quiet and then helped him close up the trailer.

"I think I will drive," Yusuf said.

"You sure you're okay?" Harvath asked.

He attempted a smile. *"Insha'Allah."*

Before they got back in the cab, Harvath had him open up the hidden compartment where his pistol and other items had been hidden.

Once he had transferred everything to his backpack, they climbed back in and got back on the road.

Yusuf didn't feel much like talking. Harvath didn't blame him. He was content to ride in silence.

The silence didn't last long. Ten minutes later, Yusuf changed his mind. "Before the border, you asked about my family."

Harvath, who had been looking out the window, turned and faced him.

"I have a wife," said Yusuf. "One son and two daughters."

Flipping his visor down, he removed a photo from inside the fabric and handed it to him

Harvath looked at Yusuf's family. They were on the chunky side, just like him, and had big, bright smiles. It was taken somewhere near the ocean. They looked happy.

"They're beautiful," Harvath said. "How old are your children?"

"The boy is nine and the girls are eleven and thirteen."

Harvath handed the photo back to him. "I'm sure you are very proud of them."

Yusuf looked down at the photo and smiled for a moment. But as soon as his smile appeared, it disappeared. He was obviously still very upset about having been robbed.

"You'll figure something out," Harvath assured him. "Don't give up."

He shook his head. "You don't understand."

"*Understand* what?"

"Never mind. Tell me about Ottawa."

Harvath laughed good-naturedly. "It's the capital of Canada. Now let's talk about your situation."

Yusuf shook another cigarette free from his pack, placed it in his mouth and reached for his lighter. "The money I lost today. I really needed it."

"That's the great thing about money, you can always find a way to make more."

The Syrian took a deep drag on his cigarette, holding the smoke in his lungs for a long time before exhaling it toward his partially lowered window. "I have lung cancer."

Harvath felt horrible for the guy. Life in Syria was tough enough without cancer. "I'm sorry to hear that, Yusuf. What's your prognosis?"

"Without treatment, it's anybody's guess. Six months maybe."

"That's what the money was for?"

He nodded and took another deep drag.

"You know, maybe you want to lay off the cigarettes."

Yusuf expelled another cloud of smoke through the window. "At this point, what difference does it make?"

The man was probably right, but still. "Tell me about your wife. What does she do?"

His face momentarily lifted into a smile. "She used to have a dress shop."

"And now?"

"The dress shop is gone. Like everything else in Aleppo. I moved my family to Damascus to find work. My wife is still looking."

Harvath wasn't a soft touch, but this guy was breaking his heart. Though he made his living pulling a trigger, he hated war. He absolutely hated it.

For the last twenty minutes of their trip, Yusuf turned the conversation back to Ottawa. Harvath only knew a little about the city, so the rest he simply made up. He didn't like lying to the guy, but Yusuf wouldn't know.

As they got closer to Damascus, everything became greener and more prosperous. This was, without a doubt, the seat of Syria's power. Or, more appropriately, the seat of non-ISIS power.

Passing a rather nice new building that looked like a school of some sort, Yusuf derisively snorted, "Iranians."

"They own that school?"

"Madrassa," Yusuf corrected him. "They have built them all over Damascus."

"What for?" said Harvath. "You have that many Iranians?"

Yusuf shook his head as he slowed for a stoplight. "The Iranians came to help prop up the regime. They want to convert everyone to Shia Islam. They set up madrassas and mosques, buy real estate, and import other Shia to live here. I think that's why the Syrian government invited the Russians in. They don't care about religion. They only care about power."

The man had no idea how right he was.

As they rolled into the city, the landscaping grew even more dramatic. Full, healthy trees were everywhere. Grass lined the medians. Palm trees lined the sidewalks. Flowers spilled from planters.

There were large apartment buildings, cafés, boutiques, and taxicabs. There were cars everywhere, as well as people walking and riding bikes.

It reminded Harvath a bit of Washington, D.C. No matter how bad things were in the rest of the country, it managed to carry on as if nothing was wrong. It was astounding.

He knew, though, that rebel-controlled neighborhoods outside the city, like Douma in the northeast, looked completely different. They were frequently targeted for shelling by the regime and resembled parts of Berlin after World War II.

"You didn't expect this," said Yusuf as he watched Harvath taking it all in.

"No."

"Have you been to Damascus before?"

He shook his head. "I have been to other parts of Syria, but not Damascus."

"Looking for bad people?"

"Yes," said Harvath.

Yusuf made another turn. "We're getting close. Where do you want me to drop you?"

Williamson had given Harvath a prepaid Syrian cell phone. Powering it up, he texted the number he had been given.

"Stop up there," Harvath said, indicating an area big enough to accommodate the truck.

While Harvath waited for a response, Yusuf pulled off the street and parked.

A few seconds later, Harvath's phone chirped. After reading the text, he asked Yusuf, "Where are we?"

The Syrian told him and Harvath typed a reply into his phone.

"Do you have another trip planned yet?" Harvath asked.

"Why? Will you need another ride?"

"Maybe. Do you have access to any other kinds of vehicles?"

"Yes," said Yusuf. "But this is supposed to be my last journey for a while."

"Because of your treatment."

The man nodded.

"How can I reach you if I need to?"

Yusuf gave him his cell phone number.

"Thank you," Harvath replied, as he reached behind his seat and grabbed his backpack.

"Are you sure you want to get out here? It's not a very good neighborhood."

Harvath smiled at him. "I'll be okay. I know what I'm doing. I'm a journalist."

The Syrian laughed.

"You're a good man," Harvath said, extending his hand.

"It depends on the day," Yusuf replied, extending his.

Harvath gathered up his backpack and camera bag. Opening his door, he climbed down.

He slung his pack, reached up for the door, and smiled once more at Yusuf. "Keep your phone turned on," he said.

Then, shutting the door, he turned and disappeared into the crowded neighborhood.

CHAPTER 52

S enator Wells stepped back into the *Meet the Press* greenroom from Hair and Makeup and helped himself to a Diet Coke. He knew most of the other guests and chatted with them briefly about what they would all be speaking on.

Last week, the Sunday shows had been consumed with the attack on American personnel in Anbar and the horrific video depicting the rape of female Embassy staffers. This week it was all about the assassination of Secretary of Defense Devon and the suicide bombing at the White House.

Out of the corner of his eye, Wells noticed his Chief of Staff engaged in a private conversation with one of the show's new producers. He had transferred in from *NBC News* in New York. Rebecca was wasting no time in getting to know him. Wells could feel the heat between the two of them all the way across the room. The woman was a force of nature and could have any man eating out of the palm of her hand within seconds.

A young production assistant interrupted his thoughts. She came in and gave the five-minute warning, and then turned up the sound on the monitors so that everyone could follow along with the program.

"You look terrific," Rebecca said, as the producer left and she rejoined the Senator. "Very presidential."

"Make a new friend?"

"He's married, so we'll see," she said with a coy smile.

Wells put his hands up. "I don't want to know."

"Sure you don't," she whispered as she leaned in and brushed some lint off his suit.

Even in a room full of people she was incorrigible. "They're going to lead with you. You'll be first up in the A block.

"They want to talk obviously about Secretary Devon and what happened at the White House. They also want to discuss what happened in Anbar and the story in the *Washington Post* this morning about President Porter possibly running his own black ops out of the Oval Office."

Lilliana Grace had tipped him late last night that the story was going to run today. Under the headline "America Under Attack," the *Post* was doing in-depth stories on the assassination of Devon and the suicide bomber at the White House.

There was a follow-up on the Anbar attack and tying it all together was Grace's story about the President's alleged program.

The reporter had spent the last couple of days methodically tracking down every lead she could. She spoke to members of the Gang of Eight, the extra-tight circle of Congress people and intel committee members the President was required to brief. All confirmed that they had been briefed on Anbar.

Off the record, Grace was able to confirm enough of what Wells had told her to pull together quite an impactful story.

In quick succession, she explained the importance of the National Security Act of 1947, the Hughes-Ryan Amendment of 1974, the Intelligence Oversight Act of 1980, and the Intelligence Authorization Act of 1991 and their impact on the interlocking webs of Congress, the Oval Office, and the intelligence community.

Instead of being dry policy-speak or legalese, she made it sexy and intriguing—like something out of a dramatic, high-stakes spy movie. She was a gifted reporter. This was going to be a great interview.

"You've been on with Alan Gottlieb plenty of times," Rebecca reminded him. "He's a great host, but he's not your friend. Okay?"

"I've been doing this since before you were born. I know how to handle the press."

Rebecca was about to respond when a middle-aged man wearing a headset and a *Star Wars* T-shirt entered the greenroom. "Senator Wells?" he asked.

"Right here," Rebecca replied, waving him over.

"Hello, Senator. I'm Abe, from Audio. Just going to get you mic'd up here if I can."

"Sure thing, Abe from Audio. Whatever you need," Wells answered.

As soon as the technician had the microphone attached to the Senator's lapel and the transmitter clipped to his waistband, he asked him to count to ten.

Wells did as instructed and Abe flashed him the thumbs-up.

"Any IFB?" the Senator asked, pointing to his ear.

Abe double-checked with the control room over his headset. "No, sir. They're not running any packages you need to listen to. You'll be speaking directly to Alan on the set. Are you ready?"

"I'm ready."

"Break a leg," Rebecca said as Abe led the Senator out of the greenroom and down the hall to the studio.

Out on the brightly lit set, Alan Gottlieb—a charming veteran journalist with a hundred-dollar haircut and a fifteen-hundred-dollar suit—was running through his opening monologue.

Abe from audio showed the Senator to his seat. A PA brought over a mug featuring the show's logo and filled with water and placed it in front of him.

As soon as Gottlieb had finished his monologue, he reached over and shook hands with Wells. "Good to see you again, Senator. Thank you for joining us this morning."

"Thirty seconds," the floor director said.

The crew took their places, cameras were adjusted one final time, and the next thing they knew, they were live.

As Gottlieb read his monologue from the teleprompter, Wells watched the video montage that the viewers at home were seeing.

It was a mash-up of news footage combined with the propaganda videos ISIS published after the attack in Anbar and on Secretary Devon in Turkey. Rounding it all out was footage of what had happened at the White House.

The red light above camera 1 came on and Gottlieb welcomed viewers to the program. After introducing Senator Wells, Chairman of the Senate Intelligence Committee, they were off and running.

The Senator struck the proper tone right out of the gate. He expressed sadness over those who had died, extended condolences to their friends and loved ones, and promised that the victims would not be allowed to have died in vain. He could have been delivering an address right from the Oval Office itself. It was that perfect.

Even though he had not been at all close with Secretary Devon, he played up his respect for the man and the "friendship" they'd shared. Rebecca had briefed him on the names of Devon's wife and children and he rattled them off as if they had spent every weekend together.

Wells was nothing if not a master manipulator, a thoroughly professional politician. Back in the greenroom, Rebecca wasn't watching the monitors. She was watching the guests as they watched the monitors. All of them were riveted, hanging on the Senator's every word.

Rebecca smiled. *Jesus, he's good,* she said to herself. They were going to go all the way to the White House together. She just knew it.

As the interview wound down, Gottlieb had one last question. "Finally, Senator, I want to ask you to comment on something."

"Go ahead, Alan," Wells replied.

"We understand that your committee may have information that the White House knew of a possible threat in advance of Secretary Devon's trip to Turkey. A, is this true? And B, what specifically did the White House know, and not only when did they know it, but what did they do about it?"

The producer bit. Rebecca had felt sure he would. The moment he had heard that a competing network was after the story, he had been hooked.

They didn't like to air gossip or speculation, but this was too big a scoop to risk not being first on. His only concern had been how to properly phrase the question so there was no blowback for Gottlieb and their team.

On set, the Senator's jaw tensed. He wanted to ask Gottlieb where he had heard that, but he knew damn well. Rebecca had told somebody. *Damn it.* They were going to have a very long talk when they left the studio.

Without missing a beat, Wells replied, "ISIS has made it very clear that they consider all Americans potential targets. Any time the President, a cabinet member, a member of Congress travels overseas, there's increased risk."

"But are you aware, sir of any specific threat that existed against Secretary Devon on his trip to Antalya, Turkey?"

Gottlieb had him between a rock and a hard place. If he said yes and Rebecca's information, which he still had not substantiated, turned out to be false, he'd be in trouble. If he said no and Rebecca's information turned out to be true, he'd look like he didn't have his finger on the pulse of what was going on. The national security cornerstone of his campaign was going to be built upon his experience as Chairman of the Senate Intelligence Committee.

So, he gave the only answer he could give. "Alan, unfortunately I am not at liberty to discuss what the committee may or may not be working on. In light of everything that's happened over the last week and a half, I'm sure you can understand."

"Of course, Senator," the host replied. "Thank you for being with us today."

After teasing the next segment, they went to a commercial and the floor director gave the all clear.

Wells took off his microphone and immediately went looking for his Chief of Staff.

• • •

At CIA Headquarters in Langley, Virginia, Brendan Cavanagh had had the television in his office on in the background.

He didn't need to rewind and play back what he had heard. He knew exactly what Senator Wells had said.

He grabbed for his cell phone, pulled up his recent call list, and hit Redial.

"We're just getting ready to leave the studio. Can I call you back?"

"No," said Cavanagh. "We need to talk right now."

CHAPTER 53

I n better times, twin brothers Thoman and Mathan Hadid could have passed for DJs or owners of a trendy local nightspot.

The handsome young men were in their late twenties. They had olive skin and brown eyes. They wore their dark hair long enough to be swept back behind their ears.

Their father was a politician who had been brutally tortured and executed by the Syrian regime. His sons had been working for the opposition ever since.

Though they were young, McGee had assured Harvath that the Hadid brothers were two of the CIA's best assets in the entire country. Before the war, they had been college students. Now, Thoman drove a cab and Mathan ran a small mechanic's shop.

Harvath found Thoman's taxicab idling three blocks from where Yusuf had dropped him. Sliding in back, he said, "I'd like to visit the Umayyad Mosque."

"At this time of day," the young man replied, "it is better to visit the Chapel of Saint Paul."

"What about the Midhat Pasha Souk?"

"It is always a good time to visit the souk."

With their authentication complete, Harvath leaned back in his seat and Thoman activated his meter and pulled out into traffic.

The young man took a long and circuitous route. Harvath watched as they passed through neighborhood after neighborhood, occasionally glancing down at the GPS on his phone to see where they were.

Eleven minutes into their ride, he made Thoman come to a stop and take a right turn. As he did, a white motorcycle zoomed past.

"He's been following us for the last six blocks," Harvath said.

"I know," the young Syrian replied.

They drove for another fifteen minutes. The streets were full of traffic. Buses, cars, trucks, taxis—everyone was honking. They honked to change lanes, to signal where they were, and to allow others to pass. It reminded Harvath of Cairo, where they did exactly the same thing.

There were people everywhere. Many of them were smokers. Both men and women appeared partial to Western fashion. A majority of women, but not all, chose to cover their hair with the Islamic head scarf known as the hijab. Some also covered their faces.

Many of the buildings they passed were run-down, and some looked downright abandoned. One dramatic high rise looked as if it had been sitting unfinished for decades. Damascus was not a booming city. It was bleeding out. Dying.

They parked the taxi in a quiet neighborhood and Harvath and Thoman proceeded on foot.

The young Syrian was wearing canvas high-tops, black jeans, and a leather jacket. Underneath he sported a T-shirt emblazoned with the face of American comedian Bill Murray wearing a pair of 3-D glasses.

They walked silently down a narrow alleyway to a set of tall wooden doors. At some point, they had been painted blue, but all the paint had long since chipped off and faded away.

Thoman removed an old-fashioned skeleton key and opened the doors. It smelled like overripe garbage and cardboard boxes. Leaning against the wall was the white motorcycle Harvath had seen earlier.

There was a small, wrought iron staircase illuminated by a cracked skylight several stories up. Thoman motioned for Harvath to follow him.

They climbed to the third floor, where he knocked against a heavy, metal door. A shadow appeared at the peephole. Bolts were then pulled back and the door opened.

Mathan greeted them dressed in blue jeans, boots, and a T-shirt proclaiming KEEP CALM AND CHIVE ON. Tucked in his waistband was a 9mm Browning Hi-Power pistol.

He stood back so they could pass and then closed and locked the door behind them. Thoman made the introductions. In addition to Arabic, both of the brothers spoke English and French.

"Hungry?" Mathan asked as he led the men into the apartment.

It was long and narrow, with exposed brick walls and timber beams. There were no bedrooms, only a large living space. The kitchen was comprised of a deep utility sink, a small fridge, a microwave, and a camping stove attached to a tank of propane.

Nonperishable food and other necessities like candles, batteries, and toilet paper, were organized on commercial metal shelving. Cases of bottled water were stacked on the floor.

"Yes, thank you," Harvath replied. He hadn't eaten since before leaving Amman.

There was an old wooden table with mismatched plastic chairs. Thoman pulled one out and invited Harvath to sit.

Mathan went to work pulling a few things from the fridge and nuking them in the microwave.

In short order he set down a stack of warm pita bread, stuffed grape leaves, and a dish of lamb meatballs in tomato sauce. They were very fortunate not to be in one of the rebel areas blockaded by the regime.

Thoman offered Harvath a bottle of room-temperature water, which he gladly accepted.

After Mathan set the last item down and joined them at the table, he gestured for Harvath to begin serving himself.

As they ate, the Hadids peppered him with questions about the conditions he had seen on his drive in. Harvath recounted all of it, including the trouble on the Syrian side of the border.

When Harvath was done with his recap, he asked the brothers about the strength of the opposition and how their fight was going.

"Russia's escalations have changed everything," said Mathan as he brewed tea. "They're here for one reason and one reason only—to protect the regime and their own interests. They do not care about anything else. Nothing."

"They're also incredibly brutal," Thoman added. "Twenty-five regime soldiers could be killed in an attack and they would do nothing. But if a Russian was so much as scratched by a piece of glass, they go and un-leash hell."

Harvath nodded. "That's the Russian way. They never forget, and they never forgive. You know the old joke, right?"

The brothers looked at him. "What joke?" Mathan asked.

"An angel appears to three men—a Frenchman, an Italian, and a Russian," said Harvath, "and tells them that tomorrow the world is going to end.

"The angel asks what they want to do during their last night on earth. The Frenchman says he will get a case of the best champagne and spend his last night with his mistress. The Italian says he will visit his mistress and then go home to a last meal with his wife and children.

"And the Russian?" Harvath asks, cocking his eyebrow and adopting a thick Russian accent. *"Burn my neighbor's barn."*

The Hadids laughed. It was a good joke, and encapsulated who and what the Russians were.

"So," said Thoman, "you're here to help create hell for the Russians."

"And hopefully ISIS too," Harvath replied.

"How?"

He held up his hand. "First things first. Let's talk about the person we asked your people to put under surveillance."

The Hadids took Harvath through everything they had learned about the subject. They showed him a map of the man's neighborhood, the photographs their people had taken, and their list of what they saw as their best options.

Harvath sat quietly and took it all in. They were about to mount a very serious operation. Nothing could be taken for granted. Every step they took had to be perfect.

When the brothers finished debriefing Harvath, he had only one question for them. "How soon can we move?"

CHAPTER 54

Despite his pride in the Armed Forces of the Russian Federation, Lieutenant General Oleg Proskurov didn't wear a uniform. Neither did the four-man Spetsnaz team assigned to protect him. They rolled in civilian clothes and armored civilian vehicles. The idea was for them to fit in. But in Syria, the gaggle of Russians stuck out like a sore thumb.

The one thing that didn't stick out, though, was a building they had code-named the "saltbox." During his interrogation in Malta, Viktor Sergun had given up both its purpose and location.

It was part safe house, part interrogation facility. Proskurov had chosen it because it was close enough to the Russian Embassy to be easily accessed, but in a part of town known to be hostile to the Iranians. Tehran was notorious for the volume of spying it conducted. The less chance the Iranians had of stumbling onto or surveilling the saltbox, the better.

It was a spoke in the wheel of a larger GRU operation. Proskurov had been tasked with eliminating ISIS. Using Sacha Baseyev to infiltrate their ranks had been his idea. The operation, thus far, had gone better than he had planned. Baseyev was an incredibly gifted operator.

Which made the email he had received from Colonel Sergun very disturbing. Sergun was suddenly having doubts about Baseyev.

Using a false American passport that had been left for him in Washington, Baseyev had flown to Rome. From there he had flown to Athens and on to Cyprus. From Cyprus, a plane was waiting to fly him to Syria. ISIS was anxious to congratulate him and celebrate his attacks on the United States.

As long as Baseyev was going to be back in Syria, Proskurov thought it a good idea that they sit down and have a talk. He wanted to measure for himself whether or not Baseyev's loyalty was slipping. And so, he had sent an encrypted email to Sergun in return, ordering him to set it up.

What Proskurov didn't know was that he hadn't been communicating with Sergun in Berlin but rather with a little person in northern Virginia named Nicholas.

For his part, Nicholas was on very thin ice. Getting into Sergun's email account wasn't a problem, nor was communicating in Russian, as it was his mother tongue. The problem was selecting the right words. That's where Vella had come in.

Vella worked very carefully to draw all the correct information out of Sergun. This included identifying any codes he would be expected to use to indicate whether or not he was under duress.

Everything appeared to have gone off without a hitch. Proskurov had requested a rendezvous with Baseyev for Sunday night and had set the saltbox as the location. After that, it was all up to Harvath.

The first and biggest problem for Harvath was Proskurov's security detail. The only advantage he had on his side was surprise. The Spetsnaz operatives were elite, far better trained than anyone Thoman or Mathan Hadid could bring to the fight.

They were going to get one shot at taking Proskurov. That one shot had to be so overwhelming that his detail had absolutely no hope of surviving.

The problem, though, was how to take out Proskurov's men without taking out Proskurov himself. For what Harvath had planned, he needed Proskurov—at least for a little while longer.

The other issue they faced was equipment. The CIA had only made certain weaponry available to the rebels. The things Harvath really wanted were impossible to get.

And even if he could get them, he didn't have nearly enough money to pay for them. In the condition Syria was in, no one was taking IOUs—especially not for the kind of sophisticated shopping list Harvath had envisioned. He would have to make do with what the Hadids had been able to rustle up.

In addition to enough radios and AK-47s to outfit the entire team, they had one 12-gauge shotgun, one Iranian Sayyad-2 .50-caliber rifle with night-vision optics, a few sets of individual thermal goggles, a box of old Soviet F-1 hand grenades, and two Yugoslavian Osas, or Wasps in English; antitank rockets with launchers.

Harvath didn't like having to hang the success of his operation on hand grenades from the Soviet days or rockets from the former Yugoslavia, but it was all they had.

Their only hope of taking Proskurov was when he was in transit. And when he was in transit, it was via armored Land Cruisers. Harvath's plan was going to have to work.

Having seen Mathan's helmet with its full face mask and shaded visor, he asked if he could borrow his motorcycle. He would only get one opportunity to drive by the saltbox and this seemed the best way to do it.

Thoman, in his cab, led the way through the crowded city streets. Harvath followed behind on the motorcycle.

When they were two blocks away, Thoman pulled over and rolled down his window. Harvath pulled up alongside him.

"At the next intersection, make a left turn. The building is halfway down on your right. You can't miss it. I'll wait for you here."

Harvath drove up to the intersection and made a left turn. Keeping the motorcycle in low gear, he moved slowly up the street.

He tried to take everything in. It would have been nice to have some sort of a low-profile video camera with him.

The neighborhood was a mix of shops and residences. If they got into it out in the street, there was a good chance innocent people might get killed.

It wasn't Harvath's first choice, but as he rolled forward, he was hard-pressed to see any other option. They had to take Proskurov and they were going to have to take him in the street.

But then, as he drew even with the saltbox, he saw its pair of solid metal gates. This wasn't just a building. It was a compound.

The curb was cut away and there was a driveway of some sort. Courtyards were a common architectural feature throughout the Middle East. While they often had a fountain, Harvath was willing to bet that this courtyard was used for parking.

It made sense. If you were smuggling people in or out, you wanted to hide as much of your activity as possible. And one of the last things you wanted to do, in a hostile nation like Syria, was to risk having your vehicle tampered with by leaving it unattended outside. If you could, securely storing it off the street was the best plan.

The rent, even by Syrian standards, must have been very expensive for this property. There were some things, though, that even the notoriously cheap Russians were willing to spend money on.

Harvath continued his slow tour past the saltbox and then around the block before circling back to Thoman.

The next thing he wanted to do was to get up onto one of the nearby rooftops.

After finding a place to park, they identified a building six doors down from the saltbox that appeared abandoned. With Thoman standing guard, Harvath went to work on the lock. In less than a minute, he had it open and they slipped inside.

The interior of the empty structure was coated in a heavy layer of dust. The unventilated air was stagnant. It was four flights of rickety wooden stairs to get to a narrow door that led out onto the roof.

Here he had an amazing view over the rooftops of Damascus. It was an ocean of satellite dishes, hot water tanks, and solar panels as far as the eye could see.

The buildings leaned right against each other, so he and Thoman were able to move from rooftop to rooftop until they got close enough to have a perfect view of the two-story saltbox.

Peering down, the first thing Harvath noticed was that he had been correct. There was a paved courtyard right in the center and it was just big enough to hold two, maybe three SUVs, but no more.

He noticed something else. There was no back door, at least not for the vehicles. They would have to go out through the gates, the same way they came in. People, though, were a different story.

No safe house had only one way in or out. There was always an additional exit. Sometimes more.

It could be through a neighboring property on either side. Through the building that abutted the saltbox in back. It could be through a tunnel or sewer system underground that people weren't aware of. It could also be via the rooftops where Harvath was right now. It could be any combination thereof. There was no way to be absolutely certain. They would have to cover all their bases.

The effective range of their shoulder-fired missiles was 350 meters. Harvath turned in a slow circle, looking at the other buildings around them. Once he spotted the perfect position, he pointed at it and said, "That's where we're going to put the Wasps. The shooters will have a perfect view of the courtyard from there and should be able to take out both of Proskurov's armored SUVs."

Thoman looked at the building he was pointing at and then back at Harvath. "There's just one problem."

"What's that?"

"None of my people have ever fired a Wasp before."

CHAPTER 55

While the operation of the Wasp wasn't exactly idiot-proof, it had been designed to be as close to it as possible. It made no difference how powerful a weapon was if the operator couldn't hit his target.

Under the stress of combat, there was a lot that could go wrong. Everything came down to training.

Two of the Hadids' men had extensive experience firing RPGs. Those were the men Harvath chose for the Wasps.

Normally, a Wasp team was made up of two people—one to load and one to fire. They couldn't afford to sacrifice that much manpower.

In addition to the two men who would be firing the Wasps, the Hadids' best sniper would be their loader. After the missiles had been fired, he would take up position behind the single-shot, .50-caliber rifle. One of the Wasp operators would pick up a pair of binoculars and act as his spotter.

The remaining Wasp operator would leave the overwatch position and close on the saltbox, staying back just far enough so that he could ambush any reinforcements that might arrive faster than anticipated.

Harvath was a big believer in the old saying that anything that could go wrong would go wrong, so plan for it.

Proskurov and his security detail wouldn't be calling the Syrians for help, they'd be calling their own people back at the Russian Embassy. That didn't mean, though, that the Damascus police and the Syrian military weren't going to come running as soon as explosions and gunshots were reported. It was going to be like kicking a hornet's nest.

Now, fully assembled in the abandoned building, Harvath went over the plan, while Mathan translated into Arabic.

Each man was given a printout of Proskurov's picture. "This is our target," Harvath said. "He is no good to us dead. Rule number one—do not shoot him. Is that clear?"

All of the men nodded.

Harvath looked at Mathan and said, "Make each one of them say it out loud."

Mathan did as Harvath instructed. He made each of the eight men they had assembled, plus his brother, pledge not to injure Proskurov.

"Rule number two," Harvath continued as Mathan translated. "Do not shoot *me*."

The men chuckled, but stopped as soon as they saw how serious he was. He didn't care how long they had been fighting and what kind of combat they had seen. They were not professionals. He hadn't come this far to be killed by "friendly" fire.

Harvath looked at Mathan, who then looked at each of the men and had them repeat rule number two. When that was done, he dove into the meat of his plan.

The saltbox had a rooftop entry similar to the building they were in now. Harvath expected the door to be bolted shut.

Back at the Hadids', he had shown the brothers how to superheat candle wax, stir in buckshot, and reload several of their shotgun shells with the mixture to create breaching rounds. Done correctly, a door could be blown right out of its frame.

The plan was for six men to enter via the rooftop stairwell. Harvath and the Hadids would make up one team. Three more men, selected by Thoman, would make up the other.

Harvath and the Hadids were the lead assault force. The second team had only one job—to hold the stairwell and make sure Harvath and the Hadids didn't get flanked.

The more Harvath thought about it, the more he believed the roof was Plan B for the Russians. If they couldn't get safely out by the front gates, that was how they'd make their escape. So, as he and the Hadids moved toward the ground floor, he expected them to be coming up—especially considering how they were going to kick everything off.

The first thing they needed to do was deny them access to the armored vehicles. Those things were rolling safe rooms. They were extremely difficult to breach without harming the occupants. And, knowing the Russians, their cars came equipped with some very nasty countermeasures.

That was why Harvath had decided to destroy both vehicles with the Wasps. As soon as he heard the detonations, they would come out from behind cover, hit the door, and make their way down into the saltbox.

On the very off chance that Proskurov's protective detail interpreted the destruction of their vehicles as the result of rebel mortar fire gone astray, Harvath had the Hadids' remaining two men posted outside. Once the fireworks started, they had been told to shoot any Russians they saw, except for Proskurov.

With their SUVs destroyed and gunmen outside on the street, the Spetsnaz soldiers would hustle their protectee to the roof. They'd leave a couple of men to engage the shooters to help give the rest of the team a head start, but they would definitely be going to Plan B.

There was just one last thing Harvath needed. Pushing his earpiece in a little further, he asked, "Am I going to have what I need?"

"I think so," Nicholas replied from back in northern Virginia.

"*I think* isn't good enough. I need you to be one hundred percent."

"I'm at ninety-nine point nine," the little man said. "Give me a few more seconds."

Even if Harvath was taking on just one Spetsnaz soldier, he'd still want every advantage he could muster. The only way he was going to win, taking on four of them, was to cheat. That was where Nicholas came in.

"We good?" Harvath asked, prodding him.

"One more second."

Harvath could picture him in his SCIF back in the United States furiously moving his tiny fingers across his keyboard.

"Got it!" Nicholas finally responded.

"Got it *you think*? Or you're *sure* you've got it?"

"Dinner on me if I'm wrong."

"Easy bet for you," Harvath replied. "If you're wrong, I'm not going to be around to collect."

"Then for your sake, I'd better be right."

Harvath smiled and shook his head. Graveyard humor. The SEALs had been merciless with jokes. The more intense the situation, the more the jokes flew. It was the same thing with the Army and the Marines, even cops he knew. It was a coping mechanism, a relief valve.

Staring the possibility of death in the eye created more than a little stress. Humor helped get operators through.

With Nicholas online and all of the Hadids' men fully briefed, they went over everything once more.

They were as ready as they were going to be. Looking at his watch, Harvath then turned to Thoman and Mathan and speaking in a heavy Russian accent said, "Let's go burn neighbor's barn."

CHAPTER 56

General Oleg Proskurov was a careful man, a planner. He understood that even the smallest, most insignificant detail could throw off the greatest of undertakings. History was replete with brilliant men undone by seemingly minuscule factors.

And so, Sergun's concerns about Baseyev troubled him. Baseyev was too important to lose.

Perhaps they were leaning on Baseyev too heavily. Perhaps he was feeling the stress of being too long in the field. His operations tempo had been excruciating. He had been asked to pull off not one spectacular feat but several. It would have taken its toll on anyone.

Proskurov had been thinking about the right way to deal with him. If Baseyev was beginning to crack, should they keep him in the game? Would a couple of days off help him catch his breath? Would he need more than that? A week? Could they even afford to take him out of play at this point?

The Americans were on the edge of getting in. He knew it. He could feel it in his bones. It was only a matter of time.

The attack on the White House was a national affront to their overinflated sense of honor. The United States could launch a thousand cruise missiles, but it wouldn't assuage the anger and humiliation felt by its citizens.

For the last two weeks, Proskurov had been watching American television news. He knew what Americans were thinking and feeling. Even the most dovish among them was admitting that ISIS had grown into too great a problem to be ignored. They were clamoring for ISIS to be dealt with once and for all.

The American President, though, was weighing his options. Proskurov understood why. This was nothing to rush into. United States citizens would be baying for blood. They would demand a quick, decisive engagement. Shock, awe, and carnage. That's all. No nation-building. Come in, kill all the vipers in the pit, and go home. They had no stomach for an occupation.

That was good. Russia didn't want an American occupation either. It needed an exterminator, not a roommate.

As soon as ISIS was defeated by the Americans, Russia could fully crush the Syrian opposition. Then, with the Syrian regime back on its feet, Russia could extend its territorial ambitions in the region. As America receded, Russia would take center stage.

General Proskurov was in his late sixties. Up until this point, he hadn't known if he would live to see such a thing in his lifetime. The idea of an ascendant Russia was beyond anyone's imagination just a few short years ago. Then came Ukraine, and now Syria. Instead of shrinking, Russian influence was growing.

But Proskurov knew that as it grew, it was important to maintain stability at home. One of the greatest domestic threats Russia faced was from Islamic radicals. That was why it was so important to keep Sacha Baseyev in the game.

His penetration of ISIS and its inner core was a great accomplishment of the GRU. But his mission wasn't over yet.

The GRU still needed him to secure the intelligence on all the Russian speakers who had come to train and fight with ISIS.

Where had they come from? How many had returned home? How many had stayed behind? How many had been killed or wounded? How were they recruited? Who had done the recruiting? Were specific plans in the works for attacks inside Russia? What and who were their targets? How did cell members communicate? How were they financed? And so on.

It was critical intelligence and no one was better positioned than Baseyev to secure it. Whatever Proskurov needed to say, whatever he needed to promise, he would. It was imperative that Baseyev complete his assignment.

The General looked out the thick, bulletproof glass of his Land Cruiser as they drove through the streets of Damascus. It was an intriguing city—exotic, but with enough modern conveniences to make it comfortable.

He liked it better than Moscow. That wasn't saying much, though. He liked any place better than Moscow.

The only place he disliked more was his hometown, Dzerzhinsk. It was a hub for Russia's chemicals industry. And with the chemical companies had come chemical weapons programs.

Dzerzhinsk, appropriately enough, had been named after the very first head of Russia's secret police. Its soil and water were polluted. Birth defects and cancer were through the roof. It was said that the death rate in Dzerzhinsk was three times the birthrate. Only Chernobyl was more toxic. Proskurov shuddered at the thought of it. He was glad to have gotten out.

But while he had turned his back on Dzerzhinsk, Dzerzhinsk hadn't turned its back on him.

A year into his first marriage he learned he was sterile. The doctors couldn't identify a cause. He, though, knew exactly what had robbed him of the ability to produce offspring—Dzerzhinsk. His hate for the city of his birth swelled.

His wife ended up leaving him because of his sterility. It was a crushing blow. As only a true Russian can, he had drowned his pain in vodka and thrown himself into his military career.

He remarried years later. She had no children and didn't want any. She was a good enough companion. She didn't mind his long stretches away from home.

When he was home, she cooked for him and they made love. All told, it would have been cheaper to keep a one-room apartment and visit prostitutes in Moscow. But knowing he was tied to another human being somewhere in the world made his assignments abroad more bearable.

It didn't, though, make any of them easier. Especially not this one.

Russia had gone all in on Syria. And after they had gone all in, they had doubled down. They didn't intend to allow the Turks, the Saudis, or anyone else to dislodge them.

In addition to the recently arrived Slava-class guided missile cruiser *Moskva*, and three more Ropucha-class amphibious assault ships based at Tartus, Russia's sole aircraft carrier, the *Admiral Kuznetsov*, was now in the Mediterranean along with her escort the *Admiral Chabanenko*, a Udaloy II–class destroyer.

Then there were the aircraft.

Ninety kilometers north of Tartus was the Khmeimim air base— accessible only to Russian personnel. In the last two days, a fleet of Su-35S supermaneuverable multirole fighters had been flown in. They were the most modern fighter aircraft in service with the Russian Air Force and this was the first time they had ever been put into operation outside Russia's borders.

Two Tu-214Rs had also been flown in. The Tu-214R was Russia's most advanced reconnaissance and surveillance aircraft. With all-weather radar systems and highly sophisticated electro optical sensors, the spy plane was incredibly adept at pinpointing hidden or camouflaged targets. It could also scoop up and monitor enemy communications and electronic signals.

Topping it all off, state-of-the-art S-400 defense missile systems had been moved into Syria to protect Russian assets.

The message Russia was sending to the rest of the world was crystal clear: *Don't fuck with us*.

It was an enormous gamble, which made Proskurov's task even more crucial. He would not be the man who let his country down.

Rolling up to the saltbox, one of the detail agents jumped out and opened up the gates.

After the SUVs were through, he closed the gates behind them. Inside the courtyard, the vehicles turned around so that they were facing out, ready to leave once Proskurov's meeting was over.

The Spetsnaz operative opened the General's door and the man stepped out with his laptop bag over his shoulder and a small cardboard box, which contained tea and a few other items from back home he thought Baseyev might enjoy.

Removing a key ring from his pocket, he unlocked one of the court-yard doors and stepped inside. There was a samovar in the kitchen. He wanted to fire it up and start heating water for tea.

He found making tea the old fashioned way relaxing. It also tasted better than using an electric kettle.

His favorite tea was Russian Caravan—a blend of oolong, Keemun, and Lapsang souchong. It had a smoky flavor to it that mimicked the tea of old, imported from China to Russia via camel caravans. During the long journey—sometimes a year to a year and a half, the tea absorbed its distinct flavor from the caravan campfires.

Placing the samovar in the sink, he filled it with water. Then, remov-ing the sack of kindling and wood chips he kept in the cabinet, he packed the cylinder in the center with just the right amount of fuel.

Patting his pockets, he realized that he had left his cigarettes, and with them his lighter, in the car. There had to be a box of kitchen matches somewhere, though.

After looking through several drawers, he finally found them in a cabinet near the coffee mugs.

Placing the samovar on the stove, he removed a match from the box, but hesitated in striking it.

The hair on the back of his neck was suddenly standing on end. He didn't know what, but something was wrong.

Setting the match and matchbox down on the counter, he turned to walk out of the kitchen. As he did, an enormous explosion detonated out-side, shattering the windows and sending an enormous shockwave through the building.

CHAPTER 57

The first Wasp had come screaming in and had detonated with such a loud explosion that they hadn't even known the second missile had been launched until it hit the second SUV with an eruption that sent an enormous fireball roiling up into the night sky.

"Now!" Harvath commanded back to northern Virginia.

Nicholas, who had hacked into the Damascus power grid, shut down the electricity in a ten-block radius. The entire neighborhood went dark.

Hitting the roof of the saltbox, Harvath gave the signal for the Hadids and their men to follow.

Charging the stairwell door, he racked his shotgun and placed it at a forty-five degree angle in, forty-five degrees down. Taking it off the safety, he looked at Thoman, who was his cover man.

When Thoman nodded, Harvath pressed the trigger and sent one of his heavy slugs flying into the area between the lock and the door frame. He then turned and mule-kicked the door. It didn't budge.

Turning around, he racked the shotgun and went after the hinges.

The weapon thundered as he unleashed three more rounds.

This time when he kicked, the door exploded inward. Thoman peered down into the stairwell, his weapon raised, ready for any threat that might have been waiting on the other side. It was empty.

Harvath handed off the shotgun and transitioned to his rifle. Tapping Thoman, who moved out of the way, he took up the point position and led the team down into the building.

The stairwell glowed ghostly gray-white in their thermal-vision goggles. Harvath had no idea if the Russians had similar equipment or not. According to the team in the overwatch position, only Proskurov was seen getting out of a vehicle carrying anything—a bag of some sort over his shoulder and a small box. If the Spetsnaz team did have night-vision or thermal equipment, Harvath hoped that they had left it in their SUVs and it had all gone up in flames.

Stepping out onto the second floor, Harvath swept his AK from side to side.

All of the windows facing down into the courtyard had been blown out. Broken glass littered the Persian rugs. The fires from outside were burning so hot he could feel the heat on his face. Dust and smoke choked the air. The building would soon be completely engulfed.

Harvath signaled for his B team to take cover and hold their position. He then motioned for the Hadid brothers to follow him. Sidestepping the glass, they moved rapidly down the hallway.

They passed two bedrooms. Both were empty. Reaching the stairs that led to the ground floor, he made a decision and said, "Wait here."

Before the Hadids could object, Harvath had disappeared down the stairs and into the thickening smoke.

When he reached the ground floor, he scanned the room. The thermal goggles allowed him to see through the smoke and dust. He could make out an overturned table, chairs, and a sofa. What he couldn't see were any Russians.

Then he heard shots fired from outside. Within seconds, it was a full-on gunfight. Proskurov and his detail must have tried to make a run for the street.

Based on the position of the two Syrians outside, Harvath knew that the Russians would be pinned down. The Hadids' men had excellent cover and concealment. They could rain lead down on the Russians all night without exposing themselves. But then something happened.

As soon as Harvath heard the explosion, he knew what it was. Someone had thrown a grenade. None of the Syrians outside were carrying any. It had to have been the Russians. *Damn it.* They weren't coming back inside the building. They were going to make their escape on foot!

Harvath began shouting instructions over the radio as he raced out into the courtyard.

There were twisted pieces of flaming metal everywhere. Columns of charcoal-black smoke twisted up into the sky.

Rounds were still being fired, but it sounded like it was coming from only one weapon.

Pulling up short against the courtyard wall, Harvath dropped to one knee. Bringing his weapon up, he leaned out around the edge of the wall and took a quick look.

At the end of the drive, just inside the gates, was a lone male firing a short, fully automatic weapon. His attention was focused across the street, where the Hadids' men had been.

From this distance, it looked like he was shooting a Bizon SMG— a 9mm submachine gun popular with Russian counterterrorism units.

He was laying down cover fire, helping Proskurov and the rest of the detail to escape. He should have kept an eye on his six o'clock.

Lining up his sights, Harvath took the shot and dropped him right at the gates. *One down.*

He heard a noise behind him and turned to see the Hadids rushing out of the building and into the courtyard.

"Where are the rest of your men?"

Thoman pointed up. "They're using the rooftops."

Mathan was carrying a thin laptop bag. "Where'd you find that?" Harvath asked.

"On the floor inside. I think it may be the bag Proskurov was carrying."

Harvath nodded and looked at his watch. As soon as the Russians had realized they were under attack, one of them would have called for a quick response team from their embassy.

In a perfect world, they would have had ten minutes. The real world being what it was, Harvath figured they had less than five. And if the Syrian army hadn't been activated yet, it would be soon.

Running for the gates, he drew even with the Spetsnaz soldier he had shot. He looked down. The man was still alive. That was a problem.

He had an earpiece in his ear, a microphone just inside his jacket, and he was babbling in Russian.

Applying pressure to his trigger, Harvath put two rounds into him, point-blank. *End of problem*.

Taking the man's radio, he stepped up to the gates and looked out.

On the sidewalk, another Spetsnaz man was down in a huge pool of blood. He wasn't moving. The Hadids' men had managed to get one. Good for them.

"Which way did they go?" Harvath asked.

"Overwatch says they went left," Mathan replied, chopping the air with his left hand.

Harvath held the radio up to his ear and listened. A quick response team, or QRT for short, was in fact inbound. They had just loaded up and were rolling out the Embassy gates. *"Shest' minuty,"* a voice said. *Six minutes*.

When Harvath nodded, the Hadids leaned out of the gates and aimed their weapons in opposite directions to give him cover.

After making sure the Russian on the sidewalk was dead, he tore across the street and took cover between two badly damaged cars. Both of the Syrians assigned to cover the front of the saltbox had been blown to pieces.

Propping his weapon up on the hood of the parked car he was hiding behind, he waved Mathan over. Once he was safely across, his brother joined them. Then, they hauled ass as carefully as they could down the sidewalk.

They had almost reached the end of the block, when Thoman and Mathan in unison said, "Stop!"

One of their men was relaying something over the radio in rapid Arabic.

"We've got them," Thoman replied.

"Where?" said Harvath.

"Apartment building on the corner."

"Do your people have eyes on?"

Mathan nodded. "Ittak is the man who fired one of the Wasps and then came to provide backup. He followed the Russians."

He was smart not to engage, thought Harvath. "Good, tell him to stay out of sight and just keep watching."

Mathan relayed Harvath's instructions as they kept moving.

Just before the intersection, they pulled up short and stopped at the rear of the building.

Harvath scanned the area through his thermals. He could make out the B team crouched behind the parapet on the roof across the street.

Pointing at them, he asked Thoman, "How's their accuracy at that distance?"

The man raised his thumb, but turned it upside down. "They're not snipers."

"They might not have to be," replied Harvath, who then pointed at the boulevard down at the corner and said, "Your man with the fifty-cal and his spotter—"

"Outha and Koshy."

Harvath shook his head. "Whatever. The Russian Embassy has a team coming in. They're going to pull up in front of that building any minute now to pick up their people. Your men need to be ready to take them out. Same thing if the army or police show up. Understood?"

Thoman nodded and immediately began radioing orders to his men.

Mathan looked at Harvath. "And us?"

Harvath glanced at the T-shirt under his jacket. "How good are you and your brother with pistols at close range?"

CHAPTER 58

S martphones in hand to light their way, the long-haired, T-shirt- and high-top-wearing Hadids strode into the lobby of the apart- ment building like they lived there.

The moment they did, the Russians were all over them.

"Hands! Hands!" the two remaining Spetsnaz operatives ordered in horrible Arabic as they shined flashlights into the brothers' faces.

The twins complied immediately and raised their hands in a "don't shoot" gesture.

"On the ground!" one of the soldiers commanded.

Mathan looked at him. *"On the ground?"*

"ON THE GROUND!" the man roared again in Arabic. He had no idea who these two were and he didn't care. He wasn't playing. The QRT would be here any second. Once it was, they could make their escape. Until then, he was in charge and these two Syrians were going to obey.

"But we live here," Thoman protested in Arabic. "Fourth floor."

The Russian put the barrel of his weapon right in his face.

Mathan appealed for calm and encouraged his brother to cooperate. Slowly, the Hadids lay down on their stomachs.

"Who the hell are you?" Thoman demanded. "What's this all about?"

"Shut up," the Russian growled.

At that moment, the twins' phones chimed with a group text from Harvath. That was their signal.

"This is bullshit," Mathan said as he began to get up.

"Total bullshit," Thoman agreed, starting to get up as well.

The Russians closed in. One drew his boot back, ready to kick the nearest Hadid. As he did, a shot rang out from across the marble-clad lobby.

Harvath, his SIG Sauer gripped in his hands, had sent a round speeding toward the Spetsnaz operative. It caught the man just above his left ear and went straight through his brain, killing him instantly.

Before the other Russian could react, Thoman and Mathan had drawn their pistols from beneath their shirts and began firing. The man never had a chance.

The brothers kept firing until their slides locked back and their weapons ran dry. Then they just stood there taking in the carnage.

"Let's move!" Harvath ordered, breaking the spell.

He had covertly surveilled the lobby before the Hadids had entered and now dragged Proskurov from the stairwell where his security team had hidden him. "Back door," he said. "Now!"

Inserting fresh magazines into their weapons, the Hadids followed.

Harvath jammed his pistol into the back of General Proskurov's flabby neck. "I know you speak English," he said as he hustled him along. "If you resist, I'll kill you. Is that clear?"

Proskurov nodded. He had trained countless soldiers on how to deal with capture.

This, though, felt different. And Proskurov was aware of what the Americans were capable of. He would need to do everything he could to stay alive.

Out on the street, Harvath steered them away from the grand boulevard and back toward the saltbox. It was about to get very nasty.

They had only made it a half block when they heard the vehicles from the Russian Embassy screech to a halt outside the apartment building.

And as soon as the quick response team leapt from their vehicles, the Syrian rebels lit them up.

The .50-caliber rounds from three blocks away chewed through their soft vehicles and the Syrians on the adjacent rooftop sprayed them with AK fire. Then they began lobbing grenade after grenade—and all of them detonated.

The Russian team was overwhelmed. They took heavy casualties. There was blood everywhere.

Through the windows of the lobby, they could see the dead Spetsnaz soldiers. Panic took over. The team gave up and pulled out.

Retreating to their vehicles, they didn't even attempt to gather their dead. They fled so fast they left tire marks.

As they fled, a van skidded to a halt in the middle of the street near Harvath and the Hadids. Two men in black balaclavas jumped out.

Throwing a bag over Proskurov's head, the men pulled him inside. Harvath and the Hadids joined them.

Reversing back up the street, they spun ninety degrees at the next corner and took off. Other vehicles were already in place to pick up the rest of the team.

• • •

They drove to the mechanic's garage Mathan operated. Jumping out of the van, he opened the rollup door. Once the van had driven through, he stepped inside, rolled the door back down, and locked it.

The garage was small and only had one lift. It smelled like spilled motor oil. There was no waiting area—just an office and supply room.

"Where are we set up?" Harvath asked.

Mathan opened the supply room and turned on the overhead lights. A black drop cloth had been hung along the rear wall. A chair sat in front of a tripod with a video camera on it. There were two stands with lights.

Harvath looked at his watch. He was in uncharted water. Vella had said the drug worked differently on different people. It could take fifteen minutes or it could take three hours. They had to just watch and monitor him.

Pulling Proskurov out of the van, they dragged him back to the supply room and secured him to the chair.

Harvath had been expressly warned not to up-dose the prisoner. No matter how long it took, he needed to go slowly. Too much of the drug too fast could scramble Proskurov's brain.

The General was wearing the hood Harvath had brought from the

Solarium in Malta. They had bound his hands, as well as his feet in the van and had placed a piece of duct tape over his mouth.

Unpacking several strips of cloth and what looked like a bottle of cold medicine, Harvath prepared everything exactly as Vella had shown him.

Once the pieces of cloth were soaked through with the synthetic pheromone, he removed them from the bowl, folded them in half twice, and then packed them into the pocket of the hood covering Proskurov's nose and mouth.

Then he adjusted the bezel on his watch and went to wash his hands. He didn't want to get any of the compound near his own mouth, nose, or eyes.

"How long does it take?" Mathan asked as he grabbed a bottle of water from the cooler in his office.

"I don't know."

"You've done an interrogation like this before?"

Harvath shook his head and took a long drink of water. After swallowing, he screwed the cap back on. "Have you heard anything? Did the rest of your men make it out okay?"

Mathan nodded.

"I'm sorry about the two you lost."

The young Syrian nodded again. "They were good fighters. It was an honorable death."

Harvath appreciated the sentiment. It was one many wouldn't understand. If you had to go, dying on your feet, for a cause you believed in, was the best way.

He was about to say as much when Thoman came running up to the office door. "Something's wrong."

"With what?"

"With Proskurov. He's sick."

Harvath set the bottle of water down and followed Thoman to the supply closet.

Even though he was still secured to the chair, Proskurov's body was convulsing wildly.

Harvath rushed over and snatched off the hood. The General's eyes had rolled back into their sockets. All he could see were the whites. Proskurov was having some sort of a seizure.

"What's wrong with him?" Mathan asked.

"I don't know."

Harvath snatched off the tape covering Proskurov's mouth and was greeted by a spray of sudsy pink foam. Everyone leapt back.

"Cyanide," Thoman stated.

Harvath had no idea what the hell was going on. Pulling out his encrypted cell phone, he tried to call Vella, but couldn't get a signal inside the garage. *Damn it.*

Tossing the phone aside, he unsheathed his knife. "Hold on to him," he ordered.

The Hadids grabbed hold of the man as best they could while Harvath cut through his restraints.

Moving everything out of the way so he couldn't hurt himself, they lay Proskurov on the floor and then rolled him onto his side. His body continued to violently jerk and contort as the pink froth oozed from his mouth.

Grabbing his phone back, Harvath told the brothers to keep an eye on him as he ran for the front of the shop.

Near the roll-up door, he was able to get one bar of service. But every time he tried to place the call, he got the same message—*call failed.*

Unlocking the door, he rolled it up a few feet and slipped underneath. He didn't like having to stand outside to make his call, but he had no choice.

Vella picked up on the first ring and Harvath explained what was taking place.

He fired back a series of health questions Harvath couldn't possibly have answered. He asked about fatigue, hypertension, blood sugar, stress.

Of course the Russian was stressed. He had just been involved in a major gun battle and had been taken prisoner.

Vella asked him to detail how he had prepared and administered the compound. He then asked how long after introducing it the seizures had begun.

Harvath answered all the questions as quickly and succinctly as he could. None of this was helping, though. Harvath needed to know what, specifically, to do.

He was stunned by Vella's response. "Nothing."

Nothing? Harvath was about to push back when Thoman ducked under the roll-up door and stepped outside.

He didn't need to ask why he wasn't back inside with the Russian. He could read it on the man's face. Proskurov was dead.

CHAPTER 59

arvath was pissed. The Hadids had lost two good men and all they got in return was a dead Russian general.

Vella didn't buy that Proskurov may have bitten down on a cyanide tablet. Nobody did that anymore, especially Russians. They made deals—comfortable sanctuary in the United States in exchange for information. Proskurov had to have had an underlying medical condition.

It didn't matter to Harvath what the cause of death was. His plans for recording Proskurov's "confession" and then using that to sow doubt, mistrust, panic, and fear throughout the ranks of ISIS were shot.

He set the laptop bag from the saltbox on top of Mathan's desk and unzipped it.

Inside was a thin, ruggedized laptop—a style popular with soldiers and spies deployed to harsh environments. Opening the lid, the first thing he noticed was the fingerprint sensor.

A lot of things had moved to biometrics. They eliminated the need to constantly change passwords.

Powering it up, he carried it back to the supply room and waited for the security prompt. When it appeared, he reached under the drop cloth, grabbed Proskurov's right hand, and swiped his index finger along the sensor.

Thinking he was good, Harvath stood up, but was greeted by a second security prompt, a picture of an eyeball with crosshairs over it. He called for the Hadids to come help him. He also told them to bring some more tape.

Putting the General in a sitting position, they propped him up against the wall. Harvath then taped his eyelids open.

He had no idea if the computer required an iris or a retinal scan and whether it was the left eye, the right eye, or both. With Proskurov ready to go, Harvath held the laptop in front of him and activated the scan. A status bar charted its progress.

Two seconds later there was a chime as the General's desktop screen came to life.

Tan folders littered a bland, medium-blue background. Everything was written in Russian.

Technically and linguistically, Harvath was nearing the outer edge of his expertise. He knew better than to push it. It was time to get a professional involved.

In order to do that, though, he was going to need better signal strength for his phone.

It took Thoman a half hour to pick up his taxi and return. Once he did, Harvath hopped in back and got to work.

Using the USB cable from his charger, he connected the laptop to his encrypted phone. Over his earpiece, he listened to Nicholas explain what he was doing as he took control of his screen.

Harvath watched as the little man back in the United States remotely opened folder after folder for him.

There were reams and reams of inane government memos. The Russians seemed to paper their employees to death in much the same way that the Americans did.

Finally, Nicholas hit on something.

"What is it?" Harvath asked.

"Something apparently worth encrypting."

"Can you decrypt it?"

"It's password protected," the little man replied. "It's going to take some time."

Harvath looked at the battery life remaining on the computer and said, "The laptop is at about thirty percent power." Making sure there was a cord in the carrying case, he turned his attention to Thoman. "I need somewhere to plug in. How long will it take us to get to the loft?"

"Twenty minutes. If there are no checkpoints."

Harvath doubted the laptop's battery would last that long. He also didn't want to run the risk of hitting a checkpoint. "Let's go back to the garage. We'll charge it up there and try again."

"I know someplace we can try," offered Thoman. "Not far from here. You should be able to plug in. Your phone should get a good signal."

"Is it safe?"

"Safe enough."

•   •   •

It was a hole in the wall. A couple of men sat at a table in back, smoking a hookah and playing backgammon.

Thoman signaled for two coffees as he let Harvath choose where he wanted to sit. He picked a table near an outlet with a good view of the front door.

"How's your signal?"

Harvath looked down at the phone. "Excellent."

"Good."

When the café owner brought over the coffees, he and Thoman spoke for several moments. As they were finishing, Thoman asked Harvath, "Do you want to smoke?"

Not particularly, thought Harvath, but as he was trying to blend in, he nodded. "Sure. Thank you."

The café owner returned and prepared the hookah with watermelon-flavored tobacco. Harvath wasn't a fan, but he took a few pulls nonetheless.

As he watched the smoke rise toward the stained ceiling, he thought about all of the cigarettes Yusuf had smoked on their ride from Jordan.

He knew where his mind was going to go next—to Yusuf having cancer and getting robbed at the border.

Though he normally liked silence, he decided talking might be better. "Why did you pick this place?" he asked Thoman.

"Because of the owner."

"What about him?"

"He grew up with my father. They were good friends."

So much for steering away from serious issues. "Where's your mom? Is she in Damascus?"

Thoman shook his head. "Paris. Moved there after the regime murdered my father."

"She can't be happy that you and your brother stayed behind."

"No. She's not happy, but I think she understands. Our father worked with the Americans. CIA. That's why he was killed."

"I'm sorry," Harvath replied.

"You shouldn't be. He was doing what he thought was right. He was an honorable man."

"I'm sure he was."

"And you?" Thoman asked.

"What about me?"

"Your father. What does he do?"

"He was a Navy SEAL. He died in a training accident."

"I'm sorry."

"Don't be. He loved it."

"And your mother?"

"She lives in California," said Harvath.

"Is she bothered by what you do?"

It was a good question. Harvath had to think about the right way to respond. Finally, he said, "She doesn't really know what my job is. What she does know is that I try to do the right thing."

Thoman smiled. "Because that's the way you were raised."

"By both of them. Yes."

"We have a few things in common."

Harvath smiled as well. "We do."

Sitting back in his chair, he was about to take another puff from the hookah when a text message appeared on his phone from Nicholas.

It was in all caps and read *URGENT. CALL ME.*

CHAPTER 60

President Porter tapped his pen on the briefing binder in front of him. "Do you have any confirmation that Senator Wells was behind the *Washington Post* story?"

"Not yet," McGee replied. "But we're going to get it."

"In the meantime, though, could the information have come from somebody else? Another member you briefed? Maybe the minority leader?"

"I know it was Wells."

"That wasn't my question," Porter said.

"Sir, you know what kind of a man Wells is. He's an absolute opportunist. He'll do anything."

"Could it have been one of the other members?"

Exasperated, McGee conceded, "Sure, it could have been one of them, but it wasn't. It was *him*."

The President didn't necessarily disagree, but every question needed to be asked. The case being built against him was incredibly serious. "Let's talk about what was said on *Meet the Press*."

"About there being advance knowledge of the attack on Secretary Devon in Turkey."

Porter nodded. "Where the hell did that come from?"

"Me."

"*You?*"

"That's how you trap a mole. You plant irresistible pieces of disinformation, watch where they pop out, and then work them backward."

"Regardless of the cost?"

McGee felt terrible. "If I had known it was Wells and that he might make it public, I would have done it differently. It was a mistake, and I'm—"

The President wasn't happy about it, but he waved the apology away and said, "How sure are you that Senator Wells is communicating with the mole?"

"He may be an opportunist, but he's not stupid," McGee replied. "Not by a long shot."

"So what's the connection between them?"

"We think it's his Chief of Staff."

President Porter removed a photo from the binder and looked at it. "What do we know about her? Other than the fact that she's extremely attractive."

"Rebecca Ritter," the CIA Director began. "Twenty-six years old. Born and raised in Davenport, Iowa. Attended St. Ambrose University and went on to earn a master's in public policy from the Kennedy School. The youngest of three children, her father owns an industrial recycling company, and her mother is in banking."

"How do you know that Ritter didn't get the information from your assistant?"

"Because Brendan Cavanagh is a good man," said McGee. "A *very* good man. He was an Eagle Scout as a boy, and not a single person who knew him was surprised when he joined the Marine Corps and was recognized repeatedly for valor in Iraq and Afghanistan. He's got three silver stars.

"In fact, if he'd achieved a degree in law or accounting, he probably would have ended up over at the FBI. But he didn't. We got him and the CIA is better for it. He's a man of impeccable integrity. That's why I chose him to be my assistant."

"But he did," Porter said for clarity, "have access to the information."

"Yes. He had access to all of it."

"And Ritter is his girlfriend."

McGee shook his head. "I think it's a lot more casual than that."

"They're sleeping together."

"Correct."

The President looked at his CIA Director, raised his eyebrows, and said, "So?"

"So I don't think that makes Brendan the leak. That's not his style."

Porter held up the picture of Rebecca so McGee could see it. "Come on, Bob. Look at her. What man wouldn't tell her whatever she wanted to know?"

"Brendan Cavanagh, Mr. President. That's who."

"How can you be so sure?"

"Because I know who he is. I know which direction his moral compass points. I know his country means more to him than anything else and I know he can be trusted."

"Did you know he was sleeping with her?"

Despite the gravity of the situation, a chuckle escaped McGee.

"So that's a no?" Porter prompted.

McGee shook his head. "Just the opposite. I not only knew about it, I encouraged him."

"Excuse me?"

"Brendan is a sharp guy. Would make a hell of a spook."

"How so?" the President asked.

"Until about six months ago, the only time Brendan had ever seen Rebecca Ritter was in conjunction with Senate Intelligence Committee business. Then she just happened to bump into him at a couple of spots he frequented.

"Like I said, Brendan is a sharp guy. He knew it wasn't an accident. Nor was it an accident that she was dressed a little more provocatively each time."

"As if she was trying to get his attention?"

"She wanted his attention, all right," McGee replied. "And then some. But when it happened the third time, he knew something strange was going on, and he brought it to my attention."

"What was strange about it?" Porter asked. "I've met him. He's a big, strong, handsome Marine."

"He's big and strong, but he isn't *that* handsome. At least he doesn't think so. Which was why he figured Ritter had a secondary agenda. After all, her boss, Senator Wells, chairs the Senate Intel Committee."

"And is not a fan of yours."

McGee shook his head again. "Not by a long shot."

"So you told your assistant to . . . ?"

"Play along."

"Meaning *sleep* with her," the President said.

"*Meaning* whatever Cavanagh thought was appropriate," the CIA Director replied. "If there was something nefarious in the works, you're damn right I wanted to know about it. I'm a spy. It's what we do."

The President smiled. "It's also why I recommended you for the job."

"Then you need to believe me. Brendan isn't the leak. It's somebody else."

Once more, Porter asked. "And you're sure about that?"

McGee nodded. "I hate doing the Sunday shows. You know that. But considering all that had happened, and more importantly because you asked me to, I went.

"On my way out of CBS, Brendan called to tell me we needed to speak ASAP. He had just seen Wells on NBC. Gottlieb had asked him what he knew about a rumor that the White House had advance warning of the attack on Secretary Devon."

"And where'd Gottlieb get that?"

"Rebecca Ritter fed it to NBC.

"How do you know that?"

"We have someone inside at NBC."

"A spy?" the President asked, not pleased with the idea of the CIA infiltrating television networks.

McGee shook his head. "A friend. Someone who wants to make sure things are kept fair. When we reached out, this person tracked down where Alan Gottlieb had gotten the question.

"Ritter had fed it to a new producer. Some guy who had just moved down from New York."

"But if it didn't come from your man Cavanagh, where'd she get the information?"

"Do you want my professional or my personal opinion?"

"Both," the President replied.

"Professionally, we have a leak somewhere within the clandestine service. It's either an employee or someone with direct access to our communications. We're looking at handful of potentials, but I hope to have an update for you soon."

"Good," Porter said. "Now, what's your personal opinion?"

The CIA Director picked up the picture of Rebecca Ritter and held it out so that the President could see it. "Whoever it is, she's sleeping with the leaker. Look at her," he said. "Who wouldn't tell her whatever she wanted to know?"

CHAPTER 61

Proskurov's laptop contained a wealth of information. The encrypted files were a treasure trove. When merged with everything Viktor Sergun had revealed in his interrogations in Malta, an amazing picture had come together.

Intelligence, though, was a tricky business. Dots didn't always connect—and even when they did, they might not mean what even the brightest minds thought they meant.

Was the information on Proskurov's laptop solid? Had it been vetted? Or was it a trap? There was a lot to digest.

Ultimately, it was Harvath's call. The President, as well as Bob McGee and the Old Man, had all said they would respect whatever decision he made.

Harvath reflected on how many people had been killed—how many Americans. The operation posed incredible risks, but the potential reward was too good to pass up.

Outside of the sheer danger he faced, his next biggest problem was manpower.

The Hadids were on the CIA's payroll. They weren't crazy about it, but they would accompany him. Not so for the rest of their men. The ones from the saltbox assault were not on anyone's payroll. Harvath had paid them in cash from the shoulder strap of his camera bag. He was now almost out of money.

That was a problem on multiple levels—not the least being that where they were going, the Hadids had absolutely no contacts. And even if they could network their way in, no one was going to risk their lives to help them without being paid, up front, and in cash.

There was only one person Harvath could think of who might help. Taking out his phone, he had dialed Yusuf.

Late the next morning, they met on the outskirts of the city and Harvath introduced the Hadids. As the three Syrians chatted, he examined the vehicle, a white, four-door Toyota Hilux pickup truck.

So common were Toyotas in ISIS-controlled territory that you would have thought that they owned stock in the company. It would help them move a little more freely. All he needed now was the right weapon.

Forty-five minutes later, in a town northeast of Damascus, Harvath handed over nearly the rest of his cash and his camera. In exchange, he was handed a modified 7.62mm Romanian PSL semiautomatic rifle complete with a suppressor that had probably been stolen from the Iraqi Security Forces.

It came with an LPS 4X6+ TIP2 telescopic sight, a Russian NSPUM night scope, and a half-empty box of ammunition.

When Harvath demanded that a carrying case be included in the deal, the old, gnarled rebel arms dealer handed him a black plastic garbage bag. *Welcome to war in Syria.*

With the rifle purchased, Yusuf drove them north. Mathan sat next to him, while Thoman sat in back with Harvath.

They were headed deep into ISIS territory and the only way for Harvath to make the journey was in disguise.

He wore black gloves and a pitch-black burka. Mathan told him he looked beautiful. Thoman told him he thought the burka made his ass look big.

Harvath told them that if they didn't shut up, he was going to shoot them both. Yusuf choked backed a laugh, lit another cigarette, and kept driving.

Once they were out of regime-controlled territory, they encountered multiple ISIS checkpoints.

Ever the accomplished smuggler, Yusuf handled them beautifully. Not a single penny changed hands.

He had brought with him his medical records and other important papers. He actually played the cancer card.

He told them he was returning home, to his village near Raqqa, to be with the rest of his family. There was nothing else the hospital in Damascus could do for him. He wanted to die in his own bed, in the house he had grown up in.

None of the ISIS fighters knew how to react. Plenty of people had begged, cajoled, and threatened in order to get out alive. They had never seen anyone, much less such a good, pious Muslim, roll up and politely ask permission to enter their territory in order to die.

It was amazing. And it worked at each of the checkpoints. Not once were they searched. Not once were they asked to get out of their vehicle.

Had they been, Harvath was the most heavily armed. It was astounding how much could be hidden beneath a burka. Then there was the drone shadowing them high overhead.

They had taken the long way. Not by choice but by necessity. By heading for the open desert, they were able to avoid many of the joint Syrian-Russian air patrols. This allowed them to pick up and maintain U.S. drone coverage sooner.

Flying at fifteen thousand feet was a General Atomics Aeronautical Systems MQ-9 Reaper carrying two AGM-114 Hellfire air-to-ground missiles and two AIM-92 Stinger air-to-air missiles in case of any contact with hostile, enemy aircraft.

The last thing Harvath wanted to do was waste the Hellfires on an ISIS checkpoint. But all the same, it was nice to know they were there, just in case they needed them.

At Tadmur, near the ancient ruins of Palmyra, they stopped, but only Yusuf got out. He purchased food and more bottled water.

Returning with it to the truck, they ate en route to al-Sukhnah, where they topped off with gas and continued on to Dayr az Zawr.

The evidence of a long-drawn-out civil war and insurgency were all around them.

Bombed-out dwellings had been reinhabited by refugees with nowhere else to go. Those fortunate enough reroofed with corrugated metal. The less fortunate used plastic tarps. The completely unfortunate used reeds, pieces of cardboard, and anything else they could scavenge.

The shells of charred, burned-out vehicles littered the shoulders of the road in both directions. As they drove, they were gripped with the quiet fear of possible IEDs, or of being targeted by a regime-aligned fighter.

The road was so badly damaged that had they not had a 4X4, they wouldn't have made it. Time after time, they were forced to go off-road and traverse long stretches of rock and sand.

Halfway to Raqqa, in the fertile corridor of the Euphrates River, south of where it flows from the Lake Assad reservoir, they stopped.

Just outside al-Kasarah was a small farm where a once-prosperous family grew dates and figs. What was left of the family now struggled just to stay alive.

ISIS had long ago confiscated all of their livestock—their goats, their chickens, even a cow. What ISIS didn't take, the regime soldiers helped themselves to when they passed through. It was like being subjected to wave after wave of locusts.

Even so, the patriarch had refused to leave his land. He was too proud. His family had farmed here for generations. Conflicts had come and gone. *Insha'Allah*, they would persevere.

When the pickup truck rolled to a stop in front of his home, he kept his wife and children hidden inside. The ISIS fighters and the regime soldiers were equally cruel and depraved. His family had already suffered too much at their hands.

Stepping outside, the man put his hand over his eyes, to shield them from the sun. His face was creased and weatherbeaten from a life spent out-of-doors. He looked much older than he really was. Squinting, he tried to make out who was in the vehicle.

A white Toyota could be anyone, but it was probably ISIS. They had increased taxes again. No one had anything left to give. Everyone he knew had been bled dry. ISIS didn't care.

The farmer's pulse began to quicken. If he didn't pay, he would be taken away. They would make an example out of him. His public torture— or perhaps even his death—would be used to frighten his kinsmen into paying up.

The thought of not ever seeing his wife or children again gripped his heart. He wished he had hugged them one last time before stepping outside. But how could he have known?

Straightening his crooked spine, Riad Qabbani prepared himself for the worst.

CHAPTER 62

I will speak with him," said Yusuf. "Okay? No one else. It is better if it is just me."

Harvath understood. Thoman and Mathan agreed. As Yusuf exited the vehicle to go talk to the old farmer, the twins got out to stretch their legs.

Harvath would have liked to as well, but for their purposes he was a woman. That meant he was relegated to second-class-citizen status. He remained behind in the truck.

It was quiet, even peaceful, here near the Euphrates. Date palms and fig trees hung heavy with fruit. The air was sweet.

The Hadids held their phones up in the air attempting to get a signal while Yusuf spoke to the farmer.

Harvath kept alert, his eyes sweeping back and forth beneath the burka, watching for trouble.

As they drove, he had tracked their position on his phone. He made mental notes of where they were. Damascus was nearly five hundred kilometers behind them. Irbil, via Mosul, was five hundred kilometers northeast. Baghdad was five hundred and sixty kilometers southeast.

They were in the middle of nowhere, surrounded on all sides by ISIS. There was no cavalry just over the hill, ready to ride to their rescue. All they had was a single drone, high and out of sight.

After five minutes of talking, Yusuf returned to the truck. "We have been invited to tea."

"All of us?" Harvath asked.

"Yes. You can trust Qabbani."

Thoman opened the door for him, Harvath stepped out, and they all walked to the small stone house.

The first thing Harvath noticed were how low the ceilings were. The next thing he noticed were all the books. The man had stacks and stacks of them.

There were carpets on the floor and pillows against the wall. The farmer invited his guests to sit down.

Retreating to an adjacent room that must have been the kitchen, he returned several moments later with a large tray. On it was a plate of dates, a plate of figs, and tea. He set it down in the middle of the floor and took a seat.

His face was gaunt and deeply tanned; his eyes sunken. He looked very poorly nourished.

Smiling, the man looked at Harvath and said in English, "It is safe here. You may remove the burka."

Harvath thanked him and pulled it off. He had no idea how Muslim women could spend all day inside those things.

Folding the garment, he set it on the carpet next to him and accepted a cup of tea.

"How long has it been?" Yusuf asked his old university friend.

"More years than I can remember."

Qabbani's English was good. Out of respect for his guest, he refrained from Arabic unless he needed to ask for a particular word.

After a few minutes of polite catching up, they got to the heart of why Yusuf was there.

"The roads are dangerous," Qabbani stated. "There are checkpoints and patrols. It is not safe for you to go to Ar Raqqah."

"We're not traveling to Raqqa," Harvath said, removing a map. Laying it out on the floor, he pointed to a town halfway there. "This is where we need to go."

The farmer clucked his tongue against his teeth. "Not safe."

"But is it possible?" Yusuf asked.

The man thought about it. "Maybe."

"Maybe?"

"There are rumors about this town. Bad things happen there. People go and do not come back. Not ever."

Harvath wasn't surprised. "Are you familiar with it?"

Qabbani nodded.

"Can you help us get there?"

"No."

"Pardon me?"

"They will kill my family if I help you. I cannot risk this."

"Is there something you need? Something I could offer you to secure your assistance?" Harvath asked.

Qabbani smiled sadly. "Can you bring peace?"

"No," he replied. "I'm sorry. I can't."

"Then I am afraid there is nothing to discuss."

Harvath took a sip of tea and then, setting the glass down, said, "How many people are in your immediate family?"

"Why do you ask?"

"How many?" Harvath repeated.

"Five. I have one wife and four children."

"How old are your children?"

"My two boys are twelve and fourteen. My girls are eight and eleven. Why are you asking this?"

Harvath looked at him. "I cannot bring your country peace. But what if I could bring safety to you and your family?"

He definitely had the man's attention. Leaning forward, Qabbani said, "Tell me how."

CHAPTER 63

The town of Furat looked like a thousand others Harvath had seen over the course of his career. The houses were square. Many had walled courtyards. They were built of mud brick. Some, usually the two-story homes, were built of concrete block.

The original drone had gone back to refuel. An identical one was now circling high above, providing imagery.

There were four roads into and out of Furat, mimicking the points of a compass. It was an old caravan stop, known for the sweetness of its water, which came from deep, cold wells.

Harvath looked at the overlays from General Proskurov's computer and compared them to the footage being fed to his phone by the drone. He spotted Baseyev's house right away. The GRU operative had chosen wisely.

The home was on the edge of the town. It was within walking distance of everything, but secluded enough to be protected if any of the other buildings were targeted in an air strike.

Proskurov had highlighted it on his map. Three old satellite dishes lay faceup, forming a triangle on the roof. Harvath guessed that they had been put there as a marker of some sort. From a Russian fighter jet, spy plane, or satellite, they weren't difficult to pick out.

Foreseeing the relentless attacks on Aleppo, Raqqa, and Dabiq, ISIS had commandeered part of the town to quietly serve as its new base of operations. That was why the town had developed a reputation for bad things happening and people disappearing. The default position for ISIS when they saw a stranger was that the stranger had to be a spy.

Yusuf had been adamant that if anyone could get them close to Furat, it was Qabbani. And he had been right.

Qabbani's family had been in the region for generations. They knew every farmer, shepherd, basket weaver, and Quran salesman from here to Aleppo. He had a network of contacts that was second to none.

The man had delivered them to a small property, long abandoned, several kilometers outside of town. Its tiny garden had been swallowed up by sand. The ramshackle, two-room house looked as if it hadn't had occupants in over a hundred years.

Righting an overturned table, Harvath discovered two scorpions mating. Before he could react, Qabbani had crushed them underfoot.

"Be careful," he warned. "Where there are two, there are always more."

Harvath heeded his advice as he took up a position near the window. Monitoring the video feed from the drone, he made notes in a small notebook.

ISIS didn't want to draw attention to itself, and so kept a low profile. There were no antiaircraft guns, permanent checkpoints, or roving teams of fighters in pickup trucks with .50-caliber machine guns mounted in their beds. That made Harvath's job a lot more difficult.

ISIS had enemies—lots of them—and its high-ranking leaders weren't about to let someone roll right up on them.

Spotters would be hidden in houses and among the townspeople up and down the streets. Every set of eyes was a potential threat. Separating good person from bad was a near impossible task.

If Harvath had been honest with himself, the best plan of all would be to fly in two pairs of F-22s and just destroy everything. Turn it all into a smoldering pile of rubble and call it a day.

But, as much as the idea appealed to him, it was dwarfed by his desire to look Sacha Baseyev in the eye. He wanted to see the man's face when he realized it was all over and he was going to die. Harvath owed that to the CIA team and the embassy staffers in Anbar, to Secretary Devon and his protective detail who were slaughtered in Turkey, and to those killed and wounded at the White House bombing.

Then there was the second thing he wanted—to cause a well-deserved shit storm for the Russians.

Based on the information Sergun had given in his interrogation, Baseyev would be back in the town tonight. Many high-level ISIS members, including its top Russian speakers, planned a meeting to honor him.

If Harvath could confirm where the event was happening, the United States could take action. Then, with Nicholas's help, they could make it look like the Russians were responsible.

The President, McGee, and Carlton had all told Harvath that they'd let him make the call, but none of them liked it. It was too risky. Just getting to Baseyev would be a major, against-the-odds accomplishment. Remaining in Furat after that, though, was suicide. They wanted Harvath out as soon as possible.

Harvath agreed. He didn't want to stay any longer than necessary. If they could pull this off, though, the risk would be worth it. Too much had been lost, too many had died, for him not to at least try.

The key was timing all of it. Getting into the town, getting the job done, and getting out.

Looking at a map of the area, Harvath needed to figure out two things. Where could he zero in his rifle? And once it was dark, how were they going to make their approach?

After discussing the first question with Qabbani and Yusuf, Harvath contacted D.C. to ask them to pull the drone back and check out the sand dunes eight kilometers east of their position.

When word came back that it was all clear, Harvath and Thoman grabbed some items to use as targets, hopped in the truck, and headed out.

As they drove, they discussed a multitude of items that could impact their assignment. Harvath explained that not only could things go wrong, they should absolutely expect them to.

He had no idea how prophetic his words would be. After he fired the first round through the PSL rifle, the next round in the magazine failed to feed.

Harvath had had his reservations about it. You didn't normally see PSLs modified to take a suppressor. It was an intricate custom job and, if not done properly, could result in problems.

But it had been the only suppressed long gun available, and for his plan to work, that's what he needed. It didn't have to be the best. All it had to do was look the part and, at the very least, function.

His first instinct was that the bolt hadn't come all the way back to pick up the next round. But when he examined it, he realized that wasn't the problem.

Ejecting the magazine, he removed the round that didn't feed and re-inserted the magazine. After charging the weapon, he focused on his target and pressed the trigger.

The weapon fired, but once again, the next round in the magazine failed to chamber. "You've got to be fucking kidding me," Harvath muttered.

"What's wrong?" Thoman asked.

"I'm going to kill your gun dealer, that's what's wrong."

He had taken a risk buying a weapon from someone he didn't know and without being able to test-fire it. *Welcome to war in Syria.*

Ejecting the metal magazine, he examined the edges at the top called the feed lips. He was hoping the problem wasn't with the rifle itself but was limited to the mag. "Do we have any pliers?" he asked.

Thoman walked back to the truck and returned with an adjustable wrench. "This is all I could find."

Harvath held his hand out like a surgeon and accepted the tool. It took five bends and several more shots to get the magazine feeding properly, but once it did, the gun performed perfectly.

As soon as he had the night-vision scope dialed in, he and Thoman leapt into the pickup and hurried back.

It was late in the day and Harvath still had a lot to do. This was the only chance they were going to get. And while he wasn't superstitious, he couldn't help but take the problems with the rifle as a bad sign.

His mind flashed to all of the ISIS videos he had ever seen—how they drowned, burned, and flayed captives to death.

He could feel a sense of apprehension growing inside him. Was this the smartest thing to be doing? Had he thought everything out? Was there a better way? Had he overlooked anything? Had he, God forbid, missed something critical?

Taking a deep breath, he held it for a couple of seconds and let it out.

He was about to walk right into the center of ISIS. They were beyond barbaric, beyond evil, and he was beyond outgunned.

What he was feeling was fear. It wasn't the first time he'd felt it. It certainly wouldn't be the last. No one was immune to it.

Courage, though, wasn't the absence of fear. It was what you did in spite of it.

The only thing he could do was to put together the best plan possible, faithfully execute that plan, and be ready to improvise if it all went to hell.

As he slammed a metal door down on his doubts and tried to focus his mind, he was left with a final, disturbing thought. *This could be the last assignment he ever undertook. Here, in the middle of nowhere, could be where he would die.*

CHAPTER 64

D o you like it?" Rebecca asked, turning in a slow circle in the center of the hotel room. "It's called a basque."

Joe Edwards didn't care what it was called. It was hot. He swallowed and nodded at the same time. *God, she was amazing.*

Rebecca bit her bottom lip as she looked at him. The lacy white basque was like a form-fitting corset that extended down over her hips. It ended in frilly garters that were attached to a pair of sheer stockings. She beckoned with her index finger for him to come to her and he obeyed.

She pressed her lips against his and pulled him onto the bed. They had never done a "nooner" before. The room had cost her a lot of money. She hoped it would be worth it.

He was clumsy undressing her. He was always clumsy. He was also a lousy lay. But at least he was quick.

Once they were both undressed, she rubbed her body against his. It drove him wild with desire. Sometimes he had to tell her to slow down. There were times when she could make him almost too hot.

Kissing down his chest, she positioned herself right between his legs, stopping when she got to his navel. Slowly, she traced her tongue around it. She could feel him pressing against her chest. He wanted her, *badly*.

And she was prepared to let him take her, but there was something she needed from him first. "Maybe we shouldn't do this."

Joe snaked toward the headboard in order to get Rebecca's mouth right where he wanted it. "Yes, we should," he whispered, as he ran his fingers through her hair and pressed her head lower.

She could feel him against her throat. "You got me in trouble."

"Shhhhhh."

"I'm serious," she replied, licking a little bit beneath his belly button. "My boss isn't happy with me."

Moving his hands from the top of her head to the sides of her face, he stopped everything. "Is that why we're here?"

Rebecca smiled and slid a little lower. "Of course not. I wanted to see you."

He stopped her. "Seriously. What's this about? What happened with Wells?"

"It's about Secretary Devon."

"What about him?"

"Wells couldn't confirm what you told me about the attack in Turkey. You know, that the White House knew about it in advance."

"Jesus, Rebecca," he said wiggling out from underneath her, the mood killed.

Reaching over the side of the bed, he fished his e-cig from his jacket that was crumpled on the floor.

"What?" she demurred.

Stuffing a couple of pillows behind his head, he propped himself up against the headboard and took a puff.

Exhaling the vapor, he pressed his palm against his forehead. "Of course he can't confirm it. Only the President and the Director of Central Intelligence knew about it. Outside a couple of their closest advisers, no one else knew."

"You're sure about that?"

"I read the actual memo. I read all of their memos—and then some. You know that. Where do you think I get everything?"

Rebecca knew exactly where he got everything. He was one of the CIA's top IT people. He was also brilliant at connecting dots. In the intelligence world, what was said was just as important as what was not said. Thirty-three-year-old Joe Edwards was a master at putting together the big picture, even when half the puzzle pieces were missing.

His parents and even his grandparents had been either career intelligence or career civil service. It had been an honor for all of them, even Joe, to serve their country.

But D.C. had changed. America, in Joe's opinion, had changed. It had lost its way. It had let him down.

As he looked around him and saw broken promise after broken promise, he began to question what he was doing and whom he was doing it for. This wasn't what he wanted. It wasn't what he had signed up for.

He had wanted to make the world a better place. Instead, he was employed by a corrupt oligarchy intent upon bending the world to its will. Other countries and other cultures had value only in direct proportion to what they could do for the United States. It was bullshit—all of it.

That's what he loved about Senator Wells. He saw in him a man who could change Washington. He could change the whole game. He had the guts to burn it all to the ground and rebuild it from the ashes—the way it should be. And Joe was honored to play a part in it.

The fact that Rebecca saw the world the way that he did was icing on the cake. They were made for each other. That was obvious from the get-go.

He understood why she needed to keep their relationship secret. Washington was full of haters, people who liked to tear good things apart.

Despite how busy she was, she always found time to see him. He knew a lot of it had to do with the sex. She always raved about how fantastic he was.

He'd never thought of himself as a monster in bed until her. She just drew the beast out in him.

They were completely in sync in so many ways, but the most important was their vision for the country.

Senator Wells had a very good chance of becoming the next President. If he did, he would be taking Rebecca with him. And if she went with Wells, she would be bringing Joe.

Rebecca was Joe's golden ticket. The opportunities at the White House were boundless. The good he could do was beyond measure. He could help steer America back on track, back to where he knew it was meant to be.

Whatever it took, he was willing. That was why he had offered to help her, to help Wells.

Of course, she had turned him down. Rebecca had not liked the thought of dealing in classified information. Joe, though, had put her at ease—even if it had involved bending the truth.

Her boss was the Chairman of the Senate Intelligence Committee. There wasn't anything he was sharing with her that Wells didn't have every right to know.

It was all aboveboard. Not that Rebecca could talk about it publicly. That was out of the question. All Joe had asked was that if, God willing, they made it to the White House, they would take him along.

Rebecca, of course, had said yes. In fact, she had done more than just say yes. She had described in wonderful detail all the things they would be able to do together once Wells was in the Oval Office.

While he found them all inspiring, his naughty idea of what they could do on *Air Force One* was something he thought could be a first in American history, and he was very much looking forward to it.

Rebecca crawled up next to him and laid her head upon his chest. "You know how the Senator is. He puts a tremendous amount of pressure on everyone."

"But especially his Chief of Staff."

She nodded, her soft hair brushing against his skin.

"Well, what if I could give you something even better? Even bigger than the Devon information?"

Rebecca looked up at him and smiled. "What would it cost me?"

Joe Edwards put his e-cig on the nightstand and turned back toward her. "That depends," he said. "Where were we?"

● ● ●

Twenty-five minutes later, Rebecca Ritter exited the hotel and turned left, heading for a sleepy café about six blocks away. The afternoon air was warm. There wasn't a cloud in the sky. It was perfect walking weather.

She almost thought she could smell the cherry blossoms from the Tidal Basin.

If what Joe Edwards had just told her was true, and she had no reason to believe it wasn't, she had landed yet another exceptional piece of intelligence. Her handler was going to be very interested in what she had to report.

Up ahead was a collection of retail shops. One of the stores had a rear door that led into a parking garage.

From there, she could access the next street over and check to make sure no one was following her. Crossing the intersection, she headed for it.

As she did, the man who had been following her at a distance spoke into a small microphone and told his team to keep an eye on the garage.

CHAPTER 65

Surrounding the town's most famous well was a small, paved square. Ringing the square were street vendors and all sorts of small shops. Harvath, in the backseat of the pickup truck, took it all in from beneath his burka.

Yusuf was driving. Qabbani sat in the passenger seat next to him. The Hadids had already been dropped off.

"Have you seen enough?" Yusuf asked, his eyes on the road in front of him. He was very uncomfortable driving through the center of town.

"Keep going," Harvath replied. "I'll let you know."

Yusuf did as he was told and continued forward.

According to the CIA, the town contained around ten thousand people. The few ISIS members he saw tried to blend in with the locals, but they were easy to spot.

Out gathering intelligence, supplies, or simply functioning as lookouts, they had a ravaged, battle-hardened look about them. Their faces were stern and their eyes took in everything.

None of them wore fatigues. They were dressed in civilian clothes. Traditional headdresses known as keffiyehs hung loosely around their necks. All of them had facial hair.

The biggest giveaway, though, was their weight. While the townspeople were sickly-thin, the young ISIS members were healthy and fit. None of them appeared to have missed any meals.

To be posted to this town meant you were plugged into the elite of

ISIS. And, as in any totalitarian system, there were two classes—those at the top, and everyone else.

The leaders of ISIS and their inner circle of fighters lived very well. They had their pick of houses, cars, and female hostages to serve as concubines. The rest of the organization, though, was suffering badly.

Because of the ongoing international efforts against it, their rank and file, aka cannon fodder, had seen their wages cut in half, their rations reduced, and their medical care dry up. But their faith kept them marching forward into battle.

Online, slick social media campaigns kept the fighters rolling in and helped to recruit followers around the globe willing to carry out attacks in their own countries. No matter how bad things got, ISIS seemed only to grow in number and influence.

"Do you want to drive by the house?" Yusuf asked as they left the square and headed north.

Harvath had a bag in his lap. Inside was his phone. He could see what the drone overhead was seeing. His earpiece allowed him to communicate back home to Langley.

"Not just yet," he replied. "Let's drive past the main mosque and then check the route out of town."

Yusuf shook his head. He thought Harvath way too brazen. But Harvath had made him the same promise he had made Qabbani.

He was going to take care of them and their families. It was an opportunity Yusuf never could have imagined. If the American remained true to his word, which Yusuf prayed to Allah he would, every risk he was being asked to take would be worth it.

Harvath had chosen this route so that they passed the tiny storefront that functioned as the local police department. With ISIS in town, the police would have been bought off. He wanted to assess their level of professionalism.

He noted two officers, seated outside, smoking. They were unkempt. Their uniforms were wrinkled and one had a large stain. These were not law enforcement officers who took pride in themselves, much less their chosen profession. They wouldn't pose a problem. The problem would come from the ISIS members themselves.

As they neared the mosque, Yusuf almost hit one of them. The man had stepped out from a parked vehicle to stop traffic. Several of his colleagues wanted to cross the street to attend early-evening prayers.

Yusuf didn't see him and slammed on the brakes at the very last second. He came so close that the man slammed his hand down on the hood of the pickup.

Oh shit was the first thing that went through Harvath's mind as the man raged at Yusuf in Arabic.

To his credit, the Syrian kept his cool, apologized, and begged for forgiveness, his eyes cast down.

The ISIS man, though, was spoiling for a fight. Grabbing the driver's side door, he yanked it open.

Harvath had already put his phone in an interior pocket, dropped the bag to the floor, and had his hands under his burka, where he was cradling an AK in his lap.

He had multiple extra magazines strapped to his chest, the PalaFox SIG Sauer tucked in the Sticky holster at the small of his back, and all the extra grenades that hadn't been used at the saltbox. If these guys wanted to rock and roll, he was going to give them the best damn gunfight they'd ever seen.

Maintaining his calm, he met Yusuf's eyes in the rearview mirror. The man was panic-stricken. Harvath nodded slowly, trying to reassure him.

The ISIS fighter yelled for Yusuf to get out of the vehicle. Yusuf put it in park and did as he was told. Two of the ISIS fighters crossing the street came over to see what was going on. Harvath assessed each one, deciding who he was going to shoot first. This was turning into a goat rodeo real fast.

Sizing up the combatants, he had decided to first shoot the guy hassling Yusuf, when he heard the front passenger door opening. Qabbani had decided to get out and intervene.

Harvath couldn't believe it. Yusuf knew how to handle these sorts of things. Harvath had seen him in action multiple times. Qabbani should have stayed in the truck. He was going to get himself and everybody else killed.

No sooner had he stepped out of the pickup than the lead ISIS fighter started yelling at him to get back in.

Harvath could see Qabbani break the beams of the headlights as he crossed in front of the vehicle. The ISIS people didn't like his insolence.

The lead fighter grabbed the front of Yusuf's shirt and snapped at one of his buddies to intercept Qabbani.

No sooner had the man begun to move than Harvath saw Qabbani reach beneath his robe.

Oh shit, Harvath thought again. *Don't let it be a gun.*

Apparently, the ISIS members were all on the same wavelength because immediately, the guns that they had kept out of public view, came flying out and were trained on Qabbani.

Harvath was now in a no-win situation. The minute he started shooting, either Yusuf or Qabbani were going to die. He could only save one of them.

Another person might have thought to save Qabbani. With his cancer, Yusuf was already dead. But that wasn't how Harvath operated.

He and Yusuf went back all of maybe thirty-six hours, but they'd been in the shit together. First and foremost, Harvath was loyal. If he had to choose whom to save, he was choosing Yusuf.

It would all be for nothing, though, if fucking Qabbani didn't stop right where he was. If he kept walking closer to Yusuf, there wasn't going to be a thing Harvath could do for either of them.

Thankfully, one of the ISIS men punched him in the chest with the nubby barrel of a Škorpion machine pistol and halted his advance.

Wrenching the crooked farmer's arm from beneath his robe, the ISIS man pulled it up into the light of the driver's-side headlamp and showed what he had been reaching for—a bag of dates.

Harvath couldn't believe it. The man had almost gotten everybody killed over a bag of fucking dates.

The ISIS men seemed to appreciate the irony as well, as they began laughing.

The man with Qabbani snatched the bag and shoved him back in the direction he had come from.

The man standing with Yusuf slapped him in the face, laughed, and pushed him back in the truck.

Arguing over the bag of dates, the three ISIS men crossed the street toward the mosque.

Yusuf sat down and pulled his door shut. Harvath didn't dare say a word. He watched the Syrian grip the steering wheel until his knuckles turned white. He was enraged and channeling every ounce of it out and through the frame of the car.

Once Qabbani had climbed back in and closed the door, Yusuf put the vehicle in gear. He made sure no one else was attempting to cross the narrow street to get to the mosque and then lifted off the clutch and rolled forward.

As soon as they started moving, Harvath asked, "Are you okay?" It was a stupid question, and he knew it, but he had to ask it anyway.

Yusuf had been forced to swallow his pride on so many occasions that he no longer choked on it for long. "I'm fine," he replied. "Let's get this over with."

CHAPTER 66

The white Toyota Hilux rolled forward, its occupants preparing to do a drive-by of the dwelling the American in the backseat had identified on his map.

They were almost to the edge of town when Harvath said, "Stop."

"I can't stop," Yusuf answered. "We might attract attention."

"Do it," Harvath ordered. "Pull over, get out, and open the hood. Pretend like something's wrong with the truck."

Yusuf did as he was asked.

"There's a building at our eleven o'clock," Harvath said via his earpiece. "Three back from the corner. Do you see it?"

"Roger that, Norseman," Lydia Ryan replied, watching the feed from the drone overhead. "We see it. What's up?"

"Somebody has a ton of screens lit up in there."

"Screens?"

"Monitors of some sort. I can't completely see from here."

"Can you get a closer look?" she asked.

"Not without getting out of the vehicle."

"What else do you see?"

Harvath scanned the vicinity for anything that appeared unusual or out of the ordinary. "Generators," he said finally. "Four of them."

"Four?" Ryan responded. Why the hell do they need that many?"

He turned his head, subtly, toward the window and tried to peer through the mesh of the burka. "I'm guessing that whatever those monitors are, they're drawing a lot of power. Plus, I can see air-conditioning units."

"Stand by, Norseman," she said.

Harvath waited.

A minute later, Ryan came back on line. "We're very interested in what's going on inside that building. Picking up lots of activity."

"Electronic?" Harvath asked.

"Roger that. Can you get a closer look?"

He was just about to respond when Yusuf closed the hood and climbed back into the truck. "We need to go."

"What's up?"

"We're being watched," the Syrian said as he started the truck, revved it like he was having trouble, and then slowly put it in gear and began moving. "As soon as we stopped, a man appeared at the front of the building with a rifle and got on his cell phone."

From where Harvath had been sitting, he hadn't been able to see him. "Good eyes."

Replying to Langley, he said, "Negative on that closer look. Going to do a pass of the objective now."

"Roger that," Ryan replied. "Be careful."

As they moved up the street, Harvath glanced sideways, taking in everything he could about the building with the AC and the extra generators. Someone had spent some serious money on it.

Nearing Baseyev's home on the edge of town, Harvath had the truck slow, but not much.

The drone had already provided them some exceptional footage. He was just getting a feel for the area at this point—who was parked where? What windows were open? Did any neighbors look too interested in what was happening outside on the street?

They were the most basic of things he needed to know before Yusuf coasted to a stop ninety seconds later and dropped him off.

• • •

"Do you have everything?" Yusuf asked.

Harvath nodded. "Just stick to the plan. It's going to get very crazy very quickly. Do what I told you, and everything will be fine."

"Here," Qabbani said, as Harvath was about to close his door. He had brought an extra bag of dates and handed them to him.

"*Shookran,*" Harvath replied in Arabic. *Thank you.*

Gently closing the door, he watched as Yusuf drove off into the darkness and disappeared. If he didn't make it back, they were going to be in a lot of trouble. *Insha'Allah*, he thought, *that wasn't going to happen.*

He had left the burka in the vehicle and was dressed like the ISIS operatives in town, in jeans, a T-shirt, and a jacket. His keffiyeh, though, was wrapped so that it covered his face. He found the Hadids right where they were supposed to be.

"Any movement?" he asked.

Mathan pointed up toward the second floor of Sacha Baseyev's house. There was a small balcony and its shutters were wide open.

"Did you see him?"

Thoman nodded. "He stepped out for a moment and then stepped back inside."

Harvath hailed Ryan. "Second floor. Northwest corner balcony. Shutters are open. Can you get a peek inside?"

"Stand by," she replied.

As they waited, Harvath glanced at his Kobold chronograph. It glowed with a green luminescence.

He tried to think what he would be doing right now if he were Baseyev. What would he be doing if he had just gotten back from a series of operations overseas?

No sooner had he asked the question than Ryan's voice crackled over his earpiece. "He's sleeping."

"Say again," Harvath replied.

"He's sleeping. Or at least that's what we think he's doing. Someone is stretched out horizontal, on a bed, in that room, and they are most definitely alive and breathing."

Harvath nodded. That was exactly what he'd be doing. He would have dozed lightly on planes, not giving himself completely over to sound sleep until he was someplace where he felt safe. Then he would collapse.

He would have a gun at hand and probably a knife, or two, but as soon as he was back to someplace he considered home, he would have stepped off the edge into the deep black abyss of complete and total sleep—until his alarm went off.

Then Baseyev would have to beat back his exhaustion, pry himself out of bed, and join his ISIS comrades for their celebration.

"Anyone else inside?" Harvath asked.

"Affirmative. Two additional tangos. One in the courtyard. Appears to be seated. And we're getting a sketchy thermal from the first floor. Looks like just one person, but they're working hard to stay away from the windows."

"Roger that," Harvath replied.

"Two bodyguards?" Mathan asked, once Harvath had signed off with Langley.

"Bodyguards or babysitters. I don't know and I don't care. I just want Baseyev," he stated. "Are you ready?"

Both of the Hadids nodded.

"Let's do it."

CHAPTER 67

Harvath was the first one over the wall. It wrapped around the entire house. Cars were meant to be parked in front and there was a lush garden in back. ISIS obviously thought very highly of Sacha Baseyev and had gifted him a very nice Syrian property. They were about to regret that—and then some.

Harvath figured the two ISIS minders at the house had probably met Baseyev at the airfield, had driven him back, and were now keeping an eye on him for whatever reason. Based on Baseyev's skill set, he didn't strike him as someone who needed protection.

Not that ISIS would have been familiar with his background, but by this point he would have proved himself exceptionally capable in battle. Bodyguards seemed a bit over the top.

That said, protection work was a plumb assignment. Perhaps the goons watching over him were affiliated with the higher-ups in ISIS. He was probably doing someone a favor by taking them on. That was usually how these things went.

Harvath didn't care. He was going to kill them both.

Moving around to the front of the house, he adjusted his thermal goggles, the same pair he had worn at the saltbox.

By now, the Hadids would be up and over the wall, taking up their predetermined positions. Harvath had been very specific about what he wanted them to do, and more important, *not* to do.

Peering into the front courtyard, he saw the man guarding the closed front gates. Beyond him was a large Toyota Land Cruiser.

The guard was leaned back in a chair, his feet up on a box of some sort. His weapon sat next to him, propped up against the wall.

Staring through the goggles, he focused on the man's torso. It rose and fell in deep, slow breaths. *Was this guy asleep too?*

Slung across his shoulder Harvath had a small canvas bag with two 1.5-liter water bottles.

Removing one, he unscrewed the cap, pulled his SIG, and placed the barrel into the mouth of the bottle: the poor man's suppressor.

It would somewhat muffle his first shot, but it would limit his range and accuracy. He'd have to be up close. And after that, he only had one more bottle.

Quietly, he crept forward. When he was about fifteen feet away he stopped. He could hear something. The man was . . . snoring. He was definitely asleep.

Holstering his weapon, he screwed the cap back on the bottle and slid it back into his bag. Then he drew his Winkler knife.

As it came out of its leather sheath, he knew the edge was being stropped one last time. Not that it needed it. It was already sharp enough.

Careful with how and where he placed his feet, Harvath moved across the courtyard.

When he had closed the distance with the ISIS man covering Baseyev's front gate, he noticed how enormous he was. The guard couldn't have been an Arab. Harvath had never seen one that big.

A couple of feet more and Harvath was able to see his bearded face. The man was in his late twenties and looked Caucasian, possibly a Chechen. Harvath didn't waste any time.

Slipping behind him, he placed his left palm across the man's mouth and tilted his head back as he plunged the knife into the base of his neck on the right side.

Then, with a flick of his wrist, he shot the knife forward. It slashed his trachea and severed his artery.

Even though he was unable to call out for help, the man still fought hard as the blood gushed from his throat.

He was so big, it took all of the strength that Harvath had to keep him seated in his chair.

When the last bit of life had finally fled the man's body, Harvath released his grasp.

Wiping his blade on the man's coat, Harvath returned it to his sheath and approached the house.

Based on the drone intel, the man on the ground floor was going to be difficult to subdue. Removing the bottle of water again, he made ready to step inside.

Stepping up to the front of the building, he looked left and then right. The Hadids were in place, and both of them indicated that he was clear to go through the front door.

Harvath tried the handle. It was unlocked. Gently, he pushed it open and peered inside.

Thermal goggles read heat, which allowed him to not only pick up people, but also the heat left behind in handprints, as well as footprints.

Following Muslim tradition, the men had taken off their boots and left them near the front door.

While Baseyev's heat signature had already faded, Harvath could make out the footprints of the man the drone had picked up moving around on the ground floor. He had just exited a nearby room and walked toward the back of the home.

Harvath wasn't sure if it was to the kitchen or some other room. A faint light glowed at the end of the hall. Careful not to make any noise, he slipped inside and closed the front door behind him.

Flipping up his goggles, he gave his eyes a chance to adjust to the light. Though he couldn't see the man, he could hear him.

There was the muted sound of gunfire and then, *an explosion*. Harvath instantly knew what was going on. The ISIS operative was playing a video game—probably a first-person-shooter simulation.

Younger jihadists loved games like *Halo* and *Call of Duty*. They binged on them—whiling away hours of boredom, believing the games helped improve their battlefield performance.

Though that part was dubious, one thing was for sure. The act of immersing yourself in a video absolutely shredded your situational awareness. The ISIS operative had no clue that Harvath had entered the room and was standing right behind him.

His rifle lay on the couch next to him, but both of his hands were on his game controller. He wasn't as big as the man outside, but he was still quite large, and about the same age. Harvath raised his weapon.

When the man let loose with a noisy, full auto burst of gunfire in the game, Harvath pressed the trigger of his SIG Sauer.

The round exploded through the water bottle and tore through the man's head.

Blood, bone, and pieces of brain matter splattered across the console, the screen, and the wall just beyond it. The back of the couch was soaked with water.

Two down, one to go, thought Harvath.

Backing out of the room, he made his way through the house, checking each room as he went.

The furnishings were cheap and threadbare, but one item caught his eye. In the kitchen, among the dented pots and decades-old pans, was a gorgeous, very expensive, Japanese chef's knife.

It was displayed like a museum piece, just as the knives in Baseyev's apartment in Frankfurt had been. Evil always wanted to possess what it could not create.

Leaving the kitchen, Harvath arrived at the darkened staircase leading up to the second story. Coming to a stop, he stood for several moments and listened. There was no sound. So, with the Hadids standing guard outside, he flipped his goggles down and began his ascent.

He chose his steps carefully, making sure to stay to the outside of each tread. The stairs were solid. Not one groaned under the weight of his boots.

At the top of the landing he stopped, looked left, and then he looked right. All of the doors were open except for one—Baseyev's.

He listened again, but still heard nothing. He had no idea if the man was awake or asleep. Holstering his pistol, he removed the black Taser X26P Williams had provided him with in Amman, and powered it up.

The floors of the hallway were covered with stone. He wouldn't have to worry about a board creaking and giving him away. Even so, he chose his steps just as carefully as he had coming up the stairs. Baseyev was so close he could almost feel him.

But no sooner had he neared the bedroom door than he realized he was in trouble. It didn't have a handle. For security, Baseyev had rigged it so that it could only be opened from inside.

"Fuck," Harvath cursed under his breath.

He examined the door itself and then the frame, looking for a latch or a switch, anything that might open it from this side. He came up empty.

Think, he told himself. *There has to be a way. There's always a way.* Then he remembered the balcony and the shutters that were open to the outside.

Retreating from the door, he retraced his footsteps to the top of the stairs and began searching for the roof access. It had to be somewhere on the second floor.

Moving quietly through each room he searched—looking for a panel in the ceiling, a ladder or some sort of hidden staircase. As he did, he tried to recall the images he had seen of the roof. *How was it accessed?*

Finally, he realized the access had to be from Baseyev's room. In fact, it probably was a trap door of some sort that he had covered up with one of the upturned satellite dishes. That meant Harvath was going to have to find another way up.

He stuck his head out the windows of two rooms before he finally found a part of the façade with enough handholds to get him all the way up to the roof. Securing all of his gear, he stepped out onto a narrow ledge and began to climb.

It only took a couple of seconds to get up and over the top.

"What are you doing on the roof?" Ryan asked from back at Langley.

Harvath looked up, though he knew he wouldn't be able to see the drone. "Long story. Is Pitchfork still in bed?"

"Roger that," she replied. "The Reaper just made a pass. He's still there."

At least something was going his way. "Roger that," Harvath whispered. "Going to zero comms."

Zero comms was code for *no further communications.* He didn't need people talking in his ear as he was preparing to take down Baseyev.

"Zero comms. Roger that," Ryan said. "Good luck."

Harvath appreciated it. With what he was about to do, he was going to need all the luck in the world.

CHAPTER 68

C limbing up onto the roof was one thing. Climbing down was something altogether different.

Harvath was forced to leave most of his gear behind. In addition to weighing him down, it rattled and made too much noise. He couldn't afford to make a sound.

Slipping over the edge of the roof, he began his descent toward Baseyev's balcony.

It was much more difficult here than the other side of the house had been, far fewer handhelds and places to put his feet.

The grips were so minimal that there were places where he was digging his fingernails into soft pieces of mortar just to hang on.

He moved not by inches but by millimeters. His hands ached and his body was soon covered with perspiration. If anyone happened by below, he'd be exposed.

Shoving the pain and the pounding of his heart from his consciousness, he kept going. The balcony was only a few more meters away.

He kept running out of places to put his hands, as well as his feet. But each time he did, he took a breath and willed himself to look around. *Find something,* he told himself. *It's here, you just have to look for it.* And each time he did, he found it.

The balcony now was only feet away. It was almost over. He kept moving toward it, ready to let go of the wall.

But no sooner had he reached it than he heard a sound from inside. Baseyev had set an alarm on his phone to wake himself up.

Harvath couldn't even manage to utter the word *fuck*. The pain in his hands was excruciating—and it was spreading. He could feel it in his legs, his arms, and his back. His entire body wanted him to give up. It was begging him to.

Each nerve ending was screaming for him to let go and just drop to the ground. The fact that he'd be badly injured in the fall made no difference. All the muscles of his body could focus on was immediate relief. *Let go,* they screamed. *Let go!*

Harvath bit down and redoubled his tenuous grip on the wall. He wasn't going to let go. He forced himself to keep moving toward the balcony.

But what about Baseyev? He strained his ears for any hint of what was going on inside.

The alarm had been silenced. Did that mean he was awake? Or had he activated the snooze feature and rolled over and gone back to sleep?

He was too close to even whisper back to Ryan to give him a SITREP from the drone. And unless the drone was making a pass right at that moment, it wouldn't be able to provide him the feedback he needed. There was only one way to know for sure.

Pushing himself the last foot and a half, he reached the balcony and eased himself down onto its solid concrete wraparound. Relief immediately coursed through his body.

He didn't have time, though, to stand there and allow his body to uncramp. He needed to move.

Stepping quietly off the surround and onto the balcony floor, he willed his stiff fingers to obey and drew his Taser. This was it. Baseyev was about to pay for everything that he had done.

Moving toward the large shutters that separated the balcony from the bedroom, he paused. There was no sound. Harvath took that as a good sign. The exhausted man had rolled over and gone back to sleep.

With his Taser tucked in to the ready position at his chest, he spun into Baseyev's room and prepared to fire.

The bed, though, was empty. In the corner was an AK-47, but no Baseyev. Harvath barely had any time to process what was happening before his target was on top of him.

Baseyev must have awoken and heard a sound from the balcony. With no time to get to his weapon, he must have simply pressed himself up against the wall to wait for his attacker to materialize. When he did, Baseyev sprang, leveraging the element of surprise for all it was worth.

He landed two devastating blows—one under the man's jaw and one to the side of his head. Harvath saw stars immediately and his already fatigued legs went rubbery on him.

Baseyev didn't give him a moment or a millimeter to collect himself. He rained the blows down like a gorilla swinging a pair of sledgehammers.

It was pure Systema—the lethal Russian martial art taught to the Spetsnaz and all of the nation's intelligence operatives.

The elbow and knee strikes came again, and again and again. Harvath's vision dimmed and he lost control of the Taser. He barely heard it fall and go clattering across the floor.

The blows came so hard and so fast, Harvath couldn't get himself into a position long enough to reach for his pistol or his knife.

He was getting his ass kicked. There was no other way to phrase it. Baseyev was an amazingly well trained and brutal fighter, relentless in his attack.

If Harvath didn't do something fast, he was going to lose consciousness. And if he did, it would be game over for him. There was only one thing he could think to do.

Planting his feet, he dropped into a squat and lunged at Baseyev, catching him around the waist and driving him over backward.

They landed hard on the concrete floor and the air raced from Baseyev's lungs. Harvath showed him no mercy.

Harvath beat him twice as hard as Baseyev had beaten him. He beat Baseyev for every American he had killed. He beat him for every loved one and family member who had been left behind.

He broke ribs and watched Baseyev vomit up blood. He grazed him with a punch across the top of his head so severe it removed a piece of scalp.

And then, on the razor-thin edge of killing the man, he stopped and rolled off him.

Baseyev gasped, trying to fill his body again with oxygen. He coughed repeatedly, aspirating on his own blood. A river of it ran from his torn lip. Some even ran out of his left ear.

Harvath had been opened up in a couple of places across his face, but he looked like a supermodel in comparison.

Struggling to his feet, he retrieved his Taser and then came back over and kicked Baseyev as hard as he could in the ribs.

The blow hit so hard he could actually hear them crack. "That's from the President of the United States."

He was tempted to deliver another kick, but he didn't want to risk puncturing and collapsing one of the man's lungs. There were still several things he needed from him.

Rolling Baseyev over onto his stomach, Harvath zip-tied his wrists and ankles, placed a piece of duct tape across his mouth, and then forced him to sit upright against the wall.

Harvath felt like he had been hit by a train. Sliding down the wall into a sitting position next to him, Harvath caught his breath and waited for some of his strength to return.

It took everything he had not to kill Baseyev right there and right then. As far as D.C. was concerned, that was a perfectly legitimate option. Harvath, though, wanted more.

Pulling out his phone, he got ready to interrogate him. But before he removed the tape from the man's mouth, he explained what his options were.

He was offering him a one-time-only deal. If Baseyev agreed, Harvath would honor his end of the bargain.

If he didn't, Harvath would leave him for ISIS and would make sure they knew he was a traitor.

"So what's it going to be, Sacha?" he asked, as he yanked the piece of tape off his mouth.

The man turned to the side and spat a glob of blood and saliva onto the floor. Turning his gaze back to Harvath, he replied, "I accept."

CHAPTER 69

arvath's original plan had been to get to Baseyev, interrogate Baseyev, and identify the location of the meeting honoring Baseyev. From there, he would call in a drone strike. Then he and Nicholas would embellish.

Nicholas would rework the drone footage to make it look like the Russians had carried out the strike. He would get it out to anti-Russian jihadist websites, forums, and chat rooms. The Islamists in all the places Russia was worried about would go berserk.

For his part, as ISIS fighters rushed to the scene of the attack to look for survivors and help dig people out of the rubble, Harvath would lie in wait with the sniper rifle. He would pick off as many as possible and then flee.

Near the edge of town, the Hadids would have staged an accident. Baseyev would be trapped, unconscious, in a rolled-over vehicle. Harvath would plant the rifle, as well as a few other pieces of incriminating Russian evidence, and they'd all be off. When ISIS found Baseyev, they would tear him limb from limb. Harvath was a sucker for happy endings.

But as things often did in the field, something changed. Baseyev revealed a piece of bombshell information.

Inside the house glowing with monitors, the one with all the extra generators and air conditioning, was the social media mastermind for ISIS—the creative force behind not only their Internet recruiting but all of their propaganda, including their horrific videos.

There was one additional factor that made him special in Harvath's eyes—he was the HVT Salah had identified. Because of him, the CIA SAD team and their pilots had been killed in Anbar. Because of him, three American women from the U.S. embassy in Amman had been brutally raped and killed. And because of him, Harvath was willing to take a huge risk. The man was too valuable a target to pass up.

At this point, the only question normally on Harvath's mind was *kill or capture?* But while killing had always provided a certain satisfaction, it no longer felt like it was enough—not after so many lives had already been lost. He wanted more than blood.

He wanted substantive revenge—against both ISIS and the Russians. That meant the social media mastermind and Baseyev were actually worth more to him alive. And so, he had made up his mind.

• • •

"Wait. You're asking permission to do what exactly?" Ryan replied from Langley.

"I'm not asking permission," Harvath clarified. "Now, can you get it done or not?"

She knew better than to argue with him. His ability to adapt under high-stress situations and prevail was why they had hired him. He was his own man, especially when he was in the field. With or without them, he was going to do it. His mind was made up.

After a quick discussion with the Pentagon, she came back online. "DoD has a Reaper in Western Iraq. It'll take them at least forty-five minutes, though, until they can get it on station over you."

"What's it carrying?"

"Four Hellfires, plus two five-hundred-pound GBU-38s."

JDAMs. Harvath knew the munition well. It was a bolt-on guidance package that turned "dumb," unguided gravity bombs into smart, precision-guided game-changers.

The DoD drone represented a massive amount of ordnance. Harvath liked that. He was a big fan of overkill. If a little was good, then a ton was even better—and it sent a hell of a message.

"The meeting starts in half an hour," he replied. "Tell them to step on it."

As Ryan signed off, Harvath's mind turned to how they were going to pull off snatching the social media guru.

According to Baseyev, there were two guards inside the house—one on the first floor and another up on the second, as Yusuf had seen.

The house also contained three racks of servers. If Harvath could grab their hard drives, in addition to the media mastermind, it would be a huge coup for the United States.

Everyone in the house, though, had explicit instructions to destroy everything if they came under attack. That left Harvath with a serious problem.

The downstairs had been converted into an open area where the social media people worked.

Besides the guru, there were six key players—two video editors, plus four operatives who monitored all the ISIS social media channels and fed ISIS propaganda to a series of sympathizers around the globe who acted as "repeater" stations.

The servers were kept in a locked room upstairs, and Baseyev gave Harvath a complete rundown of how the home was laid out.

If it was all accurate, and considering that Baseyev's life hung in the balance, and he had no reason to believe it wasn't, Harvath had the advantage. He would have the element of surprise. What he didn't have, though, was a plan.

He had beaten Baseyev so badly, the man couldn't be used as a ruse to get him inside. And while there were only two guards, the rest of the social-media people, though admittedly geeks to greater or lesser degrees, all had AK-47s. They carried them to look tough, but none of them were killers.

Even so, all it took was one lucky shot. An armed combatant was an armed combatant. Geeks or not, they were committed jihadists and Harvath wasn't going to show any of them an ounce of mercy. The only person he cared about in that house was their head of social media.

Baseyev said his name was Rafael—a twenty-seven-year-old British national of Pakistani descent. He was short and fat with a scraggly beard, greasy hair, and glasses. And while he professed to hate the West for its decadence, he could always be found wearing a vintage Western rock band T-shirt, such as The Clash or Elvis Costello. He was also known for living on huge amounts of strawberry licorice and tall cans of sugary energy drinks.

Reflecting on the details, Harvath thought, *Who the fuck lives on strawberry licorice and energy drinks in the middle of a war zone?*

Then, like a bolt from the blue, a brilliant and elegantly simple plan crystallized in his mind.

CHAPTER 70

arvath and Mathan left twenty minutes before everyone else. With the help of the CIA's Reaper, they had pinpointed the perfect spot.

The half-finished building had never been occupied. From the roof, it provided a perfect view of the street in front of Rafael's house.

They filled the pillowcase from Baseyev's with sand, and once Harvath was all set up, Mathan melted away into the neighborhood to conduct a final round of reconnaissance.

Using the Reaper's onboard equipment, Ryan confirmed back in Langley both shots Harvath would be taking. Based on how the rifle had performed out in the dunes, he adjusted for a little Kentucky windage and settled in.

He was lying on an old pallet that had been left up on the roof and was using the pillowcase as a rest for the rifle. He'd already urinated twice—once before leaving Baseyev's and again when arriving at the building. He had slugged back almost an entire bottle of water and wouldn't be able to move until his job was done.

Ryan continued to feed him a play-by-play from Langley of what they were seeing from the drone. "Pitchfork is rolling," she said. "Repeat, Pitchfork is rolling."

That meant Baseyev's Land Cruiser was on the move. Thoman would be at the wheel, Baseyev in the captain's chair behind him, and Qabbani and Yusuf in the third row.

Thoman was the most important. Harvath was counting on him to both mind Baseyev and to be immediately ready to go hot if things went kinetic. It was a tall order, but he had no doubt he was up to it.

Peering through his night scope, Harvath settled in behind the weapon and got ready to take his shots.

"Inbound," Ryan relayed. "Pitchfork. Ninety seconds. Make ready."

Harvath studied the leaves on the trees down on the street. There was a slight hint of a breeze. He adjusted his scope accordingly.

"Pitchfork. Sixty seconds to target," came Ryan's voice from northern Virginia. "Players are cleared hot. Repeat—players are cleared hot."

That was a good sign. It meant that Langley wasn't seeing any non-combatants nearby. They were free to engage anyone inside the house.

A sudden burst of air moved through. Harvath went to adjust his rifle, but the leaves settled down. Slowing his heart rate, he took long, deep breaths and placed the pad of his finger on the PSL's trigger.

"Pitchfork. Thirty seconds to target. Repeat. Thirty seconds to target."

Harvath waited for the next update from CIA headquarters. It came seconds later. "Pitchfork cellular engaged."

Focusing on the upper window across the street, he got ready to take his shot.

Ryan read the text messages as they moved back and forth between Baseyev's and Rafael's phones.

Strawberry licorice?

& Monster.

U r awesome!

Got them in duty free on my way back.

I owe you! When can I pick them up?

On way to meeting. Near ur house. Can drop them now.

Srsly?

Srsly.

U rock!

C u soon.

Ok,

Ryan then said, "All players. Fifteen seconds, Pitchfork on target. Repeat. Pitchfork on target, fifteen seconds."

Harvath watched the upstairs window and began to apply pressure to his trigger.

The biggest rule in a gunfight was that if you weren't shooting, you'd better be moving or reloading. But in his case, as soon as he got his shots off, he was going to have to haul ass.

They were beyond short-handed. The only reason he was on the roof was because neither of the Hadids was even halfway decent with a long gun. Once he took his shots, he'd have to move fast.

"Look sharp, Norseman," Ryan then said. "Pitchfork on target in five, four, three, two, one."

Opening his other eye, Harvath watched as Baseyev's Land Cruiser rolled to a stop on the street below. Three strips of duct tape on the roof formed a large N so that the vehicle could be identified from above. The same had been done to the roof of Yusuf's pickup.

"Am outside," Ryan said, relaying Baseyev's text message to Rafael.

Harvath watched as a figure appeared moments later at the upper window. "Tango, second story," he said.

"Coming out," Ryan said as the ground floor door opened. "On your mark, Norseman."

"Roger that," Harvath replied. "Stand by."

Adjusting his rifle, he focused on the door and watched as Rafael emerged. Harvath recognized him both by his physical appearance and by his T-shirt, featuring one of Harvath's favorite funk musicians, George Clinton.

Leading the way was the ground-floor security operative, who walked about two feet in front of him toward Baseyev's SUV.

"Boardwalk," Thoman said from the driver's seat of the Land Cruiser. He was using Harvath's code word to signal that the two men had cleared the building and Harvath could fire when ready.

"Roger that," Harvath replied, refocusing on the figure in the upper window. "Boardwalk," he repeated, pressing his trigger.

No sooner had the round left the barrel of his weapon than he refocused on the guard on the ground and fired again.

When the ground-floor guard's head evaporated in a sea of pink mist, Harvath ordered, "Go, go, go!"

Thoman had already partially opened the Land Cruiser's door. Upon hearing the command, he leapt out, raised Harvath's Taser, and fired at Rafael.

Simultaneously, Mathan kicked in the back door of the house, charged inside, and fired his AK above the heads of the social media jihadists.

While all this was happening, Harvath had abandoned his rifle, picked up his AK, and was racing down the stairs of the abandoned building.

Taking them three at a time, he yelled over his earpiece to Thoman, "Get inside now! Move, move, move!"

The second-row passenger-side captain's chair had been removed so that as Thoman Tasered Rafael, Yusuf could leap out, run around the back of the SUV, and restrain him.

The cancer-stricken Syrian wasn't the fastest man any of them had ever seen, but he was diligent. As Thoman dropped the Taser and ran for the house, Yusuf landed on Rafael, drove his knee into his back, and pulled out the roll of duct tape he had been given for restraining him.

Harvath caught it out the corner of his eye as he tore across the street. He watched as Yusuf, who was no fan of ISIS, landed a series of vicious body blows on the fat social-media operative.

In any other situation, he would have stopped to cheer him on, but there was something much more important happening.

When Harvath hit the door, both Hadids were already inside. "Talk to me," he yelled.

Several rounds of automatic weapons fire answered back and Harvath immediately took cover behind one of the house's columns.

Two minutes later, Thoman yelled out, "Clear!"

"Mathan?" Harvath shouted.

"Clear!" the other Hadid brother yelled.

Slowly, Harvath peered around the column and into the large, open room. It was a sea of blood, punctuated by islands of dead bodies. The Hadids had killed them all and, in their defense, Harvath couldn't see a single jihadist who didn't look as if he had been reaching for his weapon. Thoman and Mathan had done the right thing.

"Let's go," he ordered, pointing toward the second floor.

Leading the charge, Harvath raced up the stairs, stopping only long enough to check the hallway before sweeping into the room where he had shot the ISIS operative through the window.

The man lay dead in a pool of blood. Harvath's round had entered just above his right eye, gone straight through his brain and out the back of his head.

Catching up with the Hadids, he helped them pull the rest of the hard drives and then called down to Yusuf. "Coming out. Get ready."

As they exited the house with three pillowcases filled with hard drives, Yusuf was waiting behind the wheel of the Land Cruiser.

The three men leapt inside, Harvath checked to make sure Baseyev and Rafael were present, and then ordered, "Go, go, go!"

They raced to where Mathan had left Yusuf's pickup and divided up. Once they were free of the town, Harvath hailed Ryan and said, "We're clear. Light 'em up! Do it now. All of them."

CHAPTER 71

I t had been a long day and Rebecca Ritter needed a drink—a big one.

After her nooner with Joe Edwards, she had slipped away to another clandestine rendezvous. This one was all talk and no action. In fact, Rebecca had been grilled for well over an hour.

By the time she left, she had a splitting headache. Everyone seemed to feel she wasn't doing enough.

Intuitively, she knew it was part of a carrot-and-stick play. No matter how well she preformed, they were always going to want more. She was pushing the ultimate drug—*power*—and they were hooked.

Stopping at a CVS on the way back to the office, she had purchased a bottle of Naprosyn and two cans of Red Bull. She was tempted to call in sick for the balance of the afternoon, but she couldn't risk making Senator Wells any angrier.

He was still upset over the question she had planted for him at *Meet the Press* yesterday. It had taken him by surprise, which had been her intention, and he had handled it brilliantly. He had acted like a senior statesman, above the fray, and while not giving details, had assured the host and the American people that it was being looked into.

It was perfect. They had gotten the rumor into the news cycle, but without making it look like it had come directly from Wells. All of the papers this morning had run with it.

The Senator acted upset for another day or two, but in his heart, he knew Rebecca had done him a huge favor. President Porter had just been taken down another peg in the minds of American voters. A couple more leaks between now and the election, and Porter wouldn't stand a chance.

Returning to her office, she tackled the pile of paperwork on her desk and tried to winnow down her long list of phone calls and emails that needed to be returned. At five o'clock, she grabbed her purse and headed for the Hay-Adams Hotel across from the White House.

Its famous Off the Record bar was considered one of the hottest watering holes in D.C. It was known as *the* place to be seen, but not overheard.

Located on the hotel's lower level, its walls were covered with caricatures of the politically powerful—both past and present. Rebecca fully expected her own to be up there one day soon.

The bar was already filling up by the time she got there. As she entered, she turned more than a few heads. Though she'd had a tough day, none of the men in the place seemed to notice, nor would they have cared. Rebecca Ritter was a stunning woman, no matter what the situation.

Walking up to the bar, she grabbed the last stool at the end, waved the bartender over, and ordered a double Maker's Mark on the rocks.

As the bartender poured her drink, she turned to survey the room. Even in the wake of the attack on the White House, it was still a Washington power spot. She was always on the lookout for well-connected people who could expand her sphere of influence.

Her eyes came to rest on a tall, distinguished-looking man who had just approached the bar to order his own drink.

"You're Brian Wilson," she said. "*Mornings on the Mall* on WMAL."

"I am indeed," the broadcaster replied with a smile, flattered to be recognized by such an attractive young woman.

"Rebecca Ritter. Chief of Staff for Senator Wells."

As she spoke, she extended her hand.

Wilson took it politely and, sharp man that he was, noticed that she arched her back in order to subtly extend another part of her body.

"The Senator is making a lot of news lately. We'd love to have him on the show."

"Absolutely," Ritter replied, fishing out one of her business cards. "Do you have a pen?"

Wilson removed a pen from his blazer pocket and handed it to her.

Writing on the back of the card, she said, "This is my personal cell phone number."

The broadcaster didn't need to look left or right. He could feel the envious stares of all the men at the bar.

"You were fantastic at Fox and if memory serves, you also broke the story of Supreme Court Justice Sandra Day O'Connor's retirement."

"You have good taste *and* a good memory," Wilson said. "Although I think you're a little too young to remember that."

"I make it my business to know things," she replied with a coy smile as she picked up her drink and took a seductive sip through its straw. "I've always enjoyed your work. In fact, I think you'd make a terrific White House spokesperson."

Was she trying to pick him up or offer him a job? Whatever it was, Wilson was enjoying it. And whatever ended up happening, he was going to have one hell of a story to tell his cohost, Larry O'Connor, in the morning.

"So," he said, turning the subject back to work, "when can we get Senator Wells on the show?"

Rebecca was about to speak, when one of the concierges from the hotel upstairs appeared. "Miss Ritter?" he asked.

"Yes?"

"You have a phone call at the front desk. It's your office."

"My office?" she replied, removing her phone from her purse and looking at it. The signal strength appeared fine and there were no missed calls or messages.

"Yes, ma'am. If you'll follow me."

"Will you excuse me for a moment?" she said to Wilson.

"Of course."

Taking one more sip of her drink, she set it on the bar, gathered up her purse, and followed the concierge.

Upstairs, he directed her to the phone that had been placed atop the concierge desk. A husband and wife, probably hotel guests looking to make reservations for dinner or something, stood at the other end.

As she approached the phone and picked up the line the concierge had indicated, the man and woman stepped over to her.

"Rebecca Ritter," the woman stated, displaying a set of credentials, "FBI. You're under arrest."

CHAPTER 72

It was amazing how cold the desert could get at night, even after an unseasonably warm day. The rocks, the sand, all of it seemed to have released any stored heat the moment the sun had started to set.

Stretching his legs, Harvath checked his phone and noted their position. They were about one hundred kilometers from the border with Iraq.

As Thoman emptied a fuel can into the Land Cruiser, Mathan kept an eye on the prisoners.

They had parted ways with Yusuf and Qabbani hours ago. Harvath was relatively confident that the Syrians would be able to make it home without him. Just in case they ran into any problems, he had given them the rest of his cash and his Kobold chronograph.

He felt it was the least he could do—especially as he and the Hadids had kept all the weapons and the CIA's Reaper.

Having the drone overhead had proved invaluable. Always knowing what lay ahead had made it possible to avoid problems. It had also caused them to take a few wide, extremely circuitous routes to avoid potential enemy engagements. As a result, they had burned a lot of fuel. And the Syrian desert wasn't exactly populated with gas stations.

"That was our last one," Thoman said as he placed the empty fuel can in the cargo area.

Harvath had been keeping track and already knew that. "There's nothing between us and the border. We should be okay."

Thoman smirked. "Tell that to Mr. Murphy."

Harvath smiled back. The Hadids were good men. Tough, smart, and unafraid. Harvath had to hand it to McGee, the Agency knew how to judge talent. Whether or not they'd be able to tip the scales in Syria would have to be seen, but one thing was for sure: the Syrian people were incredibly fortunate to have the twin brothers fighting on the side of freedom.

Harvath respected the hell out of them. They could have been cooling their heels with their mother in Paris, but they weren't. They were right here, right in the thick of the fight.

"Okay," Harvath said as Thoman closed the hatch. "Let's get moving."

Unslinging their AKs, the men climbed back into the SUV. Changing up drivers, Harvath took the wheel, Mathan rode shotgun, and Thoman sat in back to watch over Baseyev and Rafael, who were on the floor, bound and gagged.

Harvath plugged his phone back into the cigarette lighter and placed it in the cup holder where he could watch it. Putting the vehicle in gear, he pulled back onto the desert road and continued on toward the border.

They had only gone a few hundred meters when Ryan's voice came over his earpiece. "Norseman, you've got company."

Harvath swung his head quickly from side to side and then turned to look out the rear window. "I'm not seeing anything. Talk to me."

"Russian drone. Coming in hot."

Harvath slammed on the brakes and shouted for the Hadids to get out.

"What about the prisoners?" Mathan replied.

Harvath grabbed his phone and yelled, "Leave them!" as he bailed.

With the brothers right on his heels, he ran down the steep incline from the road. Gesturing at a thick outcrop of rock five hundred meters away, he waved for them to follow.

"Hawk Four going hot," Ryan relayed, using the code name for the CIA's Reaper.

"How much time?" Harvath shouted as he ran.

"Stand by, Norseman."

"Damn it!" he cursed. "How much time?"

Ryan wasn't listening. She was completely focused on the battle unfolding above the desert.

"Russian drone, missile away," she stated clinically. And then, as if suddenly realizing the target, urged, "Run, Norseman! Run!"

Harvath didn't need to be told twice. "Hurry!" he shouted to the Hadids. "Incoming!"

They tore across the sand, running harder and faster than any of them had ever run in their lives.

"Impact," said Ryan, "in three, two, one!"

There was a blinding flash of light and an enormous explosion just as Harvath and the Hadids reached the rocks and the missile from the Russian drone slammed into the Land Cruiser.

Harvath and the brothers dove for the safety of the outcropping as a braided pillar of hot, orange flame twisted into the sky and a powerful expulsion of heat, sand, and broken rock raced across the desert with the force of a hurricane.

Harvath had made himself as small as possible, protecting as much of his body as he could. The heat from the explosion was so intense it singed the hair on his arms.

As soon as it had passed, Harvath untucked and rolled up onto his knees so he could look beyond the rocks to what remained of the SUV. There was only a smoking crater in the road.

"Fuck," he said aloud. "Fuck. Fuck. Fuck."

Everything was gone. The prisoners. The hard drives. And, worst of all, their only means of transportation out of Syria.

Above the ringing in his ears, Harvath then heard, "Russian drone inbound."

Again? What the hell was Langley waiting for? he wondered.

"Hawk Four locked on," Ryan then stated. "Hawk Four missile away. Impact in five, four, three, two, one."

Harvath had no idea where the drone dogfight was happening. All he could do was look up into the night sky. As he did, he saw a streak of orange flame as Hawk Four unleashed its air-to-air missile. It was followed, seconds later, by a brilliant explosion that illuminated the night sky.

"Russian drone destroyed," Ryan reported.

Harvath looked over at Thoman and Mathan. Both men had survived. He then asked Ryan, "What the hell just happened? Why'd the Russians target us?"

"We didn't pick up their drone until it went hot. But you're in the middle of the desert, carrying AKs, and headed toward the border. That's enough in their book."

Murphy. Harvath had a bunch of choice words he wanted to utter, especially about the Russians, but now wasn't the time. "We're not going to make it to the extraction point."

"Roger that. Stand by."

As Ryan reached out to the Joint Special Operations Command for the two stealth helicopters waiting just inside Iraq, Harvath looked again at the Hadids. Thoman was smiling.

"What are you smiling at?" he asked, not exactly finding any of this amusing.

Rolling off his stomach, he revealed two pillowcases.

Harvath then looked at Mathan, who had the third.

He was just about to smile back when he saw motion back by the crater of where their Land Cruiser used to be.

Pulling his pistol, he got to his feet and ran toward it. Halfway there, he saw them. Baseyev and Rafael were alive.

Somehow they had managed to flop like fish out of the Land Cruiser and make it to the embankment. Rolling downhill, they had managed to avoid the blast.

Slowing his pace, Harvath reholstered his pistol at the small of his back and smiled. Shaking his head, he uttered just one word. "Murphy."

CHAPTER 73

The CIA's Reaper and a pair of F-22 Raptors kept Harvath, the Hadids, and their precious cargo covered long enough for the specially modified Sikorsky UH-60 Black Hawks to pick them up and whisk them off to the safety of a covert air base in Kurdistan.

From there, a security team transported Baseyev and Rafael via private jet to Malta. Vellas was waiting in the hangar when they arrived. He had a new interrogation technique he was looking forward to trying out on them once their physicals were complete.

Williams met Harvath and the Hadids as their jet landed in Amman. While they drove into the city, Harvath double-checked that everything he had asked for was in place.

They went through the entire list, and when they got to the final item, Williams said, "I had to make a direct appeal to the Ambassador on that."

Harvath had requested a sniper, on the Jordanian side, to provide overwatch for what they were about to do. "And?"

"And it got kicked all the way up to the King."

"King Abdullah of Jordan?" Harvath remarked.

Williams nodded.

Though he had never met him, Harvath thought very highly of Abdullah. He had been extensively educated in both the United States and Britain. But even more impressive was his military experience. He had not only been a troop commander in the British Army and a tank commander in Jordan's 91st Armored Brigade, but he was a former general and Jordanian special forces commander who had also been trained to fly Cobra attack helicopters.

"What did he say?"

"Officially, the King didn't say anything. The conversation never took place."

"And unofficially?" Harvath asked.

"He was extremely moved by your story. You're going to have Jordanian overwatch."

It wasn't Harvath's story. It was Yusuf's. And Qabbani's. But that didn't matter. All that mattered was that he was going to be able to get them and their families out of Syria. He had promised.

As long as they could get to the border, there was a place for them in the United States. The men had more than earned it.

Harvath wanted to insert back into Syria to make the journey with all of them, but Yusuf had told him no. It was too risky. He knew the route and he had the little bit of money and the watch Harvath had given him, plus the money he had saved for his treatments, to bribe his way past the checkpoints. Qabbani didn't have much money, but he would use what he had to bribe his way through too.

"Just be at the crossing," Yusuf had said. "Promise me."

"I promise," Harvath replied.

That had been all that Yusuf had needed to hear. He trusted Harvath. If the American said he would be there, Yusuf knew that, *Insha'Allah,* he would.

Insha'Allah, Murphy . . . it all came down to powers outside of their hands. Even so, Harvath had no intention of failing the men or their families.

•   •   •

Smiling at the unshaven, armed thug on the Syrian side of the Nasib Border Crossing, Harvath held up his laminated press credential along with his phony Canadian passport and said, "Journalist."

He knew the man remembered him. And judging by the look on his face, he was wondering what he was doing back so soon.

Williams, who was sitting in the passenger seat next to Harvath, held up his press credential to the thugs on his side and said, "Cameraman."

You would have thought someone had just dropped hot coals down their fatigues. Like a bunch of chimpanzees, they began waving their arms and hopping up and down in unison, as several of them yelled for their commander.

"Come on out, motherfucker," Harvath whispered beneath his breath.

Right on cue, the man stepped out of the crumbling building. He was even uglier than last time. His brown, leathery face that was crisscrossed with scars seemed drawn even tighter. His mustache was so dark it looked like it was dyed with black paint.

With his right hand on the leather holster at his hip, he raised his left hand and gave it one quick jerk. The message was clear. Come forward for an "inspection."

As Harvath inched the windowless van forward, Williams tapped the wall behind his seat with three quick raps.

Pulling into the inspection area, Harvath brought the vehicle to a halt, but left it in gear. They had disconnected the brake lights back in Amman.

The moment they stopped, they were surrounded. The armed men yelled for them to get out of the car. They began pulling on the door handles but couldn't get them open. Reaching inside, they tried to activate the locking buttons, but that didn't work either.

Instantly, the van looked like a porcupine that had been turned inside out as countess rifle barrels were shoved through the driver- and passenger-side windows.

The men continued to yell for the men to open up until Harvath raised a thick, sealed envelope and moved it back and forth in front of the windshield so that the commander could see it.

He barked at his men and they backed off, removing their rifle barrels from the windows.

Stepping off the curb, he walked slowly toward the van. He had the haughty air of a petty despot. A man who, given a modicum of power, had decided to abuse it and lord it over all those unlucky enough to cross his path. He was a bully, a shakedown artist, a tyrant. He was the kind of man Harvath abhorred.

Sidling up to the van, the commander kept one hand on his holstered pistol. With the other, he played with his oily mustache.

"Monnee, monnee," he said, leaning in the window, looking at the envelope sitting in the cup holder.

"Journalist," Harvath said, just to be difficult as he pointed at the credential hanging around his neck.

Williams, not satisfied to let Harvath have all the fun, echoed him.

"Monnee!" he snapped in his terrible English. "Monnee now!"

"No money," Harvath replied, pointing at the highway. "Just go."

The commander, unaware that they were screwing with him, was confused. The journalist had waved an envelope at him. And it had been a thick one at that.

"Monnee!" he growled, pulling his pistol. It was an old, piece-of-shit Russian Tokarev. They were notorious for discharging accidentally. Anyone who knew anything about guns never carried one with a round chambered. Hell, anyone who knew anything about guns didn't carry a Tokarev, period. But that was another story.

"We might as well get this over with," Harvath said as he reached for the envelope and handed it over.

The commander took a step back, and with the Tokarev still in his right hand, ripped open the top of the envelope.

By the time he noticed he'd been had and it was only filled with newspaper, Harvath and Williams had begun shooting.

With his left hand, Harvath drew his pistol from the driver's-side door pocket. Applying pressure to the trigger, he began firing as soon as he cleared the frame.

Five rounds slammed into the commander. Harvath had zipped him up from his stomach to his face in less than two seconds. Before the last shot had even been fired, he had punched the accelerator.

As he did, both doors in the cargo area were thrown open and the Hadids, armed with fully automatic, belt-fed weapons, began firing at anything carrying a rifle. Every single thug ran for cover.

Harvath pulled a hard left and gave chase. It was an absolute bloodbath. In less than two minutes, they had mowed down over fourteen men.

Bringing the van to a stop back underneath the concrete canopy, Harvath could hear hot brass shell casings hitting the ground as the Hadids kicked them out of the cargo area.

He was about to compliment everyone when he saw six .50-caliber mounted technicals racing at them from a half-demolished building a mile back from the border crossing.

"This isn't good," he said, pointing toward the incoming vehicles.

Williams smiled. "Get out of the van."

"What?"

"You're going to want to see this," he replied. "Get out of the van."

Harvath thought he was insane, but he gave in and hopped out. Williams and the Hadids joined him.

"What the hell are we doing?" Thoman asked.

"Just watch," said Williams.

They stood there, watching, but all Harvath noticed was the vehicles getting closer and closer. They were already in range. In fact, as if they were reading his mind, the gunner in the bed of the lead vehicle began firing.

Harvath, Williams, and the Hadids were forced to lunge for cover. Pieces of the concrete canopy rained down on top of them.

"What the hell are we doing?" Harvath demanded.

"It's coming. Watch!" Williams yelled over the gunfire.

From back on the Jordanian side of the border there was what sounded like intense, incredibly loud thunder. Harvath and his team whipped their heads in its direction.

As they did, they saw one of the heavily fortified Jordanian traffic gates spring open and a sleek Cobra attack helicopter come flying out.

No sooner had it cleared the Jordanian side, than its two 7.62mm minigun pods roared to life and began chewing through the approaching technicals.

The Hadids cheered and pumped their fists in the air.

With the first two vehicles disabled, the others realized they were in trouble and attempted to turn around and head back. That was when the Cobra switched to its 70mm rockets.

One after another, the machine gun–mounted pickups and their crews were taken out. It was an incredible thing to watch.

As soon as the job was complete, the Cobra disappeared.

Harvath was beyond impressed. It had been an absolutely overwhelming show of force—something right up his alley. The Jordanians were amazing.

They stood there for several moments before Harvath looked at Williams and said, "Unbelievable. I hope someone lets King Abdullah know how awesome his pilots are."

Williams smiled back. "No one needs to let him know. That actually *was* Abdullah."

As a Jordanian team raced across to help them sanitize the scene, Harvath took out his phone to call Yusuf, who was waiting with his family and Qabbani's ten kilometers up the highway.

The border crossing was safe. He would be waiting for him on the other side. There would be no armed thugs to harass him at the checkpoint.

CHAPTER 74

CAPITOL HILL
WASHINGTON, D.C.

S enator Daniel Wells leaned forward and studied the man on the other side of his desk. "Did I stutter?" he asked.

"No," the Director of Central Intelligence replied. "You did not."

"Was I speaking in a foreign language?"

Bob McGee rolled his eyes. He'd had it with the arrogant, condescending senator from Iowa. "Let's cut the crap."

"Excuse me?"

"You heard me."

"Your agency, Director McGee, launched not one, not two, but three drone strikes inside Syria. While two of those strikes, allegedly, took out the social media capabilities of ISIS and killed many high-ranking ISIS members, including a handful from the Caucasus, you also downed a Russian drone, and diverted DoD assets including one drone and two stealth helicopters from the Iraq theater into Syria. How would you characterize your agency's actions?"

McGee looked at him. "I'd say we had a pretty damn good day."

"Excuse me?" the Senator replied.

"You heard me. Or did I stutter? Perhaps I'm speaking a foreign language."

Wells was instantly enraged. "That's it. You and I are done. For over a week, I have been waiting for an in-person update from you. Now that you finally deign to come to my office, this is how you handle yourself?

"I warned you what would happen if you chose to be a smartass. You're a shitty Director of Central Intelligence. You and your agency are now going to pay the price. You're through. Do you understand me? It's over. *You're* over."

McGee waited for the man to stop bloviating. Once he had, the DCI looked at him and said, "Now you listen to *me*, Dan."

The remark immediately got Wells's hackles up. He was about to shoot McGee the *How dare you? Call me Senator!* look when McGee froze him in place with one of his own.

"You and I are through, all right," the CIA Director continued. "But I'm not going anywhere—you are."

"What the hell are you talking about?"

McGee pretended to look around. "I didn't see your Chief of Staff when I came in."

"She has taken a couple of personal days off."

"That's what you think. The FBI arrested her two days ago at the Hay-Adams Hotel."

Wells couldn't believe it. "Rebecca was arrested? For what?"

"It will all be in the *Washington Post* tomorrow. Lilliana Grace is doing the story. I believe you two know each other."

At that remark, the Senator went right into defense mode. "I have no idea what you're talking about."

"Sure you don't, Dan."

Wells seethed at McGee's continued use of his first name. "Not only is your chairmanship of the Intelligence Committee at an end," McGee continued, "but so is any hope you ever had of running for the White House. In fact, I'd be surprised if you could even get elected dogcatcher after this is all over."

"I still have *no* idea what you're talking about."

The Director of Central Intelligence leaned back in his chair. "Your Chief of Staff, Rebecca Ritter, is a spy for the Russians."

The Senator was speechless.

"A search warrant has been issued not only for her apartment but also for your office and all of your communications together."

Wells wasn't going to go down without a fight. Collecting himself, he said the first thing that came to his mind. "You represent the Central

Intelligence Agency. Under the Constitution, you have no authority to serve any warrant."

McGee smiled. "You're right, I don't."

But as soon as he had said the words, the intercom on the Senator's phone chimed.

"Senator Wells?" the secretary in the outer office intoned. "The Director of the FBI is here to see you."

EPILOGUE

Harvath poured two beers into a Yeti tumbler and stepped out onto his patio.

"What are you doing?" Lara called from somewhere inside.

"Union coffee break," he called back. "Twenty minutes."

Moving a chair over to the railing, he sat down. From here he could see the Charles River below.

That had been his only request—something quiet, near the water.

The "quiet" part had immediately ruled out Boston Harbor. The area was fun, but too busy for his taste. When he was home, he wanted to relax.

The realtor was a friend of Lara's and had found him the perfect place. It was older, but it had character and had been well maintained. There were two bedrooms with a loft above the kitchen.

The minute Lara's son, Marco, had seen the loft, he clambered right up the ladder and declared the space "his." That was all it had taken for Harvath. He signed the lease that night.

Lara had offered to fly down to Virginia and help him move, but he knew how busy she was. Besides, he needed time alone. There was a lot to think about.

Yusuf, Qabbani, and their families had been interviewed and processed at the U.S. Embassy in Amman. When everything was in order, they were flown to Baltimore to begin their new lives in the United States.

Two Arabic-speaking families from the State Department had volunteered to help work with them and ease their transition. Yusuf had been immediately admitted to the Sidney Kimmel Comprehensive Cancer Center at Johns Hopkins. His prognosis was not good.

His medical team, though, was determined. And it was quietly understood throughout the hospital that Yusuf was an important man, someone the United States thought very highly of. Everything that could be done for him would be.

Harvath had flown home from Amman alone. Once Yusuf and company had made it safely across the border into Jordan, Williams had taken over.

He had gotten the families into a safe house and had handled everything for them at the Embassy. In the midst of that, he spent several hours talking with the Hadid brothers.

They weren't his assets to run, but it was obvious that they were being underutilized in Syria. With some additional training, they could be doing much more.

After some back-and-forth with Langley, Bob McGee and Lydia Ryan put their seal of approval on the idea. Williams was given the green light to create a new covert operations element in Syria. The Hadids would be the tip of that spear.

Back on Malta, Vella continued to extract valuable information from Baseyev, Rafael, and Sergun. The extent of what Russia and ISIS had been up to was chilling. As reports were fed back to President Porter, his anger, as well as his resolve, increased exponentially.

In the days after Harvath returned to the United States, the word *proportional* was discussed a lot. It was discussed at the White House, at the State Department, at the CIA, and at the Pentagon.

The other word, spoken only within the President's closest circle, was vengeance. It certainly lacked sophistication. It also lacked diplomatic polish. But it was accurate. The United States wanted revenge. And it would have it.

Within forty-eight hours of returning home, Harvath was summoned to the White House. He had no idea why, until he was led downstairs to the Situation Room.

Taking a seat near the President, he watched as Operation Full Justice was launched.

Bombs and missiles rained down on the Russian naval installation at the Syrian port of Tartus, as well as the Khmeimim air base just to the north. The Russian air defense systems proved utterly useless against the high-tech weapons the United States threw at them.

Ship after ship was destroyed at Tartus, as was almost every Russian aircraft at Khmeimim. It was the biggest military loss one nation has suffered since World War II.

Within a half hour, President Porter had gone on television to address the nation and explain the actions the United States had taken. He warned that any attempt by Russia to respond would be met with even more withering destruction.

After detailing the Russian's attempt to draw America into war with ISIS in Syria, he laid out a series of non-negotiable demands.

The first was that Russia withdraw from the region immediately. The second was that the nations of the Middle East must convene an immediate conference to discuss defeating terrorism by reforming Islam.

In absence of any demonstrable reformation, the United States would cease to recognize the Sykes-Picot agreement. The only nation thereunder which the United States would continue to recognize was the State of Israel.

It was the region's only democracy and an example for Muslim nations to follow. In evidence of its commitment to the security of Israel, the United States would be stepping up its weapons transfers to the Jewish state, including some of its most highly advanced and sophisticated programs.

Calling for unity in the days and weeks ahead, the President assured America, and the world, that by banding together against evil, they would ensure peace for themselves and their children.

He then ended his address by quoting Edmund Burke: "When bad men combine, the good must associate; else they will fall, one by one, an unpitied sacrifice in a contemptible struggle."

It was one of Porter's best speeches—and it came on the heels of several others that no president would ever want to give. The video of the horrors in Anbar, the assassination of Secretary Devon, the suicide bomber at the White House, and now a massive strike by the United

States upon the Russians. All of these heaped upon the losses that had been suffered by so many already.

The President prayed they were not headed to war with the Russians. He had already spoken with allies around the world and the condemnation of Moscow had been universal. They were considered a pariah. Should they try to retaliate, it would be the end of their nation.

Harvath had driven home from the White House with many of the same thoughts and concerns as the President. Fortunately, Russia did not respond. In fact, they were too involved with multiple Islamist uprisings at home.

Nicholas had doctored the footage of the strikes on the ISIS meeting, and had overlaid it with the voices of Russian pilots and combat controllers. It was a beautiful deception and had worked perfectly.

• • •

And while the CIA tried to decide what to do with Malevsky and Eichel, McGee was also working with the Department of Justice to decide how to handle Rebecca Ritter, her Russian handler, and Joe Edwards—all of whom were cooling their heels in a high-security detention facility.

Ritter was cooperating. She admitted to having done a deal with the devil. The Russians had not only paid her a fortune to spy for them, but they had also offered her the thing she wanted more than anything else.

They had convinced her that they could get Senator Wells into the White House and that from there, she could have any position she wanted. For money and promised power, she had willingly sold out her country.

And though McGee had his hands full with her and everything else, Harvath had suggested to him that he strike while the iron was hot and attempt to recruit Anna Strobl. He continued to feel she had all the right ingredients.

The ultimate get for them, of course, would be Alexandra Ivanova. Yet again, she had been forced to see how reckless and corrupt her government was. She might be very ripe for recruitment now.

McGee had told him he would take all of it under advisement and keep him up to speed on any developments.

When Harvath pulled up to his home along the Potomac, it felt alien to him. It was as if it were from another time in his life—a place out of the past. In a sense, it was. He was cutting his ties with D.C.

He had already sat down with Reed Carlton and explained his position. He had tendered his resignation, but the Old Man had refused to take it. "Go to Boston," he told him. "Let's see what happens."

And that was that.

He packed up the house—or at least those things he thought he'd need to get started. Everything else could stay behind for the time being.

Stuffing his Tahoe and pulling a trailer, he made the trip to Massachusetts—grinning like an idiot almost the entire way there. For once in his life, he was happy—truly happy.

He was pleased not only about where he was going and who he was with, but about what lay in front of him. He had the three ingredients to happiness right in the palm of his hand and he knew it—something to do, someone to love, and something to look forward to.

No matter what happened, he would never look back on his life and ask what might have been if he had only made the move to Boston.

"What's this?" Lara asked, stepping out onto the patio and interrupting his thoughts.

She was wearing shorts and a T-shirt. And, even so casually dressed, she was unbelievably gorgeous. He immediately thought about extending his break from twenty minutes to at least forty-five. He wondered if any of the neighbors could see his patio from their windows.

Lara had been helping him unpack and in her hand was a pistol suppressor.

"That?" Harvath replied. "It's a shot glass."

Lara rolled her eyes. "And this one?" she replied, holding up another.

"Bud vase. I was going to pick a flower and put it in there to surprise you."

"You know these are illegal in Boston, right?"

"Good thing I know a cop," he replied, motioning for her to come sit with him.

Setting the suppressors down, she walked over and leaned up against the edge of the railing.

"You have beautiful legs for a cop," he said. "You know that?"

"All the better to chase you with."

"No way. I'm done running. You caught me," he replied, pulling her into his lap.

She brought her lips to his and kissed him—long, slow, and unbelievably sexy—just like that last kiss they had shared in Budapest, but better. That kiss told him everything he needed to know.

There was no question. They were a great couple—smart, passionate, and electric. They were perfect for each other and they had figured out a way to make it work.

Slipping his hand beneath her T-shirt, he moved softly along her back until he found the clasp of her bra and popped it open.

"Good timing," she whispered in his ear. "I just put sheets on the bed."

"Let's christen the patio first."

Lara laughed and kissed him again. "I'm really glad you're here."

"So am I," he replied. "So am I."

ACKNOWLEDGMENTS

It has been an amazing year and I want to thank all of my fantastic **readers**. Thank you for your support, all of the great chats on social media, and for how many people you have introduced to my books.

I also want to thank all of the wonderful **booksellers** around the world who carry my novels and continue to introduce new readers to them every-day. I appreciate you more than I can ever put into words.

Once again, my very good friends **Sean F.**, **James Ryan**, and **Rodney Cox** proved invaluable during the writing of this novel. They are three of the most talented, courageous, and patriotic men I know. I am better at everything I do because I strive to meet the high standards they set for themselves.

J'ro, **Pete Scobell**, **Jeff Boss**, **Peter Osyff**, and **Jon Sanchez** have served the United States with incredible honor and distinction. I am honored to also call them my friends and to have access to their hard-won pool of knowledge. Thank you for all that you have done for me, and more important, our nation.

On the international stage, **Chad Norberg** and **Robert O'Brien** as-sisted with background on some key elements in the novel. These are two more good men whose friendship and service to our nation I am deeply grateful for. Thank you.

To those who quietly contributed to this novel but have requested not to have their names listed here, I thank you.

The characters **Lilliana Grace**, **Helen Cartland**, and **Alan Gottlieb** were named by generous contributors who helped support two very worthwhile causes I have been involved with. Thank you for your generosity, and I hope you enjoy the characters.

I owe so much of my success to the amazing people I work with. From the awesome **Carolyn Reidy** and the incomparable **Louise Burke** to the fantastic **Judith Curr**, I couldn't do it without you. Thank you for everything you and everyone else at **Simon & Schuster** have done for me.

You cannot create adventure after adventure each year without a phenomenal editor and publisher. **Emily Bestler** is, hands down, the absolute best. Thank you, Emily, for your keen eye, your great ideas, and above all your enduring friendship. You mean the world to me.

When it comes to publicists, **David Brown** is the *capo di tutti capi*. Not only is he magnificent at what he does, but also in who he is. Thank you, David, for every single thing you do for me every single day of the year.

I also want to thank the outstanding **Cindi Berger** and the entire stellar **team at PMK-BNC** for the new heights they take me to each and every year. First-rate doesn't even begin to describe what you do and how well you do it.

I have an incredible family at **Simon & Schuster** and I want to express my thanks to everyone at **Emily Bestler Books** and **Pocket Books**, including my good friends **Michael Selleck**, **Gary Urda**, and **John Hardy**, as well as the terrific **Colin Shields**, **Paula Amendolara**, **Janice Fryer**, **Seth Russo**, **Lisa Keim**, **Irene Lipsky**, **Lara Jones**, **Megan Reid**, **Emily Bamford**, **Ariele Fredman**, the entire **Emily Bestler Books/Pocket Books sales team**, **Albert Tang** and the **Emily Bestler Books/Pocket Books Art Departments**, **Al Madocs** and the **Atria/Emily Bestler Books Production Department**, **Chris Lynch**, **Tom Spain**, **Sarah Lieberman**, **Desiree Vecchio**, **Armand Schultz**, and the entire **Simon & Schuster audio division**.

When I dreamed of becoming an author, I envisioned what it would be like to have an agent. I had seen them on TV and in movies. A good agent is not only a partner in the writing process but your greatest advocate and, if you are lucky, an even greater friend. My brilliant agent, **Heide Lange** of **Sanford J. Greenburger Associates**, is all of these and more. Heide, thank you for making everything possible.

Helping Heide make everything possible are the talented **Stephanie Delman** and **Samantha Isman**. Thank you, ladies, for everything you and everyone else at SJGA does for me. My appreciation for all of you knows no bounds.

If I said thank you a million times, it would still not be enough to let **Yvonne Ralsky** know how much she means to me. Just when I think things can't get any better, she takes them to an entirely new level. It has been an absolute joy working with you, YBR, and I look forward to many, many more years to come! Thank you for all that you have done.

This novel is dedicated to one of the dearest people in the world to me, **Scott Schwimer**. Scottie has been with me since day one. He began as my entertainment attorney and grew into one of my best friends. You could not hope to ever meet a more decent, talented, intelligent, or devoted human being. God broke the mold with this man and I am grateful every day for him. Thank you, Scottie.

I have saved the absolute best for last—**my wonderful family**. As I write this, they are all downstairs hoping I'm about to put this book to bed, so we can celebrate. Day after day, through late nights and weekends, my wife, **Trish**, and our **children** have kept the world at bay so I can write. They have brought meals to my desk, have written notes in the snow outside my window, and have reminded me with each thing they do how much they love me. Thank you hardly seems enough. I love you all very much, and guess what? It's time to celebrate!

If you haven't been to BradThor.com, please stop by—and make sure to sign up for my fast, fun, free newsletter. I am constantly creating new content throughout the year and giving away some very cool prizes. It is another way I like to say thank you for all of your support.

Now we've reached the end of *Foreign Agent*. I hope you have enjoyed reading it as much I enjoyed writing it. There's now a special connection we share, and as the years go on, I look forward to bringing you many more great books.

Thank you, once more, for making the greatest career in the world possible.

—*Brad Thor*